The Taming of the Dudebro

VOLUME 1

The Taming of the Dudebro

♡

VOLUME 1

JANE WATSON

Snowy Wings
PUBLISHING

Book One

❧

THE TAMING OF THE DUDEBRO

"Thus have I politicly begun my reign,
And 'tis my hope to end successfully.
My falcon now is sharp and passing empty,
And 'til she stoop she must not be full-gorged,
For then she never looks upon her lure.
. . . And thus I'll curb her mad and headstrong humour."

- Petruchio, THE TAMING OF THE SHREW

For my mom and my sister

Chapter One ♡

"**I**S THE BROCCOLI READY?"

Patricia Verona reached for the measuring cup, gently sweeping the vegetable pieces she'd just chopped from the cutting board into the glass container. "Ready!" she declared with a grin, passing the cup to her best friend and cooking class partner, Grizz Sheridan.

"Perfect," Grizz muttered, gently shaking the chopped broccoli into the wok. "So, like I was saying, we need something really spooky and dramatic for when the ghosts appear." Her brown eyes widened as she waved the spoon in the air, exclaiming, "Smoke bombs!"

Patricia reached for the green onion and snorted. "C'mon, you know the rules. No fire hazards."

Grizz sighed, pouting her lips. "Yeah, you're right." Then she glanced at Patricia and murmured, "Sorry, I know that *you're* supposed to be coming up with all of the creative elements, and I just wrote it. I'm just *so excited* to see my story come to life!" She squealed, bouncing up and down.

Patricia laughed and nudged her, reminding Grizz to stir the pork fried rice. She tapped her chin thoughtfully. "Hey, I know: we could do stuff with the lights when the ghosts appear! Like, a different color spotlight for each one, and then dim the rest of the lights so that the stage is super dark. And—"

"Mm, I smell pork! Pork fried rice!"

Patricia groaned at the sound of the new voice. She glanced up to see fellow senior Kurt Minola standing in front of their station, rubbing his hands together eagerly as he admired their handiwork. She shouldn't have been surprised by his sudden appearance, since he showed up in her cooking class so often he might as well have been taking it himself. But that would have involved work. Instead, he always managed to appear at just the right moment to eat the food that he'd had no part in making.

Unfair, she thought, tucking a strand of dark blonde hair behind her ear as she took in the teen who stood before them. A stereotypical surfer dude, he sported cargo shorts, water shoes, and a black hoodie with a "Santa Cruz" emblem on the left lapel. *Because he clearly wants to look like a tourist in his hometown,* Patricia thought with a snicker.

As he reached for the sizzling wok, Grizz swiftly whacked his hand with the spoon. "Hands off, idiot. Are you *trying* to burn yourself?"

Kurt frowned, looking wounded. "But it smells so good. C'mon, Trixie, you'll let me have it when it's done, right?"

Patricia bristled. She absolutely *detested* being called anything other than Patricia, but 'Trixie' had to be her least favorite nickname. It made her sound like a dog. "It's Patricia," she corrected him for what was probably the thousandth time. "Go mooch off someone else."

"But your guys's smells the best!" Kurt protested.

"'Your guys's,' huh?" Patricia sighed, passing the chopped green onion to Grizz when her partner held her hand out. "Aren't you supposed to be in class right now? How is it that you waltz in here to steal the fruits of our labor practically *every single day*? Doesn't your teacher care?"

"Nah, babe, Mr. Baxter is super chill," Kurt said in his usual relaxed tone, absentmindedly picking a red pepper up from the work station.

Patricia rolled her eyes and gritted her teeth, focusing her attention once more on the recipe. She hated being called 'babe' even more than she hated being called 'Trixie.' Why couldn't Kurt go bother someone else?

"Well, you're looking at our lunch," Grizz practically growled, narrowing her heavily lined eyes at the tall, muscular teen. "So none for you."

"Aww, man," Kurt pouted, his shoulders sagging. "But I love pork fried rice."

"Kurt! Kurt!" a girl's voice called from the far corner of the room.

Patricia and Grizz both looked up to see Sophie Sinclair and her partner, Hannah Diaz, waving. "You can have some of ours, Kurt!" Sophie told him with a giggle.

Kurt grinned. "Hey, thanks, babe!"

Patricia and Grizz shared a look of disgust. The way girls flung themselves at him was revolting. Kurt *was* pretty good looking, Patricia had to admit, being six-foot-five and very well-built, with dark brown hair and hazel eyes. But as Patricia had learned years ago, he—like most of the members of the Vista High water polo team—was also an insufferable jerk who couldn't get enough of himself. A sizable portion of the girls at their school had yet to learn that, though, or else just didn't care, throwing themselves at the team every chance they got.

As he left their station to join Hannah and Sophie, Patricia stuck out her tongue slightly and made a noise of distaste. "Ech, thank goodness he's gone."

Grizz nodded and gave the ingredients in the wok another stir. "I think we're about ready for the soy sauce."

"Coming right up," Patricia said with a grin, reaching across the counter for the bottle.

As she passed it to Grizz, she overheard their cooking teacher, Ms. Hunt, snap, "Kurt Minola! How many times have I told you, you don't get to eat anything if you didn't make it! Go back to your own class!"

"But Ms. Hunt," Kurt whined with an endearing smile, causing both Hannah and Sophie to giggle, "I can't help it if I'm hungry all the time. I'm an athlete. I have to keep up my strength."

"Then pack a banana," Ms. Hunt quipped, but she turned away from Kurt and the girls to check on the rest of the students.

Grizz clucked her tongue as she watched the scene. "Ms. Hunt is way too nice to that loafer," she commented as she stirred in the soy sauce.

"Yep," Patricia agreed, turning her attention back to the task at hand. "Okay, I think we just need to add in the ginger and minced garlic, and we are done!" She reached for the small piece of ginger that Ms. Hunt had instructed them to finely chop.

Just then, there was a crackle over the intercom, and the

disembodied voice of the secretary, Mrs. Blair, said, "Ms. Hunt, is Kurt Minola in your classroom? I checked with Mr. Baxter's class and he told me to try yours."

Ms. Hunt lifted her eyes to the ceiling, as if asking for strength. "Yes," she said with a sigh. She turned her head toward the subject in question, who was leaning over on Hannah and Sophie's table and whispering, eliciting giggles from the pair. "He's here."

"Tell him the principal needs to see him," Mrs. Blair's voice said.

Patricia raised her eyebrows at Grizz, intrigued by this news. A quick glance around the room showed that she was not the only one paying attention to the intercom. Many of the other students had stopped their activities and were gazing at Kurt with interest.

Ms. Hunt nodded as the intercom clicked off. "Kurt," she called. Kurt didn't appear to hear her—he just kept whispering to Sophie and Hannah. Patricia snickered as Ms. Hunt rolled her eyes and, looking absolutely exasperated, marched over to him. "Kurt!" she snapped as she reached him.

Kurt whipped his head up, looking confused. "Wha—?"

"The principal needs to see you," Ms. Hunt told him, turning on her heel and expecting him to follow. "Come on, I'll get you a hall pass."

"Bummer," Kurt muttered. He put a hand on both Hannah and Sophie's shoulders. "Catch ya later, babes. Save me some of that rice?"

Patricia raised her eyebrows at Grizz as the two abandoned girls giggled in reply.

As soon as he'd left the room, Grizz whirled on Patricia and whispered in a singsong voice, "Oo-ooh, Mr. Water Polo Champ is in *trou*ble. I wonder what he did?"

Patricia shook her head slowly, eyes widening as she thought of the possibilities. Was it because he'd been ditching his own class for cooking? Or was it more serious? She picked up her knife to resume chopping the ginger. "Maybe he left campus during the day to go surfing again."

"Or maybe he was caught smoking in the boys' bathroom or something," Grizz suggested eagerly.

Patricia considered his cut physique and obsession with water polo. "Maybe he's been using steroids."

Caught off-guard, Grizz let out a boisterous laugh and had to cover her mouth. Quickly recovering, she paused, deep in thought. "They probably just want his parents to make another donation to the Dean's Fund," she mused glumly, adding the ginger to the wok with little enthusiasm.

Patricia wiped her hands on her apron. The Minolas were definitely one of the richer families in town. They often made large donations to the school and other establishments in the area. "But they probably just could've asked Ben to tell them that," she reasoned. Kurt's twin brother, Ben, was responsible and beloved by the faculty—the total opposite of Kurt. "I mean, Kurt would probably forget to even *mention* it to his parents, but Ben wouldn't."

Grizz thought about this, taking the minced garlic from Patricia. "Good point. Which means," she continued with a slow grin, "that our boy Kurt probably *is* in trouble." She inhaled deeply and sighed, satisfied. "That would be almost as good as this pork fried rice."

Chapter Two ♡

After lunch, Patricia sat beside Grizz in their drama class. She was carefully taking notes as Mr. Gardner lectured on *The Taming of the Shrew* when she felt a sharp poke in her right arm. She turned curiously to see Grizz brandishing her pencil, motioning for her to look at something. Patricia rolled her eyes at what she saw. Kurt appeared to be holding a four-way note-passing session with the three girls surrounding him. Each giggled shyly as their hands touched his.

Grizz shook her head in disgust. "It's like witnessing an orgy," she whispered to Patricia.

Glancing back at the foursome, Patricia had to agree. It was surprising to see Kurt in class, actually, since he skipped drama almost as much as he turned up in her cooking class. *At least he's awake for once,* she thought. Then, wrinkling her nose in annoyance, she turned her attention back to copying notes from the whiteboard.

"Well," Mr. Gardner said a few minutes later, glancing at the clock on the wall, "your homework is on the board. Take these last few minutes of class to break up into your individual groups to talk about your projects. For those not participating in the theater festival, please gather to discuss the thematic elements in Act I of *The Taming of the Shrew.*"

Quickly scribbling the homework into her day planner, Patricia stood with the rest of the class as they migrated into their groups; but she paused as she noticed Mr. Gardner approach Kurt, who was still hunched over a note, laughing.

"Mr. Minola! May I have a word with you?"

Kurt jumped at the sound of the teacher's voice. "Uh, sure," he replied, looking confused as he followed Mr. Gardner.

Ha! In trouble twice in one day! Patricia stared after them for a moment before shouldering her bag and joining Grizz, who had already chosen a spot in the corner.

"Okay, so I guess we can go over the script and I can write down what props we're going to want, and maybe how the stage should look?" Patricia suggested as she slid her backpack off and sat down.

Grizz nodded, pulling a notebook out of her messenger bag. "I had some ideas for finishing the script, too, lemme write them down real quick."

Patricia dug through her backpack and pulled out the binder where she kept all of her notes and sketches for their one-act play. While she waited for Grizz, she began to doodle ideas for how the props should be laid out on the stage. According to Mr. Gardner, how much or how little they used in their production was completely up to the director; even if it was a period piece, the cast could wear modern clothing so long as it fit the theme. However, being a known overachiever, Patricia wanted her production to look as professional as possible. She'd dreamed up costumes, props and sets that probably went above and beyond the theater festival's expectations.

"Grizelda? Patricia?"

Patricia's reverie was interrupted by Mr. Gardner's appearance. Grizz grunted and rose to her feet, her brow furrowed, but she kept her annoyance at being called "Grizelda" to herself. Patricia knew Grizz loathed her full name—it was too stuffy and old-fashioned for her taste. From a very young age, she'd declared that everyone should call her Grizz with two 'z's, and immediately shot down any other (albeit more conventional) nicknames that people had tried to stick her with. Given her fiery and sometimes quirky personality, Patricia could not imagine a more fitting name for her best friend.

"I'd like to talk to you about your project," Mr. Gardner began, folding his arms over his chest.

Patricia shared a worried look with Grizz before replying, "Oh, okay..." *Did we do something wrong?*

Their drama teacher sighed. "Well, I was looking over your outline, Patricia," he began, referring to the preliminary ideas that Patricia had turned in a few days prior, "and I saw that you had ideas for costumes and props. You were also talking about doing some actual set work, right?"

Patricia nodded, clutching her binder to her chest. "Yeah, I really want to showcase the fact that Mrs. Winchester is trapped because of the earthquake. I thought there could be a lot of debris, and maybe have a cutout that's like her door that the cast can come in through."

Mr. Gardner pursed his lips thoughtfully, which made Patricia nervous. Were her plans too over the top?

"I think it's great, but with all the ideas you have, I just don't see how you are going to be able to do this all on your own. It's quite a bit more extensive than some of the other plays, and there are only two of you." Taking a deep breath, Mr. Gardner continued, "That's why I'm assigning Kurt Minola to the project."

Patricia felt as if the wind had been knocked out of her. She looked over at Grizz. Her friend's eyes were bugged out and her mouth was agape, a sure reflection of the horror that must be showing on Patricia's own face. "Wait, what?"

Mr. Gardner held up his hands as if to calm them. "Now, I know it seems odd, but I spoke with the principal this afternoon, and it seems Kurt's parents were not happy with his quarter report card. Since college acceptances are already out, they want to make sure that he pulls his grades up so he doesn't lose his spot."

Patricia frowned. "What does that have to do with our play, though?"

"He is currently flunking this class," Mr. Gardner stated flatly, "and will have no hope of passing unless he puts in some serious extra credit. Now, I know you girls are receiving some extra credit for participating in the theater festival, but Kurt is going to have to do a *lot* more than that. Aside from redoing some assignments—and actually turning them *in*," he added wryly, "I want him to dive fully into this project. I think if he clocks in so many hours with you, I will be able to raise his grade in good conscience. I will also, of course, expect him to write a paper on his experience of working firsthand on a production. So, assign him whatever you need him to do. Building props, stage managing, running errands…"

"Mr. Gardner," Grizz interrupted, planting a sickening sweet smile on her face that Patricia knew was completely phony, "we really don't need his help. We're fine. This play is kind of like Patricia's baby, and I think she'd rather have full control."

"Oh, but she will," Mr. Gardner replied, nipping Grizz's strategy in the bud. "Patricia, you will be completely in charge. After school, on week-ends, whenever you are working on the one-act, Kurt is expected to be there. You will be supervising this portion of his grade. If he doesn't put in the work, he doesn't get the extra credit." Seeing Patricia's sour expression, he added, "Don't worry, Patricia. If he goofs off, *his* grade will suffer, not yours."

"Mr. Gardner, can't he work on someone else's?" Patricia pleaded. She didn't want to sound desperate, but she felt backed into a corner.

"You two need a lot of help if you want your production to be anywhere near your expectations," Mr. Gardner replied seriously, though not unkindly.

"Then assign us someone else!" Grizz exclaimed, tugging on a red-tipped lock of her hair in agitation.

Mr. Gardner shook his head. "I'm sorry. I'm sure Kurt is not your favorite person, but I think it is in everyone's best interest that he works on this play. You are two of my best students. You are both responsible and dedicated, and I am *confident* that you will judge his contribution to your play fairly and honestly."

Patricia sighed, closing her eyes for a moment. What he was saying was true; neither she nor Grizz were part of Kurt's little fan club. They didn't even consider themselves his friends, so there was no way that he could sweet-talk them into letting him do no work while still getting credit. And, though Patricia didn't want to admit it, she would be fair with him, and not try to spike his attempts to pass. If he was willing to put in the effort, she'd be willing to put up with him.

She glanced over at Grizz, who nodded glumly, knowing that there would be no way out of it. Finally, she said, "Sure, Mr. Gardner. We'd be happy to have him in our group."

Mr. Gardner's face broke into a relieved smile. "Wonderful. I'll call Kurt over to give you a few minutes to discuss the project."

Patricia blew a stray bang out of her eye in frustration as Mr. Gardner went to fetch Kurt.

"'Sup, Patty, Zel," Kurt greeted them when he reached their corner.

While Patricia merely grit her teeth at the nickname, Grizz inhaled sharply and spat, "You know damn well that it is *Grizz*, you—"

Patricia quickly held out her arm to stop her, widening her eyes to send a warning message to her friend. "Hey, Kurt," she greeted him, a forced smile plastered on her face.

"So, Mr. Gardner said that if I'm in your play I'll get extra credit," Kurt began in his usual relaxed tone. "I'll take a small part."

Patricia cocked a brow, shocked by his gall. *Lazy and presumptuous as always.*

Before she could respond, Mr. Gardner cleared his throat, having crept up behind Kurt without him noticing. "As usual, Mr. Minola, you appear to have selective hearing. You must participate in this production, but that does not mean you will be acting in it. And if you are, it will most certainly not be the only contribution you make. As I understand it, carpentry is a hobby of yours, is it not?"

Kurt looked taken aback by this question, slowly scratching his ear as he replied, "Well, like, I've made a couple boards." Patricia could only assume he meant for surfing. "Oh, and, like, this really sick stand for my stereo system."

Mr. Gardner turned to Patricia and Grizz and lifted his eyebrows, appearing pleased. "There, see? He can work on the sets and props for you."

Patricia grimaced. She did not at all enjoy the thought of trusting Kurt with any aspect of their play, particularly something that involved power tools.

"Though if you would like to try your hand at acting," Mr. Gardner continued, "maybe you could come to the tryouts and read for their play. If they select you, acting could be a portion of your grade."

Now this was getting ridiculous. Kurt? Act? That was most certainly *not* an option. "Um, Mr. Gardner, I don't think there's any role that…"

"Oh, Patricia," Grizz interrupted her, smiling sweetly at Kurt and Mr. Gardner, "I think Kurt should *definitely* come try out if he wants to." Turning to Patricia, she said seriously, "In fact, I have a character that he'd be *perfect* for."

Patricia stared at her as if she was crazy. *What on Earth are you up to?* she wondered, racking her brain. She'd read Grizz's drafts and could not recall any character that Kurt could pull off. But, seeing the mischievous glint in Grizz's eye, she quickly caught on. "Oh, oh! Right! Yeah, Kurt, you should definitely audition. And of course there will be lots of other things we can have you do."

Kurt nodded with a lazy smile on his face. "Sweet."

Patricia tossed her long hair over her shoulder and nodded to their teacher. "Just leave it to us, Mr. Gardner. We'll go over everything with Kurt."

"Thank you so much, both of you," Mr. Gardner replied. "Kurt, I expect to see you in my office today right after school to go over those assignments." He looked severely at Kurt over his wire-rimmed glasses.

Kurt nodded. "Sure thing, Mr. G."

With an exasperated sigh, Mr. Gardner left the group, shaking his head.

"Okay, Kurt," Patricia began, "since tryouts are on Friday, Grizz and I have a lot to prepare beforehand. Grizz will have to finish the script, and—"

She was interrupted by the loud buzz of the bell, signaling that class was over. When Kurt stood and reached for his backpack, Patricia held up her hands. "No, no, stay for just a second. Here, let's exchange numbers. We can meet up after school to work it all out, and you can see what we're going to be doing." She pulled her cell out of her pocket and glared expectantly at Kurt, who reluctantly reached into his hoodie and produced his own.

After rattling off numbers to each other, Patricia smiled, satisfied. "Okay, I can't do today, but let's meet here tomorrow, right after school. Can you make it?"

Kurt nodded without hesitation. "Sure thing, Patty."

Rolling her eyes but choosing to ignore the nickname, Patricia smiled thinly. "Great. See you then."

"Can you believe this?" Grizz said as Kurt walked away. "Argh, stuck with Kurt the Jerk for our entire play!"

Patricia wrinkled her nose in commiseration as they filed toward the door and into the hallway. "I know, but there's nothing we can do about it. Dammit," she swore under her breath.

"Why do we have to be so responsible and reliable?" Grizz demanded bitterly, only half-joking.

"No surprise that he's flunking, though," said Patricia as they wove through the throng of students congesting the hallway. "He hardly ever even shows up to drama."

"Probably thought it was gonna be an easy A that would boost his GPA with no effort while he coasted through senior year," Grizz said. "Like all the other tools around here who think that just because they got accepted to a college, their grades can tank and there won't be any consequences."

Patricia shook her head. "How stupid can you be?"

Grizz laughed, then glanced at her watch and realized the bell was going to ring any second. "Gotta run, I'll talk to you later!"

Patricia watched her friend hurry away, her red-tipped hair trailing after her. Stifling a laugh, she turned and entered her own classroom.

Chapter Three ♡

"**A**LL RIGHT, *TOUS LES MONDES*, CHOOSE A PARTNER AND DO exercise B, numbers one through five, on page two-hundred thirty-three, *s'il vous plait*," Madame Kelley instructed the next day during Patricia's final period French class.

As Patricia pulled out a clean sheet of binder paper, she felt a tap on her shoulder. Ben Minola had leaned over from his chair next to her, and he asked with a smile, *"Avec moi?"*

Patricia grinned. *"Absolument."* Clearing her throat, Patricia began to read the directions aloud in French. "Okay, so we're supposed to change the following sentences to use the conditional tense. *Numéro Un. J'irai consulter…"*

After several minutes, Ben finished writing the last answer. Craning his neck to check the clock and seeing that there were a few minutes of class left, he stared down at his textbook. "So, uh, I heard from Kurt that you're stuck with him for your one-act." He glanced up and met Patricia's eyes, his dark brows furrowing in sympathy. "That sucks."

Patricia laughed at his reaction, which pretty much summed up how she felt about it. "Yup, it does." Then she took in a deep breath and smiled at Ben. "But it's what Mr. Gardner wants. Maybe it won't be so bad."

Ben nodded, running a hand through his short black hair. "I hope not. Our parents were pretty pissed at him the other night. They laid down the law, so he'd *better* put in the effort if he knows what's good for him."

"Yeah, well, I'll find out soon enough," Patricia said with a cluck of her tongue. Seeing Ben's curious look, she explained, "He's meeting me and Grizz in the auditorium right after class."

"Patricia?" Madame Kelley interrupted them, standing at her desk with her eyebrows raised. "If you and Benjamin are done, could you write the answer to *numèro trois* up here, *s'il vous plait?*"

Patricia blinked rapidly, glad that Madame Kelley hadn't reprimanded them for chit-chatting in English. Glancing at Ben, who flashed her an easy grin, she stood. *"Oui, Madame."*

At the end of class, as Patricia sat scribbling the night's homework into her planner, a shadow fell over her. She looked up in surprise to see Ben standing next to her desk again. "Have you started on your paper for English yet?" he asked casually, shouldering his backpack as she stood.

Patricia pulled her hair up and away from her back, adjusting the straps of her bag. Then she let it fall freely down her shoulders once more and nodded. "Yeah, a little bit. All I've got is an outline, though."

"Yeah, same here," Ben said. "It's really hard to pick a theme, too. I don't know if it's senioritis or what, but I feel like my paper-writing... ness is... not good." He scratched the back of his neck awkwardly as Patricia laughed and added, "See? I can't even brain anymore. Words... hard... brain... ow..."

"Okay, that was pretty special," Patricia said with a laugh. "I do the same thing, though! Recently I've been making a ton of stupid spelling mistakes. I'm just going to blame it on being tired, because my brainpower can't have depleted that much, right?"

Ben raised an eyebrow as he surveyed her for a minute. "Nah, you don't *look* like you've gotten stupid," he told her seriously. When she bit her lip and smacked him, he grinned and held his hands up. "Kidding! But seriously, we *are* in the home stretch, and that means that the workload is just way worse. And on top of it all, you're directing your own play for the theater festival. That's got to be taking a lot out of you."

Patricia shrugged. She knew that he was right—she'd done the school play every year since she was a freshman, so she knew how hectic it could be, even when you weren't running the whole thing on your own—but she didn't regret her decision one bit. "Yeah, it'll probably keep me pretty busy, but I'm still excited. I can't wait for the festival!"

They slowed their steps when they reached the auditorium door. Patricia turned, expecting Ben to take his leave. She was surprised he'd even bothered to walk with her all that way. But she was even more surprised when he held the door open for her and followed her into the auditorium.

"Hey!" Grizz said, her eyes widening as she took in Patricia's companion. "Hi, Ben, what's up?"

Ben smiled and lifted his hand in a wave. "Hey, Grizz, how's the playwriting going?"

Grizz lifted her notebook and wiggled it enthusiastically. "Rockin'. I think I had a major breakthrough last night. I was kind of scared that it wouldn't be done in time for auditions, but now I think it'll be a piece of cake."

"Cool! What's it about?" Ben asked.

"So, you know the Winchester Mystery House, right?" At Ben's nod, Grizz went on, "Well, I toured it for the first time over break, and the idea of restless spirits haunting her was, like, way too cool. When we got to the room she'd been trapped in during the 1906 earthquake, I had such a brainstorm." Grizz made an excited gesture with her hands. "Wouldn't it be cool if *ghosts* had caused the quake?" She lifted her eyebrows. "Huh, huh? What do you think?"

"That sounds awesome!" Ben exclaimed. He turned to Patricia. "What do you have planned, Director?"

Patricia folded her arms across her chest. "I haven't fully decided yet. I'm thinking of doing a bunch of cool stuff with the lights and costumes, to give it a haunted feel. And I really want the set to look authentic, with fallen furniture and stuff."

Ben nodded, looking intrigued. "That is going to be so cool. Kurt should be able to help you with the set and props if you need stuff built. He's pretty good with carpentry."

"Yeah, that's what Mr. Gardner said," Patricia replied, though she was relieved to hear Ben confirm it.

"Speaking of which," Grizz said, "where *is* that brother of yours?"

Ben looked at his watch and frowned. "I have no idea. He was supposed to meet you right after class, right? His last class isn't far from here. He should've been here by now."

Patricia heaved a sigh and dug out her phone. "Okay, I'll text him to light a fire under it."

Several more minutes passed, producing no reply, and no Kurt.

"I'll run over to his locker and see if he's still there. He probably got distracted by some girl. You try calling him," Ben told Patricia before breaking into a jog and heading out the door.

Grizz rolled her eyes and sank into a nearby chair. "Ugh, what a pain in the ass he's already being. It's twelve after three, where *is* he?"

Patricia pursed her lips and began to dial Kurt. She bounced on her heels in annoyance as it rang several times. "Come *on*, Kurt, we don't have all day," she muttered.

Finally she heard a click and realized it was going to voicemail. "Hi, you've reached Lucy," a recorded voice that was most definitely *not* Kurt's said. "I can't get to my phone right now, leave a message after the beep!"

Patricia pulled the phone away from her ear and stared at it incredulously. "Why that stupid, good for nothing..."

"What? What happened?" Grizz asked, glancing first at the phone, then Patricia, expectantly.

"That moron gave me the wrong number! It was some girl named Lucy! Luckily I just got her voice mail."

Grizz threw her head back in frustration, looking toward the ceiling as if asking for strength. "Argh! Now what do we do?"

Before Patricia could answer, Ben returned. "He's not by his locker or his last class," he reported, panting a little from running.

"Oh, you missed the best part," Grizz called sarcastically from her chair. She pointed at Patricia. "He gave her the wrong phone number!"

"What?" Ben asked in exasperation. Patricia handed him her phone. "That sneaky bastard," he muttered under his breath as he stared at the screen. He shook his head and handed the phone back to Patricia. "That's not his number. That's not even *close* to his number."

"He deliberately gave me a fake number?"

Grizz began to mutter undecipherable curses under her breath from where she sat.

Patricia set her jaw and said to Ben, "Here, give me his real number so I can call him."

"No," Ben replied, shaking his head as he pulled his phone from his pocket. "*I* am going to call him." He held the cell to his ear, and the girls soon heard the phone pick up and noise on the other end of the line. "Hey, man, how ya doing?" Ben said. "Um, so I just have a quick question for you… WHERE THE HELL ARE YOU?"

Patricia jumped, startled. She'd never heard Ben yell like that—he was usually so calm. She raised her eyebrows and looked over at Grizz, who mouthed, "Rock *on*, Ben."

Ben stood still for a moment, frowning as he listened to Kurt. "Wha—you're on a *date*? At the *Boardwalk*? Dude, no, you're supposed to be here in the auditorium with Patricia and Grizz!" He fell silent again, letting Kurt speak. Then he rolled his eyes and said, "No, how could you forget? …Yeah, uh-huh. Just like you *forgot* your own number, and gave Patricia a totally fake one? Yeah, smooth move there, moron."

Ben looked over at Patricia with an apologetic smile before gritting his teeth and hissing into the phone, "You'd better wrap it up real quick or I'm telling Mom. And don't play the 'bro' card on *me*, Kurt. You're the one flunking, and when the teach is nice enough to offer this to you—yeah, well Grizz and Patricia have been waiting for you for *half an hour!*"

It was obvious that Ben wasn't getting through to his twin, so Patricia marched over to him and snatched the phone out of his hand with lightning-fast agility. "Kurt Minola!" she snapped into the phone, hand on hip. "Get your *butt* back to school this minute or you can kiss your extra credit goodbye!"

"Oh—uh… okay, sure thing, Patty," she heard Kurt say on the other end of the line.

"And for the *last* time, it's P-A-T-R-I-C-I-A!" Patricia shouted, pressing the 'end' button before he could reply. She took a deep breath to calm herself and handed the phone back to Ben. "Sorry about that."

Ben took the phone back, a slow grin forming on his face. "No, that was awesome. Is he coming?"

Patricia smiled in spite of the frustrating situation. "I think so."

Grizz rose to her feet and flipped a lock of hair over her shoulder. "He'd better, if he knows what's good for him."

"Thanks for calling him," Patricia told Ben.

Ben shrugged, hands in his pockets. "No problem. Sorry he's such a pain."

"It's not your fault the cosmos cursed you with him for a twin," Grizz laughed.

Ben sighed. "He has gotten so *lazy* these past few months—worse than usual! He was actually not *too* bad with doing homework and stuff 'til this year. His grades were decent enough to get into college. Now that he's *in,* he thinks high school doesn't matter anymore. His grades were worse last semester than they'd ever been, but I think my parents chocked it up to the stress of applications, so they let it slide."

"Stress, my eye," Patricia commented, folding her arms across her chest.

"Yup. But when they saw his quarter report card?" Ben lifted his hands, making an explosive sound. "There was a lot of yelling."

Grizz lifted an eyebrow. "Ouch. I would say I feel bad for the guy, except, hah, I don't."

"Well, if it makes you feel better, you aren't the only one saddled with helping Kurt. Guess who got roped into tutoring him in math and physics?" Ben lifted two thumbs and pointed them toward himself. "This guy."

"That's rough," Grizz muttered, tugging at the hem of her short-sleeved plaid shirt.

"Yeah, well, what can you do?" Ben remarked, shrugging. "Oh, here, let me give you his real number," he said to Patricia, pulling out his phone once more.

"Score. Thank you Ben," said Patricia, swiftly texting the contact information to Grizz as well.

"Great, like I really want that idiot's number contaminating my phone," Grizz grumbled, rolling her eyes. Then she cocked her head to the side. "Hang on, I hear something…"

Patricia craned her neck toward the door. She heard it, too. It sounded like… wheels?

Sure enough, Kurt soon rode into the auditorium, hopping off of his skateboard and hoisting it over his shoulder. *Really? He rode his skateboard in the hallway?*

"Hey, bro," Kurt said when he walked up to Ben. Glancing at Patricia and Grizz, he added, "'Sup, girls."

Grizz threw her hands up in annoyance, turning her back on Kurt without a word.

Ben merely shook his head and lifted his backpack from the floor. "I'll go over your homework with you after dinner," he told his brother in a flat tone, before turning toward Patricia. "See you, Patricia, Grizz." Looking into Patricia's eyes steadily, he raised his eyebrows and mouthed, "Good luck."

Patricia smiled in reply, lifting her hand in a wave. "Later, Ben." As she watched him leave the room, shaking his head and muttering something, she thought to herself, *Thank goodness he was here.* At least now they could get *some* work done.

"Okay, Kurt," Patricia said, pulling her drama binder from her bag, "how about Grizz tells you a little about the script. Then I can show you my sketches outlining what the visuals are going to look like."

Kurt had sunk to the floor, hunching over his phone and smirking as he texted. Patricia sighed heavily, pinching the bridge of her nose. "Kurt!" she shouted.

Kurt's head jerked up. "Uh, what?"

Patricia put her hands on her hips. "Put away your phone. We have work to do."

"Oh," Kurt replied lazily, sliding the phone back into the pocket of his hoodie and following Patricia up the steps to the stage, where a table and chairs had been set up.

Grizz slid into her seat and opened her notebook. "All right, so my play is about Mrs. Winchester and—"

"Who?" Kurt interrupted, leaning back in his chair, stretching his long legs under the table. Patricia scrunched her nose and scooted away when his foot brushed hers.

Grizz stared at him. "Um, Sarah Winchester. As in the Winchester

Mystery House?"

"The what house?"

Patricia shared a look with Grizz. "You know, that big, weird house in San Jose that has windows in the floor and doors leading to nowhere? There's billboards all along Highway 17 advertising it?"

Kurt shook his head. "Nope, no idea what you're talking about."

Good grief! Ben *knew about the house...* "Well, anyway," Patricia said, "it's pretty cool. I'd always heard about it, but I didn't go myself 'til a couple years ago. You should tour it sometime."

Grizz flipped through her notebook. "Moving on. Sarah Winchester was a lady whose husband was a gun manufacturer. Her misfortunes in life led her to believe she was cursed, so she visited a medium who told her she was being haunted, and that she must never cease construction on her house...or *else.*" Grizz hissed as she leaned forward in her seat, widening her eyes dramatically.

Kurt didn't react. He looked utterly bored. "So, what is your play about?"

"Well," Grizz went on, looking quite pleased with herself, "there was a huge earthquake in 1906, and it caused a ton of damage to her house. She actually was trapped in one of the bedrooms for several hours afterward. When her servants finally found her and freed her, she was in a frenzy. Boom!" Grizz slammed down her hands on the table, startling Patricia. "She stopped fixing up the front of her house. It was in shambles due to the damage from the quake, but she just left it and started gung-ho working on other parts of the house. So, *I* thought it would be cool if the cause of the quake was the vengeful ghosts, trying to exact their revenge on Mrs. Winchester because of how she got all this money from a company that ruined their lives. I wrote about three different ghosts who come to her, gave them each a little backstory, y'know."

Kurt snorted. "Dude, ghosts aren't real."

Patricia grimaced. He really shouldn't have said that to Grizz, who was a firm believer in the supernatural.

Sure enough, Grizz's eyes widened in fury, face reddening as her nostrils flared. "Listen, you—"

Patricia held up her hands, knowing that Grizz's tirades could take hours. "Kurt, it is *fiction.* Your opinion on ghosts does not matter. So, this is what we are thinking for the production…"

As she explained their ideas for the props and set, she watched carefully while Kurt blankly stared at his fingers, tracing them across the tabletop. It was obvious he wasn't listening. Sighing, she finished, "Tryouts are Friday at five-thirty here in the auditorium. We'll have short sections for both of the male roles for you to read."

Kurt nodded, finally looking up. "Okay."

"Even if you don't end up wanting to try out, I'd like you to come anyway," Patricia told him, clasping her hands on the table in front of her. "It'll be good for you to see how the process works, since you've never auditioned for a play before. You can write about it in your paper."

"Sure thing, babe," Kurt said with an easy smile, reaching for his skateboard. "So, are we done here?"

Patricia looked at Grizz in annoyance. Grizz rolled her eyes and shrugged.

"Yeah, sure," Patricia said. There wasn't much left to do right then, but she hated letting Kurt off the hook that easily. "We'll do more this weekend. Remember, Friday, five-thirty—sharp."

Untangling his tall legs from underneath the table, he stood and shouldered his skateboard. "Got it. Catch ya later."

Patricia sighed as he disappeared, keys jangling from his belt loop. Then she turned to Grizz. "I say we go get smoothies."

Grizz nodded emphatically, hoisting her messenger bag off of the floor.

Chapter Four ♥

F RIDAY NIGHT IN THE AUDITORIUM, PATRICIA CHECKED THE time on her cell phone yet again. Six o'clock, and Kurt was nowhere to be seen. No calls or texts from him, either. She didn't really *want* him to be a cast member, but if he was going to be *this* unreliable so early into the process, how was she supposed to trust him with *anything?*

"Patricia?" Mr. Gardner called from his seat in the chair against the wall. "It's your turn."

Patricia took in a deep breath and planted a smile on her face. She needed to stop worrying about that screw-off. It was time to cast her play!

Hurrying to the center of the stage, she faced the sea of students waiting to audition and cleared her throat. "Good evening. For those of you who don't know me, I'm Patricia Verona. I'm a senior, and I'm directing a one-act written by fellow senior Grizz Sheridan. It's kind of a ghost story that takes place in the Winchester Mystery House. There are four parts we're holding auditions for, two guys, two girls. One will be Mrs. Winchester herself, and then the other female role will be a young woman whose beloved was killed—and who was then murdered herself—seeking revenge for their deaths. Then there will be two male ghosts: the sweetheart who'd been shot, and a soldier who had tried to stop the war." Glancing at her clipboard to make sure she hadn't left anything out, she said, "Okay, so, everyone interested, please form a line right there by the stage steps!"

Hopping off of the steps and joining Grizz, Patricia clicked her pen nervously a few times as she slid into the theater seat. She watched each performance carefully and took quick notes. Whenever Grizz made a comment about a certain actor, she made sure to write it down alongside her own thoughts.

The process was over all too soon. As the last person auditioning for their one-act thanked them and left the stage, Patricia glanced at her phone once more and sighed. Still no messages from Kurt. "Of course he wasn't going to show," she muttered in annoyance.

She locked her phone and slid it back in her backpack. She could deal with it later—the other drama students were holding their own auditions next, and she and Grizz were supposed to stay for the entire session.

Twenty minutes later, she felt a large hand tap her shoulder. She glanced up in shock to see Kurt standing there, pulling one earbud out as he said, "Hey, made it."

"What—" Patricia began to screech, before remembering the

auditions were still going on. "What *took* you so long?" she hissed, barely above a whisper.

"I had stuff to do," he replied casually at regular volume, causing Grizz to frown and shush him with a finger to her lips.

Patricia made a noise of disgust and reached up to drag him down into the seat next to her—which was no small feat, considering how tall he was.

"Ouch!" he exclaimed as he landed half-in, half-out of the theater seat.

"Shh!" Patricia commanded, nervously looking around to see if anyone had noticed all the ruckus. "And what do you mean you had 'stuff' to do?!" she demanded quietly. "You were supposed to be here over an hour ago!"

Kurt shrugged. "Sorry, but I'm ready to audition now."

Patricia's nostrils flared in anger. "Ex*cuse* me? It's too late! The auditions for my play are over!"

"But I'm here!" Kurt exclaimed, confused.

Patricia held a finger to her mouth and whispered harshly, "For the last time, please be quiet! It's rude enough for you to come so late, but someone else is picking out people for their play now! You're being very disrespectful."

To Patricia's surprise, Kurt actually looked chagrined. "Oops," he replied in a much quieter voice, "my bad." Then he glanced around. "Well, if it's too late, I guess I'll take off." He started to stand up.

Patricia held out her arm to stop him. *Oh, no. You are so not getting off the hook that easy. You made us wait, so you can wait.* "You know what, Kurt? When everyone else is done, you can try out. I'll stay late just for you," she whispered sweetly, looking over to Grizz and winking.

"Aw, thanks, babe," Kurt smiled, leaning back in his seat and putting his earbuds back in.

Patricia quickly reached over and ripped them from his ears. "No music. And no sleeping, either. You are gonna sit right there and pay close attention."

Kurt stared at her vacantly for a second, as if not sure how to reply. Finally, he turned toward the stage and watched in bewilderment as each student took their turn and auditioned.

Patricia glanced at Grizz and grinned. Grizz held out her hand in reply to quickly high five her.

Finally, when the last audition was through, Mr. Gardner ran out to the center of the stage. "Wonderful, everyone, just wonderful," he said. "This room is filled with so much talent and excitement, it brings joy to my heart. Now, casting will be posted Monday morning on the bulletin board right outside the auditorium, so make sure and check it first thing. Good luck to you all, and have a great weekend!"

As everyone in the auditorium rose to their feet and started milling around, Patricia stood and motioned for Grizz to follow her to talk to Mr. Gardner. They had to shove past Kurt, who was still seated, legs sprawled in front of him, blocking their path. "C'mon, Kurt." She nudged him with her foot. "Time for you to show us your stuff."

Mr. Gardner looked up from his notes as the three approached him. "Oh, Grizelda, Patricia… Kurt," he greeted them. "How can I help you?"

"Kurt wants to try out for our play," Patricia explained. "But he was late, so…"

Mr. Gardner stared at Kurt disapprovingly over the top of his glasses. "Kurt, you should know better than that. You cannot expect to be allowed to participate if you do not respect scheduled times and deadlines."

Kurt shrugged. "Sorry, Mr. G."

Mr. Gardner stared at Kurt silently for a moment. "However, since this is Patricia's time and her play, it is up to her whether you are still allowed to audition." He looked at Patricia and Grizz in turn. "What is your decision?"

"Oh, we totally think he should try out," Grizz said enthusiastically, an innocent expression on her face.

Seeing Patricia nod demurely, Mr. Gardner eyed them both suspiciously. Patricia was sure he was on to their little scheme, and was relieved when he simply sighed and said, "Very well. I will be in my office catching up on grading. Please stop by when you are finished so that I can lock up."

"Thank you, sir," Patricia said sweetly. When Mr. Gardner walked away, she was pretty sure she heard him chuckle under his breath.

Turning to Kurt, she pulled a sheet of paper from her binder. "All right, get up on the stage and read for these two parts," she instructed, highlighting the sections featuring the two male ghosts. "Grizz, will you read with him?"

"Sure thing," Grizz replied, taking the audition sheet when Patricia offered it.

Patricia made herself comfortable, propping her feet on top of the seat in front of her. She wouldn't have dared to do that if Mr. Gardner had been there, but since he had left them to their own devices… *Time to have some fun.*

Grizz started off, reading the lines of Mrs. Winchester very dramatically, bugging out her eyes in terror. "'Please, spirits! What do you want with me?'"

Kurt froze, staring at the script for a few seconds. Patricia cleared her throat loudly. When he didn't reply, she rolled her eyes and snapped, "Kurt, it's your line. The one that starts with 'We have come...'"

Kurt read the lines out loud woodenly. "'We have come to take revenge for the blood the Winchester men spilled through the creation of their firearms. Blood in exchange for blood...' Whoa, man, sounds brutal."

Grizz stamped her foot and crossed her arms. "Really?"

"Stick to the script, please!" Patricia called up to the stage.

"But, Trixie, I can't help it if I speak from my heart," Kurt told her sincerely, grasping his puka shell necklace and gazing at her with wide hazel eyes.

Patricia slumped forward and covered her face with her hands. "Okay, *Kirk*, just try it again."

Kurt stared at her blankly. "Uh, my name's *Kurt*," he replied, clearly missing the point.

Grizz shrugged and nodded. "Yeah, let's get back to work, Kirk."

Before he could argue, Grizz repeated, dramatically holding a hand to her forehead, "'*Please*, spirits! What do you *want* with me?'"

"Uh," Kurt began, blinking as he stared at the script, "'We... we have come to take revenge for the blood the Winchester men spilled through the creation of their firearms! Bl-blood in exchange for—blood...'"

They ran through that scene many more times; Patricia knew full well that there was no way that he would get better, but she wanted him to see that having a part in the play was a lot harder than he thought—not to mention punish him for being over an hour late. Besides, how could she, in good conscience, sign off that he'd participated if she let him slack off?

After they'd done the scene to death, Patricia stood, clapping her hands. "All right, then."

"Sweet. Are we done, Patsy?" Kurt asked, hopping off of the stage.

"No, Burt, now you need to read the part of James," Patricia told him.

Kurt blinked at her in confusion—though whether it was because she'd called him "Burt," or the fact that he had to go through that all over again, she wasn't sure.

Patricia lifted a hand and waved him back up the steps. He took center stage again, staring at the script. "'It was your family that, uh, tore me apart from my beloved…'"

"Say it with *passion!*" Patricia commanded, pointing her pen at him.

"O-okay," Kurt mumbled, then heaved a sigh of frustration. "Ugh, I just—this is so lame. How can I even sound like I mean it? I mean, he's being so sappy. Ghost needs to get laid."

Grizz inhaled sharply, nostrils flaring. "Just because *you* are an insensitive jerk doesn't mean that someone wouldn't be heartbroken dying in the *arms of his one true love!*"

"Uh…" Kurt began to back away from Grizz slowly, his dark eyebrows raising in surprise.

"And to top it all *off,*" Grizz continued, charging forward, her eyes narrowed dangerously, "Adeline *then* gets caught in the war, trying to seek justice, and is killed herself, *by the same rifle that slew her beloved.*" She closed her eyes dramatically, her glittery eye shadow dancing in the stage lights. "How could you live with yourself for all eternity knowing that?" she asked in a hushed whisper.

"Er... okay," Kurt replied, frozen with fear at Grizz's reaction. He held up his hands as if to defend himself. "Um, calm down..."

"Okay, I've seen enough," Patricia intervened. "You can see the results on Monday. I'll talk to you in drama class to let you know when we'll meet up next."

"Cool," Kurt replied with a shrug, taking the stage steps two at a time before grabbing his bag and skateboard on his way out the door. "Catch ya on the flip side."

As soon as he was out of earshot, Patricia raced up the stairs and met Grizz in the center of the stage. Holding out a hand to her arm, she asked sympathetically, "Are you okay? Sorry he was trashing on your script."

Eyes still closed, Grizz took a deep, cleansing breath, lifting her hand and then bringing it down in front of her face as she exhaled. "I will not scream," she whispered to herself. "I will not sabotage his surfboard. Murder is bad."

"C'mon," Patricia coaxed. "Let's go binge on pizza. My treat!" Grizz opened one eye with interest.

As they left the auditorium, Patricia commented, "Either way, his acting sucks *way* more than I expected, so that's out. The play would be ruined."

"Oh, I don't know," Grizz began loftily as they walked toward Mr. Gardner's office, "I think he could really add some pizzazz to the play."

Patricia stopped dead in her tracks. "Doing what?"

Seeing Grizz's devilish smile, Patricia knew it was going to be good.

Chapter Five ♥

THE FOLLOWING WEDNESDAY, PATRICIA STOOD IN THE auditorium and directed the cast members as they read their lines. "That's good, Phillip. Just remember, you should stand right about here," Patricia came over and marked his spot on the stage, "so that the audience will really be able to see your expression."

Phillip Dizon nodded, assuming the proper place. He had been chosen to play the ghost James. "Got it, Patricia."

"Okay, could you guys take it from the top, please?" Patricia asked, holding her clipboard and walking to the side of the stage.

Grizz came up beside her. "Forty minutes and he's still a no-show," she grumbled.

"I know," Patricia said with a sigh. Grizz had described the back story of the characters to the actors while Patricia explained a little about what she wanted them to convey. She'd really wanted Kurt there so that she could show him the ropes of how the play worked, but since he still hadn't arrived, she'd decided to have everyone start reading their lines. "I think we have to talk to Mr. Gardner. Nicole, can you talk just a little louder? I'm having trouble hearing you."

"No problem," Nicole Baker, who had been chosen to play Mrs. Winchester, agreed. She smiled and flipped amber bangs out of her eyes with a toss of her head.

"Maybe he didn't like the part we chose for him," Grizz suggested with a sly grin once the actors had started reading again.

"No!" Patricia pretended to gasp, holding a hand to her chest. "We gave him the most *important* role of all!"

Grizz pulled out her cell phone. "Well, I'm sick of waiting. I'm not keeping everyone here late just because of him." She snickered as she typed out a rather menacing text. Patricia watched gleefully over her shoulder.

Just as Grizz was about to hit send, the echoing sound of wheels rolling in the hall reached Patricia's ears. She turned and saw Kurt roll into the auditorium just as he had the week before, bringing the board to a stop with his foot and kicking it up into his hands. "Hey," he greeted Patricia and Grizz with a lift of his chin.

Patricia set her jaw. Facing Natalia, Peter, Nicole and Phillip, she clapped her hands for their attention. "Okay, take five everyone."

Descending the stage steps, Patricia marched swiftly over to Kurt, who was balancing his skateboard on top of a closed theater seat. "Listen up," she snarled, all her patience gone. "You were supposed to be here forty-five minutes ago. You *do* realize that showing up late just means you have to *stay* late, don't you?"

Kurt ignored her, rummaging through his bag and producing his mp3 player and earbuds.

"Um, no!" Patricia snatched them from his hands.

"Why?" Kurt demanded, looking confused as usual. "You told us to take five!"

Patricia rolled her eyes. "I told *them* to take five so I could talk to you!"

Kurt ran a hand through his short thatch of brown hair. "About what?"

"About—" Patricia stopped herself, noticing the other actors watching with interest. She sighed and grabbed Kurt by the elbow. "C'mon back here with me."

As soon as they were behind the curtain, Patricia said, "If you expect to get a good grade in this class—heck, if you expect to even *pass*—then you need to stop doing this!"

Kurt leaned against one of the many wooden crates that were backstage. "Doing *what*, babe?"

Patricia gritted her teeth. "Well, apart from calling me 'babe'," she muttered, "you keep showing up late—*ridiculously* late! Where have you been? And don't say water polo practice, I know that the season is over."

Kurt shrugged with a lazy smile. "There were some really great waves, and I thought, 'oh, hey, it's cool, it'll be flat soon,' but they, like, kept coming, you know? And I just had to ride them out."

Rolling her eyes, Patricia snarled, "Your grade point average *cannot* handle an F, which is what you are going to get if you don't start taking this seriously. You can kiss going to college goodbye."

Kurt snorted, shoving his hands in the pockets of his baggy jeans. "Man, will you chill out? I already got into college. And my primo choice, too—ASU!"

Patricia looked him straight in the eyes. "Okay, I cannot be the first one to explain this to you: your acceptance is contingent on your grades staying the same or improving from the time you were accepted." She folded her arms. "If you do worse, you're out."

Kurt stared back at her silently, and for a minute Patricia actually thought he was taking what she'd said seriously. Then he broke his gaze, turning his head with a chuckle. "Yeah, whatever, Penelope. I'm the captain of the Vista water polo team. The ASU team is hella competitive, and the coach really wants me. I took a tour and stayed overnight with a couple of the guys—the team loves me! They're awesome. They won't revoke my acceptance when they need me."

Patricia took a step closer to him, unable to believe his sheer ignorance to the gravity of his situation. Did he think that the admissions board honestly cared about *the water polo team?*

"Um, yes, *jerk.* Yes, they will. This isn't the olden days with football where your grades can be in the toilet and no one will care. If you don't clean up your act, you can kiss Arizona State *and* their 'awesome'"—she made air quotations with her fingers—"water polo team goodbye."

Suddenly Kurt straightened, taking his hands out of his pockets and stepping closer to Patricia. She stood frozen on the spot, only able to stare quizzically into his hazel eyes as he leaned in toward her. "Well, then, you could really help me out," he said in a low voice, taking yet another step closer. "Just say I've been doing a bunch of work and it'll be all good."

She stuck out a hand to his chest to stop him from moving any closer—a bad move on her part, since she could now feel his well-defined pecs. He was dangerously close, because when she breathed in she could tell how *good* he smelled, like the ocean mixed with really nice aftershave. She felt lightheaded for a moment, and could hear her heart hammering in her chest. No wonder so many girls were crazy about Kurt. He was so tall, so cut, so *manly*. She inhaled sharply, only making it worse.

"I'll make it up to you." Kurt reached out and lightly touched her arm just above the elbow. "We could do dinner or a movie... Or I could take you to my secret spot on the beach," he told her in a husky whisper.

All at once, Patricia snapped to her senses. Taking a firm step back in her knee-high boots, she screeched, "Not gonna *work, Kirk!*" as she lifted a hand and smacked him away.

She had no idea *what* had come over her. How could any girl *actually* like him? He was hot and he knew it, and he thought that he could *bribe* her into lying and letting him get the extra credit while he never even showed up. In his mind, girls were nothing more than his tools.

Well, Patricia was just going to have to prove who was the *real* tool here, wasn't she?

"I'm not one of your little fangirls, desperate for your attention," she hissed, folding her arms across her chest. "If you keep coming late and don't do what I ask, I'll tell Mr. Gardner, and you will flunk. Your choice."

"But—"

"Uh-uh, don't wanna hear it," Patricia said firmly, holding up a hand to silence him.

Kurt simply stared at her for a moment, his jaw slackening a little bit. Then he grumbled, "Fine, what do you want me to do?"

Patricia smiled to herself, knowing that she'd won for now.

Chapter Six ♥

"SO, HE COMES OVER AN *HOUR LATE* TO THE AUDITIONS—which really ticked me off—then he mocked Grizz's script when we stayed late to let him audition, and *then* he was late to rehearsal last night!" Patricia whispered to Ben the following day at the end of their French class. When they'd finished the assignment on the board, he'd casually asked her how the one-act was going, and received a play-by-play of Kurt's shenanigans over the past week. "And then he tried to seduce me into just letting him slide."

Ben shook his head in disgust. "Of course he did. That creep."

They were interrupted by the bell. *"Ah, c'est l'heure!"* said Madame Kelley with an exaggerated sigh, earning a laugh from the class. *"Au revoir!"*

As Patricia rose to her feet and began packing away her books, Ben said, "He can't keep doing this. If Mr. Gardner expects you to help him out—"

"I talked to Kurt," Patricia informed him as they left the classroom together, "and he *seemed* to hear me. It's hard to read behind that vacant expression," she added with a sly smile.

Ben laughed, his eyes crinkling. Then his expression sobered. "I'm telling my parents."

Patricia frowned. "You don't have to, Ben. I don't want your brother to be mad at you."

But Ben shook his head, one hand tightening on the strap of his backpack. "I know he's not been doing his work. He's been B.S.ing his way through our tutoring sessions, trying to get me to give him the answers. He was out practically all weekend, not coming home 'til hella late… I need to at least clue them in."

Patricia nodded. As they walked down the crowded hallway, she smiled and said, "Well, enough of Kurt. How are you?"

Ben grinned. "Good. It's been getting sorta crazy, so I'm glad I didn't do track this year." Ben had been on the track and field team his sophomore and junior years. "I've actually got to get to a science club meeting now. Gonna do some pretty cool experiments."

"Well, don't burn off any eyebrows," Patricia teased with a laugh.

"Will do. Or not do," Ben agreed, chuckling. Lifting his hand in a wave, he turned and headed down the hallway.

Patricia waved back, staring after his tall form for a moment as he walked away.

The next day, at five minutes to seven, Patricia sat in the auditorium flipping through her notes. She was flanked by Grizz and Phillip, who had shown up ten minutes early.

"Hey, guys," Peter greeted them as he came in. Soon he was followed by Natalia and Nicole.

Patricia rose to her feet. "Okay, well that just leaves Kurt."

"Let's just start without him," Grizz said, crossing her arms. "No point in waiting, since—" She paused mid-sentence as she heard two familiar voices in the hall. "What in the…?"

Patricia turned to the door, eyes widening as Ben entered with Kurt in tow. Glancing at her phone, she saw that it was exactly seven o'clock. "Wow, right on the dot! Good job, Kurt." She stared at Ben quizzically.

Kurt snorted. "If it were up to him, we would've been here half an hour ago."

Grizz lifted her eyebrows at Patricia, clearly intrigued by the situation. "So, Ben, um… what brings you here?"

"I had to drive Kurt," Ben explained with an eye roll. "Mom and Dad took away his car keys and want me to keep an eye on him to make sure he's doing his work."

"Only because *you* ratted me out!" Kurt grumbled. "Gallant here thought that he would make me look bad in front of Mom and Dad."

Ben whipped his head around and glared at Kurt. "Hey, Goofus, I didn't *have* to make you look bad. You did it all on your own. You *still* haven't been doing your homework, and Mr. White told them you were skipping out on your English tutoring sessions, too."

Kurt scoffed. "Like I want to have to spend private time with that nerd Matt."

"Man, whatever! Just because Mr. White was smart enough not to assign you to work with some girl who was wrapped around your little finger."

"You're just jealous 'cuz you can't get any," Kurt said with a smirk, folding his arms across his chest.

"Jealous? Of *you*?" Ben drew himself up to his full height of six-foot-six and stared at his brother incredulously. "I'm not the one whose grades are so far down the toilet that Mom and Dad threatened to cut me off!"

"Only because *you* snitched! Thanks to *you*, I'm stuck without my Pacific Blue Jeep Wrangler Islander! With my lucky Tiki on the dash!" Kurt cried, looking desperate.

Grizz cocked one eyebrow. "What the hell are you talking about?"

"Oh, get over it!" Ben snapped back, rolling his eyes. "Forget about your stupid car—I'm stuck ferrying you around for the rest of forever! Or until you pass. *Whichever comes first.*"

"Kahuna is *not* stupid!" Kurt exclaimed, looking genuinely hurt by Ben's remark. Patricia had to cover her mouth to hide her laugh.

"He named his car 'Kahuna'?" Grizz whispered.

"And I'm the one whose life is ruined," Kurt continued. "Stuck with my lame little brother day and night, how uncool is that?"

Ben pulled at his hair in exasperation. "I'm only eight minutes younger than you! And do you think I *want* to be stuck spending all my free time babysitting you? I have *things* to do, Kurt!"

Kurt put on a mock pout. "Oh, what things? Nerdy little science club? Mathletics?"

"It's math*alon*, you idiot."

"Either one sounds *stupid!*" Kurt snapped, giving his brother a shove. Ben frowned in annoyance and shoved him right back, and, as everyone in the room watched with interest, the argument devolved into a shoving match, each of the Minola brothers trying to outdo each other with insults.

"Idiot!"

"Rat!"

"Jerk!"

"Nerd!"

"Moron!"

"Stop it!" Patricia commanded, inserting herself between the two of them and pushing them apart.

Kurt's chest rose and fell quickly from the exertion. "He started it," he grumbled.

Ben glanced down at Patricia in disbelief before glaring at his brother. "Did not!"

"Did too!" Kurt took a step forward, ready to brawl once more.

"*Enough!*" Patricia commanded, still holding them apart. "Go to your separate corners. Grizz, you take Kurt back to the prop closet. I'll be right there."

"My pleasure," Grizz replied gleefully, skipping forward and reaching a hand up to grab Kurt's rather large ear. "Come along, my pet."

"Ow, ow, leggo, *leggo!*" Kurt cried, doubling over as she dragged him away.

Patricia laughed before turning to Nicole, Peter, Phillip and Natalia. "Okay, guys, if you could get on the stage and do some warm-ups real quick, we'll start rehearsing in just a few."

Finally she looked at Ben with a smile. "Sorry about that." He didn't reply, merely looking down, red-faced. She followed his gaze and realized that she was still grasping him firmly around his muscular bicep. "Oh! Sorry." She dropped her hand awkwardly.

After a moment of uncomfortable silence, she told him, "I'm really sorry you got stuck with Kurt. I feel like it's my fault."

Ben shook his head with a smile. "It's not, Patricia. It's Kurt's. Besides, what I told our parents was just icing on the cake. A bunch of his teachers had called them, too."

Patricia folded her arms across her chest and leaned in to whisper, "Did your parents *really* cut him off?"

Ben nodded, shoving his hands in his pockets. "Yep. They *really* want him to go to college. Especially since everyone already knows he got in, so their reputations are on the line, now, too."

Patricia bit her lip. She knew the Minolas were wealthy, and that the family was totally into the country club, charity ball scene. It would definitely be embarrassing if one of their sons got kicked out of college before he'd even started.

"They said if he doesn't buckle down," Ben continued, "they won't pay for college even if by some bizarre chance he *did* still get in. They took away his car and cut off his allowance, and they said he's not getting another cent until he proves he is responsible enough to fix this."

"Wow. Think it will work?" Patricia asked.

Ben shrugged. "Guess we'll see, huh?"

"Yeah, well, thanks for bringing him. Maybe tonight I can actually get him to do some of the stuff on my checklist." Patricia rubbed her hands together and laughed wickedly.

Chuckling, Ben glanced around before asking in a low voice, "Sure you don't want me to stick around to kick his ass if he doesn't do as he's told?"

Patricia grinned and shoved him playfully. "Don't worry. I think we've got this."

Ben seemed hesitant. "...Okay, then. Your rehearsal ends at nine, right?" Seeing Patricia's nod, he replied, "All right, see you then."

"Bye!" Patricia replied, staring after Ben for a moment before mentally going over a checklist.

Oh, yes. Kurt had his work cut out for him.

Chapter Seven ♡

SEVERAL REHEARSALS LATER, PATRICIA WAS SEATED IN FRONT of the stage, watching carefully as the actors did a run-through. "Kurt!" she called out to the tall teen, who was standing idly by, staring off into space. "Earth to Kurt!"

Natalia, noticing he still wasn't listening, skipped over to Kurt and gently shook his arm. "Kurt," she said, flipping long platinum blonde hair over her shoulder, "I think Patricia is talking to you."

Kurt seemed to snap out of it, turning his attention on Natalia. "Oh, sorry. What'd you say, babe?"

Natalia giggled shyly, pointing offstage. "Patricia needs you."

He turned to Patricia. "'Sup, Persephone?"

Patricia gritted her teeth, gripping her pencil tightly. "Oh, nothing much, Kyle, just the fact that you *missed your cue*, again!"

Kurt stared at her blankly. "Oh, I did? Uh… what's my cue again?" He grinned as this earned yet another tinkle of laughter from Natalia.

Peter and Phillip looked at each other and rolled their eyes. "You're supposed to rattle the chains when I say, 'You, who are living on the vast fortunes of our misery,'" Peter snapped.

"*Oh*, right, right," Kurt said distractedly, still looking at Natalia.

"Okay, places, everyone! Take it from Mrs. Winchester's line, 'What must I do?'" Patricia instructed, leaning back in her chair with a sigh.

Rehearsal went on for a few more minutes, until, once again, when it was Kurt's cue, he stood there and did nothing. "Kurt!" Patricia cried. "You're supposed to do the ghostly howl right then! You know, like we talked about?"

Kurt looked sheepish. He cleared his throat. "Okay… *awww-rrrroooo…*"

Patricia turned around in her seat when she heard Ben burst into laughter. "Aren't you supposed to be doing your homework?" she asked with one eyebrow raised. To Patricia's surprise, Ben had stuck around the last couple of rehearsals, claiming he couldn't get anything done, knowing he would have to pick Kurt up in a short amount of time.

Ben lifted a fist to his mouth and pretended like he was coughing. "Um, sorry," he said, unable to hide his grin.

Patricia frowned at Ben and turned back in her seat to face the stage. "No, that sounds like a wolf. It's supposed to be like this: *eeeeeeeee-ohhhhh,*" she wailed like a banshee. "Try again."

Kurt heaved a sigh. "*E-I-E-I-O…*"

Ben's laughter that time reached the stage, and Kurt stopped abruptly. "Do I *have* to do this, Patsy? This is *so* lame. Can't you just use a stereo?"

Turning briefly to smack Ben's notebook to silence his laughter, Patricia replied, "No, *Kirk*, we can't. You are *very* essential to this production. You help to demonstrate the fact that the ghosts mean business."

Kurt's shoulders sank. "But I just can't get into this."

Patricia stood and put her hands on her hips. "You have to *try*. Like… think back to when you were little and would pretend you were a pirate, or a cowboy, or something. Could you do it then?"

Kurt shrugged, looking confused. "Yeah, sure, but that was just pretend…"

"That's what acting *is*, genius," Phillip muttered.

Patricia decided to switch tactics. "Lots of girls come to the theater festival, Kurt," she said. "*Lots* of girls. And your name is going to be in the program, so they'll know it's you…"

Raising his eyebrows, Kurt stepped forward. "They will? But"—he suddenly looked doubtful—"won't they laugh at me?"

Patricia shook her head fervently. "Oh, no, not if you do a good job. They'll think you're awesome. Knocking over stuff and making scary sounds with no synthesizer? That's really cool!"

"We came up with this part especially for *you*, Kurt," Grizz added, voice dripping in sweetness.

"And you can do a really good job if you practice. Can't he, Natalia?" Patricia looked at her expectantly.

Natalia grinned and nodded at Kurt enthusiastically. "I believe in you, Kurt," she cooed.

"Really?" Kurt brightened at the thought. "All right!"

Patricia glanced at her cell phone and said, "Okay, guys, we only have a few minutes left to use the stage, so let's just finish this page of the script."

When they were done, the cast descended the stage steps, but Patricia moved to intercept Kurt. "Kurt, you need to stay a little longer. We have a job for you."

"Bummer," he mumbled. Turning to Natalia, he whispered, "See you next time, babe," earning a nod and giggle from her.

"Okay," Grizz said as she stood from where she'd been poring over spare fabric that she'd found for costumes, "I think the storeroom will have all the plywood we'll need."

"This is gonna involve some heavy lifting," Ben, once again eavesdropping, surmised. He rose to his feet and hopped over the row of seats before him. "I'll come help."

"We can't use power tools here on campus, so we're going to need you to saw the wood and do everything else that requires your tools at home," Patricia explained as they walked to the storeroom. "Then you can bring it to rehearsal and paint it here."

Kurt merely shrugged in response.

Once inside, Grizz flipped on the light. "Man, this place is a sty," she muttered, staring at the jumbled mess of poster boards, boxes, crates, and unnamable *junk* that covered the floor. Then her eyes lit up as she noticed the tall pieces of wood leaning against a shelving unit. "Bingo!"

"That would be good for the door," Patricia mused, pointing to a sheet of plywood that was balancing precariously atop the shelving unit.

Grizz noticed a fat beam propped underneath a stack of wooden poles. "Hey, that would work, huh?"

Before anyone could react, Kurt reached his long arm behind the poles and grabbed the beam. When he tugged it forward, it knocked loose the sheet of plywood and sent it soaring toward Patricia.

"Look out!" Ben cried, wrapping his arms protectively around her as he quickly pushed her out of harm's way.

Heart hammering in her chest, Patricia kept her head down, clutching Ben's arms. After a moment or two she dared to straighten up, cheeks growing warm when she realized how close Ben's face was to her own as he peered at her in concern.

"Are you okay?" Ben asked her, his voice still a bit raspy with adrenaline.

Patricia nodded slightly, still not releasing her grip on Ben's rather muscular arms. "Y-yeah, thanks."

Grizz whirled on Kurt. "You moron! You could've killed Patricia!"

Kurt didn't answer at first, staring at Patricia with wide eyes, his face shades paler than normal. "Oh, man," he muttered in a daze. "I-I didn't mean to..."

Ben turned to Kurt, arms still protectively around Patricia. "You've gotta be careful, Kurt! I could've helped you move the wood! That was really dangerous!"

Kurt nodded slowly, still seeming dazed. "Oh, man," he repeated. "I'm really sorry. Are you okay?"

Patricia sighed, finally straightening as Ben released her. She snapped back into director mode as soon as her heart slowed back to a normal pace. "Yeah, I know you didn't mean to. Here, let's just pick out the wood and you can carry it to the car. I'll give you some drawings of how I want the pieces done, okay? Can you please have it done and back here on Tuesday so that we can start painting it?"

Kurt shook his head quickly, then nodded. "Yeah, sure thing."

Once they'd loaded the wood into Ben's car, Patricia gave Kurt detailed instructions on what she wanted done, handing him drawings and written directions so that he couldn't claim he'd forgotten.

As he got into the passenger seat, he rolled down the window and told Patricia, "I… I'm really sorry. I'll be more careful from now on."

Patricia stared into his hazel eyes, which crinkled apologetically, and she knew he meant it. "I know you will," she said with a small smile.

Before Ben got in the car, he turned to Patricia. "You're sure you're okay?" he asked her quietly, placing a hand to her shoulder.

Patricia flushed, folding her arms nervously. "Yeah, I'm sure. Thanks for rescuing me from the board of doom," she said with a laugh.

As the brothers drove away, Grizz turned to Patricia and said, "I can't believe Kurt was so…"

Patricia nodded, knowing exactly what Grizz was getting at. *Maybe there is a human buried deep inside that musclebound brain after all,* she mused with a lopsided smile.

Chapter Eight ♡

"OKAY, NOW LET'S WORK ON PAINTING THE DOOR AND the pillars," Patricia told Grizz the following Tuesday. Turning to Kurt, she asked, "Can you bring over the door you built?"

Kurt glanced at her, shifting uncomfortably. Patricia's stomach knotted. Now that she thought of it, she hadn't seen him bring anything in with him. Ben hadn't been able to drive him to rehearsal that day, so they couldn't be waiting in the car, either.

"Kurt," she began menacingly, "where are the set pieces I asked you to build?"

"Oh, *those*," Kurt replied with a laugh. "I forgot to bring them. Don't worry, I finished them this weekend like you asked me to."

Why do I not believe you? Patricia wondered snidely. Sighing, she said, "Go help Grizz with the costumes."

Groaning, Kurt slowly shuffled over to Grizz, who was sitting on the floor surrounded by patterns, thread, pincushions, and a melee of clothing.

"Come, my pet," Grizz whispered eerily, removing a pin from her mouth and carefully pushing it into the pincushion. "I have a very important task for you. I need you to measure the cast for costumes." She tossed him an electric blue measuring tape.

"Sweet," Kurt replied, starting to move toward Natalia and Nicole, who were running lines together in the corner. "Which lucky girl is first?"

"Oh, no," Grizz called after him teasingly, "not the girls. I need you to measure Peter—around his waist, his chest, then from the nape of his neck to his tail bone, please."

"What?!" Kurt recoiled in horror.

Grizz shrugged innocently. "Well, I'm making his uniform jacket, and I need to be exactly sure of his measurements."

"B-but… can't one of you chicks do it?"

"No," Patricia said harshly before Grizz could respond, "we're busy. And you are supposed to be helping us. So unless you want to be here all night long, you had better do what Grizz tells you."

Kurt looked between Grizz and Patricia for a moment, seeming at a loss. Then he heaved a sigh. "Okay. Man, Zelda, this is cruel." Cupping his hand over his mouth, he shouted, "Yo, Pete!"

Peter looked up from his script. "Yeah?"

"C'mere for a sec. I need to measure you."

Peter's eyes widened as he shook his head fervently. "No."

Kurt turned back to Grizz and shrugged, tossing her the measuring tape. "Aw, too bad. He doesn't want me to."

Grizz swiftly caught the tape and chucked it right back to him. Then she turned to Peter. "Peter," she began coyly, batting her lashes and pouting her lips, "I'm very busy making this jacket, and I need your measurements. Won't you be a sweetheart and let Kurt measure you, just this once?"

Peter stared at Grizz for a moment in silence, mouth agape. Then he slowly nodded. "Okay."

As Kurt clumsily wrapped the tape around Peter's chest, Peter growled, "One false move and I'll punch your lights out."

Kurt rolled his eyes, calling out the number as he took each measurement. "Dude, same goes for you."

When the task was done, he trudged over to Grizz. "Good job," she said. "Now I need you to sew the lace onto these sleeves." Grizz lifted an old dress that she'd found in the prop closet and was currently embellishing to be Adeline's costume. "And then the lace on the bodice as well. It's already all pinned into place, so it should be a snap."

Kurt looked at the offered dress and sneered. "Sewing is for chicks, man. I'm not doing that."

"Well, if that isn't the most sexist comment I've ever heard," Grizz snarled, brandishing her sewing scissors.

Patricia hurried over. "No, he's right, Grizz. Sewing *is* for chicks. We can't ask him to do that."

Kurt nodded. "Yeah, what she said."

"After all," Patricia went on, "he wouldn't know the first thing about sewing. It requires brain cells that he doesn't possess."

Grizz nodded slowly, catching on. "Oh, yeah, definitely. Sorry, Kurt, it's just too much to ask of you. You're not smart enough to sew on a button."

Kurt looked affronted. "Hey—"

"No, no." Patricia held up her hands. "After all, it takes a keen mind and a steady hand to do something so complex. No mere man can do it."

"I bet I could!" Kurt cried out, reaching to grab the pin cushion.

"Oh, no, you couldn't!" Grizz protested, holding the cushion away from him.

Kurt set his jaw. "I can so! Here, I'll prove it. How do you thread the needle?"

Hiding her grin as she shared a look with Patricia, Grizz showed Kurt how to thread the needle and stitch on the lace.

"So, the bellboy asks the photon if he needs help with his luggage, and the photon says, 'Oh, I don't have any. I'm traveling light,'" Ben told Patricia as he was driving the next day, glancing over at her to gauge her reaction.

Patricia threw her head back and laughed, one arm hanging out the window of the passenger seat of Ben's Expedition. "Okay, that was good."

"Really? I haven't driven you to madness yet with my dumb science jokes?" Ben asked with a grin.

Patricia made a disbelieving noise, reaching over to playfully shove him.

"Hey, watch it, I'm driving here!"

Patricia held up her hands in submission. "Whoopsie, my bad."

Glancing quickly at her before turning his attention back to the road, Ben asked, "So, what subject are you doing for your French presentation?"

"I'm thinking *Le Chat Noir*."

"Oh, yeah, that nightclub with the poster of the cranky looking cat?"

Patricia giggled at his description. "Yes, that one. What about you?"

"I'm gonna do Augustin-Louis Cauchy."

"Ooh," Patricia said in an awed voice, then grinned and asked, "Who's that?"

Ben laughed. "He was a physicist and mathematician in the 1800s."

"Cool. A subject that definitely appeals to you."

"Yep," Ben agreed. "I plan to be a physics major. Maybe even a physics and math double major."

Patricia pumped a fist in the air. "If you did both that would be so hardcore. Do it, do it!"

Ben chuckled at her enthusiasm. "The college I'm going to has an awesome program—really great resources and labs. It's gonna *rock*. But what about you? Do you think you'll do any other major besides theater?"

"Hm…" Patricia mulled that one over. "Maybe a French minor. Or something super cool, like classics!"

"Classics would be *awesome*," Ben enthused. "You could learn Latin! Man, I've always wanted to know Latin."

"Definitely."

Ben pulled into a cul-de-sac and approached a large beautiful Colonial two-story home—the Minolas' house. Patricia had voiced her suspicions to Ben about Kurt not making the set after French, and, since

Kurt was going to be at tutoring for a while, Ben had offered to bring Patricia by their house to see if he had indeed been fibbing.

"Wow," Patricia breathed as she undid her seatbelt. "You guys have a *nice* house."

Ben ducked his head shyly. "Thanks. His shed's out back, but it's easier to get to it through the house."

As they walked through the entryway, living room and kitchen, Patricia took in the cozy decorations and beautiful furniture. Ben pulled open a sliding door and led her through the nicely landscaped, fenced backyard to a large shed that looked like a miniature version of their house. "Here's where he does all of his stuff," Ben told her as he opened the door.

Once inside, Patricia could see how much Kurt really did like carpentry. There were all sorts of tools hanging from pegs on the walls, plus a table saw and a large workbench. As she passed by a surfboard propped against the wall, she ran a hand along the sanded texture. "This is really cool."

"Aw, man," Ben groaned, lifting a bunch of materials from the ground and placing them onto the workbench. "He hasn't even *started*!" Sighing, he ran both his hands through his hair in a frustrated motion. "I'm sorry, Patricia. I should have known. I'll make sure he does it in the next couple days."

Patricia shook her head, crossing her arms as she replied firmly, "Nope. *I'm* going to make sure he does it."

Chapter Nine ♡

"**N**O, KURT, YOU HAVE TO MAKE IT WIDER THAN THAT," Patricia scolded the next day as she sat with Kurt in his shed, watching his work like a hawk. He'd been pretty ticked that they had sneaked into his workshop to find out that he'd lied, but there was nothing he could do about it now.

Except complain.

"But Trixie, it looks fine this way," Kurt whined, setting the piece of plywood back down.

"No, it doesn't! The door in the Winchester Mystery House has a glass panel in the center. The cutout has to be wide enough so that the actors can walk through it and not snag their costumes or trip and knock it over. Do you want our play to look bad? Cut it wider!"

Kurt heaved a sigh, lowering his safety goggles over his eyes once again and carefully lining up the wood to the blade. Patricia grimaced and covered her ears as the saw went off. *The things I do for my play,* she thought, hating how the sound of the saw made her skin crawl.

When he was done, he slid it off the table and held it up for Patricia to test. Carefully she lifted her foot and stepped through the rectangular section that Kurt had cut out of the center of the "door." She shook her head. "About an inch and a half wider, please."

"Listen, Pam," Kurt began, pulling his goggles off and sitting down on a stool.

"I'm listening, Kyle."

Looking confused for a moment, Kurt continued, "I don't know why you are being so obsessive about this. Most people probably aren't even going to have props and sets and stuff. No one is gonna care."

"Do you really take such little pride in your own work?" Patricia asked him, standing to touch the surfboard he'd made. "You wouldn't want to make a crappy surfboard and have people see it, would you?"

Kurt scoffed, stretching out his long legs. "Yeah, but that's surfing! Something important! This play is boring. Theater is boring. I wish I'd never taken this class. I just can't get into it."

"Maybe if you *tried* to be interested in it—read the script, did *something*—it wouldn't seem like such a waste of time." When he rolled his eyes, she pulled her hair away from her face in frustration. Finally, she said, in a much calmer tone, "Okay, Kurt, what *are* you into? Besides girls and surfing," she added wryly.

"Cool things, like music, and sports, carpentry, car shows... oh, and history!" Kurt added, putting his hands in the pockets of his hooded sweatshirt as he leaned back slightly.

Patricia was taken aback. "Wait—*history?*" She was shocked that he found something so academic "cool."

"Yeah, dude, especially military history," Kurt went on, eyes shining with excitement. "Ever see a Civil War reenactment? They're radical."

Patricia couldn't believe her ears. The military history thing made sense in a strange way, but he liked Civil War reenactments? "But Kurt, that's theater!"

Kurt looked at her incredulously. "Nah, babe, it's *history*."

"But it's acting! Someone had to put together the production—build the sets, do the lighting, the makeup, the costumes, even the script. And our play is historical, too."

Kurt looked at her and laughed. "But it's about ghosts! That's not history!"

Patricia tucked a strand of hair behind her ear and replied, "But Mrs. Winchester was a real woman, and her house is a historical landmark. Grizz worked hard to add a supernatural element to a real event—the 1906 earthquake."

Kurt watched her carefully for a moment, slowly nodding. "Yeah, I guess it *is* history, huh?"

Seeing that she'd made a breakthrough, Patricia continued, "And theater can be really cool if you give it a chance. Like, there's a ton of historical plays."

Kurt looked interested. "Whoa, really?"

Patricia nodded enthusiastically. "Yeah! In fact, Shakespeare wrote several—*Henry V, Antony and Cleopatra, Julius Caesar...*"

"Sweet," Kurt muttered, running his hand absently over the plywood door. Then he sighed. "Argh—it's just, this is all so *much* work. The play, tutoring, all the homework..." He slumped forward on the work table, burying his head in his hands.

It's your own fault, you big crybaby, Patricia thought with an eye roll. But aloud she said, "Okay, just think of it this way: you just have to work hard until the end of the year to achieve your goal."

Head still on the table, Kurt turned slightly to look at her. "My goal?"

"Getting into ASU?" Patricia prodded.

"But I'm already *in*." Kurt lifted his head slightly. "It doesn't matter if Mom and Dad cut me off. I'm getting an athletic scholarship—"

"But for how much?" Patricia interrupted. She knew it couldn't be a substantial amount. When he told her, she threw her head back and laughed. "That's not even going to cover your dorm! And since your parents are loaded, I can guarantee you aren't getting any other financial aid, right?"

Kurt furrowed his brow. "Uh, yeah, I guess..."

"So you have to do this, for your goal!" Patricia balled her hand into a fist to cheer him on. "Tell me, why do you want to go to ASU?"

Sitting up straighter, Kurt said, "For everything, dude! Tempe is awesome, there's sorority babes galore, and their water polo team is the best around! The guys and coach were so cool. I did an overnight with a couple of the team members. They were even talking about doing a *theme house* next year. And did you know, with the summer Olympics just a few years away, they scout out of college? I want to play in the Olympics!"

Wow. The Olympics? Patricia blinked, surveying him for a moment or two. "Think of it this way: everything you have to do now is just work to achieve that goal," she said. "Sure, it's hard now, but it's only until the end of the year. In the fall you can apply yourself right off the bat in all your classes, and get help right away if you need it. If you play it smart, you'll never have to do something like this again."

Kurt sat up fully, turning on the stool to face her. "Whoa," he breathed. "I guess I never thought about it that way before, but you're right. I gotta do this—for water polo." Then he sighed and scratched the side of his head. "No matter how much it sucks."

Patricia put a hand to his arm. "I know it's a lot of work, and it can seem overwhelming, but it's the same for me. I want to be a theater major when I get to college—I want to be a director someday. This is my chance to get up in front of everyone and show them that I can do it. Maybe if we work together, we can make both of our dreams come true."

Kurt smiled slightly. "Sounds good to me."

"Um, am I interrupting something?"

Patricia turned quickly to see that Ben had entered the shed, holding a tray laden with snacks. "Oh, how sweet! Brownies!"

"And lemonade," Ben added with a smile, coming over to set the tray down on the workbench. "Thought you guys might need some nourishment. Mom baked these last night."

Patricia took a brownie and put a hand to her mouth as she bit into it. "They're delicious!"

"Yeah, thanks, bro," Kurt said, grabbing two at once.

Ben laughed, though Patricia noticed that it sounded a little strained. He poured a glass and handed it to Patricia. "No problem," he said. "So, how goes it?"

Before Patricia could reply, Kurt said enthusiastically, "Great! Just need to make this section a little wider, right, Patty?"

Patricia looked at Kurt in surprise. Then, with a nod, she replied, "Right!" Seeing Ben's curious look, she smiled and shrugged.

Chapter Ten ♥

GRIZZ'S EYES WIDENED AS KURT AND BEN CARRIED IN THE set pieces at their next rehearsal. "Wow, he actually did it," she said to Patricia under her breath.

Patricia nodded happily. "Yeah, don't they look nice?"

Grizz stared at the pieces as they went by. "Our play is gonna be *so* badass."

"Yo, Zelda!" Kurt called as he set down the door. "I got the stuff you wanted."

"For the last time, it's *Grizz*!" Her annoyed expression faded as he held a plastic bag out to her. Peering into it suspiciously, she saw that he'd gotten all of the paint and supplies she'd asked him to. "Wow. Um, this is great, thanks. Okay, why don't you help me paint this door, and then you can stitch some more embellishments onto Phillip's uniform."

"Sure thing," Kurt agreed easily, pulling out the paint and brushes.

"Wow, Kurt, it looks so good," Natalia cooed as she came over to admire his handiwork.

Kurt flashed a grin, twisting the cap off of a paint tube. "Thanks, babe."

"One second, Kurt!" Patricia called. "We need to lay down newspaper or something so we don't get paint on the floor. There's some in the back, I'll get it."

"I'll help," Ben offered, hurrying after her.

As they gathered old newspaper from the storeroom, Patricia commented, "Kurt sure is a lot more eager to help."

Ben nodded, holding out his arms to let her place more paper atop the stack he was carrying. "I know. He actually seems excited about the play now."

"Maybe he actually listened to me," Patricia mused as she closed the door behind them.

Ben turned to her curiously. Seeing his look, Patricia quickly said, "I gave him a pep talk the other day. Well, it was kind of more like a smackdown. I think he may actually realize now that he *will* be screwed if he doesn't do his work."

Ben broke into a surprised grin. "I hope so. That'll be better for everybody."

Patricia let out a breath with a laugh. "Don't I know it."

As Grizz and Kurt delved into painting, Patricia set the stage with the props that were ready to go, helping the actors to mark out their places and rehearse.

"Okay, remember, reach for the candlestick and hold it just so"— Patricia demonstrated to Nicole—"so that the audience can still see your reaction. Okay?"

Nicole nodded, taking hold of the candlestick. "Got it."

"Okay, let's give this part a run-through, then." Patricia skipped down the steps and took a seat.

After the actors had finished, Ben turned to her. "That was great. It's really coming along."

Patricia smiled proudly. "You think so?"

Ben grinned in return. "Definitely."

"Ben!" Kurt suddenly called from where he was busily painting. "Do me a favor, bro!"

Ben looked over to him suspiciously. "And do what?"

"I've got a Spanish test this week, can you grab my flash cards from my backpack and quiz me?"

Ben looked over at Patricia, impressed. He stood and retrieved the flash cards from Kurt's backpack. "All right, I'm gonna give you the Spanish first and you give me the English. Ready?"

"Hit me," Kurt replied, not looking up from his work.

Ben cleared his throat. *"La corbata."*

"Tie," Kurt replied without hesitating, furiously swiping his paintbrush.

"Good." Ben flipped to the next card. *"Los zapatos."*

"Uh... shoes?" Kurt asked, head cocked to the side.

"Ding ding ding!" Ben called out with a grin. "Okay, *el estante.*"

Kurt was silent, tapping his paintbrush thoughtfully. "Um... uh..."

"C'mon," Ben encouraged, flipping the card over to look at the English answer, "you can do it. It's found in a store, kind of important..."

Kurt suddenly threw his hands up in the air. "Rack!"

"Woot!" Ben cheered. "You got it!"

Patricia watched the scene and smiled, glad to see Ben so excited about Kurt doing well. Kurt really seemed to want to make a change to his life.

"Wow, Kurt," Natalia called from her spot on the stage, "you really are *maravilloso!*"

Kurt turned toward her and grinned. "*Gracias, chica!*"

Patricia rolled her eyes and returned to her notes. *Then again, the more things change, the more they stay the same.*

A couple weeks later, Patricia and Grizz were looking over the costumes, which were just about finished, except for Peter's jacket and Phillip's uniform.

"If someone had some really nice dress pants," Grizz mused, "we wouldn't have to buy or make anything."

"I'm sure one of the guys or their dads will have something like that," Patricia told her, patting her on the back. "Don't worry!"

"Hey, guys," Ben greeted everyone as he walked in the room with Kurt. "Wow, the costumes are looking great," he commented, crouching to look at them closer. "What do you think, Kurt?"

"Sweet," Kurt agreed, seeming distracted. "Oh, hey, Trixie, I checked out the Winchester Mystery House this weekend, and you were right, it *is* history. That place is off the hook, man!"

Patricia lifted her eyebrows at Grizz, who looked equally shocked. He actually went there? Because of her play? And he liked it? Patricia felt herself smile at the thought. "Well, I'm glad you enjoyed it."

Kurt grinned, lifting his hands enthusiastically. "Totally! Staircases leading to nowhere, doors that open to a straight drop down, a room with that many fireplaces? So trippy." Then he lowered his hands and looked at Grizz with furrowed brows. "Oh, but Rizzo, there's, like, a problem with your script."

Grizz bristled at the nickname. "What problem?" she scoffed incredulously.

Kurt stuck his hands in his pockets. "Well, the Winchester rifle wasn't used during the Civil War. That was the Henry rifle. Oliver Winchester didn't buy the rifle company until after the war—1866. His most famous gun model came out in 1873 and was called 'the gun that won the West.' So the ghosts wouldn't be from the Civil War. They'd be, like, Rangers, or cowboys and outlaws, or something."

Patricia inhaled sharply. She couldn't believe her ears. If that was true, then poor Grizz's script…

Patricia turned to gauge Grizz's reaction. She was just sitting there, jaw set and eyes narrowed. "What?" she finally said with a disbelieving laugh. "That can't be right." She pulled her phone out of her pocket to do an online search.

"Wait." Her hand shot out to seize Patricia's arm in a death grip. "He—he's right. No, no, no, he can't be right…"

Patricia looked at him suspiciously, all the while trying to wiggle her arm free. "How did you know that?"

Kurt grinned, oblivious to the chaos he had wrought. "History is my *jam,* man! Especially stuff about firearms and battles and all that."

Grizz rose to her feet, her heavily lined eyes bugging out with rage. "If you *knew* that, then *why didn't you say anything?!*" she screamed, balling her hands into fists that shook. "You had to keep your mouth shut until my costumes are almost finished, until the theater festival is *almost here*?! What, did you think it was *funny?!*"

Kurt scratched his ear nonchalantly. "Oh, I didn't know 'til I went to the house, and then I did some reading on it. Dad has tons of books on local stuff."

Grizz stood there on the spot, quaking for a moment. Then, suddenly, she lunged, brandishing her long, hot-pink fingernails at Kurt. *"DIE!"*

Ben and Patricia leapt to intervene, Patricia holding Grizz from behind as she kicked and screamed. "Death is too good for him," Grizz screeched, her red-tipped hair flailing about. "Tar and feather him! Give him the rack!"

Suddenly her head whipped around, her attention now focused on the costumes that lay a few feet away. "Ruined! All ruined!" Ripping herself from Patricia's grasp, she flung herself onto her knees and snatched the half-finished jacket, pulling furiously at it to rend it in two. "All this time—*wasted*! I'm gonna be a laughingstock! I'll have to work night and day—no sleep for me—to fix this idiotic mistake!"

"No, Grizz, stop!" Patricia cried, diving to grab the jacket from Grizz's hands.

Grizz held on stubbornly, tugging violently on the fabric as she whimpered, "How could *Kurt Minola* be smarter than me?!"

"Grizz, stop, stop!" Ben pleaded, forcibly lifting her to her feet by hoisting her by the underarms. "It's okay, you didn't know!"

Patricia stood and put her hands to Grizz's shoulders. "Grizz, I didn't know, either! And neither did Peter, or any of the others!"

Ben nodded and shrugged. "Me, neither. I think one of the times I went the tour guide even said something about the Civil War."

"Yeah!" Patricia nodded encouragingly. "And the tour guides talk so fast, and the house is so big! I don't think the rifles actually came up that much."

Grizz's shoulders heaved as she slowed down her breathing. Then her eyes filled with tears. "It probably was on one of those information signs out front," she said with a sniffle. "Why didn't I do more research? What kind of a writer *am* I?" Gazing at Patricia, she whispered, "I've ruined the play."

"No, you haven't," Patricia said soothingly. "Look at the gorgeous costumes you made—Mrs. Winchester's dress can stay the same!"

Grizz nodded slowly, her makeup running down her cheeks. "That's true…"

"And the guys' clothes are pretty similar," Ben told her. "I mean, we can look it up to be extra sure, but I don't think they would need much altering."

"Yeah." Then Grizz's face fell again. "But the script… my characters…"

"Well, Kurt says that history is his 'jam', right?" Turning to Kurt, who'd been standing there looking quite uncomfortable, Patricia lifted her eyebrows expectantly.

He nodded. "Yeah, and I love Westerns."

Patricia smiled. "There, see? Kurt will look stuff up and help you adapt your script."

Grizz eyed Kurt suspiciously. "You will?"

Kurt shrugged and nodded. "Yeah, sure thing. My dad has tons of books, and we can also look online. I can help with the costumes too," he surprised them all by volunteering. "I have a ton of cowboy hats and boots and stuff."

Grizz furiously wiped her face with her sleeve, taking a deep breath and returning to normal. "Well, what are we waiting for?" she declared, reaching into her bag for her keys. "Let's get a move on! To Casa Minola! Away!"

As Grizz gathered the costumes and prodded Kurt out of the auditorium, Patricia smiled and turned to Ben. "Well, hopefully that will work out."

Nodding, Ben said, "He really listens to you."

Patricia looked surprised. "Huh? No, he doesn't," she said, laughing uncomfortably.

"No, really," Ben insisted, putting his hands in his pockets. "He just agreed to helping Grizz, he's been buckling down and applying himself like you encouraged him to, and when he had me take him to the Winchester Mystery House this weekend, he wouldn't stop talking about you."

Patricia's eyebrow crinkled in surprise. "Really?"

Ben nodded and dropped his gaze to the floor, suddenly looking uncomfortable. "Um, Patricia, I…"

Patricia stared at him, holding her breath as she waited for him to finish his sentence.

Chapter Eleven ♡

Luckily for Grizz, they only had to make minor changes to the script and costumes. Grizz ended up turning the jacket she was making for Peter's character into a vest and gave him a button-down shirt, and it turned out that the dress for Natalia's character, Adeline, didn't need any changes. With the addition of Kurt's cowboy hats and boots, the costumes were finished and looked great.

In fact, as time went on, everyone in the play noticed that Kurt had begun to actually make an effort. During a dress rehearsal, Patricia kept a close eye on Kurt, who was getting better and better at his role. His ghostly moans sounded truly bone-chilling, and he was now competent at waving the chains around without causing bodily harm.

As he roamed across the stage in his costume, a long black hooded cloak so that the audience would only catch a glimpse of his ghostly presence, he seemed very into his part. *"Ohhhhh-ohhhhhhhhh,"* he wailed, knocking over a table on cue.

Patricia grinned to herself. *This is going to look* so *good when it's all done,* she thought in excitement.

Just then, Kurt dropped his chain and it fell on the stage with a clatter. "Whoops, my bad," he called out.

"Kurt," Patricia reminded him, "remember, never, ever, ever break character. If that happens during the actual show, do not say anything, just quietly pick it up and go back to haunting. People are less likely to notice mistakes if you act like nothing happened. The show must go on!"

Kurt's eyes looked a bit glazed as she was talking, but then he nodded and grinned. "You got it, chief."

After they were done rehearsing, Patricia held up her hands. "Okay, now we're going to try that with lighting, so I'm going up to the light booth for this next run-through. Grizz, can you come with me?"

Once in the light booth, Grizz clapped her hands together enthusiastically. "This is looking *so awesome.*"

Patricia grinned, turning a control. "Yeah, your costumes look so good."

Grizz gazed off into the distance, looking embarrassed but pleased. "Why, thank you." Then she sighed. "I hate to say it, but I'm glad Kurt is in our play." Seeing Patricia's horrified look, Grizz held up her hands. "No, no, he's still a tool, but if it hadn't been for him, people at the festival would've seen the big mistake I'd made."

Patricia nodded slowly. "Yeah, that's true. And the sets do look really good." She looked down and saw Ben walk in with a couple pizza boxes. "I guess everything's working out, huh?" she said with a smile.

When the rehearsal was over, Grizz and Patricia descended the precarious spiral staircase that led from the lighting booth. Kurt leapt off the stage and rushed over to Patricia. "Dude, Trixie, the lights made it choka!"

Patricia cocked an eyebrow, emitting a small laugh. "What?"

Kurt smiled. "Choka. Surf-speak for 'awesome'."

"Ohh." Patricia nodded, tucking a strand of hair behind her ear. "Well, thank you."

"Hey, everybody!"

Patricia turned her head to see Ben standing nearby, brandishing the pizza boxes. "Dinner is served," he said with a grin.

"Actors, please change out of your costumes before you eat, lest you risk my wrath!" Grizz called with an innocent smile on her face. Then she skipped over to Ben, plucking a pepperoni slice from the top box he was holding and taking a large bite. "Mm, delish! Thanks!"

"Yeah, thanks so much, Ben," Patricia told him as she joined them.

"No problem," Ben said. "There's pepperoni and," he shifted the boxes, moving the bottom one to the top of the stack and opening it, "ta-da! Hawaiian."

Patricia could feel her mouth water at the sight of the ham and pineapple pizza. "Oh, my favorite! You rock."

"The play is looking good. I think you guys are there," Ben told them, setting down the pizza boxes on a table.

"I hope so," Grizz replied, wiping the corner of her mouth with a napkin from the pack Ben had brought with the pizza, plates, and soda.

Patricia laughed, setting down her slice. "No, we *are* good. It's gonna be choka!" she said with a laugh, making a "hang loose" sign with her left hand.

≈

"Thank you so much, I'm so glad you liked it," Patricia told her English teacher as he congratulated her after the theater festival. The play had been a success, the applause afterward causing her face to hurt from grinning so much. Now all of those who had participated were lining the hallway, exchanging hugs and congratulations.

Turning to Grizz, she sighed with relief and said, "I can't believe it's over."

Grizz grinned and leaned against the wall, folding her hands behind her. "I can't believe Kurt didn't trip and knock over the set."

Laughing, Patricia smoothed the skirt of her coral-colored dress. "I know! He was actually…"

"Pretty good?" Grizz supplied grudgingly.

Patricia nodded, combing her hair with her fingers. "Yeah. I'm glad, though. Could you imagine if he'd—"

"Don't say it," Grizz warned with wide eyes.

"Ladies!" Mr. Gardner greeted them as he appeared. "Excellent one-act, truly a masterpiece. I must say, you seemed to use Mr. Minola's time well—the props were superb, and his role…" Grizz and Patricia side-eyed each other, trying not to snicker. "What an excellent use of the stage. Well done. I think working together has worked out in everyone's favor," he surmised, peering keenly at Patricia over his glasses. "Well, I won't keep you. This is a time to celebrate!"

"Thank you, Mr. Gardner," Grizz and Patricia said in unison as their teacher walked away.

"He's right, things really *have* worked out," Grizz said slyly, elbowing Patricia in the ribs.

Flushing, Patricia bit her lip and elbowed her back.

"Hey! Watch the sash!" Grizz admonished, referring to the short purple dress with black sash that she'd chosen to wear for the festival, complete with a matching black shrug and clutch.

"Um, hey."

Patricia lifted her head as Kurt approached them. He'd already changed out of his costume and was back in his street clothes of jeans and a polo shirt. *I guess this is his way of dressing up,* she thought with an eye roll. "Hey, Kurt."

Taking in Grizz and Patricia, he said, "You both look amazing."

Grizz grinned, putting a hand to her hip and striking a pose. "Don't we, though?"

"Um, Patricia?" he began, looking nervous as he shuffled in his sneakers. "Can I talk to you for a second?"

Patricia's eyes widened, feeling as if the wind had been knocked out of her. In all the time she'd known him, he had never *once* called her by her proper name. "Um, sure."

"I'm gonna congratulate Chase on his play," Grizz said, winking dramatically and trying to conceal her snicker as she passed Patricia.

Kurt shifted his weight from side to side before saying, "So, I just talked to Mr. Gardner, and he was really impressed with what you've told him. He says that this will help my grade *a lot.* I mean, I still have to finish that paper, but that'll be a cinch. Um," he mumbled, scratching his scalp and looking nervous, "what I'm trying to say is, I owe it all to you. Sorry I was being so lame before. You showed me that theater can be really cool. So… how about we go out?"

Patricia stared at him. "What, like a date?" Was that what Ben had been hinting at that time they were working on the costumes? Did Kurt… did Kurt *like* her?

Kurt nodded with a smile. "Yeah, babe. I really want to make it up to you for how much trouble I caused at first."

Patricia broke into a smile. "Aw, Kurt, that's so sweet of you! I accept your apology, but I'm afraid I can't go out with you. My boyfriend wouldn't like that."

Kurt looked dumbfounded, his jaw dropping slightly. "Your… boyfriend? Dude, I didn't know you had a boyfriend."

Patricia nodded, craning her neck to look around. "Yeah, actually, he should be…"

"Ready to go?" Ben asked as he walked up to her with a bouquet of flowers, dressed in black pants and a gray button-down shirt.

"Oh," Patricia breathed, taking the offered bouquet and cradling it in her arms, "Ben, that's so sweet!"

Ben grinned, then turned to Kurt and clapped him on the shoulder. "Good job in the play, bro."

Taking Ben's offered arm, Patricia turned and told Kurt, "Yeah, you did a really great job. We've got dinner reservations, so we have to get going, but have a good night!"

Kurt's eyes widened in sheer shock. "Wait… what…?"

"You know, I feel pretty bad for him," Ben commented as they made their way through the parking lot toward his car. "He seemed so depressed when we left. I guess he must be into you now."

As he held open the passenger door for her, Patricia shrugged.

"Well, I *do* feel bad about that, but there's nothing I can do. Don't worry, he'll find someone new soon."

Ben laughed and nodded. "Yeah, I guess you're right."

Patricia grinned. "Why, there's a lad. Come on and kiss me, Ben."

Ben's face lit up happily, and he did just that.

Book Two

♂

A MIDSUMMER NIGHT'S DUDEBRO

"Flower of this purple dye,
Hit with Cupid's archery,
Sink in apple of his eye.
When his love he doth espy,
Let her shine as gloriously
As the Venus of the sky."

- Oberon, A MIDSUMMER NIGHT'S DREAM

For Poonum

Chapter One ♡

I T WAS A WARM AFTERNOON IN LATE MAY AS THE THRONG OF
students made their way through the crowded hallway.

Grizz Sheridan wrinkled her nose as she elbowed past a tall
sophomore. Her best friend, Patricia Verona, trailed after her.

Patricia looked at the clock in the crowded hallway. "Sheesh, at this
rate we're going to be late to class! Why are there so many people?"

"The seniors are chomping at the bit since graduation is almost
here, the juniors and seniors are about to wet themselves because of
prom, and the sophomores and freshman are hanging out because
they're lemmings that do whatever everyone else does," Grizz quipped.

Patricia threw her head back and laughed. "Okay, that was pretty
awesome."

As they made their way through the doorway, Grizz replied with a shrug, "What can I say? I have a way with words."

Patricia groaned at the crowd in the doorway of the theater classroom. "Why are they all standing in a clump?"

Grizz rolled her eyes. "See previous." She flicked a lock of her red-tipped hair over her shoulder and squeezed through a small group of students. As she struggled to make her way to the usual row they sat in, she snapped, "Sit your muffets on your tuffets and get out of my way!"

Standing in the aisle, Patricia clutched the strap of her messenger bag and glanced around. "Where is Mr. Gardner?"

"Hey, guys!"

Grizz's eyes widened, and she cursed inwardly. "Run!" she whispered urgently to Patricia.

Patricia gave her friend a sardonic look as she was pushed slightly forward into the theater seats. "Where?" she mumbled back. Plastering a civil look on her face, Patricia awkwardly pivoted on her heel, trying not to trip in the tight space. "Oh, hi Kurt."

Kurt Minola rubbed the back of his neck shyly as he smiled at Patricia. "What are you dudettes up to on this sunny afternoon?"

Patricia glanced away from him, feeling awkward. Even though she was dating his twin brother, Ben, Kurt seemed to have developed a little crush on her during the theater festival.

"Oh, you know, just trying to find a seat," Grizz replied grouchily.

"Sweet," Kurt said, casually shouldering his backpack.

Mr. Gardner bustled into the room, clutching a stack of books and papers. "I'm here, I'm here." He paused, lowering his glasses to stare at the sea of bodies that milled about in the small theater. "All right, I know that the school year is almost over, and you all are itching to get out there in the sand, sun, and surf—especially you seniors," he added with a wry smile. "But if you would all cut the chatter and take your seats, the lesson would go by much more quickly."

Patricia sighed as people pushed all around her to find their way to their seats. Kurt tried to follow them down the aisle, but his plan was thwarted when the chairs around them filled. With a disappointed glance aimed at Patricia, he made his way to the row ahead of them and sat directly in front of Grizz.

Kurt pulled out his things, uncapping a pen as he flipped through the spiral bound notebook. Grizz frowned as he leaned back in the seat, half expecting him to crush her legs. *I knew Kurt would try to sit by us,* she thought in annoyance.

Mr. Gardner smiled and assumed his place at the podium. "Very good. Now, when we last left off, we were summarizing the events of Act Three of *A Midsummer Night's Dream.*"

Grizz took careful notes as he lectured. Her concentration was interrupted when a ball of paper whizzed past her face and landed in front of her on Kurt's desk.

Patricia rolled her eyes when Grizz shared a look with her, and they both watched as Kurt lifted the note and glanced around for the sender. When he saw his friend a few rows back wave to him, Kurt smiled, but shook his head and shoved the note in his pocket.

"Wow, he's being a good boy," Patricia whispered.

Kurt chose that moment to glance at Patricia over his shoulder.

"All right, class, can anyone tell me what some of the main themes are in *A Midsummer Night's Dream?*" Mr. Gardner asked as he wrote on the white board in electric blue marker. He scanned the classroom, eyes landing on Kurt. "Mr. Minola, how about you?"

Kurt sat up straight in his seat. "Oh, uh, sure Mr. G. Well..." He scratched his large ear as he thought hard. "I would say jealousy is definitely a big one."

Mr. Gardner lifted his eyebrows, pleased. "Jealousy? Can you give us some examples?"

Kurt flipped through his copy. "Well, that Helena girl is pretty ticked that De—Dem..."

"Demetrius," Mr. Gardner supplied, pen poised to write down Kurt's suggestions.

"Oh, thanks. That Demetrius chose Hermia over her. But like, he just doesn't dig her, man." Kurt shook his head. "And then Demetrius is jealous of Lysander, because he wants Hermia for himself. She must be some babe," he muttered.

Mr. Gardner covered his mouth with a fist, clearing his throat to hide his laughter. "Thank you very much, Kurt, those are excellent points." He turned and wrote "Helena, Demetrius, Hermia, Lysander" on the board across from the word "Jealousy."

Grizz nudged Patricia, raising her eyebrows and nodding to Kurt, impressed that he had been paying that much attention to the play. Then she mouthed the words, "She must be some babe," and broke into a peal of giggles. Patricia held up a finger to her mouth to shush her.

Her efforts were too late. Mr. Gardner's eyes came to rest on Grizz. "What are some other themes that we have seen thus far, Grizelda?"

Grizz's giggles halted immediately, and she froze for a moment. She glanced at her notes to collect herself. "Well... I think love is a pretty present theme. But not just being in love with someone, the different aspects of the emotion—trust, betrayal."

Mr. Gardner wrote "Love" on the board and nodded. "Such as?"

"Hermia and Helena grew up together like sisters, so they really care about each other. But when Demetrius loves Hermia instead of Helena, Helena is hurt, and starts to resent her closest friend." Grizz waved her hands with excitement as she went on. "And when Puck places the spell on the boys to fall in love with Helena, Hermia feels that Helena has betrayed her, and Helena is upset because she can't believe her sister would think she'd do something like that to her."

"Fantastic," Mr. Gardner said, writing her points on the board. Kurt's hand shot up, and Mr. Gardner nodded to him. "Yes, Kurt?"

"I think Zelly hit the nail right on the head," Kurt began, earning an eye roll from Grizz. "Oberon also is feeling betrayed by his wife. He wants her attention, and she has that kid that she's obsessed with."

Mr. Gardner nodded. "I like your point. Is there even more about that relationship you would like to touch upon?"

"Um…" Kurt paused as he read through his notes. "Aren't they, like, cheating on each other, too?"

"They both appear to be having extramarital relations, yes," Mr. Gardner said, adding Kurt's points to the board.

Kurt nodded enthusiastically. "So, yeah, there's a lot of trust issues in that marriage. They need to see a shrink." Several students tittered at his comment.

"Thank you, Kurt, you elaborated on Grizelda's point quite well," Mr. Gardner said with a chuckle.

Kurt leaned back in his seat to look at Grizz, giving her the thumbs up. Grizz drew her knees into her chest to avoid being crushed by the back of his chair, grumbling. Patricia patted Grizz on the arm to console her.

Kurt kept his chair at a slight incline, missing Grizz's knees by mere inches. She was tempted to rest her feet on the back of his chair. Maybe she'd cuff him across the head by "accident." *Just a couple more weeks of school,* she chanted mentally. *Just a couple more weeks…*

The following afternoon during lunch, Patricia slid in to join Grizz at a picnic table outside, basking in the warmth of the sun. "Hey, what are you doing?"

Grizz tapped the magazine in front of her. Patricia read over her shoulder and realized it was the pamphlet for Arizona State University. "Are you still torn between ASU and Florida State?"

Grizz shook her head, lifting the pamphlet. "I've been thinking it over, and I've decided Arizona State is the one for me!" She flipped through it. "I mean, look! They have so many cool clubs!"

Patricia smiled. "That's awesome, Grizz. I'm selfishly relieved you're not going to Florida." She sniffled. "I don't think I could handle my bestie across the country. I mean, it's bad enough we're not going to the same school..." Thinking about that made her think about Ben, and her stomach clenched. She hadn't even brought up the topic of what school she'd chosen, fearing what the future held for their relationship. She sighed. It sucked that they had just started dating, at the end of their senior year. She wished that he'd asked her out sooner, or that she'd told him she liked him months ago.

Grizz squeezed her hand and smiled. "I know, girl, but we're going to visit each other a lot. Plus we'll both be back in Santa Cruz over breaks, so it's not like we're never going to be together." She pulled a hair tie out of her pocket and drew her red-tipped hair back into a stylish bun. "But it's going to be scary going to a new school, not knowing anyone."

Patricia cleared her throat, not sure if she should voice her thoughts. After all, the guy in question was someone Grizz could barely stomach. "Um, you're going to know at least one person." Seeing Grizz's curious look, Patricia said, "Remember how ASU is Kurt's 'primo choice'?"

Grizz's eyes widened, and Patricia realized she seemed to have forgotten that little detail. "Kurt's going to ASU?" Patricia nodded, and Grizz was silent for a moment. Then she scoffed. "Oh, whatever, like I'm going to even see him," she said with a wave of her polished fingers. "ASU's campus is freaking huge, and we're going to be in totally different departments." She smiled like a cat. "He'll probably never be out of the pool anyway, what with his obsession with water polo."

Patricia laughed. "Very true. Is Tempe pretty?"

Grizz nodded enthusiastically. "It's gorgeous, Patricia! And the campus is way cool." She pulled her smart phone from her pocket and searched through her photos. "Here's a pic of me in front of their fountain."

"Ooh, I love it!" Patricia took a bite of her sandwich as Grizz showed her the pictures.

Grizz arrived at the photos they'd taken of each other while out shopping for their prom dresses.

Patricia thought hard with a frown, staring at the photo of her gorgeous sky blue dress. "Should I wear my hair up or down?"

Grizz studied her friend critically, holding up her hands to put Patricia in a frame. "Definitely down."

"Do you think you could curl it for me?" Patricia asked. She was terrible at curling her own hair.

"Soft ringlets… gorgeous!" Grizz rested her chin on her hand. "I think I'll put it in a half-up half-down, maybe with a little braid on one side. I still can't decide what kind of jewelry to wear." She blew a lock of hair out of her eye with a puff of breath. "Boys have it so easy. All they have to do is wear a suit or tux. If they don't have one, they can just rent it." She paused. "I wonder which kind Peter is wearing." Grizz was going with her good friend, Peter Fields. She furrowed her brow. "I hope he has the sense to wear a plain black suit if it's not a tux. Could you imagine if he wore a bright color, or"—she shuddered—"a white tux?"

Patricia laughed. "Well, double check with him, but Peter doesn't strike me as the type who would be caught dead in anything but a standard suit. I wonder what Ben is wearing?" She bit her lip, imagining her tall, handsome boyfriend in formal wear.

"Let's get our nails done, Patricia!" Grizz suggested eagerly.

"Okay. I'll try not to chip them before the dance is over," Patricia said with a laugh. Her eyes widened. "Quick, duck!"

Grizz lowered her head just in the nick of time. A ball whizzed past, missing them both by a mere inch. "Dear God!" she exclaimed, looking around wildly to see who'd thrown it.

"There's your culprit," Patricia hissed, pointing behind Grizz.

Grizz turned to see Tuck Robinson smile and shrug innocently. "Sorry, ladies. Guess I threw it a little low."

Another guy jogged over to where the ball had landed. "Found it!" he called back to his friends.

Grizz warily watched the small group from the water polo team toss the ball back and forth. "He's lucky my juice had a cap on it," she grumbled, righting the tipped glass bottle.

"Tuck's such a pain," Patricia said, sliding her sunglasses on her face as she watched him.

"Oh, look, one of their kin is approaching," Grizz said with a frown.

Patricia turned to see Kurt stroll out of the breezeway. She hoped that he wouldn't try to join them. He paused to talk to someone sitting at a picnic table several feet behind them.

Tuck saw Kurt and grinned mischievously. "Hey, Kurt, think fast!"

Grizz and Patricia watched in terror as the ball went speeding toward an unsuspecting Kurt. With lightning reflexes, he turned his attention to it at the last moment, lifting his hands to catch the ball. He chuckled and tossed it back to Tuck, who caught it with a blank expression.

"That was pretty cool," Patricia had to admit.

"Yeah, for a moment there I thought Kurt was going to get K-O'd," Grizz said as she watched two girls leap to their feet and run over to Kurt, squealing. "Then again, that might not have been so bad."

Patricia nudged her, laughing to herself. "But think of the girls lining up to give him mouth-to-mouth."

"It would turn into a cat fight," Grizz mused, scrunching her nose in disgust at the thought.

"I wonder who Kurt is going to prom with?" Patricia said as she watched him make his way to his teammates.

"I bet I know who he wishes he was going with," Grizz mumbled slyly.

Patricia turned beet red, burying her face in her hands. "There is not an 'ew' loud enough," she said, her voice muffled.

"I'm sorry," Grizz said, patting Patricia's back. "Don't think of him—prom is nigh." Grizz took a satisfied sip of her juice. "I can't wait!"

Chapter Two ♥

Lights in pastel colors crisscrossed the ceiling from one corner to the other, casting a soft glow on the prom attendees below. The large hall was filled with gauzy draperies, shimmering balloons, and large cutouts of castles, dragons, and trees, completing the fairy tale theme.

Patricia leaned against the long table the prom committee had set up against one wall, waiting for the line to clear before she and Ben partook of the buffet. She'd had a pretty big dinner before the dance, but when she got a look at some of the dessert options, she knew she had to have some before it was all gone.

After loading up their plates with tasty treats, Patricia and Ben walked over to the cluster of tables on the edge of the dance floor to join their friends, Teddy Torres and Lita Melosa.

"Hey guys," Patricia greeted them, pulling her curled hair off of her shoulders as she sat.

"Whew!" Ben loosened his necktie, nodding to Teddy. "I think I'm danced out."

Patricia pouted. "We've only been here for an hour and a half. You can't be done yet!"

Lita narrowed her chestnut brown eyes and chimed in, "Yeah, Ben, way to be a downer."

Ben grinned and nudged Teddy. "I see that you two are being wallflowers, so who are you to judge?"

Lita folded her arms and shot Teddy a disgruntled look. "I wouldn't be, if it weren't for him."

"It's just this food is so good," Teddy replied with a mouthful of cheese.

"Don't worry, Patricia, we'll let the wimpy boys have their rest, then we'll hit the floor," Lita whispered conspiratorially to Patricia.

Patricia took a sip of her punch and glared at Ben mischievously. "You'd better, buster."

Ben laughed and held up his hands. "I'll be good once I have some food." He took a bite of the piece of bread that was drizzled in melted chocolate. "That's the stuff."

Teddy laughed. "It's going to be hard to keep me away from that fondue pot."

Lita looked at his empty plate that was full of dirty skewers. "You've already been back to it five times," she said with a laugh.

Teddy shrugged his muscular shoulders. "It's taking all of my willpower to not dive onto the table and stick my head underneath the chocolate fountain." He opened his mouth wide. "Aah!"

The group dissolved into laughter, and Teddy glanced around and grinned.

Patricia lifted her head, face hurting from laughing so hard. She froze when she realized that someone had joined them. "Uh, hi, Kurt…"

Kurt sank into the empty chair across from her with a depressed sigh. "Hi, Patricia."

Patricia exchanged a glance with Ben, who eyed his brother warily.

"Hey, man," Teddy greeted him with a nod.

"Hi, Kurt," Lita added.

Kurt glanced around at the table, shoulders slumped. "Hey, guys," he mumbled.

Patricia frowned, wondering why Kurt, who was usually in a good mood, seemed so down.

"Have you tried the food yet, Kurt?" Teddy asked, taking a large bite of his fondue.

Kurt shook his head, eyes cast forlornly on Patricia.

Patricia tried her best to ignore him, turning to Lita and tucking a strand of hair behind her ear. "So, um, Lita, did you guys go to dinner first?"

Lita nodded, her pretty face breaking into a dazzling smile. "Yeah, we actually ate at your parents' restaurant, Patricia."

Patricia smiled. "That's cool!"

Teddy smiled at the memory. "I had the best stuffed crab."

Lita poked her boyfriend in the arm affectionately. "And yet you're putting away the snack table."

Teddy shrugged good-naturedly. "All that dancing made me starving."

"What about you guys?" Lita asked.

"Ben and I went with Grizz and Peter to Bertoluccis." Patricia replied.

"Oh, I'm so jealous!" Lita squealed. "I've always wanted to eat there!"

"Did you and your date get dinner before you guys came, Kurt?" Teddy asked. Then he frowned, glancing around. "Say, where *is* your date?"

"Over there." Kurt pointed across the crowded dance floor to the girl grinding with two different guys, their ties hanging loosely from their necks, and their jackets tossed aside.

"Whoa, did she *ditch* you?" Lita asked incredulously.

"Maybe she's just dancing with... a couple... other guys right now?" Teddy suggested lamely.

Kurt shook his head, shoving his hands in his pockets. "Nope. I tried to cut in, and she told me to get lost."

"Damn!" Teddy and Ben exclaimed in unison.

"I'm sorry, bro," Ben told Kurt.

Patricia's eyebrows knit together as she watched his date dance the night away, feeling a pang of sympathy for Kurt. "That was mean of her. I thought Jenna was really into you."

"Why didn't you go with Natalia?" Ben asked with a frown.

Kurt sighed. "She asked me, but I turned her down. I was planning on going with someone else," he added in a pathetic tone, his hazel eyes turning to rest on Patricia.

Patricia felt very uncomfortable under his intense stare, shoving a skewer of chocolate in her mouth out of stress.

"Well, forget about that biatch," Lita said in her usual peppy tone, patting his shoulder. "You can hang with us."

Patricia's eyes widened at her offer, and she took a swig of her punch.

"Thanks, guys," Kurt said in a small voice. "It *would* be nice not to be all alone... on prom night..."

"What you need, dude, is some chocolate," Teddy said cheerfully.

Patricia leaned back in her seat, shoulders slumping. She felt backed into a corner. She resisted the urge to peel off her manicure, choosing instead to fiddle with her earring, nerves on edge.

When a new song started, Ben reached for Patricia's hand. "Shall we?"

Patricia smiled gratefully and leapt to her feet. "See you guys later!"

Ben pulled her along until they were in the middle of the dance floor. He craned his neck and looked around. "I think we're safe now," he said with a chuckle.

Patricia smiled. "I thought you were too tired to dance," she teased.

Ben shrugged. "I got a second wind." Then he added in a quiet voice, "And I don't like the way he was staring at you."

"Didn't you, now?" She took a step closer to Ben, eyes shining. Placing a hand on his arm, she stood on tiptoe...

"Hey, guys."

Patricia pulled away from Ben as if she'd been electrocuted.

Ben cleared his throat, cheeks red. "Um... hi?" he said to Kurt, who had appeared out of nowhere.

"You going to get back out there and dance, Kurt?" Patricia asked in an exuberant tone. "Show that Jenna that you don't care if she ditched you?"

Kurt stared back at her with puppy dog eyes. "There's not really anyone free to dance with..."

Patricia glanced around wildly, trying to find any spare girl in the vicinity. She came up with nothing.

Ben scratched the back of his neck. "Where are Teddy and Lita?"

Kurt nodded to the snack table. "Teddy wanted to attack the fondue pot again."

Patricia shook her head and smiled pleasantly. "Well, the night is young, let's dance!" She bobbed her head to the music. Surely Kurt would find some other friends soon. *He won't be a third wheel forever,* she reasoned.

After several songs, she slowed her steps and glanced at Ben with a sigh. Kurt seemed to have no intention of leaving their side, and she was getting sick of it. The fact that Kurt had a crush on her made it about fifty times worse.

"Whew, all that dancing has made me really hungry," Ben said pointedly. "Come on, bro, what do you say we go and get some food?" He put a strong arm around Kurt's shoulder and steered him toward the refreshment area.

Standing on the tiptoes of her glittery pumps, Patricia scanned the room for Grizz. She spotted her best friend tossing her hair as she danced with Peter.

Patricia made her way through the throng of dancers. When she reached the pair, Peter paused in his dancing and tapped Grizz on the shoulder. Grizz turned in confusion, then grinned when she saw who it was. "Hey, girl! Why don't you and Ben join us and boogie?" She began to shimmy her hips in time to the music and throw her hands in the air. Then she stopped and furrowed her brow. "Where *is* Ben?"

Patricia sighed, tucking a strand of her curled hair behind her ear. "He's busy keeping Kurt away from me."

"What?" Grizz's heavily made up eyes narrowed. "Why is he trying to mack on his brother's girl, when he's got a date to boot?"

"Well, that's the thing, his date ditched him to flirt with a bunch of other guys."

Grizz snorted, before dissolving into giggles. "His date *what?*" She leaned on Peter for support as she laughed. "Oh, I'm sorry, that's too funny. Mr. Playboy himself getting a taste of his own medicine? Hee hee hee."

Patricia smiled thinly. "It would be sort of funny, except now he won't leave me and Ben alone!"

Peter whistled lowly. "That sucks."

Grizz stomped her foot. "This is your special night with your man! You can't let that surfer boy spoil it!"

Patricia sighed. "I know, but I have no idea what to do about it. I mean, I do feel sort of sorry for him."

Grizz chewed her lip for a moment as she thought. "I've got it." She turned to her date. "Peter?"

Peter raised his eyebrows. "What?"

"Would you mind dancing with some other people while I run interference?"

Peter nodded amiably. "Sure thing. Sounds like Patricia's going to need all the help she can get."

Grizz patted his shoulder. "Thank you." She linked arms with Patricia and pulled her off the dance floor.

"Wait, Grizz, are you sure? I don't want to ruin both your nights," Patricia protested as Grizz led her to the refreshment table where Ben was chatting with Kurt.

Grizz rolled her eyes. "Peter has plenty of friends to hang out with for a little bit, and it's not as if we like each other or anything. This is your and Ben's only prom!" Grizz gripped Patricia by the shoulders and shook her gently. "Ever! It's supposed to be special and romantic! And Kurt-free." Casting a glance to the teenager in question, Grizz's lips curled in an impish smile. "Besides, this will be fun..."

Patricia narrowed her eyes suspiciously. "What wicked scheme are you plotting now?"

Grizz winked. "Don't worry, I've got this." She skipped lightly in her silver heels over to Kurt, who was leaning against the wall, glumly sipping his cup of red punch. Landing daintily in front of him, Grizz widened her eyes dramatically and exclaimed, "Why, if it isn't Kurt Minola! Just the boy I've been looking for."

Kurt straightened up, looking at Grizz in surprise, then glanced at Patricia forlornly. "Oh, hey, Zelda, what's up?"

Ignoring the nickname, Grizz pouted her glossed lips and said breezily, "I've just been itching to dance, and no one will dance with me..."

Patricia had to hide her snicker at Grizz's total lie.

Grizz batted her long lashes at him. "Will you do me the honor?"

Kurt blinked slowly, and Ben came up to him, taking the punch cup from his brother's hand. "Aw, come on, Kurt, how can you turn her down?" he said with an exuberant slap on Kurt's back.

Kurt was absolutely still for a moment as he processed this, then nodded. "Okay, sure thing, Rizzo."

Grizz grit her teeth, but luckily Kurt didn't seem to notice. "Great," she cooed, wrapping her hands tightly around his muscular bicep. "Let's hit the floor! See you guys!" she called over her shoulder as she dragged Kurt to the middle of the room.

Ben approached Patricia with a small smile on his face. "You should get her a mug for graduation," he said as he watched Grizz holding Kurt's hands and swinging with him to the music. "'World's Greatest Best Friend.'"

Patricia laughed. "She definitely earned that award. I hope she doesn't mind."

Ben bumped her shoulder with his. "I don't think she would have offered if she did. We'll spell her in a little bit. Besides, it will be good for Kurt to be with someone so energetic as Grizz—he's looked so miserable all night."

Patricia nodded. "That sucks about his date. I mean, not like he's probably never done that to anyone before, but still..."

"I don't think that's why he's so down," Ben muttered, casting his eyes sideways at his girlfriend.

Patricia slipped her hand in his and gave it a squeeze. "Are you going to talk about your brother all night, or are you going to dance with me, Mr. Minola?"

Ben's handsome face broke into a grin. "Shall we?"

As Ben and Patricia danced to the fast beat of the music, she found herself relaxing and really enjoying her prom. She was glad the pumps she had chosen were comfortable to dance in, while still looking great with her blue dress. She grinned as she looked up into Ben's deep brown eyes, and he smiled and spun her around.

After a few songs, Patricia found herself scanning the dance floor for Grizz and Kurt. Expecting to see Kurt ignoring her or just halfheartedly dancing, she was pleasantly surprised to see Kurt laughing as Grizz showed him a complicated dance move, reaching for his hands when he fumbled with the steps. Patricia noted happily that Grizz seemed to be enjoying herself, too. She and Ben had a little more time together before they had to rescue her.

When a slow song started, Patricia found her steps faltering, cutting her eyes to the floor shyly.

Ben tapped her elbow. "May I have this dance?" he asked with laughing eyes, and Patricia's nerves melted away as she took his hand. After several moments, she found herself relaxing in his arms. Slow dancing was always awkward, but she found it to be much more comfortable when it was with your actual boyfriend.

As they danced, Patricia's mind began to wander in the silence, and she found herself focusing on a topic she wasn't sure she wanted to bring up. What if it ruined their night? "Um, about graduation," Patricia began, swallowing to try and relax her sudden dry mouth. "Have you narrowed down your college choices?" She hadn't even mentioned to Ben which schools she'd been accepted at, and she had no idea what schools he'd even applied to. She was afraid to ask in case it was somewhere thousands of miles away.

Ben took a deep breath, glancing away from her. "Um, I had it down between two, but I'm going with my top choice." Looking down into her blue eyes, he asked quietly, "Have you picked where you're going?"

Patricia nodded, biting her lip. "Yeah... it's got the best theater program, and also has lots of clubs and stuff. Plus the campus is really pretty." She carefully avoided saying where it was.

"Yeah, I looked into the physics department, and even took a tour of the lab when I was looking at schools with my parents a few months back." Ben asked shyly, "Um, so where are you going?"

"Where is it?" Patricia asked at the exact same time. They met each others' eyes and laughed. "Okay, you go first."

Ben shook his head. "No, you go first."

Patricia could tell he was just as nervous as she was.

"Um, Patricia, I want you to know, that wherever it is..." he began, squeezing her hand gently. "That I don't want us to, um, break up... I mean, I totally understand if you want to, I won't be mad or anything, I just..." He trailed off, ducking his head. "I just really like you..."

Patricia's heartbeat sped up, feeling so happy when he said that. "I really like you, too. I don't want to break up either."

Ben stared at her, then grinned slowly. "Really?" Seeing her nod, he said, "Well, I'm sticking to the West Coast, so if that means anything..."

"You are? Me, too!" Patricia said excitedly. "I'm actually sticking to California."

Ben's smile widened. "So am I! Wow, this is great. Okay, I realize California is huge, but, that's better than nothing, right?"

Patricia sighed and squeezed her eyes shut. "Okay, no more beating around the bush. The school I chose is UCLA."

She let out a squeal of surprise when she felt Ben pull her into a tight hug and spin her around. Opening her eyes when he finally set her down, his strong arms still around her, Patricia laughed and asked, "Okay, is that a good sign? Are you going somewhere in SoCal too?"

Ben grinned, seeming unable to contain his excitement. "No, Patricia, you don't understand. I'm going to UCLA, too!"

Patricia's eyes widened, unable to believe her ears. "You—you're serious, right?" He nodded. "You're not just saying that... that's your first choice, right?" He nodded, seeming even more excited. "Really?" She reached out and grabbed his shoulders. "Really, really?" Ben laughed and nodded, and she threw her arms around his neck. "Oh, my

God, I was so terrified to tell you! I thought we'd end up on opposite sides of the country, and we just started dating, and..."

Patricia heard him chuckle as he snaked his arms around her waist to hug her back. "I know, me too! I didn't want to ask you where you were going because I thought you might want to break up or something." He laughed as Patricia shook her head and hugged him tighter.

Patricia leaned her head against his shoulder as they finished the slow dance. "This is the best prom ever," she said with a grin.

Grizz bobbed her head rhythmically to the beat of the song, glancing at Kurt as she did. To her annoyance, he wasn't even looking at her; he was craning his neck, glancing around the dance floor, looking for Patricia, she assumed.

Oh, no you don't, Bub. Grizz thought. *You are not ruining your brother's night just because you've decided you're hung up on his girlfriend!* She realized he might not be doing this if his own date hadn't abandoned him, but she was taking time out of her night to dance with him. The least he could do was actually *pay attention* to her. "C'mon, Kurt, get in gear!"

Kurt didn't reply, so she repeated herself. He looked at her as if he noticed her for the first time. "Oh, sorry, Zelly."

An idea came to Grizz. With a secretive smile, she said, "Oh, that's all right. I know how hard it must be for you to dance. I mean, following the beat is really hard."

"I can dance," Kurt protested with a wrinkled brow.

"No, it's totally okay, I get it. I mean, just because you're coordinated in the water doesn't mean that you can strut your stuff on the dance floor," Grizz said with a dramatic sigh, spinning herself around.

"I can so!" Kurt insisted, the glum expression vanishing from his face.

Seeing that it was working, Grizz watched him like a cat about to pounce and said, "Oh, really? Like this?" She began to shimmy from side to side to the beat.

"Amateur, Ginny," Kurt said with a smirk, following her lead.

Grizz laughed as he got more into it, moving his head from side to side and bending his knees. The song changed, and Grizz jumped up and down. "All right, Kirk, get ready for a dance-off! I love this song!"

Kurt grinned, hazel eyes lighting up. "So do I!"

They energetically danced to the next few songs, Grizz pleased by the DJ's music choices. "I just love 80s music!" she exclaimed happily, tossing her hands in the air.

Kurt raised his eyebrows. "You do? Me, too! This is great, Zel!"

Grizz laughed when he grabbed her hand and spun her around. "So, Kurt, are you excited to graduate?" she asked, stepping slowly from side to side.

Kurt shrugged. "Yeah, I mean, I'm ready to be done with school for awhile, but I'm gonna miss my peeps, you know?"

Grizz felt her heart sink, thinking of Patricia and all her other friends at Vista High. "Yeah, I definitely know what you mean. That's why we've gotta live it up now, right?" With a grin she lifted her hands and clapped to the beat.

Kurt got into the spirit of things. "Dance, Riz, dance!"

Grizz laughed, turning herself in a circle. "Yes, sir!"

"I'm so done with classes though," Kurt said after a few minutes as he moved to the music.

"How do you feel about the final for theater?" Grizz asked, reaching for Kurt's hand.

Kurt took it, and they swung hands back and forth. "Kind of overwhelmed. I've been digging *A Midsummer Night's Dream*, but some of the plays we read months ago..." He chuckled, seeming ashamed. "I don't remember them that well."

Thinking of all the work Kurt had been putting in to play catch-up, and how dedicated he'd been, Grizz said, "Some of us were going to do a study group. We're doing summaries of every play and going to read off bullet points and talk about themes and stuff." She pointed a finger at him, her sparkling polish glittering in the lights on the dance floor. "If you're willing to put in the work, be there on time when we meet and all that jazz, the final should be a snap."

Kurt's eyes widened. "Really? You'd let me be part of the group? Thanks, Zelly, you're the coolest. Which play should I summarize?"

Grizz smiled, pleasantly surprised. "I don't think anyone has picked *A Midsummer Night's Dream* yet. I'll have to check. You've been taking notes?"

He nodded.

"Then let's say that. We were planning on getting together next Saturday afternoon, is that okay?"

"Super. Hey, we could meet at my house!" Kurt said with a grin.

Grizz shrugged, knowing that the Minolas' house had plenty of space. "If you don't mind, that sounds great!"

"You're a life saver," Kurt said. "Study groups and stuff are really awesome, I wish I'd known about them sooner!"

Grizz bit her lip to keep from commenting. How could he not have known about them? "No problem."

"Check this out!" Kurt sang out the lyrics to the song currently pounding through the speakers and shuffled his feet to the rhythm.

Grizz laughed and imitated him. When the song ended, she still was rolling her shoulders until she realized that the beat had slowed down considerably. A red alert sounded in her mind. *A slow song?!*

She dropped her hands awkwardly and stared at her shoes, hoping she could peel herself away from Kurt and hide in the corner. Probably no chance Peter was free, but she could at least wait the song out. To her surprise, she felt a tap on her shoulder. Lifting her eyes, she saw Kurt still standing there. He smiled tentatively. "Want to dance?"

Quickly she weighed the options in her mind. Did she really want to be in Kurt Minola's arms? No. But Patricia and Ben were trying to have their alone time, and besides, if she didn't dance with him, he had no date and would probably follow her to sit on the sidelines. What harm could befall her? She nodded, trying to be friendly. "Sure."

He stepped closer to her and put his hands on her hips. She grabbed them and lifted their position. "Too low, buddy."

"Oh, sorry."

Pursing her lips, she awkwardly put her hands on his shoulders as he pulled her to him. Her fingertips met solid muscle beneath the suit, and she lifted her eyebrows as she slid her hands behind his neck. As she locked her fingers together, she inhaled and was overwhelmed by how nice he smelled, her skin beginning to tingle. She closed her eyes and felt herself go limp in his arms, lost in the moment, until she remembered whom she was dancing with. She snapped to her senses and stood up straight, staring at a spot over his shoulder, praying for the song to end soon.

Chapter Three ♥

THE FOLLOWING MONDAY AT LUNCH, PATRICIA AND GRIZZ carried their trays outside. "Let's go over there," Grizz suggested, pointing to a shaded table.

"I don't usually like the caf food, but there's something about their pizza and salad," Patricia commented as she sat down, opening her can of soda.

Grizz took a large bite of her pizza and said with her mouth full, "I'm glad ASU hash good food. I sheckthed."

Patricia squinted. "I only understood about half of that."

Grizz swallowed and laughed. "Sorry, girl. I said I ate at the cafeteria at ASU, and it tasted *super* good, so I'm excited."

"Yeah, that's important since you'll be subsisting on it for the next four years," Patricia said. "I liked UCLA's coffee shop. I also had dinner on campus. It was yummy." She patted her stomach fondly.

"Speaking of yummy, wasn't dinner at Bertoluccis fabulous?" Grizz asked, sipping her water.

Patricia nodded. "It really was. I was terrified of spilling on my dress, but thankfully I didn't." She paused, remembering what had happened with Kurt at prom. She'd lost track of Grizz after that. "So, you never told me how the rest of prom night went."

Grizz smiled. "It was a lot of fun. Entertaining Kurt for a little while actually wasn't so bad." Unbidden, she was hit with a memory of his arms around her, and the smell of his surfer boy cologne. She shuddered. She vowed never to breathe a word about slow dancing with Kurt Minola to anyone. "After a while some girls popped out of the woodwork to flirt with him." She snickered. "Where were they sooner, I ask you?"

Patricia laughed. "So Peter wasn't mad?"

Grizz shook her head. "Nope! We danced the night away." She wiggled her eyebrows suggestively. "How was your evening with Ben?"

Patricia grinned, bouncing up and down in her seat. "Oh my gosh, it was *so* much fun! Thank you for running interference. I don't think I realized how stressed out Ben was about Kurt. I mean, I know he didn't want to leave him hanging, because he felt bad for him. But it seemed like Kurt felt a lot better after hanging out with you."

Grizz recalled his smiling face as they danced. "Yeah, I think he did. Oh!" She set down her drink. "Patricia, I hope this is okay, but I kinda-sorta offered to let Kurt join our study group."

Patricia's jaw dropped. "Y-you..." she spluttered. Her shoulders sagged with a sigh. "Yeah, that was nice of you. If he still has his act together, it should be fine."

Grizz looked at Patricia through narrowed eyes. "We just can't seem to escape him, can we?"

Patricia took a french fry and nodded. "Our fates seem to be tied to Kurt Minola's."

Grizz nudged her. "Especially since you're dating *his twin*."

Patricia reddened and pushed back. "Well, come this fall we'll be free of him for awhile." Her blue eyes widened. "Wait—I will, but you won't!"

Grizz froze. "Oh, whatever. We're not going to be in the same classes or anything, and who knows how long he'll even last? Besides, since you and Ben won't be around, there will be no need for me to keep him away. I'll probably never see him." She smiled impishly. "*You're* the one he thinks is hot."

Patricia groaned, face flushing. "Please, stop rubbing it in!"

"All right, all right," Grizz conceded with a snicker. "But the important question is"—her voice grew quiet—"do you know where Ben is going yet?"

"Hey guys!" Ben slid in next to Patricia. "What's up?"

"Oh, hi Ben," Grizz said, throwing Patricia a meaningful look.

"Hi," Patricia bumped his shoulder with hers. "Actually, Grizz was just asking where you're planning on going to school," she said, running her fingers through her ponytail casually.

"Oh," Ben replied, and Grizz noticed with suspicion that he seemed to be trying not to grin.

"Well, out with it, man!" Grizz exclaimed, reaching across the table to poke Ben in the chest.

Ben laughed, holding up his hands in an attempt to stop Grizz's attack. "Okay, okay. I'm going to UCLA."

Grizz nodded, taking a sip of her soda. "That's cool. Wait—" Her eyes narrowed. "*You're* going to UCLA, too?"

Ben and Patricia glanced at each other and blushed, both nodding.

"Is this just… a coincidence?"

Patricia laughed. "Yeah, isn't that crazy? We're both going to the same school, and I had no idea he'd even applied there!"

Ben grinned. "I didn't know which schools Patricia was looking at."

Grizz clapped her hands together. "It was fate! Wow, that's so awesome, guys! I'm so happy for both of you!" Though she was really excited, her chest felt a funny squeeze. "But… I'm going to miss you two…" Tears welled in her eyes. "I wish *I* was going there, too, now! What am I going to do without you?" she whispered, reaching for Patricia's hand across the table.

Patricia felt like crying herself. "Oh, Grizz, we're going to be best friends forever!"

"It'll be okay, Grizz. Fall is still a few months away, and there's lots of vacations. You guys can visit each other, too!" Ben said encouragingly. Then he paused. "Where are you going, Grizz?"

Grizz sighed heavily. "Arizona State."

Ben smiled. "That's not that far!" He gave a start. "Wait a minute— you're going to ASU, too? That's where Kur—"

Patricia put her hand on his shoulder. "She knows," she whispered.

Grizz sank forward, burying her face in her hands. "While you two are romping through beautiful SoCal, I'm going to be miles away, stuck at a school with an idiot." She lifted her head to cast Ben a sympathetic glance. "No offense."

"But, Grizz, think of all the awesome things that you were telling me about," Patricia said, trying to cheer her up.

Grizz twirled her straw around her glass. "That's true, I really am looking forward to it."

Ben smiled encouragingly. "Well, the ASU thing is probably going to work out in our favor all around: I'm going to be visiting Kurt a lot, and he'll visit me, too—so Patricia can come with me, and you can come with Kurt."

Grizz's nostrils flared. "Never!" She wiped the tears from her eyes and said furiously, "You can come visit me all you want, you two, but I refuse to be stuck in a car for six hours with KURT MINOLA!"

Ben whistled lowly. "You could always fly—then it would only be, like, an hour."

"Not in a car, not on a plane..." Grizz growled.

"Not by boat, not by train...?" Patricia rhymed with a teasing smile. Grizz's scowl deepened.

"You two think you're so funny, don't you?" she hissed, slamming her hand on the picnic table and rising to her feet. "But mark my words, come fall, the name Kurt Minola will mean absolutely nothing to me!" She gathered her tray of food and flounced away.

Ben looked at Patricia with lifted eyebrows. Patricia shrugged and handed him the extra pudding cup she'd taken for dessert, which he gratefully accepted.

That Saturday, Grizz rang the doorbell to the Minolas' house. The cherry wood door opened, and Mrs. Minola broke into a wide smile. "Grizz! Come in."

Grizz smiled as she followed her into the entryway. "Hi, Mrs. Minola."

"Your play was wonderful, sweetie," Mrs. Minola said warmly. "I just loved the storyline between the ghosts; it was so heartbreaking."

Grizz ducked her head shyly. "Thank you."

Mrs. Minola shook her head. "Makes me feel sad just thinking about it. That's the sign of an excellent writer."

Grizz felt her cheeks warm. "But I made such a stupid mistake!" she blurted. "Writers shouldn't do things like that."

"Oh, no, no! Don't talk that way. It was an easy one to make, I wouldn't have even known. And, I must say, Kurt really buckled down when helping you research. He became so invested in your story that he wouldn't stop talking about it!" Mrs. Minola smiled and whispered conspiratorially, "He's thinking about majoring in history when he gets to college." She winked. "It's all thanks to you, honey."

It's more thanks to Patricia, Grizz thought, but she just clutched the strap of her messenger bag and said, "Thanks, Mrs. Minola."

"You're the first one here. Kurt is waiting on the back porch. I'll bring you all some snacks in a little bit."

Grizz thanked her and made her way through the spacious house. An orange and brown calico cat rose from where it had been curled up on a chair in the family room, stretching its paws toward her.

"Hi, Marmalade," Grizz said softly, reaching out to pet the cat.

Marmalade blinked large, blue eyes at Grizz and began to purr. Grizz had gotten to know the cat when Kurt helped her fix the scripts and costumes for the play. She'd seemed skittish at first, but now she and Grizz were good friends. "Are you having a lazy day? I envy you. I have to study with stupid Kurt," she whispered, hoping Mrs. Minola wasn't in earshot. "Speaking of which, I'd better go out there. Bye bye." Grizz turned and walked toward the dining room.

Hearing a jingle, she pivoted and saw that Marmalade had hopped off the chair and was following her. When she got to the french door, she said, "You stay here. You're an indoor kitty." When Marmalade wouldn't move, Grizz walked quickly toward her, shuffling her feet loudly. "Scoot!"

Marmalade gave her an indignant look, flouncing off with her nose in the air. Grizz laughed and opened the door to the large covered porch.

Kurt was hunched over his phone on the wicker couch, but he sat up eagerly when the door opened. When he saw that it was Grizz, his shoulders sagged slightly. "Oh. Sup, Gertie," he said glumly.

Grizz rolled her eyes, knowing whom he was so eager to see. "Hey, Kyle." She pulled her bag off her shoulder and sank to the chair opposite him. She noted with approval that he had all of his books and notes on the wicker table in front of him. "Guess I'm kind of early, huh?"

Kurt shoved his phone in his pocket and nodded. "I've just been chilling, it's cool to enjoy the breeze. Summer's almost here." He stretched his arms over his head and yawned.

"Yeah, I can't wait until finals are over. Prom made it feel like we were done. It was hard to go back to school Monday." She leaned back in her chair, and silence settled over them. Kurt pulled out his phone again after a moment, and Grizz sighed, wishing she hadn't been so early. She found herself looking around to amuse herself. Her eyes wandered past the porch railing and landed on a cluster of rosebushes. "Wow, those are gorgeous!" She leapt to her feet and hurried out in the yard. When she reached the roses, she sniffed the coral blossoms.

Hearing footsteps, she turned to see that Kurt had joined her, hands in his pockets. "Yeah, mom spends hours out here. They're pretty sweet, though." He pointed to one that was so dark it was almost black. "That one is especially sick."

Grizz walked over to the dark rose, stepping on something in the lawn. "Ack—oh, hey, check it." She picked up the flying disc and wiggled it in her hands. "You up for it?"

Kurt grinned. "You know it, Riz."

Grizz rolled her eyes and handed it to him, choosing to ignore the nickname as she jogged to the far end of the yard. "Show me what you've got!"

Kurt tossed the disc, and it soared toward Grizz a few feet above her head. She leapt up and caught it, squealing gleefully.

"Whoa, that was bitchin'!" Kurt exclaimed, clapping and whistling.

Grizz laughed and gave a bow. "Thank you, thank you!" She threw the disc back to him.

Kurt broke into a run to catch it, nearly running into the arbor before he caught it. "Ha ha!" he laughed, pumping the disc into the air. "Ready, Gwen?"

Grizz nodded, putting her hands on her knees as she readied herself. "You bet, Kev!"

Kurt chuckled as he spun in a little circle, letting the disc fly.

"Ow!"

Grizz turned around in surprise to see Patricia standing there, clutching her head in pain. "Patricia! Are you okay?"

"Oh, shit!" Kurt raced across the lawn, stopping at Patricia's side. "Patricia! I–I'm so sorry!" He put his hand on her arm. "Are you okay? Do you need ice?"

Patricia pressed her lips into a thin line, taking a large step away from Kurt. "No prob. I'm fine. Totally fine." She quickly put on her sunglasses, and Grizz got the feeling that it was her way to hide from Kurt.

Kurt's cheeks reddened. "I'm really sorry. Guess I just don't know my own strength," he added as he rocked on his heels, glancing at her out of the corner of his eye.

Patricia clutched the strap of her bag and backed away. "Yeah, um, actually, before the group starts, I'm going to go find Ben." She turned and hurried back to the house.

"He's not here."

Patricia's steps slowed, and she pivoted to look at them. "He's not?"

Kurt shook his head. "Nope. He said he wouldn't be back until after dinner. Library, or the lab, or... something." He shrugged. "Don't know, wasn't really listening."

Grizz snorted.

"Well, I'm just going to put the book I borrowed in his room really quick." Patricia rushed off before Kurt could protest.

Kurt's shoulders sagged. "Aw, man," he muttered.

"Want to play some more?" Grizz asked, crouching to retrieve the disc.

Heaving a sigh, Kurt shrugged. "I guess."

"Hey guys!" Phillip called, their fellow classmate Rebecca in tow.

Saved by the gang, Grizz though to herself. "Hi!" she said with a wave.

Kurt nodded to them. "Sup, Phil. Becca." He turned to Grizz. "Is that everybody?"

Grizz shook her head. "Peter is coming, too."

"Well, you guys can set your stuff on the porch. I thought we could work there since it's so big, and it's such a nice day," Kurt told the group, walking to the steps.

"Thanks for having us over, Kurt," Rebecca said as she chose a spot on the love seat. Grizz sank beside her and dug through her messenger bag for her things.

"No sweat, happy to be of service," Kurt mumbled, eyes fixed on the porch door for Patricia.

Grizz followed his gaze and muttered under her breath, "Get over it, idiot." She cleared her throat. "So, I'm covering *The Three Sisters*; Phillip, you've got *The Taming of the Shrew*, right?"

Phillip lifted his notebook and nodded. "I've got it in bullet points."

Rebecca flipped through her books. "Mine are so funny, I was busting up writing the outlines."

"That's because you got all of the short comedies," Phillip teased.

"Well, I've been taking notes on *A Midsummer Night's Dream*." Kurt slowly turned the pages of his copy. "So trippy, man. Was it really all just a dream?"

Phillip shot him an incredulous look. "Uh, what?"

"Well, you know, bro, Puck's line at the end, 'And this weak and idle theme, no more yielding but a dream…'"

Before Phillip could respond, the porch screen slid open, and Patricia joined them. "Hey guys!"

"Yo, Patricia! Grab a seat!" Kurt called, sitting up straight, and Patricia realized with panic that the only free spot was on the wicker couch, next to Kurt.

Grizz noticed the stricken look on her friend's face, and was about to fling herself onto the couch when she spotted Peter coming up the porch steps behind them. "Peter!" Grizz exclaimed, far too enthusiastically, leaping to her feet and reaching out to him. "You're here! Come, sit a spell!"

"Yeah, I ran into Mr. Minola out front, and he let me in through the gate..." Peter mumbled, furrowing his brow as Grizz pushed him down on the couch next to Kurt.

Patricia smiled gratefully to Grizz and sat on the other side of Peter. "Hey, Peter."

Peter smiled, catching on. "Oh, hi, Patricia. How goes it?"

"Aw, man," Kurt grumbled, slumping in his seat.

"Okay," Grizz said brightly, sitting again and opening her notes. "Who wants to start?"

Kurt surprised everyone by saying, "Why not? I'll go. Take notes, dudes, it's gonna get your minds wrecked. So much shit goes down..."

Grizz couldn't help but smile at his enthusiasm. "That's the spirit, Kurt, let's get excited."

Phillip snorted as Kurt began to outline the play. "Like we didn't already read this in class," he mumbled. "This is just a review." Thankfully, Kurt couldn't hear him.

Grizz leaned over and poked Phillip.

"So, like, it's a love triangle, right?" Kurt scratched his head and frowned. "Nah, maybe it's a love square... either way, the King and Queen of the fairies decide to butt in, and then it really gets hilarious."

"Why couldn't you just let him flunk?" Phillip grumbled, crossing his arms.

This time Grizz kicked Phillip in the shin. He clutched his leg in pain and glared sulkily at her.

Kurt paused in his summarizing, chuckling as he stared at his book. He glanced up and was met with blank stares. "Oh, sorry, I was just laughing at Demetrius' line from Act 5, 'No wonder, my lord. One lion may, when many asses do.'" He snickered. "I just got that. Well, it's true, the characters in the play *do* kind of make asses of themselves..."

Grizz burst into laughter, then stopped abruptly when she noticed the rest of the group, save for Kurt, staring stonily at her. "What?" she mouthed grouchily at Patricia, who pressed her lips into a small smile in reply and raised her eyebrows at her.

Grizz slumped forward and rubbed her temples, knowing one thing for sure: she would be glad to be done with drama class, and helping out Kurt Minola.

Chapter Four ♡

P ATRICIA SLID OUT OF THE PASSENGER SEAT OF BEN'S Expedition, stomach fluttering with excitement.

"Party! Party!" Grizz chanted as she slammed the back door closed.

Ben laughed, hitting the button on the fob to lock his car. "I can't believe we're done with high school," he said in a dazed tone.

"Almost done," Grizz corrected him. "We still have Grad Night awaiting us," she sang, flinging her arms in the air.

"May I say you ladies looked lovely accepting your diplomas?" Ben said as they walked through the parking lot toward the Boardwalk entrance.

Patricia tossed her hair over her shoulder and laughed. "Why, thank you, Mr. Minola."

"They called me Grizelda," Grizz said with a shudder.

Patricia put her arm around her. "You still looked awesome," she said comfortingly.

"As for me, I felt like the Scarecrow when they handed me that diploma," Ben said, putting a finger to his temple and reciting the Pythagorean Theorem.

Patricia nudged him, giggling. "As if you didn't know that already!"

Grizz pulled the pamphlet for Grad Night out of her purse. "This is going to be so—freaking—awesome!" she declared, hopping up and down excitedly.

Ben put on his sunglasses. "We are ready to par-tay! What should we do first?"

His question was interrupted by a horn honking. Patricia jumped slightly at the sound and turned.

Kurt had pulled up in his Jeep Wrangler just a few feet from where they stood. The top and windows were down to accommodate the warm summer night. "Check it out, dude and dudettes!" he called to them. "Kahuna and I have been reunited!" He opened the door and hopped out, running over to the front of the Jeep. "It's all right, Kahuna," he murmured, patting the hood gently. "Daddy will get you a new wax job and everything to make up for it."

Grizz stuck her finger down her throat. "Oh, please. Gag me."

Ben covered his mouth with a fist to hide his chuckle. "That's great, Kurt," he said sincerely.

"Thanks, bro," Kurt replied, pausing when he saw Patricia. He ran a hand through his hair and adjusted the hem of his blue tee shirt that had "Vista High Water Polo" scrawled across it. Grizz noticed with a snicker that the color almost exactly matched his car.

Kurt cleared his throat and said shyly, "Hey, Patricia."

Patricia, who had been putting something in her purse, gave a start. "Oh, hey, Kurt," she answered, not meeting his eyes.

Ben heaved a worried sigh.

Grizz set her jaw and skipped over to Kurt, grabbing his upper arm. She lifted her eyebrows, impressed when she felt the solid muscle mass under her fingertips. She linked arms on the other side with Patricia. "Well, let's go hit the party! Grad Night awaits!"

Patricia breathed a sigh of relief, motioning to Ben. He offered her his arm, and the four of them walked to the Boardwalk in a line.

"So, um," Kurt began, trying to peer at Patricia over Grizz's head as they neared the entrance, "do you know what all is going to be happening tonight?"

Grizz said, "There's going to be all of the regular Boardwalk stuff, but since Vista is hosting it, we're going to be getting a bunch of free tickets, and then everything else will be discounted."

"Plus there's going to be live music," Ben added, straying a little from the rest of the group with his long legs. Grizz was keeping a tight grip on Kurt's arm, so they were moving at a snail's pace.

"I think it said that the teachers are going to have special booths and stuff, too," Patricia added, trying to keep up with Ben while still linked with Grizz.

"Really?" Grizz wrinkled her nose as Kurt leaned over to try to say something to Patricia. She squeezed his bicep and kept him right where he was.

"Damn, Rizzo, you're strong!" he grumbled.

At last they reached the line outside the entrance. Grizz cast Kurt a suspicious glance before letting go of him. She stepped away from Patricia to give her some breathing space.

Kurt rubbed his bicep and shot Grizz a pouting glance.

Patricia nudged Grizz and nodded her head to get her to come away from Kurt. "Don't run interference tonight, Grizz," she whispered urgently. "I want you to have fun, not feel like you need to babysit Kurt."

Grizz nodded. "Don't worry, this isn't like prom—there's going to be plenty of man-hungry girls about. Plus all of his 'bros'." She made quotation marks angrily with her fingers. "We'll be rid of him soon enough." Then she smiled cleverly. "And if he tries to horn in, be as disgustingly in love as you can be. Hold hands, nonstop. Hug Ben and squeal. Share his food. Make him carry you around, piggy-back style. Whisper sweet nothings—"

Patricia kicked her lightly in the shin, pretending to gag. "Gross! Besides, we aren't going to be glued to each other's sides all night. He's got his own friends, you and I have our friend circle…"

Grizz sighed dramatically. "Very well."

The group stopped at the end of the line. Patricia rocked back and forth on her heels as she watched her classmates at the front of the line get their student IDs checked, before being presented with a wristband.

"Dude, I thought this was a sober grad thing," Kurt said, shoving his hands in his pockets as he stared at the check-in.

Ben furrowed his brow. "It is."

Kurt lifted his sunglasses. "Then why are they checking our IDs, man? We're not old enough to drink yet. I don't think anyone at Vista is, unless we've got someone who flunked senior year like four times or something."

Patricia's face scrunched up as she tried to hide the laugh that was threatening to burst free.

Grizz rolled her eyes. "They're checking our *student* IDs, genius. It's so that Vista students get all the discounts and freebies, but no other teenagers sneak in."

Kurt punched his hand, muscles flexing. "Like SCH!" he hissed. Santa Cruz High was Vista High's rival.

"They also want to make sure it's only actual Vista High *seniors*," Ben added.

Kurt's eyes scanned the line, which was growing longer by the minute. "Yeah, just wait, little guppies, your time will come."

Though she'd been reminded of it all day, thinking of being done at Vista forever made a funny knot curl in Grizz's stomach. Kurt must have been feeling something similar, since he suddenly wrapped his strong arms around the three of them. "I'm going to miss you guys," he choked.

Ben laughed awkwardly, and, seeing Patricia's panicked gaze, inserted himself between her and his brother. "Aw, it's okay, Kurt."

Grizz's heart hammered as she stood pressed against his chiseled form. Her eyes grew wide, and she tried to push herself away from him.

"Hey, Minola!"

Both Ben and Kurt turned their heads at the voice.

Kurt let go of his friends to shout back, "Yo, 'sup Quince!"

Quincy Peterson, one of the members of the water polo team, lifted his hand in a wave. "A bunch of the guys are going to do a laser tag challenge. You in?"

Kurt grinned. "You know it!"

Patricia breathed a sigh of relief. She'd be rid of Kurt soon.

The line moved quickly. Soon they were walking around the Boardwalk, taking in the sights and smelling the fried food.

Grizz thumbed through the brochure. "Ooh, Patricia, look at all of this stuff! A live band, karaoke, a sand castle building contest, a fortune teller—"

"And food," Kurt added with a dreamy smile, closing his eyes as he inhaled the tantalizing scents of the Boardwalk.

"Hey, guys!" Lita called out, running over to them. Teddy trailed after her.

"Hey, Lita, Teddy," Grizz began, then cleared her throat. "Or should I say, Your Majesties?" She lifted the hem of her sundress and curtsied. Teddy and Lita had been elected Prom King and Queen.

Lita waved her hand with a blush. "Oh, you know we're not into the whole title thing."

"I left my crown at the Royal cleaners," Teddy said with a teasing smile, running a hand through his short black hair.

"Well then, you'll pardon me if I don't bow," Ben replied, and he and Teddy began playfully rough housing.

Patricia laughed as she watched them, and turned to Lita. "What are you two up to?"

"We got in just a few minutes ago. There's so many fun things! I was kind of thinking of entering the sand castle building contest..." Lita cast her eyes to her boyfriend. "But Teddy doesn't really want to..."

Teddy folded his muscular arms across his chest, grinning sheepishly. "I'm kind of hungry."

Lita rolled her eyes and looked pointedly at Patricia.

Ben laughed. "I am too, man."

Grizz said eagerly, "I'd love to build a sandcastle!"

Patricia nodded and linked arms with Grizz and Lita. "We'll go do that, you boys go fill your bottomless pits."

"What are you doing, Kurt? Want to eat with us?" Teddy asked.

Kurt was watching Patricia with a dazed look, oblivious to the fact that Teddy was talking to him.

Ben rolled his eyes. "Earth to Kurt!" He snapped his fingers.

Kurt furrowed his brow. "What?"

Teddy frowned in confusion, and repeated, "Want to come eat with us?"

Realization dawned on Kurt's features. "Oh! I'm going to play laser tag in a little bit—can't decide if I should fuel up beforehand while I wait for the guys, or if I should fast, and claim dinner as my victory."

Ben held up a fistful of coupons and beckoned to him. "Eat something first. They gave us lots of coupons."

Kurt flipped through his stack of coupons and tickets and proclaimed, "Two for one hot dog special? What are we waiting for?"

"We each got one of those, right?" Teddy asked eagerly as the boys walked in the opposite direction. "Because I'm not sharing!"

"It's just as well," Grizz reasoned. "Those boys wouldn't be able to build an artistic masterpiece."

"Teddy would probably step on it," Lita added with a giggle.

"Cameras ready?" Patricia asked.

Grizz and Lita held up their smart phones.

"Let's go!"

"Minola! Minola!" Kurt exited the arcade to a series of cheers and claps from his water polo teammates.

"That was sick, Kurt!" Quincy exclaimed, clapping Kurt on the back.

Kurt stretched his arms over his head. "Thanks, dude."

Tuck shoved his hands in his pockets and grumbled, "I almost had you."

"He creamed you, bro," Nick Toda, one of their other teammates, pointed out.

Tuck sneered, casting a sour glance in Kurt's direction. "Well, I'm heading to the beach," he muttered. Several of the others fell into step with him.

Kurt walked down the Boardwalk, flanked by Quincy and Nick. "Gotta admit, this is a pretty sweet party," he said with a grin.

Nick nodded, about to say something when his phone beeped. Sliding it out of his pocket, he quickly scanned the text. "Oh, sweet, my girlfriend's here. Sorry, dudes, got to go meet her at the front!"

"Bye, Nick!" Kurt and Quincy called after him.

"So what do you want to do next?" Kurt asked, flipping through his coupons.

"Maybe a ride?" Quincy suggested. "We could hold off on eating so we don't puke our brains ou—" His sentence was interrupted when a girl hugged him from behind. "Oh, hey, Faye!"

Faye Jones laughed and unhooked her arms from around her boyfriend. "Hi, Quincy. Hi, Kurt."

"Sup," Kurt greeted her.

"What are you up to?" Quincy asked with a smile.

She shifted her weight from one foot to the next, her bobbed blonde hair bouncing with the motion. "Actually, I was wondering if we could maybe ride the Sky Glider? Um, that is, unless you guys were busy."

Quincy glanced at Kurt, raising his eyebrows hopefully.

Kurt sighed, knowing that Quincy wanted to hang out with his girlfriend. "You two go ahead. I'm going to meet up with some other friends anyway," he lied.

"You sure, dude?" Seeing Kurt's nod, Quincy grinned. "All right, see you later!" He and Faye went off arm in arm.

Kurt felt his shoulders slump as he watched them. *Every guy's got a girl, it seems. I wonder where Patricia went off to?* He sighed, feeling depressed. *Man, I never used to care so much about this kind of junk!* He straightened his shoulders, trying to psych himself up. *Yeah, I'm as free as the waves! I'm sure I'll run into some peeps soon...* Though he tried, it didn't seem to help. "Just a single guy, man, trying to make my way in this world..." Kurt half-sang tonelessly under his breath, shuffling slowly down the drag.

Grizz clutched the gift certificate tightly to her chest. She, Lita, and Patricia had won second prize in the sandcastle building contest for their mermaid masterpiece. They each had been awarded a ten dollar gift certificate to a local pizza parlor. "It's so beautiful," she whispered, almost teary eyed. "I hate to leave it..."

Lita crouched and blew kisses to the turrets they had so painstakingly carved with the tools. "Be strong, my beauty. Soon you will be returned to the waves, where tiny mermaids may live within you."

"*Aloha 'Oe*," Grizz sang softly. "*Aloha 'Oe, until we meet again...*"

"Aw," Teddy said, crossing his arms as he watched them.

All three girls turned to glower at him, not sure if he was being sarcastic or not.

"Dry your eyes, let me get one last picture of you with your masterpiece!" Ben told them, lifting his smart phone and motioning for them to stand around the castle.

Patricia smoothed the wrinkles out of her shirt as she put her arms around Grizz and Lita.

"Great," Ben said with a grin, walking over to show them.

Patricia smiled as they flipped through the photos. "Okay, I'm ready," she told Ben.

Lita looked sorrowfully at the castle one last time. "Me too."

"Finally," Teddy muttered under his breath, but not softly enough to go unnoticed by his girlfriend.

Lita, at six feet tall, was just a couple of inches shorter than him. She glared at Teddy and began to charge after him, long legs pumping as she ran.

"Ack! It was a joke, I swear!" he cried as they disappeared down the beach.

"I hope she doesn't catch him," Ben said with a low whistle.

"Her high kick is something fierce," Grizz added with a smirk. Lita was on the cheerleading squad. She then waved to Rebecca and Stacey, who were walking toward her. "Okay, I will leave you two alone for now—we're going to be hitting a bunch of the rides."

"I think I want to look at the booths," Patricia said, casting her eyes to Ben.

He nodded. "Sounds good."

"Want to meet up again on the beach in a couple of hours?" Patricia asked them.

Rebecca adjusted her large glasses. "Definitely!"

Grizz began to walk backwards, waving to Patricia and Ben. "Okay, we'll see you soon!"

"I'm kind of hungry," Stacey commented as they walked down the busy drag.

Rebecca glanced around. "We should probably just stick to food carts so that we have more time to do everything."

"Good idea," Grizz said. She fanned through the coupons. "Ooh, so many options—free bubble tea if you buy a muffin, deep-fried twinkies… that's a recipe for heartburn, but sounds so good…"

"I think I want churros," Stacey said, twirling a lock of curly hair around her finger as she eyed the stand not too far from where they stood.

"Bubble tea and muffin for me," Rebecca said with a grin.

Grizz found a coupon for a free soda with a soft pretzel. "Ooh," she breathed, already able to taste the salty bread. "I think I'm going to go for a pretzel."

Rebecca shouldered her plaid purse. "Should we split up and meet by the Ferris Wheel?"

"So we have time to process our food before we hit the hardcore coasters?" Stacey asked with a mischievous grin.

Grizz laughed. "Okay, see you two in a bit." She looked at her coupons again as she walked, trying to find the pretzel cart. She'd been to the Boardwalk plenty of times before, but she didn't have the location of everything, specifically the smaller things like the food carts, memorized.

"Hey, cutie," she heard someone say.

She frowned and didn't bother looking to see who'd said it, walking faster.

"Where you going?" A tall teenage boy suddenly crossed her path. She took in his short blond hair and stocky frame, vaguely recognizing him as a football player from Vista.

"Away," Grizz said curtly, narrowing her eyes at him. When he didn't move, she hissed, "What the hell are you doing? Is this the only path on the whole freaking Boardwalk? Move."

"Aw, you're kind of hot when you're mad," he slurred. "Why don't you come party with some of my friends?"

Grizz sighed, glancing around to see if there were any teachers or workers nearby. If worse came to worst, this guy could use a punch in the face. "Not happening."

The guy took a step closer to her, and she maneuvered out of his way, wrinkling her nose in distaste. *Do you want the blow to your groin or your nose?* she thought.

"Hey, leave her alone."

Grizz's eyes widened as she saw that Kurt had appeared out of nowhere, clamping a hand down on the guy's shoulder.

"Who is this jerk?" The party was supposed to be alcohol free, but this guy had clearly pre-gamed. Kurt grimaced as he swung too close to his face and caught the scent of his reeking breath. Slowly he read the text on Kurt's tee shirt. "Oh, you're on the water polo team?" he sneered. "Why don't you move along, loser, and I'll keep this hottie company."

Grizz watched him in disgust, wanting nothing more than to bash his face in. She began to worry that Kurt was feeling the same way, watching him grit his teeth and narrow his eyes as he leaned down to glare at the football player. She wondered if their Grad Night would end with a trip to the police station.

Kurt, to her surprise, kept his temper, taking a step closer to Grizz and putting an arm around her shoulders. "She told you no, dude. Now, you'd better knock it off and move along before I get really pissed." He lifted his eyebrows threateningly.

The football player frowned, swaying slightly as he took a step away from them. "Whatever," he muttered as he walked away.

Kurt watched him leave with satisfaction. Something about the way he'd been talking to Grizz made his blood boil. "Are you okay, Zel? It sucks that you can't even enjoy yourself without random creeps like him popping out of the woodwork. Being a girl is no joke." He took in Grizz's sparkling brown eyes and flowing hair. His face, for some reason, began to feel hot. "Just because you're pretty, they all want to bother you... Well, that's their problem."

Grizz was frozen on the spot for a moment as she stared up into his tanned face, aware of how her heart pounded in her ears. She came to her senses a second later, shrugging out of his grasp. "Thanks, Galahart, but I can take care of myself."

Kurt looked confused. "Um, I think you mean Galahad."

Grizz could practically feel the steam shooting out of her ears at his correction. How dare he pull out the smart words! She grit her teeth. "Well, *Galahad*, why don't you get back on that horse of yours and ride away. Aren't you supposed to be playing laser tag?"

Kurt reached his arms over his head and stretched. "We finished. I was one of the guys who won. The guys who lost were kind of miffed, and took off." He patted his stomach. "But all that exercise made me hungry again." He turned to her and asked, "What are you up to, Zelly? Weren't you hanging out with your friends?"

Grizz shuffled in her purple flip flops. "I'm meeting Rebecca and Stacey at the Ferris Wheel. Just as soon as I find the freaking soft pretzels…"

"Oh, I walked past those," Kurt said, starting off in that direction. "They look awesome! Did we get a coupon for them, too? Bitchin.'"

Grizz mouthed "bitchin" with a laugh as she followed him. Soon they'd reached the cart, and Grizz's mouth watered at the sight of the plump pretzels on display. "Ah, you found it. Thanks," she said, playfully punching his shoulder. She expected him to leave, but he just stood there, staring at the pretzels. *I guess he's getting one, too,* she thought, pulling out her phone to group text Rebecca and Stacey. *"Sorry I'm running kind of late. Had a little incident."*

"I can already taste the salty feast," Kurt said, running a hand through his hair as they moved up in line.

Grizz laughed. "Me, too. So, what are you doing for the rest of the night?" She hoped he had plans. While she was grateful that he'd helped her out with the drunk football player, she didn't know if she wanted to be stuck with him for the duration of the party.

"As soon as I get my pretzel, I was going to head over to the beach—my teammates went over that way, I think."

A little warning bell went off in Grizz's mind. Ben and Patricia had said they were heading to the beach. *Then again,* she reasoned, *he'll be with his friends and Ben and Patricia will be together. Surely Ben has enough of a backbone to tell his brother to get lost.*

"That's cool," Grizz said with a smile, looping her thumb through the strap on her shoulder bag. "I'll probably do that later. The girls and I were going to hit all the rides—Caveman Train, buckets, log ride…"

"Sweet," Kurt said, then realized they'd reached the front of the line. "Oh, you go first, Zelly. You were looking for it before me."

"Aw, shucks." Grizz stepped in front of him and handed the guy her coupon. Soon she was holding a toasty pretzel, waiting for her soda. "Hot," she hissed when she went to take a bite. "But—must—taste…" She opened her mouth, then cringed and retracted, only to reach out desperately with her mouth once more.

She stopped abruptly when she heard a snicker. "What?" she demanded with a hand on her hip.

Kurt put a fist to his mouth, pretending he had a cough. "Nothing! Oh, look your soda's up."

"Hmph." Grizz carefully switched the pretzel to her other hand, cooling her burned fingers on the cold soda cup. She side-eyed Kurt as he stepped up to the cart to get his own pretzel.

"You're right, Gwendolyn, it is pretty hot," Kurt commented as he came away, double fisting a pretzel and soda. He cocked a brow as he stared at the pretzel, before taking an enormous bite.

Grizz stared dumbfounded as his face froze and turned bright pink. He choked, eyes watering. "Dirty lickings!" he gasped.

"The hell did you just say, Klaus?" she muttered, before patting his back. "Drink your soda, your soda!"

Kurt nodded and put the straw to his lips, before ripping the lid off and downing half the drink in one gulp. He exhaled in relief, sniffling. "Good call. Thanks."

"No problem," Grizz replied. "You knew it was hot, what were you even doing?"

Kurt sighed, staring at the pretzel forlornly. "My stomach thought first. Man, the roof of my mouth feels like it's going to peel off. Ahh." He lowered his jaw, as if he could air it out somehow.

Grizz snickered, pulling off a piece of her treat and blowing on it. She touched it to her cheek and nodded in satisfaction before popping it into her mouth. "Mm!" She closed her eyes as she chewed. "Heavenly!" She began walking toward the Ferris Wheel.

"No fair, I can't taste mine now," Kurt whined as he trailed after her.

"That's what you get for having no resistance," she said loftily. "You don't have to walk me to the wheel, I can see it from here."

"Nah, it's okay. I'm headed that way anyhow. I don't think you should be by yourself in case that dude in the gray suit is around."

Grizz furrowed her brow. "He wasn't wearing a suit."

Kurt glanced at her and laughed. "Nah, Rizzo, that's surf speak for shark. And that guy is definitely a shark on land."

Grizz took a sip of her soda, remembering that football player's creepy eyes as he'd leered at her. "Wise words, surfer guru. Wise words." She regarded Kurt, who was eying his pretzel forlornly. "Canst thou feeleth thine tongue now?"

Kurt furrowed his brow, clearly not understanding her.

Grizz rolled her eyes. Half of her jokes were lost on his pea brain. "Is your mouth feeling any better?"

Recognition dawned on his face. "Oh. Um." He took a small bite of his pretzel, chewing thoughtfully. "Thort of," he mumbled, mouth full.

Grizz threw her head back as she laughed. Her eye then caught Stacey and Rebecca, who waved to her excitedly. "Oh, we made it!" She jogged over to them, Kurt shuffling after her. "Hey, girlies! Sorry I'm so late."

"Oh, no problem," Rebecca said, lifting her drink. "The line for the bubble tea was hella long, so I just got here."

"Hi, Kurt," Stacey said in surprise.

"Hey," Kurt lifted his fist as way of greeting. Being so tall, he was able to scan the area quickly with his eyes. "Oh, sweet, there's a cop. I'm gonna go report that Noah. Don't want him ruining anyone else's fun. Later, Zelly."

Grizz smiled and nodded. "Thanks, Kurt!" She watched him hurry over to the woman in uniform.

"What guy?" Rebecca asked with raised eyebrows. "Someone named 'Noah'?"

Stacey looked intrigued, nudging Grizz. "What were you doing with Kurt?"

Grizz sighed, turning her back to Kurt. "It's a long story."

"All right, we're on the beach," Mr. Gardner said, a whistle around his neck.

Patricia laughed. Her drama teacher looked ridiculous in a Hawaiian print shirt and board shorts.

"Thank you, Captain Obvious," Tuck muttered under his breath as he stood among the group of seniors that had congregated in the "Fun by the Seashore" section that the teaches had set up.

"And just a few feet away is the ocean, where anything can happen," Mr. Gardner said ominously. "You could innocently be out in the surf on your board, waiting for the perfect moment…"

"Sounds like Kurt," Ben noted with a laugh.

"When all of a sudden, the biggest wave you've ever seen comes out of nowhere, and you wipe out! But what if, instead, out of the water leaps Jaws, the terror of the deep?" Mr. Gardner paused for effect, looking at the group of students. "So we are going to play a little game called surfer, shark, wave. It's like rock, paper, scissors, but bigger and better! You will break up into groups and select a group leader for every turn. Then your group will wander the beach until it bumps into another group. The leader will have three seconds to discuss which move you are going to make to face your opponent. Will it be surfer" — Mr. Gardner mimed balancing on a board—"shark"—he slapped his hands together, then flapped them like jaws—"or wave?" He hopped in the air and swung both of his arms forward. "With me so far?"

The crowd nodded and murmured. Patricia rubbed her hands together excitedly. She had never played this game, and it looked like a blast.

"Sweet, my kind of game!"

Patricia threw her head back. *No! Why?!*

Ben exchanged a glance with Patricia. "Hey, bro, what's up? How was laser tag?"

"Epic. I won!" Kurt held up his prize, a gold token.

"Show off," Tuck muttered.

"Are we going to be on teams?" Kurt asked, hazel eyes hopeful.

"Yeah," Tuck said brightly, scooting closer and putting his arms around them. "What do you say we all team up together?"

Patricia heaved a sigh. Sadly, she preferred Kurt's company to Tuck's by far.

"Whichever team loses will then join the winning team, and the group will elect a new leader for the next round. The goal is to have one enormous group. Whichever team collects the rest, wins!"

"Sweet," Kurt said. "What do you say, guys? Are we going to win this thing?"

Patricia shrugged herself out of Tuck's grasp and brushed her hair over her shoulder, wrinkling her nose at Tuck. "Uh, yeah, sure…"

"We've got a surfer on our side, how can we lose?" Ben said with an amiable smile.

"This will be fun," Tuck replied.

"Now, to start off," Mr. Gardner began, "I would like you to divide up into teams. What state are you attending college in? If it's California, please stand over here," he indicated an area of the beach to the far left of him, "and, for instance, if it's Washington, stand over here. Be sure to keep shouting out the name of your state so we don't get mixed up!"

"Oh, bummer," Tuck said, slipping away from the group to stand over in the Nevada section.

No! Kurt thought, glancing around for an Arizona section. *Patricia… Maybe she will be in Arizona, too?* he wondered hopefully.

"And if certain states only have a few, we will combine to make larger groups," Mr. Gardner called out.

Patricia and Ben walked over to the largest group. "This must be California," Ben muttered with a laugh.

"Gee, it's almost as big as the state," Patricia joked.

Kurt saw them together and his shoulders sagged. "She's going to be in Cali?" He sighed heavily. "Bummer, man."

Mr. Gardner walks around surveying the groups, tapping his chin thoughtfully. "New England, combine," he said, gesturing to the stragglers milling about.

The students gravitated toward each other, but so did several other groups.

"No, no, New England!" Mr. Gardner shook his head as New York and Pennsylvania tried to join them. He pinched the bridge of his nose. "Where did your geography teachers go wrong?" He held up his fingers and began to count off, "Connecticut, Rhode Island, New Hampshire, Vermont, Massachusetts, Maine." He left them to wander to the West Coast states.

Mr. Gardner heaved a sigh. "I should have known this would happen," he muttered. "California, you're dominating this game. Divide by Northern and Southern, please, and we'll see if that balances it out."

Kurt rocked back and forth on his heels and watched them intently. "Are they both going to be in the same part of California?" he found himself wondering aloud. Patricia and Ben stayed glued to each other's sides as half of the group split off and walked a few feet away. "No way!" he groaned, running a hand through his hair. "They are?"

Tuck, who was just steps away from Kurt, looked keenly interested, his grass green eyes flitting from Kurt to Patricia. "Yo, Patricia!"

Patricia turned her head and eyed Tuck warily. Was he about to tell a stupid knock-knock joke? "Yeah?"

"Where are you going to college? I'm going to UNLV."

His question was so ordinary, it caught her off guard. "Oh, UCLA."

Kurt, who had been listening, dropped his eyes to the sand. He realized with a heavy heart that she was going to the same school as Ben. "I guess it was meant to be, huh? Bummer, man..."

"Aw, what's the matter, Kurt?" Tuck asked, coming up to him and lightly punching his arm. "You seem upset."

"All right—on your marks-get set—go!"

Kurt lifted his eyes and regarded Tuck as the groups began to take off in various directions down the beach. "What? No, man, I'm not. I just, uh, realized, I have somewhere to go..." He turned and slowly walked away, shoving his hands in the pockets of his khaki cargo shorts.

He walked down the beach away from the ongoing game, ignoring the squeals of laughter he could hear. The wind picked up, and he felt a spray coming off from the ocean lightly mist his features. Even the sea couldn't brighten his mood.

"This bites. I'm supposed to be having the time of my life..." he said under his breath, the sight of happy students causing him to sink further into depression, "Why am I so crushed on my brother's babe?"

"Come one, come all! I am the great fortune teller, Tatiana! The past, the future, it is all clear to me! Ask anything! Love, fortune, adventure! It can all be known!"

Kurt slowed his steps, turning to see where the voice was coming from. To the right of him was a small tent with vibrant stripes, adorned with scarves and bells. A banner hung across the opening in the tarp, reading "Tatiana the Great: Fortunes Inside."

The woman seated inside saw him lingering. "You there, young man! Come in, come in. You wish to know your future?"

Kurt glanced over his shoulder, then nodded when he realized she was addressing him. "Whoa, ma'am, how did you know?"

Tatiana pushed a curl behind her ear and smiled mysteriously. "I know that questioning look in your bright eyes, my child. Sit, sit. Let us consult the crystal."

Kurt took in the rich colored silk swags that hung from the ceiling. As he made his way to the plush stool in front of the table, something brushed his head, and he cried out. He breathed a sigh of relief when he saw that it was just a plastic dragon looped to one of the pieces of fabric. Slowly he lowered himself onto the stool, heaving a long sigh.

"You seem sad, my boy," Tatiana surmised, staring at him critically.

Kurt slumped in his seat, shoulders sagging. "Is it that obvious?"

"Ask the crystal the question that is weighing so heavily on your heart."

Taking a deep breath, Kurt began, "Well, it's like this. I've never been super close with my bro, but we always got along, you know? I mean, sure, Mom and Dad are sometimes annoying with how they fawn over his nerdiness. 'Oh, isn't Ben so great? He got first place in the science fair! He's on the honor roll! Oh, he got this scholarship!' But, like, who cares, man? I never wanted any of that stuff. But now…" Kurt sighed heavily. "Now, he's dating this amazing girl. Whenever I see them together, I feel totally raked out. I know it's wrong to be crushing on my brother's girlfriend, but I can't help it."

Tatiana leaned forward, her many bracelets jingling with the motion. "You want what your brother has."

Kurt thought back to Ben and Patricia laughing and cheering as they played surfer, shark, wave. "Yeah, she's great…"

The fortune teller shook her head. "No, my boy, it's not the girl. What you want is *happiness.* You see your brother happy with his new girlfriend, and you wish that you had someone like that in your life."

Kurt frowned, resting his chin on his fist. "There's plenty of babes," he mumbled. "But none of them hold my interest like she does…"

Tatiana gave him a wry smile. "Let me consult the crystal." Mumbling a chant under her breath, she waved her hands back and forth over the ball.

"Whoa!" Kurt breathed as the crystal first turned a brilliant blue, then a deep purple.

"I see a young lady in your future. One who shares many of your common interests, one with whom you can laugh easily and be comfortable with. She will genuinely care for you, but also keep that ego of yours in check." Tatiana glanced at Kurt as she said this, but he was too mesmerized by the changing colors of the crystal.

"You do?" He knit his eyebrows together. "I don't see anything."

Tatiana made a clucking noise with her tongue. "That is because you do not have the gift. Now hush before I lose the vision!"

Kurt sat up straight in his chair, eyes wide. "Yes, ma'am."

"She will steal your heart. You will care for this girl as much as she does for you. Her happiness will be the most important thing to you."

Kurt nodded slowly. "Whoa… what else? Who is this girl?"

Tatiana shook her head, sitting up. "The vision fades. But take heart, my boy. You need not envy your brother. Let him be happy, for you will have a special someone soon enough."

"B–but…" Kurt began, standing up when Tatiana rose to her feet, "How will I…?"

Tatiana shooed him away with a wave of her billowing sleeves and jangling bracelets. "No more, my child, I must rejuvenate my psychic energies. Off with you! And enjoy Grad Night," she added with a mysterious smile, before pulling the curtain to the tent closed in his face.

Kurt turned away to stare out at the choppy waves of the ocean, the sunset casting golden hues on the water. "I wonder what the fortune teller lady meant?" he muttered, walking away slowly.

Chapter Five ♡

"WHOO-HOO!" GRIZZ CHEERED, CLAPPING ENTHUSIASTICALLY as the cover band finished the song with a flourish.

Ben put his arm around Patricia and pointed to the sky. Patricia jumped a little and covered her ears when a boom resounded. She smiled when she saw the blue and yellow fireworks unfurl in the air.

Grizz grinned, jumping up and down. "Isn't this the best night ever?"

Patricia nodded, grimacing at the noise from the fireworks. "Sorry, sensitive ears," she said with a shrug.

"Check it dudes! That one's shaped like a sea lion!"

Grizz looked to see Quincy, Kurt, Tuck, and several other water polo players standing in a group near them. Kurt looked their way and waved shyly.

"What is Kurt doing here?" Grizz mumbled under her breath. "As if I didn't know..." She shifted her eyes to Patricia.

Patricia elbowed her. "Why are you always so quick to assume it's me? *You* seem to be getting pretty chummy with Kurt lately," she said slyly.

Grizz felt her cheeks grow hot, though she was convinced Patricia hadn't seen them slow dance at prom. "Yeah, right," she scoffed. She glanced at him, recalling how Kurt had helped chase off that creepy football player, and felt a bit more charitable with him.

"Go Vista High! Sea Lions roar!" the middle-aged man on the microphone shouted, pumping his fists in a complicated motion Grizz recognized as a cheer guys did during sporting events at the school. He must have gone to Vista himself years ago.

Kurt and his friends let out a whoop and mimicked the cheer, and Patricia noticed that even Ben joined in. She also saw that Kurt and his posse had inched closer, joining them in the audience.

"All right, kids, you've heard enough of me singing. We're going to switch it up a little with some karaoke performed by you!" the singer said with a grin, pointing to the audience.

Grizz's eyes lit up as the crowd murmured excitedly. "Karaoke?" She turned and grabbed Patricia by the elbow. "Patricia, you *have* to sing with me."

Patricia's eyes widened, and she shook her head fervently. "Please no."

"Pa-tri-cia..." Grizz whined with pouted lips.

Patricia paled and whispered, "I can't, I'm sorry." She glanced sideways at Ben and gave Grizz an imploring look. Singing in public—particularly in front of her boyfriend—was a terrifying prospect.

Tuck, who had been eavesdropping, said snidely, "The theater girl has stage fright? Classic."

Impromptu karaoke isn't the same thing as performing in a play, you jerk! Patricia thought, feeling hot tears sting her eyes.

Kurt frowned, about to tell Tuck off, but Ben beat him to it.

"Why don't you go jump in the ocean, Robinson?" Ben said, dark brows furrowed as he stared down at Tuck.

"Oh, look, Tuck, I have something for you." Grizz pretended to reach into her purse before delicately lifting one finger in the air.

Kurt hooted as the rest of the group emitted an "ooh." "Good one, Zel!"

Grizz accepted Kurt's high five, then shrugged at Tuck's glare and turned on her heel, sashaying over to the stage steps to wait in line.

Ben reached for Patricia's hand and gave it an affectionate squeeze. She smiled gratefully at him, finding herself laughing at Grizz's fantastic comeback for Tuck. "Go Grizz!" she shouted, pumping her fist in the air.

Tuck crossed his arms, face reddening to match his hair as he stared at the stage.

"I wonder what song she's going to pick?" Patricia said.

When the opening chords to the song began, neither Ben nor Patricia recognized the song at first.

"Dude!" Kurt turned to them excitedly. "I *love* this song!" Taking in their blank expressions, Kurt rolled his eyes. "You seriously don't know it?"

When Grizz started singing, Patricia said, "*Oh*, yeah!" She glanced at Kurt, impressed he was able to recognize it instantly. "You're good, Kurt."

Kurt's head was already bobbing to the rhythm as he watched Grizz, oblivious to Patricia's compliment.

Patricia shrugged when he didn't reply, clapping her hands to the beat. The audience was cheering and clapping along with her.

As Grizz hit a high note, Ben raised his eyebrows. "She's great!"

Kurt's gaze was riveted to Grizz on the stage, whose eyes were closed as she crooned. She lifted her free hand in the air, her hair swaying about as she danced. He cupped his hands around his mouth. "Sing it, Gwen!"

Several of Grizz's friends who were near him gave him a funny look when he shouted that, but he didn't notice.

Kurt furrowed his eyebrows when he heard someone talking to him. When he felt the person nudge his arm, he turned his attention away from the stage to see Patricia motioning to him. She stood on her tipstoes to tell him over the music, "I said, we should get her to sing another one!"

Kurt nodded, mildly annoyed that Patricia was talking while Grizz was singing. He looked back at the stage and grinned to himself as Grizz danced to the melody of the music, the stage lights bringing out the bronze undertones of her complexion.

All at once what he was doing hit him, and he froze. *Wait—why am I so annoyed Patricia's trying to talk to me? That's not right—I should take advantage of it!* Even as he thought this, he was unable to tear his eyes away from Grizz on the stage. *Patricia's the one I dig—isn't she?*

He crinkled his brow, noticing for the first time how his heart was hammering in his chest when he looked at Grizz. The fortune teller's words rang in his ears.

"I see a young lady in your future. One who shares many of your

common interests, one with whom you can laugh easily and be comfortable with. She will steal your heart."

Kurt remembered how they'd danced at prom, and that it had been oddly fun helping Grizz fix her costumes for the play, staying up late poring through books as they adapted her script to be period accurate. *Whoa, man! Do I like... Zelda?* The realization hit him like a ton of bricks.

He stared, dumbfounded while Grizz finished the song. He needed to talk to her, as soon as possible. He had so much to say... so much to do...

Grizz gave a bow to the cheering audience, hurrying off the stage to join her friends.

"You were incredible, Grizz!" Patricia squealed, throwing her arms around her.

"Thanks!" Grizz said with a grin.

"You've got an impressive set of pipes," Ben said, giving her a high five.

Grizz rested her hands on her hips. "Aw, shucks."

"You did great," Quincy added.

Grizz waved her hand in embarrassment, cheeks flushing as she glanced around at their smiling faces. She cocked her head when Tuck began to say something, then closed his mouth. "Oh, look, I've even struck little Tuck dumb!"

Tuck folded his arms across his chest and frowned. "Well, you weren't the worst thing ever," he said grudgingly.

"Ha!" Grizz smiled smugly.

"Kurt recognized the song immediately," Ben said, nudging his brother.

"Really?" Grizz turned to look at Kurt, eyes wide with excitement.

Kurt stared at her, unable to say a word. He wanted to tell her how much he'd loved her singing, but he felt frozen. He racked his brain, trying to remember how to form a coherent sentence.

"Hey, Grizz!" Lita called out, squeezing between the throng of people to flag her down.

Grizz squeezed Patricia's arm. "Okay, I'm off for now. I'll see you guys later!"

Patricia and Ben waved to her. "Bye! See you in a bit!"

Kurt's eyes widened as he realized that Grizz was walking away from them, and he shook his head, righting his senses. "Whoa, wait!"

"Why wait?" Quincy wondered, scratching his shaved head.

Kurt had already lost sight of Grizz and Lita, so he barely looked at Quincy when he said hurriedly, "I—I have to go. Er… I'll text you guys in a bit." He took off, pushing his way through the crowd.

"Dude?" Quincy frowned, then shrugged and turned to the others. "Guess he's in a hurry about something."

"Free at last," Patricia muttered under her breath, smiling at Ben as they watched the fireworks.

Grizz stretched her arms over her head. "I love that one," she said as she stepped away from the Caveman car.

"Caveman Train rocks," Lita agreed.

"What next?" Rebecca asked, hugging her sides. "Brr, it's getting chilly."

"Hm," Grizz began, gazing around the Boardwalk. "How about—"

"There you are!"

The three girls turned their heads to see that Kurt had joined them.

Grizz fought to keep herself from groaning. How many times was she going to have to see him in one night?

"Hi, Kurt," Lita said.

Rebecca looked pointedly at Grizz before saying, "Fancy seeing you here, yet again."

Grizz wrinkled her nose and nudged Rebecca.

Kurt's eyes flicked from Lita to Rebecca, finally resting on Grizz.

She noticed with a frown that his shoulders were rising and falling, and he seemed out of breath. "Did you just run a marathon or something?"

"I—" The words died in his throat. He'd jogged all over the Boardwalk trying to catch her, but now that he had, all the things he'd wanted to tell her flew from his mind. He scratched his neck self-consciously. "Er—what are you ladies up to?"

Grizz frowned in suspicion. He was probably looking for Patricia, and now that he saw she wasn't with them, he couldn't come up with an excuse.

"Just going to hit a few more things before the night ends!" Lita replied cheerfully. "Want to join us?"

He won't, Grizz reasoned with a smile.

Kurt lifted his eyebrows and said eagerly, "Sure!"

Well, that's weird, Grizz thought as they resumed walking. She surreptitiously looked at Kurt out of the corner of her eye, noticing with annoyance that he had chosen to walk alongside her. She took a large step to the side to put more distance between them. *Maybe he thinks that we're meeting up with Patricia…*

"So, um, Zelly..." Kurt began, trying to sound casual as his heart thudded in his ears. *Stop being such a grommet!* he scolded himself. *I'm acting like I've never talked to her before. I just need to chill!*

Grizz pinched the bridge of her nose. "My name is not Zelly."

Kurt furrowed his brow. "Oh. Oh, right. So, um, Guinevere..."

Lita covered her mouth to hide her giggle. Rebecca rolled her eyes as they got in line for the ride.

Grizz heaved a sigh. "Yes, Kristoff?"

Lita nudged Rebecca and raised her eyebrows at Grizz's comeback. "Kristoff," she whispered, trying hard not to laugh.

"Well, I've been thinking a lot these past couple of weeks. The play was awesome, and it's really given me like, drive, you know? School can be cool when you focus on your interests..."

Grizz nodded disinterestedly, taking a few steps as the line moved up.

Kurt shoved his hands deep in his pockets, and cleared his throat. "I think the reason that I was so stuck on it was because a certain girl made me see, like, the error of my ways, man."

Grizz turned to face Kurt, unable to take this nonsense any longer. She had to get it out in the open. "Okay, I get it, you really like Patricia." She blew a stray bang out of her eyes with a frustrated puff of breath. *Gently, girl, gently...* "I feel bad for you, Kurt, honestly I do... but Patricia is *dating* your *brother* and they're super happy together. Sooner or later you have to accept that, and stop bothering her!" She looked up into his eyes, the bright lights from the Boardwalk casting flecks of light within the hazel pools. She paused for a beat to let her words sink in.

He stood motionlessly staring at her, the wind picking up and ruffling his hair.

Grizz wrapped her sweater tight about her body. *What, did he think I was going to help him woo Patricia? Enlist the best friend to brainwash the girl you like?*

Kurt blinked, urging himself to finally speak. "…No, Zel, you don't get it. I *thought* it was Patricia, but it—"

"Tickets, please?"

Kurt turned in surprise to see that they had reached the front of the line. The ticket taker held out his hand expectantly. He reached into his pocket and produced the tickets.

Grizz frowned when she realized that Lita and Rebecca must have gotten on the ride while she was talking to Kurt. *Oh, great. I'm going to be stuck on this ride with him,* she realized, shoulders sagging as she stamped her feet quickly in annoyance. With pouting lips she dug through her purse and handed the worker her tickets.

As Grizz followed Kurt through the gate, he thought with excitement, *I'm going to be riding with Rizzy? Rad!* His mind was a blur as they sat side by side in the car.

Grizz frowned and scooted as far away from him as the seat would allow, squishing her purse between them.

When the ride started, Kurt turned to Grizz. "So, like I was saying…" He froze when his stomach did a somersault. He knew it wasn't from the fact that he was finally alone with Grizz. "Wa—" his voice came out in a squeak several pitches higher than normal.

Grizz furrowed her brow.

Kurt cleared his throat, feeling sweaty all of a sudden. "Wait—what ride are we on?" He dared to look down and saw that their legs were hanging high up in the air. He felt a rush of vertigo and gripped the bar in front of them.

"We're on the Glider," Grizz replied. *How did he not see what line we were in?* She saw how pale he had become. "Whoa… are you okay, Kurt?"

Kurt swallowed hard, feeling beads of perspiration form on his forehead. "I…" He turned to her, struggling to focus on her features and not look down.

"Oh… are you afraid of heights?" Grizz asked, brow furrowed in sympathy.

This is so uncool, man! I don't want to admit I'm clucked of anything in front of her! Unconsciously, Kurt glanced down, and felt his ears ring. He squeezed his eyes shut. "I—I just don't like them that much," he croaked.

Grizz bit her lip fretfully, noticing that Kurt's usually tan complexion was turning a sickly shade of green. "Do you want me to try to flag the ride operator and get us off this thing?"

Kurt shook his head, gripping the bar so tightly his knuckles turned white. "I'll be okay," he said, feeling his stomach lurch.

"Try not to think about it," Grizz urged, staring at his arm muscles bulging as he held the bar for dear life. "You're going to hurt yourself! Here, here." She pried one of his hands free and held it in hers. She thought for a moment on how to calm him, before saying soothingly, "You're not in the air at all, you're in the water, riding a huge wave, the biggest one you've ever seen." She gazed out over the sparkling ocean as she spun her tale. "You're not afraid of it—you're feeling the rush, the wind in your face, the refreshing spray touching your toes as you conquer that thing. A crowd has gathered on the beach to watch you, Kurt Minola, King of the Waves!"

Kurt took a deep breath, her words taking over as he felt his stomach calm and his mind clear. He could really imagine it—him rushing through the water on his board, surfing that monster wave as people cheered him on. He slowly opened his eyes to see Grizz staring at him, eyes shining with concern. He smiled.

"Feel better?" she asked cautiously.

Kurt nodded, realizing with a pounding heart that she was still holding his hand. "That was great, Zelda."

Grizz grinned, for once not annoyed that he'd called her by the wrong name.

"Dude, you really made me feel like I was out there in the water," he continued, the color returning to his face. "How did you do that?"

Grizz shrugged nonchalantly. "Well, I *am* a writer after all."

"You're awesome," he said.

Grizz was grateful that he turned away from her, because she knew she was blushing.

He dared to look out over the ocean. "It is totally awesome up here," he commented.

"See? Just don't look down," Grizz warned.

Kurt exhaled slowly, leaning back against the seat as he relaxed. "See, this is what I meant."

Grizz knit her eyebrows. "What?"

He glanced down at their hands, and Grizz flushed, pulling hers free.

"I had it all wrong. The play was cool because of *you*. Trixie just helped me to see…"

A warning bell sounded in Grizz's mind. Why was he suddenly calling Patricia "Trixie" again?

He scratched his ear and laughed. "I feel bad for all the grief I probably put Ben through... the fortune teller lady was right," he said, bravely turning to face her. "I wonder if she knew I'd find that special someone so quickly?"

Fortune teller? What the hell is he babbling about? Her thoughts raced, heart pounding in her ears. *Special someone? Does he mean...* She stared wordlessly back at him, the horrible reality crashing around her as she saw the earnest look in his shining eyes.

"I guess it was destiny, man," Kurt said with a smile.

Grizz felt her eyes widen to the size of saucers. *No. No. NO!* She had to get off of this ride, now. She saw with relief that they were descending, about to touch the ground. She reached for her purse and began rustling through it, willing her heartbeat to slow back to normal. *I am not having a panic attack,* she told herself sternly. *I am not.* She refused to look at him, but luckily he was keeping his big mouth shut, apparently too shy to keep spitting his psycho babble.

The moment the car halted, Grizz practically flung the safety bar off of herself, much to the irritation of the ride operator. She hopped off and broke out in a run.

"Rizzo! Wait!" Kurt called, scrambling to his feet.

"I have to go home!" she screeched over her shoulder, not slowing down. "I'm going to turn into a pumpkin!" She hoped Ben and Patricia had their fill of fun, because she had to leave. Immediately.

Kurt heaved a sigh, heart sinking as he watched her disappear down the beach. "Well," he muttered, brightening, "she just had to get home. Her parents are probably really strict or something." He smiled dreamily to himself. "We have all summer for our love to blossom."

Chapter Six ♡

"OH, CHECK OUT THAT PURSE," GRIZZ SAID A FEW DAYS later as she and Patricia strolled downtown, pointing to a large ocean blue shoulder bag with silver buckles hanging in a window display.

Patricia slowed her steps, sipping her smoothie as she stared at the bag. "It's so pretty! And I love that dress," she added, gesturing to the mannequin in the window.

"That does it, we're going in," Grizz declared, grabbing Patricia's hand and hurrying into the boutique. "I may be short on cash, but I need some retail therapy to forget the other night," she muttered as they looked around the store, decorated stylishly for the summer. They'd been shopping for a couple of hours, but she still hadn't found that special something to erase Kurt Minola and his sudden confession from her mind.

"Here's more of the dresses," Patricia said, walking over to a rack and fingering the soft fabric. She glanced about surreptitiously before reaching into the folds and peeking at the price tag. "Ooh!" The boutique's prices were pretty fair. "Grizz, Grizz," she called to her friend, who was looking around wildly for the bag that had caught her eye.

Grizz turned to look at Patricia, who was holding the coral sundress up to herself. "That would be such a good color on you!"

"You think so? Should I try it on?" Patricia asked, biting her lip.

Grizz nodded. "Now to find my prize!" She rounded a corner and found a wall display with several of the blue shoulder bags, as well as a multitude of other purses in various sizes and colors. "Jackpot!" She raced over and carefully lifted one from the rack. She placed it on her shoulder and admired herself in the mirror. She'd dyed the bottom of her hair aqua the day after the grad party to signify the beginning of summer, and the two shades of blue complimented each other perfectly. She walked over to the dressing area to wait for Patricia, loving the way the bag felt on her shoulder.

"Grizz, you there?"

Grizz grinned. "Yep, I'm ready."

Patricia pulled back the curtain, and Grizz let out a soft gasp. "You look *gorgeous*," she told her.

"Really?" Patricia broke into a smile and did a little twirl. The skirt swayed with her as she moved, the fabric resting a few inches above her knee. "It's *so* comfortable… I wonder if I can wear it out of the store?" She paused, noticing Grizz's accessory. "Is that the purse? It's so cute! Get it!"

Grizz bit her lip, squeezing her eyes shut. "I'm afraid to look at the price tag."

Patricia scoffed, beckoning her over. "I'll do the honors." She dug through the stuffing inside the bag and pulled the tag free. "Not bad!" She read the price to Grizz.

Grizz opened one eye hopefully. "That's a good price, right?" Then she stamped her feet, squirming all over. "Argh! I know I shouldn't—I need to be saving up my money for fixing my car."

"I doubt that thirty dollars is going to go very far toward a new alternator and brakes," Patricia said wryly, speaking of the car Grizz's grandmother had bequeathed to her that was currently up on blocks in the shop.

"Yeah, that makes total sense," Grizz reasoned eagerly, running her fingers over the smooth material. "And it's the perfect color for summer!" she squealed, shimmying from side to side.

"We may both be doing something naughty," Patricia said as they made their way to the front counter, "but I think I can wear this dress all the time, don't you?"

Grizz nodded, reaching for her wallet and sliding the new bag off of her shoulder. "Perfect for going out and about, or on a romantic excursion with Ben," she added slyly.

Patricia elbowed her, stepping up to the counter. "Can I wear this dress out?" she asked.

The sales girl smiled and nodded. "Sure, let me just hit the tag really quick!" Patricia turned and let the girl scan the tag.

As they left the boutique, Grizz moved her things from her old purse to the new one. "Besides, this will be paid off by my first paycheck," she reasoned.

"See? Perfect," Patricia agreed, sliding her sunglasses on her face.

"Plus, it's a great size to fend off muggers," Grizz added with an evil grin, swinging the bag swiftly.

"With all the stuff you keep in your purse, it could be a fatal blow," Patricia deduced. "We'd better keep Kurt away from you."

Grizz stopped short, whirling on Patricia as her nostrils flared with fury. "Don't tempt me," she hissed. Her skin crawled as she remembered yet again being stuck on the Glider with Kurt during Grad Night when he'd confessed that he'd turned his affections to her. She was doing her best to avoid him. She knew it was too much to ask that she wouldn't see him again for the entire summer, but she could always hope. It might be hard to swing because of Ben, but Ben and Kurt seldom hung out together on their own, so she was keeping her fingers crossed. "I foolishly thought that he was finally becoming tolerable," she seethed, striding quickly down the street. "I didn't even mind running interference too much for you and Ben, because he was kind of fun, in a cosmic sort of way."

Patricia bit her lip, holding up her hands in supplication. "I'm sorry, I was trying to be funny! If I'd known that he liked *you* now, I would have never left your side!"

Grizz tossed her bangs out of her eyes and sighed. The fact that Kurt had decided she was the one he liked was disconcerting, to say the least. The first half of the night, he'd seemed like he couldn't get enough of Patricia. *I wonder what changed?* she mused. *Oh, well. Don't dwell on the workings of that moron's brain.* "Very well. But I need to be kept away from that doofus, or else I refuse to be held accountable for my actions!" she said, rubbing her palms together gleefully.

Patricia smoothed her dress as they resumed walking. "As for me, I think buying this is my treat for enduring that horrible couple at the restaurant last night," she muttered with a grimace.

"I can't believe they did all that and then didn't even leave you a tip," Grizz seethed.

"Waitressing is not exactly my idea of a dream job," Patricia said dryly. She was helping out at her parents' seafood restaurant like she did every summer vacation. "Though the extra spending money is good. Especially since I'll need it at school this fall." She put on a high pitched voice as she whined, "'More water! More butter! I specifically asked for *gluten free* biscuits! What do you mean they *are*? They don't taste like they are!'" Patricia made a face and grumbled, "When they're made well, they're not *supposed* to taste like they are, that's the freaking point!" She put on the voice again as she continued, "'Is this your best lobster? Are you sure?'" She tossed her braid over her shoulder and sighed. "Luckily we don't get people like them very often."

"Let's pray they're from out of town," Grizz said. "I really hope they aren't coffee drinkers."

"I sincerely doubt those two would *deign* to grace a shop called 'The Merry Mule,'" Patricia said flatly. "Unless it's more high class than it sounds?"

Grizz laughed. "It's a really cute place, but I don't think it could ever be considered 'high class.' Our uniforms are brightly colored aprons."

Patricia giggled. "I think you're safe."

Grizz slid her cell phone out of her purse and checked the time. "Speaking of which, I had better get going pretty soon. We're having a staff meeting tonight, and Mr. O'Shea—I mean, Obediah," Grizz corrected herself—her boss wanted the staff, which consisted mostly of high school and college students, to call him by his first name, which was hard for Grizz to get used to— "wants to show us the ropes and have us get to know each other. One big, happy family and all."

"One *merry* family!" Patricia teased.

Grizz walked through the french doors of Merry Mule Coffee Roasters and glanced around. She didn't recognize anyone, which she supposed she should have expected. *I wonder where Obediah is?* she thought, clutching the strap of her new purse tightly. The tables had been pushed to the edges of the shop, and there were about ten or so chairs that had been placed in a large circle. Aside from two girls who were seated side by side deep in conversation, everyone else was just milling about. She wandered over to the group of chairs and figured she would just stand until Obediah showed up.

She found herself staring at the photos on the blue walls of the Wharf and the Bay, as well as trees and wildlife. She'd only been in the coffee shop a few times, but she'd always really liked it.

"Hi."

Grizz turned to find a guy about her age standing there. Her eyes scanned him—tall and lean, with curly brown hair and blue eyes. A very *cute* guy. "Oh. Hi!"

"I take it you're one of Obe's new recruits?" he asked with a smile, revealing a row of even, white teeth.

Grizz nodded. "Yep. So you've worked here before?"

He shrugged his shoulders. "For about two years. It's a lot of fun." Sticking out his hand, he added, "I'm Dimitri."

Grizz smiled, fighting the butterflies in her stomach as she shook his hand. "Nice to meet you. I'm Grizz."

"Grizz?" Dimitri raised his eyebrows.

"G-R-I to the double 'Z.' It's short for Grizelda," she explained, sticking her tongue out in disgust.

Dimitri chuckled, blue eyes sparkling. "Cool name," he said appreciatively.

Grizz felt her cheeks warm. "Thanks." She cleared her throat, playing with a lock of her hair absentmindedly. "So, where do you go to school?"

"Actually, I just graduated from Santa Cruz High," he replied with an easy smile.

"Oh, I just graduated, too!" Grizz said. "But from Vista."

"Uh-oh, our rivals," Dimitri said with a chuckle. "But don't worry. I won't hold it against you."

Grizz laughed. "I appreciate that. I wouldn't want to make an enemy right away starting a new job."

Dimitri began to say something else, but Obediah suddenly emerged from the back room and clapped his hands. "All right, is everyone here?" His gray eyes scanned the room, and he nodded in satisfaction. "Have a seat, and we'll get started."

Grizz joined the group and sat in one of the chairs. She noticed with delight that Dimitri had chosen the seat next to hers.

Obediah took his seat in the middle chair, adjusting his glasses. "All right, several of you are new to the Merry Mule family, so first off, will my veteran mules please give the new foals a hand?"

Grizz shook her head as Dimitri and a few of her coworkers clapped for them. *I'm a mule now? Oh, excuse me, a foal?!* She reminded herself to not roll her eyes while in the coffee shop. Just then, Dimitri caught her eye and smiled, and she found herself smiling back, ducking her head to thank him for his applause.

"Tonight we'll get to know each other, and I'll show you foals the ropes of making coffee. I'm sure you all will be great. We're trying some new advertising gimmicks this summer, so it should be a busy one. Let's keep those drinks pouring!"

The group clapped and cheered, and Grizz grinned from ear to ear, surreptitiously glancing at Dimitri.

"Let's start with some ice breakers to get to know each other. The Merry Mule runs like a well-oiled machine when everyone isn't stumbling around not knowing the other's names," Obediah said, peering at them over his wire rim glasses. "So here's what I want us all to do. Remove your left shoe, or flip flop, sandal," Obediah went on, waving his hand, "whatever you're wearing, and toss it into the middle of the circle." He looked expectantly around when no one moved. "Well, what are you waiting for?"

Amidst excited murmurs, Grizz shrugged and unbuckled her gladiator sandal. She dared a glance at Dimitri, who was tossing his loafer into the middle of the room. She did the same, laughing when it connected with someone else's shoe, making a satisfying *thwack*!

"Now, I want you all to walk—or hop, as the case may be," Obediah began, "to the pile of shoes, pick a shoe that is not yours, and find the owner of said shoe. Then, you will ask each other the following questions: What their name is, their favorite season, favorite junk food, and one of their hobbies. Everyone got it?" Seeing a chorus of nods, he said, "Good. Go!"

Luckily Grizz's sandals were flat, so she didn't have to hobble to reach the pile. She crouched and retrieved a white sneaker with orange stripes. "Hm, who do you belong to?" she muttered to the shoe, searching the room for a right foot bearing its mate.

She found the owner to be a teenage boy a few inches shorter than her with black hair, wearing jeans and a gray tee shirt. He was looking around the room wildly, holding an ankle boot.

Grizz smiled and wiggled his sneaker in front of his face. "This is yours, I take it?"

He grinned. "Yep! I'm Frank Talampas."

"Nice to meet you, Frank. I'm Grizz Sheridan."

"Cool name," Frank said. He furrowed his brow. "What were the other questions? Your favorite junk food, hobby, and...?"

"Season," Grizz replied. "Well, I love candy, but Reeses Peanut Butter Cups are my addiction," she said conspiratorially. "I like to write and sew, and I think my favorite season is spring."

"Ah, Reeses," Frank said knowingly. "Those are some of the best. I think my junk food of choice would have to be cheesy popcorn, though. Hobbies... um..." Frank shrugged sheepishly. "Sorry, I blank when put on the spot."

"Don't worry about it," Grizz assured him, and Frank smiled.

"I like video games," he said finally. "And reading! Let's see... I guess my favorite season is summer."

"Well, then it's upon you," Grizz laughed, and Frank joined in.

He lifted the ankle boot. "Okay, guess I'd better find the owner of this boot." He paused, lifting his eyebrows at Grizz. "Now that you have nothing to do, want to join me?"

"Jolly good," Grizz said teasingly, scanning the room. She saw a girl standing lopsided just a few feet from them.

The girl turned and grinned. "At last!" Taking the boot, she hopped to a nearby chair and beckoned Grizz and Frank closer. "I'm Hayley."

Frank lifted his hand. "I'm Frank."

"Grizz," Grizz added with a smile.

Lacing up her boot, Hayley said from underneath a curtain of honey brown hair, "Welcome to the Merry Mule team!"

"Oh, you've worked here before?" Grizz asked.

Hayley smiled and nodded, standing up when her boot was completely buckled and laced. "Yep, for about six months. It's a lot of fun."

Frank said, "What is your favorite junk food?"

Hayley smiled mischievously. "I can't get enough of Toblerone."

"Ah, chocolate lovers unite!" Grizz cheered, high fiving Hayley. "I love Reeses."

"What about you?" Hayley asked Frank.

Frank replied, "Cheesy popcorn. But you know, I love those special sets you can get at Christmas time that also have the caramel corn and the buttered along with the cheesy corn." He sighed. "Deliciousness."

Grizz laughed. "What about your hobbies and season of choice?"

"Hm…" Hayley chewed her lip thoughtfully. "Shopping, tennis, painting…" She counted off her fingers. "And I think my favorite season is autumn."

Frank grinned, pointing to Grizz. "She's spring, I'm summer. We're just missing winter!"

Hayley giggled, her hazel eyes sparkling. "Well, did we all finish our shoes?"

Grizz and Frank both nodded. "Whose shoe did you have?" Grizz asked her.

Hayley smiled and pointed. Grizz turned and saw Dimitri standing a few feet away, talking to someone. "Dimitri." She shrugged. "Kind of silly, since I of course already know him. He's worked here awhile."

"Yeah…" Grizz murmured, finding herself taking in Dimitri's tall form.

He turned around and caught her eye, causing her to blush and avert her gaze. He smiled and walked over to them. Her heart did a funny leap in her chest, and she willed herself to remain cool.

"Hi, Dimitri," Hayley greeted him.

"Hey, Hayley," Dimitri replied, stopping in front of them and putting his hands in his pockets.

"Do you know Grizz and Frank?" Hayley asked him.

Dimitri nodded. "How's it going, Frank?"

Frank grinned and playfully punched Dimitri in the shoulder. "Great, dude."

Grizz watched them with interest. *It seems like everyone knows Dimitri,* she mused.

Dimitri turned his attention to Grizz. "And I just had the pleasure of meeting Grizz tonight."

Grizz smiled at him, tucking a strand of hair behind her ear. *Maybe this summer won't be so bad after all,* she thought as she took in Dimitri's handsome features. *Nothing like a new hottie to get my mind off of Kurt the Jerk.*

Chapter Seven ♡

T HE FOLLOWING WEEK, GRIZZ CAME OUT OF THE BACK ROOM of the Merry Mule, tying her brightly colored apron around her waist. Whether it was for school or work, getting up early was not her favorite thing, but at least now she had coffee at her fingertips.

She almost bumped into someone as she walked to the counter. "Oh, excuse me," she mumbled, rubbing the sleep from her eyes.

"No prob," the person responded.

Grizz recognized that voice. Lifting her eyes, she exclaimed, "*What* are *you* doing here?"

Kurt lifted his chin, trying to appear cool. "Hey."

Grizz put her hands on her hips. "No, no 'hey.' What. Are. You. Doing. Here. Oh, whatever," she grumbled before he could reply. She waved her arm in front of the staff door. "This area is for employees only. You go to the front counter to order coffee." Then she glanced at the clock. "And you're here too early, we don't open 'til 9."

"I'm not here to get coffee, Grizzy," Kurt replied. "I—"

"Get you gone, then!" Grizz waved her arms, his newest nickname for her making her skin crawl. "I have work to do, and there's a strict no loitering policy to non-paying customers." She marched past him.

"I work here, too."

His words made her freeze in her tracks. Slowly, she turned, setting a cold, furious glare on him. "*What* did you say?"

"I work here," he repeated.

Grizz felt like she was being gaslighted. *Kurt works here? But… he wasn't at the staff meeting! Why would Obediah hire another barista suddenly? Did he find out that I work here, and decided to copy me?* She blinked rapidly. "You do?"

"Yep. Today is my first day on the job! But, whoa," Kurt shuffled as he added, "I didn't know you worked here, too. What a coincidence! This is going to be off the hook!"

Seeing his pleasantly surprised and earnest expression, she knew he was telling the truth. *Ben gets to live another day. Patricia will appreciate that. A cosmic coincidence. Of freaking course.*

"Yeah, off the hook," Grizz said sarcastically. "Making coffee is a total rush." She felt stricken with worry. Were they going to be the only two working that day?

"Oh, I won't be making coffee," Kurt replied.

Grizz furrowed her brow. "You won't…?"

Kurt shook his head. "Nah. I'm the official new mascot for Merry Mule coffee!" Hands on his hips, he puffed out his chest proudly.

Her eyebrows lifted as a wicked smile slowly graced her lips. "The mascot, eh?"

Kurt nodded, pleased at her interest. "Yep. Well, my parents really wanted me to get a job, to 'keep me engaged for college,'" he said, moving his fingers like quotation marks. "And as I was searching I saw that this one called for someone tall with a lot of endurance." He grinned. "So I knew I was perfect for it."

Before Grizz could make a clever crack, Obediah popped his head out of the back room. "Oh, good, Kurt, you're here. I've got your suit ready."

"Duty calls, babe," Kurt murmured, brushing past her.

Grizz curled her hand like a claw and swatted at him as he passed. She walked behind the bar and got everything ready, waiting with bated breath for Kurt to re-emerge.

Frank came in through the side door, running to the counter. "Sorry, sorry. I overslept." He ran his hands through his thick black hair, trying to tame his bed head. He glanced around curiously. "Where's Obe?"

Grizz leaned forward, beckoning Frank to come closer. "He's in the back. Wait 'til you see what's in store."

Frank raised his eyebrows, curious. His expression became one of shock as he stared in the direction of the back room, and Grizz knew Kurt must have emerged. She turned around, her cheeks puffing as she busted up.

Obediah emerged behind him and shot Grizz and Frank each a look that instantly sobered them, though Grizz had to cover her mouth with her hand to hide her expression.

"So, what do you think, Zelda?" Kurt asked, his voice muffled from the grinning mule head he wore. He was covered from head to toe in brown fur, the suit sporting a bright blue tee shirt covered by a yellow apron that read "Merry Mule Coffee Roasters" in spray paint font. Kurt held his arms wide, turning around proudly so they could all get the full effect. The costume was completed by the long, thin tail that hung from behind, lifting in the air as he spun.

Grizz had to cough to hide her snort. "I've never seen a cuter farm animal," she said sweetly.

Kurt clapped his large gloves together in excitement. "Really?"

Grizz nodded, a fake smile plastered on her face.

"Oh, um, I'm Frank." Frank held out his hand, trying to keep a straight face.

"Kurt." Kurt clumsily took his hand, having trouble making the hooves curve.

"Burt?" Frank asked.

"Sounds about right," Grizz muttered with a devilish twitch of her eyebrow.

"We're trying some new promotional ideas for the summer," Obediah continued. He handed Kurt a stack of coupons. "We'll switch out the coupons every couple of days, and also have a specialty drink and pastry of the day. The coupons will usually correlate with the specialties, but sometimes they'll be related to different items."

Though Grizz couldn't see Kurt's expression under the mule head, she knew he was getting confused.

Sure enough, Kurt cocked his head. "What?"

Obediah pushed his glasses up the bridge of his nose. "You don't need to worry about it, Kurt. Just hand out the fliers to people walking by." He went behind the counter and came out with a large, colorful poster board. "Wave this around, too."

Kurt reached for the board, then realized his hands were full. He clumsily shoved the coupons in the pocket of his apron and took the poster. "Cool," he said.

"Oh, and here, you'll need this," Obediah went into the back room, coming out with a large boom box that looked like it was at least twenty years old. "Now go out there, play the music, and do your thing!"

"Sweet! Old school," Kurt exclaimed, clumsily reaching for it and putting it on his shoulder. He strode jauntily out of the shop to the snickers of Frank and Grizz.

"Here come our first customers," Obediah said, cutting their fun short. "Grizz, Frank, I'll leave them to you." He peered over his glasses at both of them before heading to the back room. "I'll be up front soon."

"Hello, sir, what can I get you?" Grizz asked the elderly man who came to the counter.

As she was counting his change back to him, her eye caught movement out the front window, and she giggled at the sight of a giant mule dancing while waving a poster board. To her surprise, he seemed to be really enthusiastic about playing the part.

The customer frowned, and Grizz cleared her throat. "I'm sorry, sir. We'll have your drink right out for you."

"I never knew working here would have so much entertainment!" Frank commented with a quirky grin, taking the cup from Grizz, gaze riveted on the front windows.

Grizz snorted. "I guess him being here won't be as bad as it could have been," she said with a shrug.

The following morning, Ben opened the hatchback to his Expedition, pulling out Grizz and Patricia's body boards. "Here you go."

"Thank you, sir," Patricia said, taking it and tucking it under her arm.

"Feel that sea air," Grizz said with a smile as they walked from the parking lot to the beach. "I can't wait for my first boarding of the summer!"

"It's a perfect day for it," Ben agreed. "Not too hot, but definitely warm enough for the water."

When they reached the sand, Grizz scanned the area. "Where should we set our stuff?"

Patricia pointed to a spot closer to the ocean. "How about right there? There aren't too many people around."

"Great," Ben agreed, setting his boogie board in the sand to claim the spot.

Grizz unbuttoned her loose cotton shirt to reveal the periwinkle top to her two-piece, then laid her large beach towel on the sand. "What a relaxing day we have ahead of us!" she said, flinging her arms above her head happily. She wasn't working for three glorious days, and planned to live every Kurt-free minute to the fullest. She sat down cross-legged and began to fold her shirt carefully to put it in her bag.

Patricia peeled off her coverup and pulled out her sunscreen. "I hope I don't miss any spots," she said with a nervous chuckle, glancing at the sky. There were plenty of clouds, but she knew she burned just as badly on overcast days.

Someone forcefully staked their surfboard in the sand near them, and Grizz absentmindedly glanced over. Her eyes widened when she saw who it was.

Kurt looked over just then, locking gazes with her. His mouth spread slowly into a surprised grin. He wordlessly lifted his hand in a wave.

Grizz, after a moment of staring at him in utter shock, tore her eyes from his and whirled on Ben. "What is *he* doing here?" she mouthed at him.

Ben cocked his head in confusion, before turning to see Kurt. "Oh! Hey, Kurt."

Kurt, who was still making goo-goo eyes at Grizz, started at the voice. "Hi, bro. Hey, Patsy," he said with a wave.

"We're back to that, are we?" Patricia muttered crisply. She noticed that the moment he got over his crush on her, he stopped calling her by her proper name.

Kurt ran a hand through his thatch of brown hair. "Whoa, I didn't know you guys would be here." He smiled shyly at Grizz. "Rad!"

"We didn't know *you* would be here," Grizz replied tightly, pursing her lips as she turned away from him.

"Yeah, I got here awhile ago, but needed a new leash for my board," Kurt explained, tapping the long black cord with the thick cuff dangling from his surfboard. "Are you guys going to surf?" he asked eagerly.

Ben shook his head. "We're just going to swim, maybe boogie board a little."

Kurt's shoulders sagged. "Aw, bummer." He shielded his eyes with his hand, staring out at the water. "The waves are really pumping today," he said, pulling his shirt over his head and kicking off his water shoes.

Grizz ducked her eyes at the sight of his chiseled muscles, feeling her cheeks warm involuntarily. She frowned, looking at Ben, who was peeling off his own tee shirt. Though he was almost as cut as his brother, she didn't feel embarrassed seeing *him* shirtless. Maybe because Ben didn't irritate her.

"Akaw!" Kurt suddenly called out, and Grizz was snapped out of her reverie.

"Why are you a bird?" she asked, tilting her head to look up at him.

"I just spotted the most awesome wave!" he replied hurriedly, picking up his surfboard. "BRB!"

He ran out into the waves, holding his enormous surfboard effortlessly under one arm. Grizz found herself staring at his form as he lay down on his stomach and paddled on the board out to sea. Within moments a wave had picked him up and he effortlessly hopped to his feet. *Got to admit, that's pretty cool.* She felt a funny little jump in her gut. *I am not jealous of Kurt.* Grizz told herself with a scoff. The mere thought sent her senses afire with irritation. She couldn't believe that Kurt was there. First he ruined her perfect summer job, now he was ruining their perfect beach day. "How did this happen?" she demanded, rising to her feet to stare at Ben, hands on hips.

Ben shook his head earnestly. "I didn't know he was going to be here! He's been gone all morning, I thought he was hanging out with his friends or something!"

Grizz rolled her eyes, then turned to stare at Kurt out in the water in disgust. "I should have freaking known and told you two no. Of course surfer dude would be at the beach."

"He's not always," Ben replied. "Though I know it may be hard to believe."

Grizz tossed her hair over her shoulder. "Okay, fine, you get a pass."

Ben smiled in relief. "I appreciate that." He frowned, looking at his things laid out on the sand. "Shoot, I forgot my towel in the car. I'll be right back!" he promised, jogging up the beach.

Patricia waved to him, rubbing the sunscreen on her arms.

Grizz sank to her knees and sighed. "I suppose it was too good to be true to think I could avoid him all summer," she mused. She wiggled her hands and wailed dramatically, "He's everywhere!" Remembering his dazed smile when he saw her there, she stopped. "Maybe if I play dumb, even if he keeps googling at me, as long as he never actually asks me out, I'm in the clear!" She paused and watched the waves lap onto the beach in horror. "Except I won't, since we are going to be at the *same school* for the next four years!" She slumped forward, running her hands through her hair as she groaned. "He must never know! Keep your trap shut," she spat, pointing at Patricia as she stared at her from under a curtain of hair, "And tell Ben to keep his shut, too!"

Patricia dropped the sunscreen bottle in her lap and held up her hands. "I won't tell Kurt, I swear!"

Grizz leaned back on her elbows and let out a short puff of breath. "If I stick to my side of campus, and he sticks to his... But what about Orientation?" She fell flat on her back. "Argh, it's no good. I can keep the facade up for the summer, but sooner or later... I need to go somewhere else," she decided emphatically, waving her arms and making a demented sand-angel. "Anywhere else!"

"Grizz! Don't change schools because of Kurt," Patricia urged. "You knew he was going there and it didn't bother you before."

"That was before he started stalking me," Grizz seethed.

"He's not stalking you," Patricia replied, trying to calm her down.

"Him working at the Merry Mule was a coincidence!" *A freaky coincidence,* but Patricia kept that to herself. "Besides, look at it this way: he's going to be in that costume all day, you won't even have to look at his face! And he didn't know we were coming to the beach today, but Ben and I should have thought of that before we planned it." She furrowed her brow apologetically. "If you really don't want to be here, we can totally leave."

Grizz gazed out over the ocean, focusing on Kurt riding a large wave. He turned his form effortlessly to follow the curve of the water. "No," she said with a sigh, eyes still glued to Kurt. "He's doing his thing, we'll do ours."

"That's a great attitude to have," Patricia said encouragingly, reaching for her boogie board. "And if he actually gets up the nerve to ask you out, just let him down gently," she suggested. "You could say you like hanging out with him, but you're not interested in him."

"Oh, sure. Because *you* did that when he liked you," Grizz snapped back irritably, unbuckling the straps of her sandals.

Patricia shrugged helplessly, leaning forward to rest her arms on the top of her board sticking up in the sand. "I'm dating *his brother,* how much clearer do I need to be? Besides, to be fair, he never made a play for me after I told him I had a boyfriend."

"No, he just stared at you and pined away hopelessly," Grizz retorted.

Patricia couldn't think of how to respond to that, so she just said, "Well, if you tell him that you're not interested and he's still bugging you, just let Ben know if he gets out of line, and he'll kick his ass."

Grizz considered this, pleased by the thought. She rose to her feet and brushed off the sand, reaching for her board. "Enough of that dude. Let's hit the water!"

≈

An hour later, Grizz hopped off of her boogie board, wiping the salt water from her face. She turned to watch Patricia and Ben, who had abandoned their boards and were standing in the shallow surf splashing each other. She laughed and walked over to their spot on the beach, picking up her towel and lightly drying herself off. She scanned the waves absentmindedly, seeing that Kurt was still carving it up. She frowned. "He looks so cool, it's not fair," she admitted grudgingly. As she watched him, she became more and more determined, imagining herself flying on the water effortlessly atop a surfboard. She walked out into the surf, the water lapping around her knees as she joined Ben and Patricia.

"Hey!"

The group turned to see Kurt cupping a hand around his mouth as he straddled his board. "Don't be a bunch of paddlepusses! Conquer these waves!" Before they could reply, he was in position, paddling toward a wave.

As he leapt to his feet and began to surf, Grizz curled her hands into fists. "That does it!" she decreed. "It can't be that hard if Kurt's doing it. I've always wanted to learn." She looked over her shoulder to the surfboard rental up the beach. "Get me a freaking surfboard, I'll show him!"

Ben and Patricia followed her out of the water, sitting down on their towels. "You're going to surf?" Patricia asked, wringing her hair out.

Grizz nodded, grabbing her wallet out of her bag. "Yep." She marched up the beach.

Patricia exchanged a look with Ben and shrugged. Ben leaned back on his elbows and watched Kurt as he rode the wave inland. He clapped as Kurt picked up his board and waded toward them. "That looked great, Kurt."

Kurt grinned, setting his board on the sand. "Thanks, bro." He looked around. "Where's Zelly?"

Patricia stood up, lifting her boogie board. "She should be back any minute. She went to rent—"

Kurt scanned the beach and saw her heading back from the board rental. He took in her toned physique in the periwinkle two-piece as she hefted the surfboard under one arm, her aqua-tipped hair trailing behind her in the wind. He felt his cheeks warm.

Grizz set down the board in the sand with a gleeful shout. "Check it out, gang!"

"Wow, that one is pretty," Patricia said, admiring the yellow Hawaiian flowers on the aqua paint.

"It matches your hair," Ben said with a laugh.

Grizz struck a pose. "Thank you, that's why I chose it." She waded into the water, lugging the board behind her.

"I think I'm ready to board some more. Want to join me?" Patricia asked Ben.

Ben cocked his head thoughtfully. "No, you know what, I think I'll just lay back and admire your skills."

Patricia blushed and crouched to pick up her boogie board, giving him a quick peck on the cheek before racing toward the surf.

Kurt finally came to his senses, picking up his own board and following Grizz out to where she stood waist-deep in the water. "Er, have you ever surfed before, Zel?"

Grizz cast him an annoyed look. "I've body surfed. It's not rocket science."

Kurt made a move for her board. "Here, let me give you some pointers."

Grizz slapped his hands away, climbing onto the board. Kurt wrapped his hands around her waist and pulled her off.

Grizz reddened under his touch, clawing at his hands as he set her back in the water. "What are you—get your hands off of me, you Neanderthal!"

Kurt slid his hands from her waist to her elbows, turning her around to look into her eyes. "But Zelda, you could get hurt. Surfing is no joke, man." He stared out over the ocean. "There's a lot of tragic stories out on those big, blue waves."

She frowned, ignoring the way his touch seemed to make her skin tingle. No, it wasn't tingling—it had to be crawling. "Okay, okay."

Kurt breathed a sigh of relief and let go of her. "Great. Let's start with paddling." He adjusted his board so that it was directly in front of him, moving slightly as the waves gently lapped in. "Knowing how to lie on the board and paddle properly is super important, because this is going to be how you travel in the water to and from the waves, and if you can get the knack of it, you'll be able to catch a wave quickly."

Grizz blew a bang out of her eyes, trying to retain what he was saying, but still irritated by the fact that Kurt knew something she didn't. She didn't care that he'd been surfing for years, he wasn't allowed to have the ability to teach her something! It reminded her of when he'd discovered the huge mistake she'd made in the script of her play for the theater festival. He'd actually been nice helping her research, but the memory still made her bristle.

"Here, I'll show you." Kurt expertly hopped onto his red board, stomach first.

Grizz watched him, noticing with irritation how toned his muscles were as he gripped the board.

Kurt glanced at her. "See? You make sure your body is centered on the board, and you want to be back a little bit from the front so that the nose of the board is coming out of the water just a couple inches. Then you kind of lift your legs like this." He demonstrated.

Reaching for her own board, Grizz nodded. "Okay, step one, lie down. Easy enough." Kurt rolled off of his board and stood next to her. Fidgeting for a moment, she took a deep breath and hopped forward. "Ow!" Her stomach smacked down hard on the material before the surfboard shot out from under her. She sank head-first into the water.

"Whoa!" Kurt pulled her out of the water. "Are you okay?"

Grizz coughed, wiping her face. "Water up my nose," she whined.

Kurt grimaced, patting her back. "I hate that. Oh, shoot, lemme get your board." He quickly waded after the board, which was being washed out to sea.

Grizz sniffed, her sinuses still out of whack. She was annoyed that she wasn't able to show off in front of Kurt.

When he returned he held out her board with a smile. "Once you get the hang of it, we'll put the leg rope on you and your board won't get away from you."

She sighed and took it, ready to try again.

And again. And again. "Argh, it just keeps shooting out from under me, like it's slathered in butter!"

"Don't worry, Rizzy, it just takes a lot of practice. This happens to everyone." He snapped his fingers. "I have an idea." Kurt gripped the side of her aqua board. "Now hop on."

Grizz looked at him warily. "Ok, fine." She poked it to make sure Kurt was indeed holding it steady, then leapt on. "Ha ha! I'm on!"

"Great job!" Kurt grinned. "Okay, now, you have to get the proper position, or else you'll torpedo."

Still laying on the board, Grizz turned her head to look up at him, cocking an eyebrow. "Translation, please?"

Kurt cleared his throat, ears turning red. "Your board will shoot out when you try to paddle, hitting innocent surfers."

Grizz nodded. "Ah."

"You want to make sure you're not too far up the board, but not too far back, either." He tapped a spot a few inches higher than she was. "I'd say shimmy up so that your shoulder is right about here, and see how that feels."

Grizz obeyed, feeling stupid as her body barely was able to move in her wet bathing suit. She prayed both pieces were on securely—she wasn't about to give Kurt a show.

Kurt studied the nose of her board. "Okay, perfect—see how the tip of the board is a couple inches out of the water? That's what you want, don't ever let it dig in." Kurt studied her form for a moment, nodding in approval. "Okay, ready to practice paddling?"

Grizz nodded.

"Think of it like gently pulling your board through the water, one hand at a time. I'm gonna let go, okay?"

"Okay." She nodded again, narrowing her eyes in determination.

"If you ever feel like you're dragging, slide back a tiny bit on the board. Try it, one hand in the water at a time."

Grizz tentatively brought one hand forward, sweeping it through the sea as she zoomed forward. "Whee!"

"That's pretty good, Zelda," Kurt said, wading after her. "Only, um, can I…"

Grizz glanced up at him suspiciously. "What?"

"Well, your hands are digging in too deep and it's making you wobble." Kurt held out his own hand with an embarrassed look.

Grizz froze, realizing he meant to touch her hand. Stiffly she held one aloft. Kurt gently took it in his own large hand, heart pounding in his ears. "See, almost like you're doing a free stroke, but really smooth and gentle." He guided her hand and pulled it through the water. "That's it. Chill, man. Soothing."

Grizz made a face at his words and tore her hand away. "I get it." She did a few strokes.

"Perfect! Okay, let's practice that for a little bit, then you can try to get on the board a few more times," Kurt said with a grin, hopping on his own board.

Grizz rolled her eyes. "Whatever you say."

Heaving a tired sigh and setting her boogie board on the sand, Patricia sank to join Ben where he lay collapsed on the beach. She wrung out her hair with a towel and pulled on her coverup, glancing at his prone form. With a laugh she reached over and poked his bare chest.

"Ack!" Ben sat up straight and lifted the sunglasses from his face. "Oh, Patricia! Are you done already?"

Patricia's eyebrows knit in confusion—she'd been body boarding by herself for almost forty-five minutes. "Oh!" She patted his shoulder. "Sorry Ben, were you sleeping?"

Ben laughed and wiped his eyes. "I hadn't meant to, but apparently I drifted off there. The sand was just so soft..." he blinked slowly. "And the sun was nice and warm..."

Patricia gave his shoulder a gentle shake. "I'm losing you again."

Ben covered his mouth and yawned. "I'm alive, I swear. Mr. Johnson had me in the lab later than normal last night sorting through slides, since his meeting had run late."

"Do you want to go home?" Patricia asked. "I can drive your car if you're too sleepy."

Ben shook his head and stretched. "No, I'm fine. It's a really nice day today and I want to enjoy it. Maybe lunch would wake me up. Then we could board some more?"

Patricia nodded enthusiastically.

Ben grinned and pulled on his shoes. "Great. Do you think Grizz and Kurt want to join us?" His brown eyes scanned the waves. "Where did they go?"

"Kurt was helping Grizz learn to surf," Patricia said with a snicker.

Ben's gaze locked on to two figures in the waves. Kurt was lying on his board, then shot up to his feet, checking to make sure Grizz could do the same. She pushed up and wobbled, before falling sideways off of her board into the waves. "Apparently it's a work in progress."

Patricia followed where his finger pointed with her eyes, and laughed incredulously when she saw Kurt helping Grizz out of the surf. Grizz threw up her hands in protest and dove onto her board once more, paddling away from Kurt, who waved his arms in the air and called after her. He shrugged and grabbed his own board, following her.

"Grizz seems to be holding her own," Patricia commented. She rose and brushed the sand from her skin, trotting to the edge of the beach. "Hey, you two choka surfers!" she called out to them. Hearing Ben snicker, she turned back to him, hands on hips. "What?" she demanded with a laugh.

"We've got to get you away from the beach, you're sounding like Kurt," Ben teased.

"Bite your tongue." Patricia turned her attention back to Grizz and Kurt. "Hey, Grizz! Kurt!" With a sigh she trudged back to Ben. "It's no use—we've lost them to the irresistible call of the waves."

Ben stood and shook his head, pulling on a tee shirt. "What can you do?" Then he grinned and tapped Patricia on the shoulder. "Race you to the Boardwalk!"

Patricia's jaw dropped as she broke into a run after him. "No fair— you were on the track team!"

Ben cackled wickedly as he disappeared up the beach.

Oblivious to Ben and Patricia's activities, Kurt and Grizz were absorbed in their lesson. "Pop up, Rizzo, pop up!"

Grizz pressed her lips together, determination blazing in her eyes. She pushed herself up and balanced on her board. "I—I did it! I did it!"

Kurt pumped a fist in the air. "Great job, I knew you could do it!" He glanced at her feet and nodded approvingly. "Goofy footed!"

Grizz cut her eyes to his and glowered. "What did you just call my feet?" she hissed.

Kurt laughed. "No, you're just like me. 'Goofy' means you balance on your board with your right foot forward. 'Natural' is with the left food forward."

Grizz wrinkled her nose. "Some of these surfing terms are just plain stupid."

Kurt scratched his neck with a chuckle. "Surfing is its own culture, Zelly. It's brought people together worldwide for decades."

Grizz rolled her eyes. "Cowabunga, dudes."

He used his hand to shield his eyes as he scanned the waves. "Yup, there's some pretty calm ones rolling in. I'd say you're ready to practice catching some waves. We'll do the dinky waves by the whitewater so that you won't get hurt. Oh, be sure to put on your leash."

What am I, a dog? Grizz thought, but said instead, "Aye aye, *mon capitan.*" She waded into shallow water, then crouched to attach the leg rope to her right ankle.

"Oh, wrong leg," Kurt corrected her.

She paused and wrinkled her nose at him. "But I like this leg."

"But you're goofy footed," Kurt explained, mimicking balancing on a board. "Which means your right foot is forward. You need to put it on your back ankle so that you don't get tangled."

"Okay. Left. That's right, right?" She grinned, knowing she'd confuse him.

Scratching his head, Kurt just smiled. "Technically, you don't need to wear your leash when you're an expert, but it's safer to. Safety when you surf, man."

Grizz nodded, making an x over her heart with her pointer finger. "I swear to never surf without my leg rope."

"Good on you," Kurt said approvingly. "Let's paddle over there so you can get more practice," he said, pointing to a calm spot before he pushed through the water and leapt on his board. Grizz followed suit, grinning when she got it right on the first try.

This is really relaxing, she thought with a smile as she propelled herself forward in the water.

As they stood and waited for the oncoming waves to roll in, Kurt said, "Don't be clucked, Zelda."

Grizz furrowed her brow. "What?"

Kurt's hazel eyes softened as he bumped her shoulder gently with his fist. "Scared of the waves. I'm here with you."

Grizz set her jaw. "I fear nothing and no one!"

Kurt nodded with a smile. "You'll be awesome. Oh, here comes one. Okay, turn to face the beach, and lay down and start paddling. Then just let it carry you inland. Don't try to stand up yet, just ride it on your stomach. Okay?"

Grizz nodded, trying to bring back her bravado from moments before. She turned and assumed position, pushing her board toward the beach as she laid on it stomach first. "Eee!" she squealed with adrenaline as she felt the wave pick her up.

"Way to go!" She heard Kurt call after her.

When she reached the shore, she lay there on her board for a moment, reveling in how it felt to surf. It was like boogie boarding, only better, because she knew that soon she would be standing up on the board. She pushed herself up and lifted her board, eager to try again.

"Here comes the champion!" Kurt said, clapping as she approached him. "If you practice that a few more times, you'll be ready to ride one standing!"

"Yes!" Grizz pumped her fist in the air. "Let's do this thing!"

After five successful rides in the whitewater, Kurt waded toward her. "There's some waves just a little bigger rolling in now. Why don't you try standing up on one? I think you can do it."

Wiping the water from her eyes, Grizz nodded, following him as he led her further out.

"Before you go, Zelda," he began, running a hand through his hair, "you should practice paddling, then popping up while the board is moving."

"Okay, check it!" Grizz leapt onto her board and began paddling through the water.

"Great! Now pop up!"

Steeling herself, Grizz pressed upwards to a standing position. "Whee! Okay, one more time." She bent her legs to crouch and lie down again, but faltered, the board tipping sideways as she fell. "Ah!"

"Whoa!" Kurt threw his arms out and caught her, stumbling in the waves slightly.

Grizz opened her eyes and stared up into Kurt's face, which shone with concern. She hadn't realized he'd followed her out while she was practicing.

"You..." his voice came out half hoarse and half squeaky, and he cleared his throat.

Grizz's heart pounded, and she was pretty sure it wasn't from the fall, which was only a couple of feet. Unconsciously she realized that her hands were flat on his bare chest, his muscular arms strong around her. "Um... sorry..." she stammered, tearing her eyes from his.

Kurt's cheeks flushed as he found his voice. "Y-you almost wiped there, Zelda. Are you okay?"

Grizz regained her senses, pushing out of his arms. "Yeah, I'm fine." She turned her back to him, shaking her head. What kind of surfer voodoo did this boy possess? She needed to see Dimitri and be reminded what a real man was, because Kurt was actually starting to look halfway decent to her, which meant she was losing it. "I—I think I want to stop for the day. I'm..." she tried to walk away from him, then felt a tug on her ankle and realized she was still wearing the leg rope. She crouched in the water and quickly unhooked it, mumbling, "I'm hungry, and tired, and..." she dared to look at him, his eyebrows raised as he stared at her, hazel eyes shining with confusion. "I just... I've gotta go." She waded as quickly as she could inland, ignoring Kurt as he called after her.

Chapter Eight ♡

"THANKS, DAD," GRIZZ SAID AS SHE HOPPED OUT OF THE passenger seat, shouldering her purse.

"Have a good day, sweetie! I'll pick you up when your shift ends," her dad called back, pulling away from the curb.

Grizz waved to him, walking up the street toward the coffee shop. Luckily her dad had dropped her off a few stores away. She'd had a fluttery stomach ever since she'd gone surfing with Kurt, and it had kicked into overdrive when her alarm woke her up that morning and she realized she'd have to see him at work.

Sure enough, he was suited up and in front of the shop, handing out fliers as he bobbed his head to the music. Grizz panicked, the memory of being in his arms all too fresh. She slid her sunglasses on and pulled the hood of her pink sweatshirt over her head, walking swiftly to the side doors and out of his line of sight. When she crossed the threshold, she breathed a sigh of relief. *That stupid mule*, she thought irritably.

"Hey, Grizz!"

Grizz leapt about a foot in the air to see Frank had come up to her.

Frank laughed, taking in her outfit. "Are you a vampire or something?"

Grizz pulled off her sunglasses, tilting her head. "Yeah, ha, ha. Light!" She pretended to hiss and recoil. "I'll go clock in."

She slid the hood off her head, combing her bangs back into place with her fingers. As she passed the front counter, she noticed with a jump that Dimitri was working. She bit her lip to keep from squealing, hurrying into the back room. He was just what she needed to forget all about that stupid surfer boy. She took a deep breath and signed her time card, putting her purse and cell phone in her locker.

When she came out of the back, she saw Frank had joined Dimitri behind the counter, and they were deep in conversation. Grizz walked behind the espresso machine and took the cup Frank handed to her. As she made an Americano, Frank and Dimitri kept talking.

"Dude, just because you were publicity officer doesn't mean you are a shoo-in for student body president!" Dimitri said with a chuckle.

Frank shrugged as he put a pastry in the microwave. "But if you put a good word in for me, maybe write a letter of recommendation..."

"That's not how it works," Dimitri quipped, sliding the customer's credit card.

"Well, I'll just tell everyone I'm your best friend, use your popularity and just assume your place," Frank said with a sly grin. "Hey, you'll be gone! You can't protest!"

Dimitri laughed, going around the front of the counter when the last customer paid and walked back to their table.

When he was out of earshot, Grizz sidled up to Frank. "Oh, Frank," she whispered in a sing-song voice.

Frank turned curiously. "Hm?"

"Are you really Dimitri's best friend?" she asked nonchalantly.

Frank chuckled. "Nah. I actually only know him through student council. He was student body president."

"Are you going to run for it this year?" Grizz asked, wiping down the equipment.

He shrugged. "I like student council, but I don't know if I actually want to be president. I was just kidding. I'm probably not popular enough, anyway."

Grizz frowned and ruffled his hair. "I'm sure you're popular! I've only known you for a few weeks, and I already love you."

Frank wrinkled his nose and attempted to smooth his flyaway hair. "Aw, shucks! But Dimitri is way more popular. He is—well, I guess he *was* on the soccer team, and so he knows a lot more people." Frank shrugged, not seeming fazed by it. "But I like being in charge of publicity, so I'll probably run for that again."

Grizz nodded. "That sounds like it was fun. I was on the school paper a couple of years." She bit her lip, feeling wistful. "I'm going to miss high school."

Pouring hot water over a tea bag in a mug, Frank replied, "College will be way better."

Grizz considered this. "You think so?"

Frank nodded, setting the mug on the counter. "English breakfast for here!" he called out before saying to Grizz, "That's what my brother says. There will be lots of clubs and activities to get involved in."

"I'll miss my friends, though," she told him as she started making a mocha.

"You'll see them on vacation!" Frank replied encouragingly. "And maybe in between if you're not too far apart. Where are you going to college, anyway, Grizz?" he asked as he crouched to get more cups from the cupboard.

Grizz had started the steamer just as he asked the question. "Arizona State," she shouted over the noise.

"What?" Frank asked, rocking back on his heels to stare up at her.

Grizz cupped a hand to her mouth. "Ar-i-zo-na State!"

Frank hopped to his feet when the steamer had been turned off. "Oh, my aunt and uncle live in Arizona. It's really nice there."

Grizz grinned, feeling excited for college again. "I definitely am looking forward to it." Her eyes swept over the counter to the middle of the cafe where Dimitri was cleaning a table. She willed herself to not feel sad that she was leaving in a couple of months, and he probably was, too. She needed to live in the moment.

"Dimitri is H–U–N–K–Y," Grizz whispered to Frank as she put a domed lid on a plastic cup and filled it to the top with whipped cream. "Do you think he's into me?"

Frank knit his eyebrows together. "Isn't it kind of late to start a relationship if you're leaving in September?"

"Haven't you ever heard of a summer fling, Frank?" Grizz demanded, waving a bottle of chocolate syrup at him before she drizzled it violently on top of the iced mocha.

Frank laughed as she did a 180 and calmly placed the drink on the counter, calling out in a sweet voice that it was ready.

"So, do you?" Grizz lifted her eyebrows expectantly. "Think he's into me?"

Frank looked past her. "Well, I don't know him well enough to say for sure, but based on the way he keeps glancing at you when you're not looking and then smiling like an idiot, I'd say yeah."

Grizz's heartbeat sped up, and she whipped her head wildly around to see where Dimitri was, only to realize that he was walking back to the counter.

"Hey, guys," he greeted casually, checking the glass case that held the pastries. "I'll go see if Obe has more in the back," he commented when he noticed the stock was low. He winked at Grizz as he passed.

Frank raised his eyebrows and said when Dimitri was out of earshot, "Yep. Methinks he likes you."

Eyes widening, Grizz could feel her cheeks heating up as a wild, bubbly feeling surged in her stomach. She tried to remain cool on the outside, humming to herself as she made a cappuccino.

"Tall cappuccino for here!" she called as she set the ceramic mug on the counter.

Dimitri set the trays on the counter and began refilling the display case.

"I'll help you, Dimitri," Grizz said. If it was going to only last the summer, she couldn't miss out on a second of flirting time.

Dimitri smiled, his blue eyes lighting up. "Thanks!"

"Wow, you've got to admit, Kurt really knows how to bring it," Frank commented.

Grizz handed Dimitri a tray, then followed the direction of Frank's gaze to the large windows in the front of the shop. She burst into giggles when she saw Kurt, decked out in his mule costume, bouncing up and down, managing to juggle a large poster board while he handed out coupons to passersby. She squinted when she saw two people come up to him and start dancing as well, mimicking his excited gestures. When Kurt patted the guy on the back with his mule glove, Grizz shook her head. "Well, well, well, I guess they couldn't resist for long, hm?"

Shortly after, Ben and Patricia walked into the Merry Mule, clutching brightly colored fliers.

"Grizz!" Patricia called, waving the piece of paper in the air. "I just met the strangest creature. It was dancing and told me to use this coupon to get fifty cents off a blended drink." She put her hand to her mouth and said in a stage whisper, "I decided to do what he said, I didn't want him to get violent."

Grizz snorted, holding her hand out as she came to the register. "Gimme, silly girl. All this fresh air has gone to your brain. What do you want?"

Patricia squinted as she stared at the board above Grizz's head, hand written with an array of rainbow colored markers. Little drawings of coffee mugs, sea creatures, and beach balls decorated the corners. "Wow, the board is really pretty," she commented. She'd never been inside the coffee shop before.

"You can thank Grizz for that," Dimitri said, rising to his feet and patting her on the shoulder. "Obe put her in charge of it last week."

Patricia raised her eyebrows at Grizz, intrigued. Once Dimitri had walked off, she mouthed, "Is that him?"

Trying to remain nonchalant, Grizz tossed her head, winking ever so slightly.

Patricia winked back, then said, "Wow, there's so much to choose from. Is there a special blended drink every day?"

Grizz tapped her aqua nails on the register. "Yes, ma'am. Today the special is Red Velvet Dream Cake."

"That sounds too good to pass up. Could I get a sixteen ounce?"

"Don't you mean a 'Molly'?" Grizz asked with a snicker. Seeing Patricia's perplexed look, Grizz pointed to the board. "A 'Foal' is twelve ounces, a 'Molly' is sixteen, and last, but certainly not least, a 'John' is a twenty ounce."

"The donkey decor in here is too much," Patricia teased.

Typing away on the cash register, Grizz clucked her tongue. "Mule decor, Patricia! A mule is the offspring of a donkey and a horse."

Patricia raised her eyebrows, handing Grizz her money. "You are quite the expert."

Grizz shrugged. "It's all ol' Obe's influence. Oh, here, let me get you a punch card." She pulled a blue and yellow card from a stack and punched it with a music note hole punch.

Patricia took it from her, laughing. "This is so freaking cute!" The coffee shop's logo, a cartoon mule, smiled at her from the card.

"Seems like it's pretty fun to work here," Ben said with a grin, walking to the counter with cups of water. He handed one to Patricia, who thanked him and moved aside so he could order. "Could I get an Americano?"

"Must you be so boring, Ben?" Grizz intoned, rolling her eyes exaggeratedly.

Patricia nudged him. "Behold the bounty of options before you!"

Ben's eyes focused on the chalkboard menu and widened. "I... damn, there's a lot of choices. Um... um... what do you recommend?" he asked meekly with a shrug.

"You've got a coupon from the merriest of mules, don't you?"

Grizz asked with a smirk.

"Oh, duh, that's right. Fifty cents off of blended drinks?" He squinted at the board, clucking his tongue as he searched for the blended section. "Ah, still too many options…"

"Your girlfriend is getting today's special, the Red Velvet Dream Cake!" Grizz informed him.

Ben glanced at Patricia, then said, "Sure, that sounds good. I'll get a twenty ounce, please."

Patricia elbowed him. "Don't you mean a 'John'?"

Ben furrowed his brow for a moment. "Oh, that's a male mule, huh? Clever."

As Grizz rang him up, he glanced over his shoulder to watch Kurt through the window and said, "Kurt seems to be having a blast. Has he been bringing in a lot of customers?" He took a large gulp from his water glass.

Grizz's eyes quickly scanned the coffee shop, which was full of customers happily sipping their drinks. "Yeah, I think so. Gotta admit, he does his job well." She smiled innocently as she said, "I can't think of a better guy to play a jack ass than your brother."

Ben's eyes widened as he choked, putting a fist over his mouth so he wouldn't spray water everywhere.

Patricia patted his back. "Are you okay?"

Ben nodded, coughing a little. He locked eyes with Grizz and pointed at her. "Good one."

Grizz shrugged. "I try."

Ben and Patricia found an empty table in the back of the shop. Grizz busied herself with helping Frank make their drinks. When they were done, she carried them to their table.

"Wow, hand-delivered and everything!" Patricia said, impressed.

"Thanks, Grizz," Ben said, clinking cups with Patricia before taking a sip. "Mm, that's really good."

Grizz was about to reply when she became distracted by a six and a half foot mule entering the cafe. Kurt removed the mule head and ran a gloved hand through his hair. "Whoo! Hey guys."

Taking in his flushed cheeks and rumpled hair, Grizz couldn't help but giggle.

Ben leaned back in his chair and scrutinized his brother. "How's our mascot doing?"

"Noodled, man," Kurt said with a sigh.

Patricia snorted mid-sip and poked herself in the roof of her mouth with her straw.

Grizz cocked a brow expectantly. "Excuse me?"

"My arms hurt from waving that board," Kurt explained. "Oh, Rizzo, could I get some more fliers? I ran out." He held up his empty hooves as proof.

"Sure, Kyle, sure." Grizz said, rolling her eyes and shuffling to the back room.

"Obe, we need more fliers!" she called as she came through the doorway, only to be greeted by the sight of Dimitri lifting a tray full of dirty dishes, his arm muscles flexing.

He lifted his eyes and nodded to her. "Hey."

Tucking a strand of hair behind her ear, she replied, "You've got your arms full." She scanned the room with her eyes. "Um, where's Obe?"

"Right here."

Grizz screamed as her silver haired boss popped out from behind a shelving unit full of boxes.

Obediah peered over the glasses perched on the bridge of his nose. He didn't seem perturbed by her shriek. "What do you need?"

Grizz put her hand on her chest. "Um, uh..." her fright made her forget why she'd come looking for him. An image of Kurt dressed as Flute the mule flashed through her mind. She snapped her fingers. "That's right. Flute needs fliers!"

Obediah nodded and wandered over to the table, rustling through a box. He produced a large stack of paper. "Here you are."

Kurt was engrossed in a conversation with Ben and Patricia when she came up to him. Grizz tapped him on the shoulder. "Here you are. Now, Flute, you'd better scoot before you lose your hide. You're still on the clock."

"Thanks so much, you're a lifesaver," Kurt told her before donning his grinning mascot head once more. He saluted her and strolled out of the cafe.

Grizz shook her head and made her way back to the front counter. After serving several more customers, Patricia came up to the other side of the counter near the espresso machine.

"You're going to Teddy's party, right?"

Grizz looked thoughtful, pumping chocolate syrup into the mocha she was making. "I haven't decided yet," she said loftily.

"Please?" Patricia begged with puppy-dog eyes. "Ben will give us a ride!"

"Won't I be a third wheel?"

"What? No! We don't make you feel like that ever, do we?" Patricia asked in concern.

Laughing, Grizz told her, "No, you don't. You're the least

sickening couple I know."

Patricia sighed with relief. "Thank God. So, you'll come? We were thinking of heading over around nine-thirty."

Grizz pretended to think about it some more, then grinned and nodded. "I'm in."

"Yes!" Patricia high fived her over the counter before glancing at the clock. "Okay, I need to get going, I'm working tonight."

"Have fun with the fishies," Grizz teased. She watched Ben and Patricia leave, only to stop next to Kurt and take a selfie with him in all his merry mule glory. She laughed and got back to work.

Chapter Nine ♡

A FEW DAYS LATER, GRIZZ WALKED INTO THE MERRY MULE to begin her afternoon shift. The bells that Obediah had tied to the door tinkled as the door swung open. Shouldering her purse, she surveyed the tables that were full of patrons. She half-wondered who would be working with her that day.

Dimitri spotted her and waved. "Hey, Grizz!"

"Oh, hey Dimitri," Grizz said nonchalantly as she headed to the back room to drop off her purse. She pulled a hair tie from her pocket as she slipped past him, catching his eye for just a second before she disappeared through the doorway. He cast her a wink, and her heart leapt in her chest. "Yes! Yes! Yes!" she chanted as she skipped over to her locker, tying her hair in a cute side ponytail. "Nailed it."

She emerged from the back room, adjusting the straps of her apron.

She studied Dimitri's fine form as he worked at the espresso machine. *Oh, darn. Dimitri's working, too.* She smiled gleefully to herself, approaching the bar as she waved to Hayley, who was wiping down a nearby table. She stopped short, furrowing her brow. Dimitri and Hayley weren't the only ones working. Another tall guy was there, too. He turned, and Grizz's eyes widened.

Kurt saw her and froze for a second before a stupid grin crossed his face. He held his hand up in a wordless wave.

Grizz walked behind the counter with a frown. "What are you doing out of uniform, son?" she said, taking in the Merry Mule apron tied on over his street clothes.

Kurt saluted. "Hey, Rizzo! Obe told me he didn't want me to get heatstroke out there!" They'd been hit that entire week with a heat wave—the weather that day was cloudless and sweltering. "I've been promoted to the bar."

Dimitri placed a cup on the counter. "Sixteen ounce machiatto!" He turned and began to remove his apron.

Grizz realized with a sinking heart that he was leaving. *I must be replacing him for the shift.* She groaned. *Don't tell me—I'm stuck with—*

Obediah came over to them. "Grizz, can you please show Kurt the basics?"

Kurt's brows lifted as his eyes got an eager gleam to them.

Grizz's nostrils flared when she saw his reaction. *Why can't Hayley do it?*

As if reading her thoughts, Obediah turned to Hayley, who had just finished wiping down the tables and was heading for the counter. "Hayley, I need to do inventory and would like your help, please."

Hayley wiped her hands on her apron and adjusted her ponytail. "Sure thing."

Grizz felt as if she were a tea kettle, the steam rising and about to blow out of her ears any second. Obediah seemed to be doing this on purpose! *Kurt could help you with inventory instead! Don't you value your customers' health and safety?!* "The basics of cashier or working on bar...?" she asked dejectedly. She didn't know which she worried about more—Kurt handling money or Kurt handling machinery.

"Teach Kurt the basic recipes," Obediah replied. "I'm sure he'll catch on quick. The two of you should be enough to handle it for awhile. If it gets really crowded, holler in the back for us, okay?"

Grizz tried to smile. "Um, sure thing."

Obediah adjusted his glasses and nodded to Hayley. "Let's get started!"

Grizz heaved a sigh and walked over to the bar. "Here is where we keep the recipe list," she told him in a lifeless tone.

"This is so sweet of you to help me, Zelly," Kurt said bashfully.

Grizz pursed her lips and pointed to her name tag. "Can you not read? What does this say?"

Kurt squinted. "Grizz," he read, letting the 'z' drag, sounding like a buzzing bee.

"Ah, so you can read," she said with a slow nod, turning her back on him. "That will be useful. What's your favorite kind of coffee?"

Kurt scratched his ear. "Aw, you don't have to make me coffee."

"I'm not going to make it. You are." Grizz said with a coy smile. "Now tell me, so I can show you."

"Um, I like Mexican mochas a lot. They're not too hot to handle for me," Kurt added, lifting his eyebrows proudly at his clever joke.

Grizz stuck her finger in her mouth while her back was to him, walking to the machinery. "Here's the espresso grinder. You take a scoop of coffee beans, like so, and it will grind." She turned on the machine, grimacing at the loud noise. When she flipped off the switch, she said, "We grind fresh beans for every single drink, that's really important to remember. Then you use this little, um," she racked her brain, trying to remember the word for the portafilter. "Um…" She waved the portafilter in the air. "You take this thing, and you fill it to the top. Then you use the tamper," she held up a metal object, "and squish down the grounds." She held it out to him. "Here, use your surfer strength and give it a shot." She giggled at her pun.

Kurt tried to concentrate as she explained, but became distracted as he stared at Grizz's pretty features when she laughed. He blinked in confusion when she began to snap her fingers in front of his face.

"Earth to Kurt! Come in, Kurt?" Grizz put her hands on her hips and tapped her foot impatiently.

"Oh, sorry, babe." Kurt rubbed his eyes.

"I'm not your babe," Grizz hissed. She pinched the bridge of her nose. "Show me what you've got."

Kurt nodded obediently, taking the portafilter full of grounds and the tamper. Following Grizz's instructions, he pushed the grounds into an even puck.

"That's good," Grizz said, pulling down a stack of metal cups and continuing with her lesson. It was nerve-wracking to be teaching someone when she hadn't learned that long ago herself, so she hoped she remembered it all.

"And that is pretty much the basics," Grizz told him. "If you have any questions, ask me or someone else. Practice makes perfect, and all of that." The bell jingled, and Grizz noticed customers entering the shop. "Oh, shoot," she muttered under her breath. "Okay, Kurt, you practice making your mocha, and I'll handle these guys. If I taste your coffee and it's semi-decent, I may let you make some real stuff. Got it?"

Kurt nodded, saluting her before studying the list once more.

Grizz heaved a sigh and plastered a smile on her face. "Hi, what can I get started for you?" she asked once she was at the register. Glancing at Kurt, she saw him carefully pouring milk into the cup. *Well, this is taking you three times longer than it should,* she thought as she counted back the customer's change. *Be nice, be nice, he's new,* she chanted to herself. She frowned when she saw the line seemed to be getting longer. She couldn't ask Kurt to make drinks yet… this was such a stupid idea. "I'll be with you in just a mo—"

"Argh!"

Kurt's cry was drowned out by the squeal of the steaming wand, and a weird gurgling sound. Grizz turned to see that there was milk everywhere—on the floor, the machinery, and all over Kurt. She held up a hand to the customers and hurried over to him. "Are you okay?"

Kurt squinted as milk dripped down his eyelids. He lifted the metal cup with a frown. "Wipeout," he muttered with a groan.

Grizz nervously gnawed on her lip, handing Kurt a towel before she headed for the back room. "*Obe!*"

Obediah set down a box and hurried to the doorway, followed by Hayley. He ran a hand over his face, shaking his head as he surveyed the damage.

Hayley's eyes grew as wide as saucers as she peered over his shoulder.

"As you can see," Grizz said, "We need some help."

Kurt looked at his boss and grinned crookedly, lifting a hand in a wave as flecks of milk flew through the air.

Grizz couldn't help but laugh at the sight of him. *As if I couldn't predict this,* she thought with a sigh.

Chapter Ten ♥

"**W**HAT DOES 'OBD' STAND FOR?" KURT ASKED GRIZZ A few days later, pointing to the scrawl on the plastic cup that Dimitri had set next to the espresso machine. "Oh, it's short for 'Obediah,' right? Is this for the big boss man?"

Grizz held up a pointer finger, starting the steaming wand to froth the milk for the drink she was making. When she was finished, she took the cup from him. "It's 'Ocean Berry Delight.'" She pointed to the menu board. "That's one of the seasonal drinks."

Kurt scratched his head. "I've never heard of an 'ocean berry' before."

Grizz pulled out the recipe list and propped it in front of Kurt. "There's no such thing. Obe made it up for the drink. The smoothie has pineapple, raspberry, blueberry, and mango."

"Sounds tasty," Kurt muttered as he studied the recipe, turning to the blender to gather the ingredients.

Grizz sighed and pulled out the whipped cream and syrup. "Caramel soy latte!" she called out, setting the cup on the end of the counter.

"I don't know what to get..." Grizz heard a familiar indecisive male voice.

"Well, it's really hot out, so I think iced or blended, at least for me."

"Are you guys ready to order?" Dimitri asked Ben and Patricia, who were standing a few feet away from the counter.

Patricia looked expectantly at Ben, then took a step forward. "Um, I am. He's still deciding."

"Hey, you two." Grizz came to stand next to Dimitri behind the cash register. "It's okay, Dimitri, I know these troublemakers. I'll handle it from here."

"Oh, sure thing," Dimitri said with an easy smile, walking over to the espresso machine.

"Could I get a blended cinnamon mocha?" Patricia asked.

"What size?" Grizz paused when reaching for the cups.

"I'll get a 'John' this time," Patricia replied with a grin. "I have a mighty thirst." As Grizz labeled the cup, Patricia leaned in and whispered, "How has Kurt been doing in the store?"

Grizz glanced at Kurt, who was talking to Ben while working on the smoothie. "He's okay. He only turns in his mule mask when the weather is foul. Curse the elements," she muttered. "Oh, give me your punch card."

"That looks good," Ben commented, arms crossed as he stood on the other side of the bar while Kurt finished up the smoothie. "What is it?"

Kurt put a plastic lid on the top and reached for a straw, carefully pushing it through the top. "An Oceanic Blast Delish."

Dimitri shook his head, reaching around him for a lid. "It's an Ocean Berry Delight," he corrected. "And it's probably melted by now," he muttered.

Kurt reddened. "Oh yeah. It's that." He set the cup on the counter. "Ocean Berry Delight," he called out.

"What does it have in it?" Ben asked, moving out of the way when the woman who'd ordered the smoothie came to pick it up.

Kurt thought for a moment. "Uh, blueberries, mango, pineapple..." he snapped his fingers. "And..."

"Raspberries," Dimitri chimed in, pushing past Kurt to get to the syrups.

Ben said to Kurt, "That sounds pretty good, I think I'll order one."

Patricia walked over to Ben. "Hey, Kurt. How goes it?"

Kurt smiled and nodded at her, wiping down the equipment. "Sup, Trixie. Y'know how it is, I'm mule-ing it up one day, making drinks the next."

"Cool," Patricia said. "Do you know what you want?" she asked Ben.

"I think I'm going to get an Ocean Berry smoothie," Ben said with a nod. He turned to the line and grimaced. "Ouch, it tripled in like, two minutes."

"Yeah, it's been pretty busy all day," Kurt commented, scooping espresso beans into the grinder. "But Zelda and I can handle it." He smiled to himself as he put the lid on the machine. "We make a great team."

Patricia caught Ben's eye with raised eyebrows.

"John blended cinnamon mocha," Dimitri said, holding out the large drink to Patricia.

"Thanks," Patricia replied, taking a sip. "Ah, that's the stuff." Ben reached for the cup, but Patricia was too quick for him. Holding the cup close to herself, she said, "Uh-uh, get your own."

Ben frowned, eyes flicking to the long line. "It's not my fault you're indecisive," she teased. Laughing, she linked arms with him and pulled him toward the line. "I suppose I can let you have a sip or two."

Within forty-five minutes the rush ended, and soon Grizz was straightening up the area of the store where there were two armchairs and a couch, with a large coffee table between them. She swept crumbs from the table into the dustpan. She sighed when she saw crumbs on the furniture as well. "It can be done!" she said with a nod, gently brushing the specks of food from the upholstery.

The doors jingled, and Grizz glanced up to see Obediah bustle into the shop, followed by a woman with curly brown hair that was graying at the temples.

Grizz smiled and waved. "Hi, Mrs. O'Shea!"

"Hello, Grizz," Mrs. O'Shea greeted her warmly.

Grizz smiled. Mrs. O'Shea was one of the few Vista faculty members who ever called her Grizz instead of Grizelda.

"Could you help me unload the car, please?" Obediah called to Kurt, who was cleaning off a table.

"Sure thing, boss," Kurt said amicably, following Obediah out the front doors.

"How are you liking working here, honey?" Mrs. O'Shea asked as Grizz fluffed the pillows on the couch.

"Oh, it's great," Grizz replied. "Everyone is really nice."

"That's wonderful," Mrs. O'Shea said, just as a movement by the door caught her eye. She hurried over and opened the french door for Kurt, laden with two boxes stacked on top of one another.

"Thanks, ma'am," Kurt said, shuffling toward the back room. Grizz followed him and held the door open.

Kurt set the boxes down next to a file cabinet. "Thanks, Gwen," he said with a smile.

Grizz rolled her eyes, heading back to the couches. "No problem, Kris."

Kurt followed her, pausing when he saw Mrs. O'Shea. "I'm Kurt," he said, offering his hand for her to shake. Then he frowned. "Whoa, ma'am, it's trippy, but I feel like I've met you before…"

Mrs. O'Shea shook his hand with a puzzled smile.

Grizz chuckled. "Yeah, it's Mrs. O'Shea? She teaches at Vista?" Then she remembered that Mrs. O'Shea taught creative writing. "Oh, that's right, you never had her."

"Lovely to meet you, Kurt," Mrs. O'Shea said kindly.

"Tatiana, honey, can you help me with this sign?" Obediah called from the front door.

Kurt's eyes widened with recognition. "'Tatiana'? Dude! You're the fortune teller! You changed my life, ma'am."

Grizz furrowed her brow, wondering what Kurt was talking about.

Tatiana paused with a blank expression before realization dawned on her. "Oh!" She coughed lightly. "Oh, nonsense. You just needed a little guidance, that's all."

Grizz wondered what they were talking about, becoming more curious by the moment.

"Your prediction was totally on the nose, ma'am. I definitely think I've found the right one." He cast his gaze casually to Grizz.

Tatiana hesitantly looked at Grizz, eyes widening as she caught on to his meaning. "Ah—is that so?"

Grizz felt her jaw drop as she watched the exchange, getting a horrible idea of what they were talking about. *"The fortune teller lady was right... I wonder if she knew I'd find that special someone so quickly?"* Kurt's words from Grad Night pounded in her ears. Mrs. O'Shea was the fortune teller?!

"Well, that's wonderful," Tatiana said, noticing Grizz's furious expression. "I—I have to go help my husband now. It was nice seeing you, honey," she added, laying a hand on Grizz's shoulder before hurrying out of the cafe.

Mrs. O'Shea had been one of Grizz's favorite teachers, so she tried to ignore the mutinous feelings that now simmered inside of her. "What exactly were you and Mrs. O talking about, Kurt?"

Kurt turned to her and blushed, rubbing the back of his neck. "What? Oh! Nothing, nothing. I didn't realize one of our teachers had psychic powers, though. 'With great power,' man..."

Grizz stared at him incredulously. "That was an act! For Grad Night!" This from the guy who claimed he didn't believe in ghosts? Grizz herself was open to the idea of people possessing clairvoyant powers, but she had never heard Mrs. O'Shea claim to have them, or practice such a craft. Whatever Mrs. O'Shea had spouted at him was *not* written in stone. "All of the teachers come up with gimmicks for the senior class, it's a requirement or something."

Kurt didn't seem to hear her, smiling to himself.

"Hey, guys."

Grizz suppressed a groan when she saw that Tuck had entered the cafe. "Hi, Tuck," she said in a listless tone.

"What's happening?" Kurt said with a grin.

Tuck shrugged. "I just got off work." He glanced between Grizz and Kurt. "I didn't realize you guys worked here, or together, for that matter."

Kurt looked at Grizz and ducked his head. "Yep, Rizzy and I are proud servers of Merry Mule coffee!"

Grizz elbowed him lightly. "Oh, come, Burt, *you're* the company mule usually."

"Grizz!"

The trio turned to see Dimitri signaling from the front register. Grizz noticed that a line had formed. Dimitri caught her eye and gave her an imploring look.

Grizz giggled, twirling a lock of hair around her finger. "I've got to go help Dimitri," she told Kurt and Tuck, practically skipping up to the front of the store.

Kurt watched her leave with a frown, his shoulders sagging slightly. Grizz went around the back of the counter and got to work making drinks, stealing glances at Dimitri all the while.

Tuck studied Kurt's expression, before looking at Grizz. "So, Kurt, what would you recommend I order?" When Kurt didn't answer, he nudged him. "Kurt?"

"What?"

Tuck looked suspicious. "Never mind. I'm going to get in line now."

Kurt put the ceramic figurines back on the coffee table and sighed. He brightened when he saw Grizz wave to him from behind the counter. Straightening his shoulders, Kurt came up to her. "Hey, Zelly." He smiled, summoning up his courage. "So, um, I was thinking…"

Grizz cut him off by thrusting a mug with a sticker into his hands, her expression frazzled. "A white mocha for here."

Kurt sighed, realizing Grizz wasn't listening. He dejectedly began making the drink.

When Tuck ordered, he wandered over to the edge of the bar. "So, Kurt," he began off-handedly, "I noticed Ben and Patricia were outside on the patio."

"Uh-huh," Kurt replied distractedly, drizzling syrup on the whipped cream. "White mocha for here," he called out.

"Too bad she didn't sit inside, so you could try to talk to her," Tuck went on, leaning against the counter, a sly smile on his face.

"The patio has those nice beach umbrellas, of course she and Ben wanted to sit outside," Kurt replied, lifting a paper cup off of the edge of the bar and reading the instructions on it under his breath.

Tuck frowned, folding his arms as he fell silent.

"So, I noticed you rode your bike today, Grizz," Dimitri commented after he rang up a customer.

Grizz smiled to herself as she put spoons in an ice bath. "Oh, yeah, I was riding in the area and decided to just come to work that way."

"When do you get off tonight?" Dimitri asked, looking at her out of the corner of his eye.

Grizz almost dropped the can of whipped cream she was holding. *Could he be…?* "I work until closing."

Dimitri whistled lowly. "It will be dark by then. I can give you a lift home, if you want."

Grizz felt her heart pound with excitement. Trying to be

nonchalant, she said, "Oh, if it's not too much trouble, that would be nice."

"Hey, it's no trouble for *you.*"

Grizz giggled, about to reply when a horrible noise filled the cafe.

Kurt was standing in front of the espresso grinder with a dazed look, clutching the lid tightly in his hand. The bin was filled to the top with beans, far more than there should have been for a single or even a triple shot. The worst thing of all, however, was that he had failed to put the lid on tightly. It had popped off and flown over the counter, and beans were shooting off in every direction!

Grizz ran to Kurt, covering her face to avoid having an eye taken out with a bean. "Kurt, what the hell!" she exclaimed, reaching around him to shut off the machine.

Obediah hurried over to the front counter, which was now a sea of half-ground coffee beans. "What happened here?" He sighed when he saw Kurt standing at the machine. "I thought you'd figured out the machinery by now, Kurt," Obediah said, shaking his head. "How many scoops did you put in? Where was your mind?"

Kurt looked up at him, specks of coffee clinging to his face. "Sorry, boss," he said with a cough.

"There's never been more merriment in this place," Tuck said with a snicker.

"I'll have to clean out the grinder," Obediah said, furrowing his brow. "What a mess." He looked at Kurt, whose gaze was riveted to the cash register. Turning, Obediah saw Dimitri brushing off Grizz's shoulders as she laughed. He shot Kurt a sympathetic glance. "Ah. Well, no harm done. Kurt, why don't you get the broom and dustpan? I'll clean the grinder, and we'll set this to rights."

"O-okay. Thanks, Obe," Kurt mumbled, walking slowly to the store room.

Tuck followed him with his eyes, a mischievous glint reflected in them.

≈

Later that evening, the sun had set, and Kurt, Grizz, and Dimitri were tidying up the cafe. Kurt effortlessly lifted the chair and turned it upside down on the table as Grizz passed him with the dust mop.

"As soon as you're done cleaning, you guys can clock out and go home," Obediah told them, looking at his watch. He straightened his papers on a tabletop. "I've got some paperwork to do, so I'll lock up and alarm the shop."

Soon I'll be getting some one-on-one time with Dimitri, Grizz thought gleefully, tucking a layer behind her ear as she crouched to get at the dust under a table leg. She surreptitiously glanced at him heading through a side door with two full trash bags.

"Rizzy, can I have the dust pan?" Kurt asked. "I can't put these chairs on this dirty table."

Grizz extracted herself from underneath the table, stretching to handing him the pan. "Sure thing, Cary."

"Thanks!" Kurt said, holding the pan to the edge of the table and sweeping crumbs off of it with his hand. He wiped his hand on his apron, bits of food and dirt spilling to the floor.

Grizz rolled her eyes. "It will be easier if you use the little broom. For you and the rest of us," she added under her breath. "Now where did I put that thing?"

Kurt began looking for it as well. "There it is!" he exclaimed gleefully, picking the handheld broom up from one of the tables.

Grizz smiled. "Good. Now let's sweep, sweep, sweep up the dirt, dust, and grime," she sang, tidying the mess Kurt had made.

When she heard Kurt chuckle, she cut her eyes to him. "What?"

Kurt quickly shook his head, pretending to focus on sweeping the table. "Nothing! Um, I liked your little song, that's all. 'Sweep, sweep...'" he repeated, taking the full dustpan to the trash bin.

Grizz couldn't help but laugh. "Okay, then." She noticed Dimitri walking past just then, and quickly straightened her posture, trying to catch his eye.

A few minutes later, Grizz and Kurt had finished, and were putting the cleaning supplies back in the closet. Kurt went into the break room, and Grizz followed him to fill out her time card and clock out.

She retrieved her purse, bike helmet, and sweater from her locker, turning her cell phone back on. *Dimitri time!* her heart practically sang. She looked over her shoulder when she saw movement, but frowned in disappointment when she saw it was just Kurt pulling his things out of his locker.

Grizz hurried out into the main cafe, looking for Dimitri. She frowned, wondering if he was outside. She went out the side door. "Dimitri?" she called, not wanting to be too loud. She walked down the covered patio area, glancing all around. "Dimitri!"

She came back inside and shut the door behind her with a frown. *Maybe he's in the bathroom,* she reasoned, leaning against the counter and shouldering her purse. She clicked her nails against the counter top as she pulled out her phone and looked through her text messages.

When a shadow fell in front of her, she eagerly lifted her eyes, only to see that, once again, it was just Kurt.

"Are you staying to help Obe or something, Zelly?" he asked curiously, noticing that she was clearly waiting around for something.

Grizz slid her cell phone into her bag. "Um... I'm leaving with Dimitri..."

Kurt frowned, but tried to keep his tone indifferent. "Oh, okay." He rocked back on his heels and looked around, realizing he hadn't seen Dimitri for awhile. "Is he in the back room or something?"

Grizz shrugged. "I guess so. Or maybe the men's room..."

"I'll check for you," Kurt replied, pivoting and heading toward the bathroom before she could protest.

She blew a bang out of her eye and slumped against the counter top, getting tired of waiting. Finally she walked into the break room, pausing in the doorway.

"Do you need something, Grizz?" Obediah asked kindly from his spot at his desk.

"Oh, nothing, just..." she paused, standing on tiptoe as she gazed around the room. "Where's Dimitri?"

Obediah adjusted his glasses as he flipped through a pile of papers. "I think he left."

She was taken aback by his statement, sure he was mistaken. She turned silently and walked back into the cafe.

"Have a good night, Grizz!" Obediah called after her.

"...You, too!" she replied after a long pause.

Her brows knit together. He couldn't have left, he was supposed to give her a ride home. Obediah had to be wrong.

Kurt emerged from the hallway, shaking his head at Grizz. "He's not in the bathroom."

"Did he… leave?" she asked incredulously.

Kurt shrugged, walking over to the front windows. "Um… there's only two cars left in the parking lot," he began hesitantly. "Mine and Obe's."

Grizz felt her jaw drop. "Did he *completely forget* that he offered to give me a ride home?!"

Kurt cringed. "Looks like it."

He didn't even say goodbye! Grizz hated to admit it, but the thought that Dimitri would blow her off like that stung. She wanted to be mad, but a stupid part of her felt sad and disappointed. She didn't want to believe that Dimitri could be so inconsiderate. *Maybe he had something really important to do, and he had to leave right away, and was so preoccupied that he wasn't thinking straight? An emergency?* Her mind raced as she stared off into space. *I've been stranded!* "I called my dad on my break and told him not to bother picking me up because I had a ride!"

"That sucks," Kurt said, annoyed that Dimitri was flirting with Grizz in the first place, but even more annoyed that he had bailed on her. Then he brightened. "I'll give you a ride home!" he said with a smile.

A wave of relief rushed over her before she realized what that would entail. Then again, what other choice did she have? *Aside from asking Obe,* she thought dismally. *No, thank you!* "Um, but my bike…" she began hesitantly.

Kurt waved his hand, beckoning her to follow him out the french doors. "We can put your bike in the back of Kahuna. No one should wander around alone after dark."

Grizz nodded, putting her sweater on when she felt the chilly night air. "Okay, thanks."

Kurt smiled easily as they walked to the bike rack. "No sweat, babe—"

Grizz shot out a hand, clutching his bicep. Kurt stared at her, intrigued, until she squeezed hard. "Ow!"

"If you ever call me babe again, your arm won't be the only thing I break. Got it?"

Kurt frowned, nodding mutely.

Grizz relaxed her grip, patting his muscular arm before pulling away. "Good boy." She unlocked her bike from the rack and wheeled it across the parking lot.

Kurt pulled his keys from the pocket of his cargo shorts and hit the fob. His Jeep's lights flickered as the doors unlocked. "This is your first time riding in Kahuna, right?" Grizz rolled her eyes and nodded. "Well, you're in for a treat. She's got a new speaker system; it's radical."

"Did I take a trip back to the nineties?" Grizz mumbled under her breath, heading for the back of the Jeep, frowning as she wondered how she was going to get her bike up there.

Kurt appeared at her side and reached for the bicycle, effortlessly lifting it up and over the back compartment, the flexing of his shoulder muscles visible through his shirt.

Grizz raised her eyebrows, impressed at his strength. She was about to say as much, then stopped herself. No need to pump his already enormous ego. She walked to the passenger side and paused. Her car was an old, beat-up Ford, so she couldn't help but admire the sleek, pacific blue paint job. She opened the door and balked at how high up the seat was compared to her car. Smirking, she reached for the overhead bars and swung herself up and into the seat easily. She set her purse and helmet at her feet and drummed her fingers on her knee as she waited for Kurt.

Kurt shrugged on his Santa Cruz hooded sweatshirt and hopped in on the driver's side, starting up the car. "What's your favorite station?"

"What, you don't have a Beach Boys playlist?" Grizz asked with a smirk.

Kurt rustled in his pocket and pulled out his smart phone. "Wow, you know me so well, Zel!" he said with a grin, plugging his phone into the stereo.

Grizz couldn't help but giggle, shaking her head. *It's not my fault you're a total stereotype,* she thought, studying the interior of his car. Decals of Hawaiian flowers decorated the passenger window, while a Santa Cruz bumper sticker adorned the back windshield, and a surfboard medallion hung from the rear view mirror. She had to admit, the theme of his car was actually pretty cool. The seats were even the same shade of blue as the exterior. She tapped the miniature surfboard with her fingers, then gave a start when she saw a gruesome looking little statue glaring up at her from the dashboard. "What *is* this thing?" she murmured in disgust, reaching for it.

Kurt shot his hand out. "Don't touch Kona!" he cried out.

Grizz quickly leaned back against her seat, eyes cutting to Kurt. "Who the *what* now?"

Kurt took a deep breath. "Sorry." He gave the statue a pat. "Kona is very sensitive. He's my good luck Tiki. He makes sure that no matter where Kahuna takes me, we always make it back safe."

Eyes wide and heart still pounding from Kurt's sudden outburst, Grizz nodded, trying to placate him. "Okay, hands off the Tiki. Got it."

Kurt smiled at her, adjusting the volume dial. "Thanks, Rizzo. I knew you'd understand."

"No problem, Kirk," she muttered. Kurt just laughed and shook his head, apparently missing her point yet again.

"I first found Kona in Hawaii years ago when my parents brought me there. Surfing, man. Surfing in Hawaii is no joke. You could get thrown against the rocks and totally destroyed, just like that." He snapped his fingers.

"Yeesh," Grizz muttered with a grimace. "That does sound scary."

"But it's so awesome to watch."

She cocked a brow. "People getting squished against the rocks?"

Kurt shook his head fervently. "Oh, no, I meant surfing in Hawaii when it goes well. You ever been to Hawaii?"

Grizz tried to squelch her jealousy. "No, but I'd really like to," she said wistfully.

"Oh, you'll love it when you do go. The sky is unreal. I think it's because of all the, uh…" He fell silent as he struggled for the right word.

"Volcanic activity?" Grizz supplied.

Kurt nodded with a grin. "Yeah, that. You're so smart," he said admiringly.

Normally Grizz would have been flattered, and a part of her wanted to preen with pride. She resisted the urge and rolled her eyes. Glancing up, she noticed that the top of the Jeep was off, so she could see the starry night sky. She rolled down the window and rested her arm on the ledge.

Kurt put the Jeep in reverse and looked over his shoulder as he backed out of the parking space. Grizz realized with alarm that she had never ridden in the car with Kurt before. Given his usual attention span, she braced herself for a nerve-wracking trip, pressing her lips tightly together so as not to talk and distract him.

"So… work today was fun," Kurt commented after a few minutes of silence, keeping his eyes on the road.

Grizz, who had started to relax slightly—since Kurt had driven smoothly thus far—replied, "Yeah, it was. Especially when you broke the espresso grinder," she added with a sly smile.

Kurt's cheeks flushed, and he gripped the steering wheel tightly. "I—I didn't break it," he said finally. If she knew the real reason he'd screwed up so badly...

Grizz laughed. "I'm just teasing you, it's fine! We've all had our share of on the job catastrophes."

Kurt stuck out his lower lip, not believing her. "No, you haven't. I bet none of you guys have done anything dumb like that."

Grizz stared at his crestfallen features, and realized she'd really hit a nerve. "Have so! The first day I worked with Frank, he dropped a mug! Obe was pretty upset." Each of the mugs were ones that Obediah had hand-picked over the years from various thrift stores and gift shops. "Frank wanted the floor to open and swallow him up."

Kurt cringed, glancing at her for a second before he signaled to turn. "That's rough, man." Then he frowned. "I bet *Dimitri*," he said the name in a high-pitched tone, "has never screwed up."

Bristling, Grizz remembered how Dimitri had ditched her for who knows what reason. "I'm sure he has," she said in a salty tone. "But he's worked there for a couple of years, so his screw-ups were probably before we knew him."

"He sure as hell screwed up tonight," Kurt said tightly as he rolled to a stop for a red light.

Grizz nodded, her eyes feeling strangely hot and moist. "Yep." She cleared her throat, desperate to change the subject. "And I couldn't figure out how to pull espresso shots for the longest time. I thought I had it, but off and on the layers separated, or they would be icky and watery."

"You're already such a pro," Kurt said with a smile. "I guess if even *you* messed up at first, I've got to get better."

Grizz was happy to see that he had seemed to cheer up. "Exactly!"

"Oh, shit," Kurt muttered, glancing at Grizz. "What's your address? I'm such a dope."

"Oops," Grizz said with a laugh. "That's important to know, huh?" She glanced around at the street signs. "Okay, keep going straight, and make a left hand turn in two blocks."

Kurt nodded. "Got it."

Grizz studied him as he cleanly merged into the left lane. *It's kind of hard to believe that this derp drives so well, but I guess it makes sense, seeing how much he adores his car,* she thought with a smile. *Can't let Kahuna get hurt!*

Soon they'd pulled up in front of Grizz's house. "Thanks for the ride, Kurt," Grizz said, unhooking her seatbelt and reaching for her purse and helmet. She opened the door and hopped out of the car.

To her surprise, Kurt turned off the engine and opened the driver's side door.

"You don't have to walk me to the door," Grizz said incredulously, stopping in front of the car.

Kurt scratched the side of his neck as he stepped out. "But your bike..."

Grizz felt like a moron. "Oh. Right."

Following him to the back of the Jeep, she realized with a start that there was a Tiki, much like Kona, on the side of his car. *Good grief, his car is Hawaiian-surfer themed down to the last detail!* She reached out and patted the decal. "Good boy," she whispered with a snicker.

Kurt opened the back hatch and pulled out her bicycle. Grizz reached for it, but Kurt stopped her. "I've got it!"

With a cluck of the tongue, Grizz nodded. They made it to the front door, and just as she was pulling out her keys, the door opened to the sound of barking dogs.

"Hi, honey," her mom greeted her with a warm smile.

"Hi, Mom," Grizz said, feeling awkward that Kurt was there.

Sure enough, her mother turned to look at Kurt. "Hello, you must be Grizz's friend."

Kurt stuck out his hand with a grin. "Hi, Mrs. Sheridan, I'm Kurt."

"Thank you so much for giving Grizz a ride home," Mrs. Sheridan said. "Oh, let me open the garage for you, sweetie, so you can put your bike away. Please excuse the dogs," she added with an apologetic smile, as the dogs continued to bark with booming voices.

Kurt chuckled. "No worries, they're protecting their territory."

"Be right back," Mrs. Sheridan said, closing the front door.

Grizz wrinkled her nose, annoyed that her mother had abandoned her on the front porch with Kurt. "Um, let's head to the garage," she mumbled, beckoning for him to follow.

"Sure thing," Kurt replied, following her.

As the door rose, Grizz wrung her hands together, hoping that the garage was tidy. She and her mother had a lot of boxes filled with crafting supplies stored inside, and it tended to get messy. To her relief, everything seemed orderly when the door was fully opened.

"Where does it go, Rizzy?" Kurt asked as they walked into the garage.

Grizz noticed with irritation that her mother had gone back inside.

Her mom was never one to hover, but she wished that, just this once, she would have. "Over there," Grizz pointed to a far spot on the wall.

Kurt wheeled it into position, and Grizz took it from him, pushing the kickstand into place with her foot. "Thanks."

Kurt paused, turning to the work bench. "Whoa, this is choka," he said, reaching out to touch a blue and white bulletin board.

"Oh, thanks," Grizz said, putting her helmet in the bicycle basket. "The edges started to come apart, so I had my dad glue it." She came over to inspect it. "Yay, good as new!"

Kurt touched a wooden, hand-painted crab that was glued to one corner. "Did you make this yourself?"

"Yeah. A few years back. I just took an old picture frame and painted it, then attached a piece of corkboard to the back." She shrugged. "And I added all of the embellishments, of course."

Kurt grinned, locking eyes with her. "It's awesome."

Grizz felt her mouth go dry under his stare. She tore her eyes away after a long moment. "Thanks. And thanks again for the ride home."

Kurt put his hands in his pockets. "No sweat." He stepped away from the workbench, and Grizz followed him out to his car. "Oh," he said, pivoting to face her once again, "I was thinking of hitting the beach this Saturday," he said off-handedly, trying to keep his tone even, "I'll ask Ben—do you and Patty want to come, too?"

Grizz quickly weighed the pros and cons in her mind. It sounded like fun—but did she really want to hang out with Kurt Minola all day? Then she remembered the rush of surfing. Kurt was a pretty good teacher; besides, she'd been with him all day today, and lived to tell the tale. Unbidden, the feeling of his arms around her when she'd fallen off of her surfboard hit her, and she felt herself flush. *You were suffering from dehydration and hunger that day,* she insisted. *Nothing more. It won't happen again.* Seeing his hopeful look as he waited for her answer, she found herself saying, "Sure, that sounds fun. I'll ask Patricia." Then, without letting him say anything in reply, she turned and hurried inside the garage to flip the automatic door opener.

Kurt grinned, staring after her as the door lowered.

Chapter Eleven ♡

"SO, WHEN I GAVE THEM THE BEEPER TO TELL THEM WHEN there would be a table available, the old man handed me a walkie-talkie, the really fancy kind," Patricia added as she and Grizz walked down the beach. "And told me to call him on that!"

Grizz snickered. "Clearly wanted to make use of those things. So, did you?"

Patricia shrugged helplessly. "He and his son were so insistent! You could tell they were really proud of them. He was like, 'Now, young lady,'" Patricia began, imitating the elderly man's voice, "'I'm entrusting you with this. Call us the moment it's ready. Rest assured, it will come in loud and clear no matter where we are on the Boardwalk.' It was actually pretty fun. If those things weren't so expensive, I'd say Mom and Dad should use those instead of beepers."

Laughing, Grizz slowed her steps as they neared the water. "Now where should we—"

"Hey, Rizzo, Trix, you made it!" Kurt said, appearing in front of them with a grin.

Seeing that he was wearing a tee shirt over his trunks, Grizz added, "I hope you weren't, like, waiting around for us or something." She hadn't been clear on what time Kurt wanted to meet.

Kurt shook his head with an easy grin. "Nah, I'm just taking a breather. There's some really good waves out there today, not too gnarly." He glanced around. "Where's my brother from the same mother?"

Patricia burst into a fit of giggles, doubling over.

Grizz patted her on the back, rolling her eyes. "He dropped us off in the parking lot. He said he saw a sign that he needed to get a better look at."

"Oh, okay. Well, get ready for a fun day ahead," Kurt said enthusiastically. "Wait 'til you see my stick."

Grizz's eyes bugged out in horror. "See your what?!" she shrieked, recoiling from him. Just what was he proposing?

Kurt was already walking away from them. "My board," he called over his shoulder. "I gave it a good wax job."

Grizz put a hand to her chest and breathed a sigh of relief, sharing a look with Patricia. They chose a spot nearby and began setting down their things.

"I'm not sure why I agreed to this," Grizz muttered, laying her towel out on the sand.

Patricia gave her an incredulous look. "I thought you loved surfing! You've been dying to get back in the ocean all week!"

Grizz stuck out her lower lip, peeling off her coverup. "Okay, okay, fine, you're right. It's just the realization is sinking in." She pointed to Kurt, who was approaching with his red surfboard tucked under his arm. *Then again,* Grizz thought, drinking in his chiseled muscles with her eyes, noticing his evenly tanned skin from his head to his waist, *I guess I can suffer through it.* Then she realized what she was thinking, and shook her head. *No. What you like is surfing. That's it. Kurt is just an annoying necessity.*

"All right, dudettes," Kurt said with a grin, putting his board upright in the sand for them to admire.

"Very nice, Kurt," Patricia said as she kicked off her sandals.

Grizz took a step closer and felt the board. "Ooh," she said in a voice dripping with awe, "Smooth."

Kurt blushed from her compliment. "Thanks! You two ready to stop being beach leeches and catch some waves?"

Patricia laughed. "Yep. Well, Ben and I are going to be lame and just body board."

"Aw, you don't want to learn?" Kurt's shoulders sagged. "Too bad, we could've party waved."

"Well, maybe when you've made Grizz a champ, then I'll join you guys," Patricia said, squinting up at him in the sunlight as she poured sunscreen in her hands.

Grizz preened. "Well, I am a natural."

Kurt nudged her shoulder. "Nah, Rizzo, you're goofy."

Patricia furrowed her brow as Kurt and Grizz dissolved into laughter.

"Oh, I've got to go rent my board," Grizz remembered, crouching to pull her wallet from her beach bag.

Kurt grinned, pumping a fist in the air. "Yeah, go get it! I'm so amped to get you back in the water!"

Grizz laughed, feeling excited herself. "Okay, I'll be right back." She headed up the beach.

Patricia waved to Ben, who was jogging toward them.

"Sorry that took so long."

"Oh, no worries." Patricia replied as she rubbed sunscreen on her face. "Did you find whatever it was you needed to find?"

Nodding, Ben turned to Kurt. "I saw the sign announcing that surfing contest you were talking about."

Kurt's hazel eyes widened. "Really, bro? Where?"

"Right by the parking lot entrance." Ben wasn't surprised he'd missed it, given his brother's short attention span. "It said that sign ups start this afternoon."

"YES!" Kurt punched his hands in the air in a complicated pattern. He pointed to Patricia and Ben in turn. "You heard it here first. I'm going to win that thing."

Patricia laughed and shrugged. "Okay."

Grizz appeared at their sides just then. "Hey, guys. No one rented her, so we are reunited!" She lifted the aqua board slightly.

Whooping, Kurt clapped. "That's great, Zelly!" He turned, using a hand to shield his eyes. "The waves are perfect right now." He headed for the surf, then paused and pivoted, looking at Grizz with raised eyebrows. "Well, little Wahine? You coming?"

Grizz narrowed her eyes, nostrils flaring. "Did you just call me a whore?"

Kurt frowned, confused. "Um, no, it means 'Female surfer...'"

"Oh." She closed her mouth, but shot him a suspicious look as she followed him to the water.

Patricia watched them and shook her head. "Let's hope Kurt lives through this lesson." She turned her attention to Ben. "Ready to hit the water?" She massaged the last of the sunscreen into her arm and stood. "I think I won't turn into a lobster now."

Ben nodded. "Sure thing." He held out his hand to her, helping her to stand.

"We'd better keep out of the way of the advanced class," Patricia joked, boogie board securely under her arm as they walked toward the breaking waves.

Kurt gestured for Grizz to follow him, paddling out to where low waves were rolling into the beach. "So, we'll pick up right where we left off," he said.

Grizz flushed, remembering what had happened during the last lesson. She felt butterflies in her stomach, and she was pretty sure it wasn't fear of falling—it was fear of being caught by a certain muscular someone.

She felt Kurt watching her, and kept her focus trained on the water lapping about her knees.

"Don't be afraid," Kurt encouraged, seeming to mistake her uncomfortable demeanor for nerves. "When you wipe, get back on the board, I always say."

"Is that like when you fall off a horse?" Grizz asked sarcastically, finally able to look at him. *It's just Kurt,* she reminded herself, heartbeat thudding. *Kurt the Jerk, remember?*

"Yeah!" Kurt said, having completely missed her tone. "It's exactly like that. If you wait too long, sometimes your nerves get the better of you."

Grizz nodded, knowing she had to face her fears and try again. What her fears were exactly, she couldn't say.

"Here, I'll show you. The key is to not stand up too soon or too late. When we get to bigger waves, I'll show you how to sit up like this and swivel to surf them." To demonstrate, he expertly straddled the surfboard. "This is a good way to be out in the deep water, waiting for incoming waves." He turned in the water and began to paddle when he saw an incoming wave. "Pay attention to my timing," Kurt called to her, popping up when the wave carried his board inland.

Grizz stared after him as he rode the small wave, trying to focus on his technique, and not his physique. She blinked rapidly. *What the hell are you doing? FOCUS!*

Kurt waved as he lifted his board and prepared to paddle back to her. Grizz lifted her hand, chuckling hollowly. She turned and waited for a wave, quickly pivoting toward the beach when she felt a good one rolling in. She began paddling quickly, the rush of the oncoming wave driving Kurt from her mind.

Later that afternoon, Grizz hauled her board to where she'd stashed her things, limbs tingling with fatigue from surfing for so long. She awkwardly set the board in the sand as she detached her leg rope, sinking to the ground once she was free. "Whoo," she exhaled, pulling her fingers through her damp hair.

"You rocked those waves, Zel," Kurt said, pumping his fist.

Grizz smiled to herself. Coming from the surfing guru himself, that was quite the compliment. *Maybe he's just trying to butter me up because he likes me*, she thought suspiciously. Looking into his earnest hazel eyes, however, she could tell he was being sincere. She'd seen him flirt with girls before, and that wasn't how he went about it. Drying her face with her beach towel, she replied, "Thanks."

"You're no frube, that's for sure," Kurt added, setting his board next to hers.

Grizz held up her hands. "Not even going to ask." She smiled to herself, shoulders relaxing. "Surfing is such a rush. I wonder if I'll ever be able to do one of those cool spinny things…" She moved her arms back and forth excitedly.

"Oh, an aerial?" Kurt grinned. "It'll take lots of practice, but I bet you can."

"Cool." Grizz stood and wrapped her beach towel around her waist. "Where are Ben and Patricia?" she mumbled, chewing on her lip.

Kurt turned toward the water, and pointed to two figures in the white water. "Still frolicking in the surf."

Grizz laughed. "Well, we'll let them be, hm?"

Taking in her smiling face, Kurt summoned up his courage. "So, all that surfing wiped me out," he began nonchalantly. "Do you want to go get…"

"Grizz?"

Grizz turned at her name, freezing when she saw Dimitri standing before her. "Oh. Dimitri," she said, annoyed at how her chest felt like it was being squeezed.

Dimitri shoved his hands in the pocket of his plaid Bermuda shorts. "Um, didn't think I'd see you here today. Hey, Kurt," he added.

Kurt, who had been glowering at Dimitri, barely grunted in reply.

"Can I talk to you, Grizz?" Dimitri asked in a low tone.

Grizz licked her lips, tossing a damp bang out of her eye, taking a small step backwards. "I'm kind of busy."

Kurt tried to hide his grin. *You tell that jerk, Zella!*

"Please, Grizz?" Dimitri asked, reaching out to touch her elbow.

Kurt frowned at the movement, looking at Grizz's reaction.

His fingers made her skin feel like it was on fire. "Um," she began, tingles shooting up her spine. "I—" She looked up at him, his lips pouting slightly as he waited for her answer. "I guess we can talk. Just for a minute."

Dimitri sighed in relief. "Great." He turned his attention to Kurt. "Do you mind?"

Grizz looked over her shoulder to see Kurt staring at Dimitri, his eyes narrowed. "Um, walk with me," she told Dimitri, walking away from Kurt.

The wind picked up, and Grizz pushed her hair out of her face before saying, "So, what did you want to talk about?" She couldn't quite get the iciness out of her voice.

"Don't be mad, Grizz," Dimitri said imploringly. "I don't blame you—it was totally dumb of me to leave like that the other night, when I'd promised to give you a ride home."

Grizz nodded. "I can't refute that." She felt so confused—she was mad at him, but not sure if she wanted to keep snipping at him. What if she missed her chance? She folded her arms across her chest. *Hear him out, hear him out…*

"I can't believe I did that—leaving a girl all alone to get home by herself—did you get home okay?" Dimitri asked.

"Kurt drove me home," Grizz replied, trying to keep her tone civil.

"Oh." Dimitri's eyes wandered back to where Kurt stood, then flicked to Grizz. "Uh, that's great. See, when I got to my locker, I turned on my phone," he began, wringing his hands together. "And I had about a million texts from my mom. She needed my help, because a pipe burst in the basement, and it flooded."

Grizz relaxed her shoulders a little bit, processing what he said. She supposed she could let it slide if it had been something important like that. "Oh, no!"

Dimitri made a face. "Yeah, it's been kind of a pain, we had to move a ton of stuff so that it wouldn't get wrecked."

"Was anything damaged?" Grizz asked in concern.

"Thankfully no. The water didn't get too high up, and most of the stuff stored down there is in plastic."

"Smart move," Grizz replied, all the iciness that she'd felt in her chest melted. She felt guilty for having been so mad at him. *I probably would have forgotten about everything else, too,* she reasoned.

"But I still should have driven you home," Dimitri went on, taking a step closer. "I'm sorry to have made a gorgeous girl like you mad."

Grizz felt her temperature rise through the roof. Her eyes locked with his, and she faltered. "Um, it's okay. I understand now," she stammered.

Dimitri looked relieved. "Good. So, are you hungry?"

Grizz smiled and nodded. "Let me just go get my stuff," she said, turning from him and squealing to herself.

Kurt watched Grizz walk off to talk to Dimitri, a heavy feeling settling over his chest. *First he blows her off,* he seethed, *Then he shows up out of nowhere and interrupts us!* He could see Dimitri saying something to her, and found he couldn't stand to watch.

He dug through his bag and pulled out a tube of sunscreen, violently rubbing it on his arms and chest before pulling his tee shirt on. *She'll be back,* he chanted to himself, trying to focus on other things. *And then we can go get lunch.* He sat on his towel and occupied himself with games on his phone while he waited.

Kurt's head shot up when he heard someone walking toward him a few minutes later. "Hey, Grizzy," he said with a smile, feeling relieved when she approached him.

"Hey," she said, seeming distracted as she crouched, shoving her things quickly in her beach bag.

Kurt watched in confusion as she pulled her street clothes on over her bathing suit. "Hey, what's the rush?" he asked with a chuckle. *Maybe she somehow knew I wanted to hit the Boardwalk...* he thought.

Wringing out her hair, she answered as she absentmindedly tried to comb her bangs, "I'm going to grab lunch with Dimitri."

Kurt felt like he'd been punched in the gut. "What?" His smile faded slightly. "But I thought we were surfing..."

Grizz waved her hand. "Oh, don't bother waiting around for me. I may not be back for awhile." She cast Dimitri a glance as she said it, biting her lip slightly.

"Wait—am I missing something?" Kurt managed to ask after a moment, his voice angrier sounding than he wanted it to be. "Weren't you mad at Dimitri for forgetting about you the other night?"

Buckling her sandals, Grizz said hurriedly, "Oh, it turns out his basement was flooded. It's all cool now." She rose to her feet and wiped the sand off of her legs.

Kurt furrowed his brow. "But—"

"So, now you can do whatever you want!" Grizz told him as she put her bracelets back on her wrist. "I don't want to waste your day making you teach me to surf..."

Kurt shook his head, taking a step closer. "It's not a waste of—"

Shouldering her bag, Grizz turned away and hurried up the beach. "Bye!"

Kurt sighed and turned on his heel as Grizz sped out of his sight, a wave of depression settling over him. "But I was going to ask you to go get lunch," he mumbled glumly, kicking a stray stick out of his way. His stomach felt tied up in knots at the thought of Grizz and Dimitri basically on a date.

"You know what your problem is, Kurt?"

Kurt leapt in surprise as Tuck walked up to him. "Shit, man, you scared me."

Tuck held up his hands, flashing a row of perfect, too-white teeth as he smiled. "Sorry, dude. I just couldn't help but notice your little encounter with Grizz there."

Kurt frowned, not wanting to be reminded. "Uh, yeah. We were surfing, but she, uh, had to go."

Tuck shrugged. "No, I totally get it, bro. She obviously doesn't get what a cool dude you are."

Kurt thought of Grizz's scowl any time he was near her, the way she giggled around Dimitri. He heaved a sigh. "Yeah, I guess she'll never be into me, huh?"

"Not necessarily," Tuck said breezily, taking a step toward him.

"She may just need a little persuasion." He slid his backpack off of his shoulder and rummaged around, finally pulling out a small bottle of purple liquid.

Kurt furrowed his brow. "What is that?"

Tuck chuckled, holding the bottle up and giving it a tiny shake. "This, my friend, is a love potion."

"A love potion?" Kurt repeated with wide eyes.

"Exactly. Just a few drops of this, and Grizz will be all yours."

"Really? Whoa," Kurt breathed, eyes fixed on the bottle. "Er— you're not pulling my leg rope, right?"

Tuck looked genuinely offended. "Nah, man. Look at me. Would I lie to you?"

Kurt considered this, then slowly shook his head. "Wow. A love potion, this is incredible! It... won't hurt her, will it?"

Tuck shook his head, playfully punching Kurt. "Of course not. She won't feel a thing. Except crazy about you," he whispered. "It will just give her a swing in the right direction—she'll become annoyed with Dimitri, and be all about you."

Kurt cocked his head. "How does it work?"

Tuck pointed to the label on the bottle. "It's simple. Just put a couple of drops in a drink for yourself, and then some in a drink for her."

"Wait—why do I have to drink it? I already am..." Kurt reddened, ducking his head as he mumbled, "I don't need a potion to like her."

Tuck clucked his tongue. "You don't get it, dude! The potion won't work unless you take it, too. That way she falls for the right guy."

Staring at the bottle, Kurt nodded. "Okay. We both have to take it, so that she falls for me. Got it." The idea of Grizz liking him back was too exciting to bear. Then he felt a flicker of doubt. *Is it really okay to do something like this?* "Um, I don't know, Tuck, maybe I shouldn't."

Tuck swiftly put the bottle in his pocket, turning on his heel. "Okay, fine, if you don't ever want Grizz to go out with you and just keep thinking you're lame, sure."

"Wait!" Kurt shot out his hand to stop Tuck. "Okay, okay, I'm desperate. How much?"

Tuck turned to face him, lips curling into an innocent smile. "For you, old buddy? Only fifty bucks."

"Whoa, what a steal," Kurt muttered, reaching into his pocket for the cash.

As they traded hands, Tuck grasped Kurt's in a firm shake. "Thanks. Good luck, my friend."

"No, man, thank you," Kurt said with a grin. "This is fantastic! Grizz is finally going to like me!" He turned and hurried away, feeling a rush of adrenaline.

He was too far away to hear Tuck's snicker.

Chapter Twelve ♡

"HI FRANK," GRIZZ GREETED HER COWORKER WHEN SHE came into the Merry Mule the following Tuesday.

Frank grinned, pinning his name tag to the lapel of his shirt. "Hey, Grizz! Have a nice weekend?"

Unbidden, a memory of having lunch with Dimitri flashed through her mind. "Fantastic," she said dreamily. She cleared her throat. "I mean, I had a lot of fun. Went to the beach, surfed, you know. What about you?"

Frank shrugged, going behind the counter. "I worked on Saturday, but I went with my family to San Jose for the day on Sunday."

Grizz wiggled her eyebrows. "Did you go to the Winchester Mystery House?"

Frank shook his head. "I'd love to go there again, though. I haven't been since I was little."

"It *is* awesome," Grizz said, walking into the back room. She passed the schedule posted on the wall and paused. *Frank and I... who else is working today?* she wondered, quickly reading it. *Oh. Hayley.* She was disappointed that Dimitri was not working, but relieved that Kurt wasn't, either. *Should be a relaxing day,* she concluded, walking to her locker and pulling out her apron and name tag before setting her things inside.

She switched the sign on the french doors to say "Come in, We're Open", before joining Frank behind the counter.

"I thought Hayley was working today," Grizz commented, eyes cutting to the clock on the wall after they'd served a few people. She was late for her shift—very late.

"She's sick, so Obe had to call around to find a replacement for her," Frank explained.

Hm, maybe Dimitri, Grizz thought excitedly.

When the bells jingled, Grizz looked up, scowling when she saw that it was Kurt walking through the door. *Maybe he's here to be the mule,* she thought hopefully. *I can't always get stuck with him when he works on bar. Right? Right?!*

Kurt caught her eye and grinned like a doofus. "Hey, Riz!"

"Hi." she said curtly, turning her back on him and busying herself with pulling a ceramic mug off of the peg board.

Kurt frowned at her reaction. *Aw, man.* Then he steeled himself. *No! You have the power of the potion now. Courage!* He strode into the back room.

Grizz busied herself with making the customer's latte, when a movement caught her attention. Kurt had emerged from the back room.

She rolled her eyes when she saw that Kurt was putting on an apron instead of his mule costume. *No!*

"So, that's too bad about Hayley being sick," Kurt commented as he came over to her and Frank.

"Tragic," Grizz said through gritted teeth.

"What do you guys need help with?" Kurt asked.

"Can you make this Mexican mocha?" Frank held up a sixteen ounce cup.

Kurt grinned. "Sure thing! They're my specialty." He looked at Grizz and lifted his eyebrows. "Right, Zella?"

"Definitely, Chirp," Grizz replied in a salty tone, focusing on finishing the drink she was making.

Kurt shrugged, starting on the mocha. *She may still like Dimitri now, but as soon as I give her some potion, she'll forget about him,* he reasoned. *I wonder how I can give it to her? Maybe on her break…*

"Molly cappuccino for here!" Grizz called out to the tables, setting the large mug on the counter. She found herself staring at Kurt while he searched the toppings before pulling out the cinnamon with a grin, sprinkling it vigorously atop the whipped cream.

Realizing what she was doing, she shook her head and went to the blender to make an Ocean Berry Delight, relaxing when her back was to him.

"Mexican mocha!" Kurt placed the cup on the end of the bar, then began wiping down the equipment.

Quincy walked up to the counter, reaching for the cup. "Hey, man, what's up?"

Kurt lifted his eyes and grinned. "Yo, Quince!" The two bumped fists over the counter. "What are you doing?"

Quincy shrugged. "Just hanging out." He took a sip of his coffee. "Wow, that's good. Did you make it?"

Kurt nodded proudly. "Sure did."

"And we all thought you were just a pretty face," Quincy cooed with a chuckle. "By the way, love the apron. It brings out your eyes."

Kurt jokingly scowled and flicked the damp rag at Quincy, who held up his hands and walked back to his table, laughing.

"Have you seen it?"

Grizz turned off the blender when she heard the voice. "Hm?"

Frank, who was now at her elbow, repeated, "I said, that new superhero spoof movie. Have you seen it?"

Grizz shook her head, reaching for a lid and punching a straw through the plastic. "No, is it good?"

"I haven't seen it yet, but Dimitri told me that it was hi-la-ri-ous," Frank said.

"Dimitri did?" Grizz asked, her heart thudding like it always did when she thought of him.

Kurt, who was putting a slice of coffee cake in the microwave, frowned. He didn't like Grizz's tone when she said Dimitri's name.

"Yeah. Hey, I have an idea," Frank said excitedly. "Maybe we can all go see it this Friday."

"Oh, I can't," Grizz told him, putting the drink on the end of the bar, "I have plans."

Frank shrugged amiably. "No big deal. Next weekend?"

"Sounds fun!" Grizz agreed. "Do you think Dimitri will come too?" she asked hopefully.

Kurt felt his heart sink as he pulled the pastry out of the microwave.

"I'm sure he will," Frank said.

Kurt quickly grabbed a fork and napkin and hurried out into the cafe, setting the coffee cake on the customer's table.

"Thank you," the woman said, pleasantly surprised.

"No problem," he replied listlessly, walking to Quincy's table. Sighing heavily, he sank into the empty chair across from him.

Looking up from his book, Quincy cocked a brow. "Aren't you working?"

"Life sucks," Kurt replied vehemently, ignoring his question.

"Whoa, what's wrong?" Quincy asked, leaning closer.

Kurt looked over his shoulder to where Grizz was restocking the water glasses by the cooler. "Can I ask you something?"

Quincy nodded, dark brows furrowed. "Sure."

Kurt tugged self-consciously at the collar of his apron. "Have you ever really, really liked a girl who liked someone else?"

Quincy whistled. "No, can't say that I have."

"Figures." Kurt folded his arms over his broad chest. "This guy is a total jerk, but she just doesn't see it," Kurt rushed on. "She's all, '*Oh, Dimitri, you're so fine!*' Give me a break!"

"That's rough," Quincy said sympathetically. "Who is it?"

Kurt turned to face the water cooler, casting forlorn looks at Grizz.

"Grizz?" Quincy asked loudly in surprise.

"Ssh!" Kurt hissed, looking around wildly.

"Wow, I didn't know you liked her," Quincy said in a softer voice.

Kurt leaned back in the chair. "Yeah, one day it just hit me, right here." He pounded the left side of his chest with a fist. He shrugged helplessly. "But what can I do? I stupidly got my hopes up because Tuck gave—"

"Kurt!" Obediah called from the front. "Get back to work!"

Kurt heaved yet another sigh. "Coming, boss! See you, Quincy."

Quincy frowned in concern at his friend. "Good luck, man."

Kurt shuffled back to the front counter. "What do you need?" he asked in a lifeless tone.

Grizz started at his sudden change in demeanor. *What's his problem?* She stared at him critically, before he turned to face her. She felt her heartbeat pound wildly at his intense gaze, and dropped her eyes to study the paper cup she held. "Let's see, hazelnut latte with no whipped cream, and almond milk." She crouched and opened the door to the mini refrigerator. "Where is that pesky almond milk?" she muttered to herself. "Oh, I guess I need to get more."

"Grizz, can you grab some more of the syrups, too? We're pretty low," Frank asked, before attending the cash register once more.

"Sure thing." She rose to her feet and walked into the store room, where Obediah was sorting through boxes. "Hi, Obe," she greeted him. "Too bad Hayley's sick, huh?" she commented, glancing at her boss.

Obediah didn't look up. "It's a good thing I got a hold of Kurt. It seems pretty busy out there."

Grizz blew a bang out of her eye with a frustrated puff of air. "Yeah…" She searched the shelves for the vanilla syrup, trying to forget about Kurt for the moment.

Meanwhile, Kurt pulled out the can of whipped cream, furrowing his brow as he stared at the lid of the plastic cup. "How do I get the whipped cream on this?" He poked the nozzle at the straw hole. "Oh." He tore off the flat lid and replaced it with a domed lid, filling it to the brim with cream. "John iced mocha!" he said loudly.

"Thanks," the guy who came to claim the drink told Kurt.

Kurt looked up and saw that the guy, who looked around his age, was wearing a maroon sweatshirt with the words "Arizona State Sun Devils" in gold and white. "Sweet, man!" Kurt whooped, pumping a fist in the air. "Arizona State! Represent!"

The guy lifted his eyebrows. "Oh, you go to ASU, too?"

Kurt shook his head. "Not yet. You're looking at an incoming froshie."

"Awesome!" The guy stuck out his hand over the counter. "I'm Jared."

"Kurt." They shook hands briskly. "What year are you?"

"I'm going to be a junior," Jared replied. "It's the best, you're going to love it. What major are you going to declare?"

"History," Kurt replied.

"Cool," Jared said easily. "I'm Anthropology. Same campus. Well, I'll let you get back to work, but I'm excited for you."

"Thanks, dude," Kurt said.

"Go Sun Devils!" they said in unison.

Kurt grinned, waving to Jared as he went to find a table.

"You're going to Arizona State, Kurt?" Frank asked, leaning against the counter.

Kurt nodded distractedly, pulling the next waiting cup off of the espresso machine. "Yeah."

"Awesome," Frank said, folding his arms across his chest. "Like I was telling Grizz, I think you'll really like Arizona. I've spent a few vacations there with my aunt and uncle, and the weather is neat. It does get pretty cold at night," he warned. "So make sure to bring warm clothes, and lots of blankets and stuff."

"Oh, for sure," Kurt muttered absentmindedly, filling a portafilter to the brim with espresso grounds. Finally what Frank had said caught up to him. "Wait—why were you telling Zelda that I'd like Arizona…?"

"Zelda?" Frank furrowed his brow in confusion. "Oh, you mean Grizz! I wasn't saying that *you'd* like Arizona, I told her *she'd* like Arizona." He turned back to the cash register. As he rang up a customer, he said over his shoulder, "It's cool you guys are going to the same school."

Kurt's eyes widened, a dazed smile crossing his features. "We *are?*"

"Well, yeah—" Frank turned to face him, but froze when he saw Grizz had appeared behind Kurt, arms laden with cartons and bottles, staring at Frank with a look that could only be described as murderous. He realized all too late that Kurt apparently hadn't known about Grizz also attending ASU. Judging by her expression, that information was not supposed to be divulged. "Uh… hi, Grizz."

Her nostrils flared and she narrowed her eyes at Frank, setting the carton of almond milk and the bottles of chocolate, vanilla, and hazelnut syrup violently down on the counter. She made a swiping motion across her throat to Frank as Kurt swung around. "You're going to ASU too, Rizzo?" he asked, unable to believe his ears.

Grizz saw red, feeling like a bull about to charge. Her gaze flicked from Kurt to Frank, then back to Kurt. He was looking at her with hearts practically dancing in those puppy dog eyes of his. *When I get my hands on you Frank—!* "Your espresso shot is going to expire," she spat at Kurt, stomping toward the break room in fury, a strangled cry emitting from her throat.

Completely missing her angry reaction, Kurt grinned slowly and nodded at Frank. "We're going to the same school? That means parting *won't* be 'such sweet sorrow,' man!" *And now I have a way better chance than that kook, Dimitri!* He couldn't believe his luck. *It's destiny!*

Frank looked wildly around to make sure there was no one in line before scrambling past Kurt and into the break room.

"Grizz?" he called out tentatively, wringing his hands as he glanced around the room.

Grizz popped out from behind a shelving unit, giving him the Evil Eye. "What?"

Frank jumped, and his face crumpled. "I'm so sorry! There was a guy from Arizona State here, and he and Kurt started talking. I didn't know it was a secret!" he said mournfully.

Grizz felt a pang of guilt and came over to him. She folded him into her arms, resting her head atop his. "Aw, it's okay, Frank, don't be upset. I should have told you I didn't want Kurt to know." She pulled away and sighed. "I suppose I couldn't keep it a secret from him forever." *Though I'd always hoped.*

Frank sniffled. "So, you're not mad?"

Grizz exhaled, knowing she couldn't take out her frustration on poor Frank. "No, I'm sorry for flipping out."

"It's okay," Frank said, the waver mostly gone from his voice. "I understand."

Grizz smiled, putting her arm around him. "Let's get back to work before Obe makes *us* the new mules." *It was going to happen sooner or later,* she thought in resignation. *I just wish it had been later rather than sooner.*

Chapter Thirteen ♡

GRIZZ STOOD IN THE LIVING ROOM OF HER HOUSE, EYES flitting between the large front room window and her phone as she waited for Patricia and Ben. Headlights reflected in the glass just as her phone dinged.

"We're here! :)"

"Okay, Mom: Patricia and Ben are here!" Grizz called, lifting her purse and jacket from the couch.

Her mother hurried into the room to give Grizz a hug. "Okay, bye, honey! Text me when you get there." She tucked a strand of her curly black hair behind her ear as her eyes crinkled in concern. "Do you have everything? Will you be warm enough?"

"It's still pretty hot out, which is good since it's also kind of a pool party," Grizz told her. "But I'm bringing a jacket." She gave her mom a hug and slipped out the front door.

Her brown eyes widened as she realized that it wasn't Ben's Expedition parked in front of her house, but Kurt's Islander.

Kurt leaned forward and waved at her, honking the horn. Ben, who was sitting in the passenger seat, playfully shoved his brother before opening the door and hopping out. "Hey, Grizz."

Patricia waved to Grizz from the backseat as Grizz made her way down the sidewalk, narrowing her eyes at Ben. "I thought just *you and Patricia* were picking me up," she hissed.

Ben shrugged apologetically. "Since he was going, too, Mom and Dad said we all had to go together. Which makes sense..."

"But that *goon* is driving and not you?" Grizz accused.

Ben looked chagrined. "He begged."

Kurt called out the window, "Hey, Rizzy! Kahuna awaits!"

Grizz sighed and lifted her hand in the "hang loose" gesture. "Cowabunga."

Patricia pushed the seat forward so that Grizz could climb in back. "Thank you," Grizz whispered when she was safely seated. She was grateful to not be stuck sitting next to Kurt.

Kurt turned around in his seat to grin at Grizz. "This party is going to be off the hook!" he sang, pumping a fist in the air. "I'm so glad you're coming too, Zelly."

Grizz leaned against the window, looking up and noticing with a start that the top was on the Islander. *If I'd known we'd all be stuck together like this, I might not have,* she thought with a grumble. *I was looking forward to partying with my friends, not being followed around all night by this goofball.* Between work and socializing, would she ever get a break from him? "Yeah," she said with the smallest hint of a smile, watching as Kurt ran a hand through his hair before starting the car.

After a few minutes of driving, the silence in between the conversation grated on Grizz's nerves. "Hey, Ben!" she barked.

Ben turned around in his seat to look at her. "Yeah?"

"Put on some music," she commanded with a cackle. "Let's get this party started!"

Ben smiled good-naturedly. "Okay." He turned on the radio.

Kurt had apparently had the volume turned up pretty high the last time he drove Kahuna, because the song came in loud and clear through the speakers. The melody was slow and pretty, and though Grizz usually didn't like listening to slower songs in the car, she found herself humming along, a warm feeling spreading throughout her, lightening her heart. Her mind filled with visions of twinkling lights hanging from the ceiling, and a tall, attractive someone holding her close.

Glancing at Kurt in the rearview mirror, she could tell that he, too, recognized it as the song they danced to at prom.

"T-turn the channel!" she found herself shrieking.

Ben leapt in his seat. "Uh, okay!" He fumbled with the controls, trying to turn it to a better station before Grizz lost it.

"Here, let me just put on my music," Patricia said quickly, passing her phone to Ben, who plugged it into the coaxial cable.

Grizz exhaled slowly, leaning back against the headrest, ignoring Patricia's questioning looks.

Soon they pulled onto Teddy's street.

"Whoa," Ben muttered when he saw that the block was filled with cars. "We're going to have to walk quite a ways. Maybe we should have gotten here sooner…"

"No sweat, you're talking to the party pro," Kurt said. "It's better to get to the party later so that more peeps are there. We don't want to act like eager little froshies, desperate for a night out."

"Rub it in, mister popularity," Ben grumbled and shared a look with Patricia.

After driving for several minutes, they finally found a parking spot around the block.

Grizz unhooked her seatbelt and waited for Ben to get out.

"Ah, if only Kahuna were a four-door," Patricia whispered to her.

Grizz nodded, about to climb in the front seat when she saw Kurt still behind the wheel. She poked him in the shoulder.

Kurt turned with lifted eyebrows. "Yeah?"

Grizz frowned. "You need to move so I don't kick you." *Though the thought is tempting.*

"Oh, sure thing," Kurt agreed, opening the driver side door and hopping out.

Grizz rolled her eyes and wiggled her way into the front seat. "This is—oof!—awkward," she grunted, kneeling in the driver's seat.

"Ack!" Patricia cried when Grizz kicked her in the shoulder.

"Oh! Sorry, Patricia," Grizz groaned, trying to shimmy forward. "Whoever invented cars like this should be tarred and feathered!"

Ben popped his head in the open door. "Need help?"

Grizz waved him away, wriggling her leg over the seat. "I think I've got it." Inching toward the open driver's door, she reached for the bar to swing herself out. "I'm free!"

Just as she said the words, her foot caught in the seatbelt, and she fell out of the car. "Aah!"

"Whoa!" Kurt stepped forward and caught her in his arms.

Ba-dump. Ba-dump. Grizz felt her heartbeat race, senses overwhelmed by his cologne and the feel of his strong arms around her.

She was usually pretty coordinated—what was it about Kurt that made her accident prone? She felt discomfort, and realized it wasn't from being held by Kurt—her foot was still stuck, causing her leg to be suspended in the air at an awkward angle. "Help," she whined.

"I've got you!" Patricia came through from the back seat and grabbed the strap of the seatbelt, pulling her foot free.

"Oof!" Grizz stumbled forward slightly, but Kurt kept his grip on her. Once both feet were safely on the ground, she pushed herself out of his arms and cleared her throat. "Um, thanks," she mumbled, avoiding his eyes as she adjusted her clothes.

Kurt turned away. "No problem," he replied, rubbing his neck. "You okay?"

"Yep, fine," Grizz told him hurriedly, rushing around the car to where Ben stood. "Next time, I'll accept your help," she muttered to him, causing Ben to chuckle.

"Let's not have anymore accidents," Ben said, stepping closer to the car and taking Patricia's hands. "Kahuna is dangerous."

"Aw, she didn't mean it!" Kurt pouted as he closed the driver's door.

With Ben's assistance, Patricia made it out with no problems. "Good girl," she intoned, patting the Jeep on the hood.

As they walked to Teddy's house, Grizz fell back, trying to avoid any sort of contact with Kurt. To her annoyance, her heart was still pounding.

Patricia slowed her steps to link arms with her. "This will be fun! What do you want to do first? Swim, eat..."

Grizz forced a smile, urging herself to get into the spirit of things. She'd been looking forward to this party for awhile—she couldn't let

Kurt spoil it for her. "Let's play it by ear, but maybe the pool pretty soon," she replied, eyes wandering unconsciously over to Kurt. Her face flushed. "I—I'm kind of hot," she stammered.

When they got near Teddy's house, they could hear the faint beating of music, and had to weave through people chatting on the front lawn.

"Hey, how's it going," Kurt greeted a group of boys.

"Hi, Kurt!" a girl's voice called.

"Sup," Kurt replied amiably as he made his way to the front door.

"Hey, dude!" Quincy lifted his hand in a high five as Kurt approached him.

"Yo, Quince!" The boys did a complicated handshake.

Grizz sighed with relief. *Of course he would run into a ton of people,* she thought gleefully. *I don't have to worry about him.* She practically skipped into the Torres' large entry way. Like the Minolas, the Torres' had money, and their house showed it. Her parents would freak out if she tried to have a party this size, but Teddy's house could handle it easily.

"Let's find Lita," Patricia said to Grizz, her sandals clicking on the marble tile.

"Yeah, got to greet the hosts," Ben agreed, walking with them through the living room.

Grizz looked around at the paper lanterns and streamers that decorated the banister and ceiling. "Lita's outdone herself again," she said with an admiring nod.

"Hello Ben, Patricia, Grizz," Mrs. Torres said warmly.

They slowed their steps. "Hey, Mrs. Torres. Thanks for having this party," Patricia replied.

"Oh, it's our pleasure," Mrs. Torres said. Grizz knew that Mr. Torres was wandering around, making sure the festivities didn't get out of hand. "Help yourself to some food," she told them, pointing to the dining room table that had been extended with leaves and was laid out with an array of chips, cookies, and appetizers. "And I think Teddy and Lita are by the pool."

"Thanks!" Ben called to her as he followed the other two through the house to the patio.

Though night had fallen, the Torres' large backyard was brightly lit with path markers and lamp posts, as well as twinkle lights hanging from the patio overhang. Grizz knew that was Lita's doing.

Lots of people were hanging around the pool, either dangling their feet or actually swimming, while others were drinking from their cups and munching on snacks.

Grizz jumped when she heard a loud splash followed by squeals of dismay. She turned to see two girls in street clothes who'd been standing a few feet from the pool, soaking wet and spluttering.

Tuck popped his head out from the pool, putting his arms over the side. "Aw, what's the matter, girls? Didn't you know this was a pool party?"

"Tuck!" one of them shrieked. "You creep! Wait until I get my hands on you—!"

Tuck snickered.

"Hey!"

Tuck stopped short when Lita came over to him, hands on her hips. "Listen, Tucker Eugene Robinson," she said severely.

Tuck flushed and glanced around, annoyed at her use of his full name.

Lita continued, "Keep it up, and you'll be on a one way ticket out of here in a box, disassembled. Got it?"

"I'm beginning to see why Teddy keeps you around," he said dryly, ducking underwater and kicking off from the side to swim away from her.

Grinning, Grizz tapped Lita on the shoulder. "I've never seen Tuck leave so fast. Good one!"

Lita turned around in confusion, eyes lighting up when she saw Grizz, Patricia, and Ben. "Hey, guys! You made it!" She hugged Grizz and Patricia briefly.

"Love the decorations," Patricia told her with a smile.

Brushing curly hair off of her shoulders, Lita replied, "Thanks! It was so much fun, oh my gosh. I found these really cheap lanterns at the store, and I painted designs on them. Then I switched out the bulb—"

"Whassup?!" a voice growled behind them, as arms wrapped around Patricia and Grizz from behind and squeezed.

"What the—" Grizz began to scream, then stopped short when she saw that Teddy had sneaked up behind them. "Oh, it's just you."

"Thanks for the warning," Patricia cut her gaze to Ben, who was chuckling.

"Sorry to startle you two," Teddy said with a good-natured grin. He slapped Ben high five. "Thanks for coming."

"Oh, don't carry around your purses all night," Lita said, nudging Teddy. "You can stash them in Teddy's room."

Grizz looked to her ocean blue bag, which was weighing heavy on her shoulder. "Oh, right! Thanks."

They made their way back into the house and up the Torres' large staircase, the beat of the music softer upstairs.

"I think I'll keep my phone," Patricia commented as they stepped into Teddy's bedroom, slipping her purse off of her shoulder and placing it and her sweatshirt on Teddy's desk. Grizz left her bag next to Patricia's and followed her out of the bedroom.

"I'm kind of hungry," Patricia commented as they descended the staircase.

"Well, we can…" Grizz paused on the stairs, heart beating rapidly.

Patricia, who had just reached the ground level, turned to look at her questioningly. "Grizz?"

"He's here," Grizz whispered urgently, gesturing.

Patricia looked around until she spotted Dimitri standing a few feet away from them, sipping a soda and talking to someone Patricia didn't recognize. "What is he doing here?" she asked curiously.

"I don't know," Grizz replied, voice tinged with excitement and confusion. "He didn't go to Vista!"

Patricia raised her eyebrows, watching Dimitri with interest. "Must be a friend of Teddy," she mused. "Are you going to go say hi to him?"

Grizz descended the last few steps quickly, grabbing Patricia's arm. "I don't know… is my hair okay? Is my outfit…"

"Grizz, you look fantastic," Patricia told her. "You could walk up to him right now and blow him away. If what you told me about your little lunch date the other day is any indication…"

Grizz bit her lip as she watched Dimitri laugh at something his friend said. She hated her hormones—just looking at him made her feel jittery, and the idea of waltzing right up to him and striking up a conversation made her slightly nauseous. "Where did my confidence go?" she demanded under her breath.

Patricia put a hand on Grizz's arm. "You don't have to! We can just hang out, dance, eat, and see how it goes."

Grizz nodded, walking with Patricia into the living room. When Dimitri was out of eyesight, she began to relax.

"What is this song?" Patricia wondered, cocking her head as she listened to the beat. It sounded familiar, but she couldn't put her finger on it.

"Elementary, my dear Watson," Grizz said, lifting her nose in the air. "You shall find that it is 'Straight Up,' by good ol' Paula Abdul."

"Wow, that's impressive," Patricia said admiringly. "You're as good as…" she stopped short, realizing Grizz wouldn't like it if she compared her to Kurt.

Grizz looked at her curiously. "Good as…?"

"Hey, Grizz!"

Grizz felt her spine tingle at the voice, reaching out to squeeze Patricia's hand.

Patricia glanced surreptitiously over her shoulder at Dimitri, before whispering to Grizz, "Mr. McHottie is summoning you."

Grizz squealed under her breath. "Give me a few minutes alone?" she whispered back.

Patricia grinned, nodding and walking off nonchalantly.

Grizz ran her fingers through her hair self-consciously, taking a deep breath before turning to walk to Dimitri. "Hi, Dimitri," she greeted him.

"What a pleasant surprise," Dimitri said with a grin that made his blue eyes sparkle.

Trying to keep her cool, Grizz replied, "Totally. I had no idea you'd be here."

Dimitri shrugged. "Yeah, Teddy's cool. We went to elementary school together. Oh, this is Leon."

The beefy blond guy next to him smiled. "Hey."

Grizz nodded at him. "Nice to meet you."

"So, how do you guys know each other?" Leon asked.

Dimitri smiled, eyes resting on Grizz. "We work together."

Leon laughed. "Ah, so you work at the Whistling Donkey, too, huh?"

"Merry Mule," Grizz and Dimitri said in unison, causing Dimitri to grin and Grizz to blush.

Kurt wandered into the backyard, bobbing his head to the music that was coming through the Torres' outdoor speakers. He spotted Teddy talking to some people near the gazebo.

"Hey, Teddy, great party," Kurt said when he reached him.

"Thanks, man!" Teddy said with a grin. "I'm glad so many people could come. It's like a graduation shindig!"

"Yeah, free at last, dude!" Kurt replied, slapping Teddy's outstretched hand. He turned his attention to the party-goers in the pool. "It's the perfect night for the water. I think Quincy was going to round up some of the boys later so we could do some racing."

"Awesome, count me in. Oh, but don't play water polo in the pool," Teddy warned. "Ever since the window broke, Dad kind of wants a 'no ball' policy at parties…"

"Sure thing, Teddy," Kurt agreed. "We'll behave."

Teddy clapped him on the back. "Good." He turned his head at the sound of his name, seeing his dad signaling him from the patio door.

"Dad needs me. See you in a bit."

"Later." As Teddy walked off, Kurt did a circumference of the yard.

"Hey, Kurt!" A bikini-clad girl greeted him.

"Sup, Angie," Kurt said with a smile, walking past her. Since Quincy had left him to round up the others, Kurt figured he would try to find Grizz. So far, no luck. "Where are Ben and Penny?" he muttered to himself. "She's probably with them…" As he walked, he suddenly felt something snuffling at his feet.

"Hey, Minnie," Kurt greeted the black Labrador-Staffordshire terrier mix, crouching to pet her. "Who's a good girl?"

Mrs. Torres came over to them and laughed. "Just letting her out for some fresh air."

"You want to see what all the excitement is, huh?" Kurt asked, petting the dog's silky head. Minnie looked up at him and wagged her tail. After another minute or so of pets, Minnie wandered away from him, following her nose. "She's off," he said with a chuckle, waving to Mrs. Torres. "If only she could tell me where Guinevere is…" He looked around the yard once again and shrugged. "Better find some of my posse."

Kurt made his way back into the house, pausing by the buffet to pick up a handful of potato chips. "Maybe the guys are in the den," he guessed, walking slowly through the crowded room.

When his eye caught a flash of aqua, Kurt gave a start. *Oh, sweet, there's Grizzy!* Walking toward her, he slowed his steps when he saw that she was talking to someone. He did a double-take when he saw that someone was Dimitri. "What the hell, Teddy?" he muttered under his breath, stepping backward as his mind reeled. *He went to SCH! They're the enemy!* He watched them dejectedly as they talked and laughed,

Grizz tossing her hair over her shoulder. He sighed. "Guess love really is a battlefield, huh?" *I was hoping to spend some time with her*, he thought. *Who knew Teddy would be such a turncoat, man! They'll probably hang out all night with my luck. She'll never like me back...*

Suddenly he remembered the love potion. Quickly his eyes darted all around until he felt it was safe. He poured some cola from the two liter bottle on the table into a cup, then reached for the potion in his jeans pocket. *No time like the present to try this stuff out.* His hazel eyes scanned the small printed label. "Put three drops into any drink, and stir counter-clockwise." He frowned, thinking hard. "Oh, got it." He twisted the cap off and tipped it carefully over the cup, smiling with satisfaction before popping the bottle back in his pocket. He grabbed a clean plastic fork from the table and stirred in the potion. "Oh! That's right. Have to make some for me, too." He did the same for a second cup of cola. "At least I don't have to worry about the cups getting mixed up," he said to himself with a nervous chuckle.

"Then, we zero in, and I pass to Dimitri..." Leon told Grizz.

"And then I kick, and the goalie totally couldn't block me." Dimitri said with a small shrug.

"So you scored the winning point?" Grizz asked. Truth be told, soccer wasn't one of her greatest interests, but the story was pretty exciting.

"Yup." Dimitri looked embarrassed. "It was a great send-off for my last game, ever."

"Aw, well that's great," Grizz told him, boldly patting him on the arm just above his elbow. "Do you think you'll play soccer in college, or...?"

Dimitri glanced at her hand, then caught her eye and smiled, sending a thrill throughout her body. "Well, actually…"

"Hi, guys."

Grizz bristled. *Of course you would interrupt us,* she seethed, glaring at Kurt.

Kurt held out a cup of soda with a smile. "Here, Rizzo, thought you might be thirsty."

She took it from him with a stony gaze. "Thanks," she said flatly. She stared at him pointedly, hoping he would take his leave. To her annoyance, he stayed where he was.

"Oh, hi, I'm Kurt," he said to Leon, offering his free hand.

Leon clasped it for the briefest of seconds. "Leon."

"So, guys, how's it hanging?" Kurt asked casually, taking a sip from his soda. He willed himself not to stare at Grizz, praying she'd drink her soda soon and be rid of Dimitri.

Dimitri shrugged. "Good."

Kurt rocked on his heels, trying to figure out what to say. "Yeah, it's a great night for a party, huh?" He chuckled nervously.

"Mm-hm," Grizz murmured, feeling annoyed, especially when he ran a hand through his hair and she noticed how *good* he looked with his dark button-down shirt rolled up at the elbows. She cut her eyes back to Dimitri, who looked equally good—no, *better,* in his v-neck shirt tucked in at the waist.

"So, you guys friends of Teddy?" Kurt asked them with a light chuckle.

Leon snorted. "Nah, dude, we just were tooling around the area, saw a party, and invited ourselves in."

Seeing Kurt's confused look, Dimitri elbowed Leon. "Stop ribbing him, bro. Yeah, Teddy and us go way back."

Kurt didn't really have a response for that, so he just nodded. *I should have planned my battle maneuvers before I walked right into the thick of it,* he thought helplessly.

Grizz took a swig of her soda, pleased that Kurt had chosen cherry cola, her favorite. Lifting her eyes from the cup, she saw Kurt's gaze riveted on her, and flushed with annoyance.

Kurt held his breath. *It won't be long now,* he thought hopefully.

Patricia picked up a cupcake with chocolate frosting sprinkled with cinnamon. "Mm!" she exclaimed as she took a bite. "Mrs. Torres always makes such good things!"

"This is a pretty fun party," Ben agreed. "Want to go for a swim later? After enough time has passed, since we're eating…"

Patricia laughed. "Safety first, and all that."

"Well, I don't want you drowning," Ben said. "And I wouldn't be able to rescue you, since I've just eaten. And vice versa."

Patricia playfully rolled her eyes, licking frosting from her fingers.

"We'll make Grizz be our lifeguard," Ben teased as he lifted a cheese quesadilla off of the large platter. "Where is Grizz, anyway?"

"Talking to Dimitri," Patricia replied, lifting her eyebrows meaningfully.

"Ah, so you want to give her some private time," Ben said knowingly. "I get it, I get it."

The pair wandered down the hallway as they munched. Patricia's eyes swept the room, but she did a double-take when she saw a certain tall brunette with Grizz and Dimitri. She realized with alarm that she recognized that profile. "Oh, no. Red alert, red alert!"

"What?" Ben asked with a mouthful of quesadilla.

"Your brother has horned in on Grizz's flirting time," Patricia told him, frowning as she noticed Grizz's furious expression.

Ben sighed, exasperated. "He's good at that, isn't he?"

Patricia grabbed his arm. "Rescue mission. Let's go."

Ben hurriedly finished his food, tossing the napkin in a trash can.

Patricia walked over to the four of them, saying in a cheerful tone, "Hi, everybody!"

Grizz looked at her in relief.

"Hey, Trix," Kurt greeted her.

Leon stood up straighter, eyes landing on Patricia with interest.

Ben appeared at her side. "How's it going? Oh, I don't think we got to meet the other day," he said with a smile, squeezing himself between Kurt and Grizz as he focused on Dimitri. "I'm Ben."

"Hi, I'm Dimitri." Dimitri flicked his eyes from Ben to Kurt curiously, furrowing his brow at their similar features and heights.

Seeing his look, Grizz said, "They're twins."

"*Oh,*" Dimitri replied.

"Fraternal," Ben added. Noticing Leon's mouth agape as his eyes were riveted on Patricia, he said, "And this is my girlfriend, Patricia."

Patricia felt her heartbeat spike. It still excited her when she heard Ben call her his girlfriend. "Hi. Nice to meet you."

Leon cast his eyes downward, clearly disappointed. "I'm Leon," he muttered.

"So, has anybody tried these cupcakes yet?" Patricia asked, trying to make conversation. "They're divine!" She took a happy bite.

Grizz laughed. "No, but I definitely will."

A silence fell over the group. "Well, this is cool, us all getting to hang out," Grizz said, trying to get everyone talking. At least now she had a buffer from Kurt. As she sipped her soda, she caught him staring at her yet again, and he looked away quickly. No matter how many times he did it, it still made her skin feel hot.

Patricia and Ben nodded, but they each struggled with what to say.

"I see someone is a sports man," Dimitri finally said, pointing to Ben's blue and silver letterman jacket.

Ben glanced down at his jacket and shrugged. "Guilty."

"What sport?" Leon asked eagerly.

"Track and field."

"Oh." Dimitri shared a short look with Leon. "We were on the soccer team."

"That's cool," Patricia commented, wiping the frosting from her hands with a napkin.

"Nice sardine," Leon said with a snicker.

Ben furrowed his brow, then glanced down at the lapel of his jacket, which depicted a sea lion sitting atop the letters "VHS."

"It's a sea lion," Kurt said unnecessarily.

"Whoever drew it doesn't know what a sea lion looks like," Leon scoffed.

Patricia furrowed her brow. *What a jerk.* "Lay off Seymour," she said defensively. "He's adorable!"

"Yeah, no need to be rude," Ben added.

"Like you want an adorable mascot," Dimitri said, looking skeptical.

Kurt nudged Ben, who had set his jaw. "Oh, like yours strikes fear into the hearts of the opponents?" Kurt shot back. "It's a little bird!"

"We're the Cardinals. The original Angry Birds," Dimitri quipped with a shrug.

Grizz giggled. "You're right, it totally looks like them!"

Kurt watched in horror as her lips parted into a smile, watching Dimitri with a coy expression, her eyes shining. Taking in his gel-slicked hair, which gave the impression that he'd been caught in a rainstorm, plus his deep v-neck shirt tucked into Bermuda shorts with sockless loafers, Kurt thought he looked *extra* douchey. *What's going on here? She's agreeing with these tools? This is so uncool!*

Kurt gripped his plastic cup so tightly it sloshed. "Yeah, well we Sea Lions would eat you for lunch."

"Sea lions eat fish, not birds," Dimitri said with a smirk, blue eyes glinting.

"They might if the bird is a pain in the *ass*," Kurt hissed.

"Oh, let it go, Kurt, high school is a thing of the past," Grizz said, nudging him a little too roughly. *He needs to go away so I can have some alone time with this hottie!*

"It's okay that you guys went to the losing school," Dimitri quipped, lips spreading into a smile. "We won't hold it against you."

Patricia furrowed her brow. She wasn't even a follower of a lot of the sports, but knew Vista did really well. How were *they* the losers? She glanced at Grizz, wondering how the conversation had devolved into this, but Grizz had her gaze riveted on Dimitri, twirling a lock of hair around her finger.

Setting his cup down on an end table, Kurt thought, *I'm ready to show this punk who's the real man.* "Well, you guys weren't so cocky when we whooped your asses in the finals," he replied sharply.

Dimitri and Leon shared a look. "Who cares about water polo?"

Leon asked. "That's not even a real sport. It's all about soccer. We won the championships the last two years."

"Excuse me?" Kurt demanded. "What do you mean it's not a 'real sport'?" He scrunched his fingers into air quotation marks. "Water polo is like rugby in the water, dude. It's *intense*."

"And Vista has won the Water Polo Championship the last *three* years," Ben chimed in, eyes narrowed.

Patricia was starting to feel defensive of Kurt thanks to Leon and Dimitri's digs. "And that's pretty much thanks to Kurt, the star player. He was *scouted* by the coach at ASU."

Kurt titled his head in her direction. "Thanks, Patty."

Patricia nodded, folding her arms across her chest. "You're welcome."

"Oh, an athletic scholarship, huh?" Dimitri asked with a snicker.

Grizz watched Dimitri narrow his eyes in Kurt's direction, holding her breath. He seemed to be extra annoyed with Kurt—did he know that Kurt liked her, and was trying to get him to back off? *He really must like me!* she thought hopefully.

"No one receives a free ride for water polo," Ben replied, a hard edge to his voice. "Sorry nobody came to scout you for soccer, but you don't need to take it out on my brother."

Patricia watched this little exchange with wide eyes. She'd never seen Ben get so riled up. It was kind of hot.

Grizz wound her way to Patricia, nudging her in the side. "Isn't Dimitri smexy?" she whispered.

Patricia tore her eyes from her boyfriend and wrinkled her nose. Dimitri, in her opinion, was acting like a jerk, and also wasn't her type *at all*, but she was afraid of offending Grizz. She lifted her eyebrows.

"Don't you think this is getting out of hand?" she muttered back.

Grizz sighed. "Fine." Clapping her hands, she moved to stand between Dimitri and Ben. "Boys, boys. This is a party! Stop throwing insults, and forget about your rivalry. We've all graduated, and are moving on to bigger and better things!"

Ben wasn't in any mood to back down, but when he felt Patricia's hand on his arm, he looked into her imploring eyes and exhaled. "I'm cool," he said, his voice tighter than normal.

Seeing Grizz's intense expression, Leon shrugged. "No hard feelings."

Dimitri cast a look to Kurt, who stared silently back at him.

Grizz took their silence as a truce. After a few moments, she said, "So, Teddy sure knows how to throw parties, huh?"

If you count near bloodshed, it's a blast, Patricia thought wryly.

Ben took a deep breath, determined to make an effort to keep the peace. "Hey, Kurt, maybe Mom and Dad will let us throw a couple parties. We could even do an end-of-summer barbecue as a last hurrah before we all go our separate ways."

Ben's words made Patricia's chest squeeze, thinking that soon she and Grizz would be in separate states. She stepped closer to her friend and clung to her arm, leaning her head on her shoulder. Grizz smiled and tilted her head to rest against Patricia's.

Dimitri watched them. "Aw, so sweet. Besties will be separated."

Leon looked at Ben. "Are you and Patricia going to try the long distance thing, or just get the most out of the summer?" He wiggled his eyebrows suggestively.

Patricia's head shot up, and she shared a look with Ben. Ben cringed, and she could sense he felt as disgusted by Leon's suggestion as she did.

Jaw tight, Ben replied, "Actually, Patricia and I are both going to UCLA."

Dimitri whistled. "Going to the same school?" He shared a smirk with Leon. "That's hardcore."

"Damn, can't stand being apart, huh?" Leon asked, nudging Dimitri with his elbow.

Patricia didn't like his tone. *Apparently it's not just sports you're an ass about.* Looking at Ben, she saw his eyebrow twitch, and he seemed incapable of answering. "We didn't do it on purpose," she explained. "We both just happened to pick the same school."

"Yeah, Ben and Patsy aren't attached at the hip. They're both very independent," Kurt added in a cold tone.

Ben cut his eyes to Kurt. "Thanks, bro," he muttered to him.

"Just kidding," Leon said, lifting his hands defensively.

"Where are you going to college, Dimitri?" Grizz asked, hoping it would be somewhere nearby.

"I'm taking a year off, I think," Dimitri replied with a shrug.

"Oh, going to keep on at the Merry Mule?" Grizz asked. *Maybe then I'll see him over Fall Break!*

"Or do you have an internship or something?" Patricia wondered.

Dimitri shrugged. "I think I'm going to backpack through Europe. Couch-surf. You know."

Grizz felt her heart sink. *Europe? Wow. That's a lot farther than just a state or two...* Things seemed to be going well, but would he really be interested in dating her if he was leaving soon? *What's the big deal?* she chided herself. *You just want to go on a few dates with him, not marry him.*

Kurt frowned, nudging his brother. "He's going to surf on a *couch?*

Won't it sink?"

Ben turned his back to the group to whisper, "No, 'couch-surfing' means he's going to crash on random people's couches all over Europe. You know, *be a bum.*"

Patricia had to fight to keep from rolling her eyes. "If your parents are made of money, I guess they don't care," she grumbled under her breath.

"Yeah?" Kurt straightened up, a good few inches taller than Dimitri. "Well, Zelly and I are going to ASU." He gently bumped shoulders with her.

Grizz felt her nostrils flare as she glared at him. *I knew he'd be insufferable if he found out.*

"Wow." Dimitri's gaze rested on Grizz, and she felt her heart stop. "Talk about coincidences."

"Yeah," Grizz said breathlessly. "You got that right. *Total* coincidence."

Dimitri grinned, seeming a bit relieved, in her opinion. He shifted his weight, now standing closer to her.

Kurt didn't like the way this was going one bit. *Why hasn't that stupid love potion kicked in yet?* he wondered desperately. He stole a glance at Grizz's cup. It was almost empty.

Leon snorted. "Well, I'm going to CSU Monterey Bay. I'm sure they'll want me on their soccer team. How could they say no?"

Patricia began to roll her eyes, then squeezed them shut. *I can't take this anymore...*

"Hey, Patricia!"

She breathed a sigh of relief when she looked over her shoulder and saw her friend Nicole waving to her.

"Coming!" she called in a cheerful tone. She took Ben's hand and gave it a squeeze, trying to signal to him that she wanted to leave.

Ben caught on quickly. "We've got to run, maybe we'll see you later?"

Grizz lifted her eyebrows at Patricia, glancing rapidly between her and Kurt.

Patricia nudged Ben, who sighed. "Coming, Kurt?"

Kurt kept his gaze riveted on Dimitri. "Be there in a few," he said coldly.

Ben shrugged to Grizz, waving vaguely. "Later, guys."

Patricia supposed she should have felt bad, but that whole encounter made her skin crawl. *If Grizz wants to hang out with him, I personally think it's better if she has a chaperon.*

Traitors, Grizz thought, peeved that Kurt was still there. *No, you can't let Kurt ruin your night. Just ignore him.* Easier said than done.

"Have you guys heard of the big surfing competition coming up?" Dimitri asked.

Grizz shook her head, but Kurt replied, "Hell yeah! I can't wait to try out my moves."

Leon chuckled. "You're going to enter?"

Kurt didn't like his tone, or the smirk he was giving him. "Yeah, of course." He squinted at Leon. "Are *you?*"

Leon shrugged. "No, but I know my man Dimitri is."

Of course he is, Kurt thought in frustration.

Just then, Leon's phone buzzed. "Oh, shit, I've got to answer this. Catch you later." He swiped his phone to answer it as he walked away.

"You surf?" Grizz asked, turning her attention to Dimitri.

Kurt grit his teeth at the awe in her voice. *Notice you're not like that around me. I surf!*

Dimitri shrugged. "I picked it up when my family was vacationing in Fiji."

"Wow," Grizz breathed, sipping her soda.

"Do *you* surf, Grizz?" Dimitri smiled at her.

"Well, I've just started," she admitted. "But it's really cool."

"She's great," Kurt added.

Grizz felt herself blush, pleased by Kurt's comment. "I'm decent."

Dimitri glanced at Kurt as if he'd forgotten Kurt was there. Then he turned his attention back to Grizz. "You definitely should come out on the water with me, Grizz. Maybe even later tonight."

"Oh!" Grizz could hardly contain her excitement. Was he asking her on a date?

"You don't seriously mean to bring her surfing out in the ocean at this time," Kurt said incredulously.

Dimitri didn't seem fazed, sipping his soda. "Night surfing is cool."

Kurt stared at him incredulously. *Is this guy full of it, or just the biggest idiot I've ever met?* "Noahs *hunt* at night, dude. And the fin of surfboards in the water looks like fish swimming. That's just asking to get eaten."

"Maybe for chickens," Dimitri said nonchalantly.

Kurt bristled. "It's not *chicken* to surf safely," he shot back.

Grizz looked back and forth between them, not knowing what to say. "Um, guys..."

With a smirk, Dimitri replied, "You can't live in a bubble. Some of life's greatest risks are also life's greatest rewards. It's so peaceful to surf at night, with the moon shining down..."

Kurt scoffed. "It's peaceful due to the fact that there's no one else surfing, because, did I mention before? *It's not safe.* But hey, if you want to be shark bait, who am I to stop you?" He turned to Grizz. "But Zel, please don't ever do that," he asked in the most serious tone she'd ever heard him use. "It's not worth it."

Grizz felt lost in his hazel pools, shining fiercely as they focused on her. *I hate it when he pulls out the smart words,* she thought, realizing she had to agree with Kurt. Surfing at night seemed dangerous. Swallowing hard, she looked at Dimitri and replied, "Yeah, I don't think so. I'd like to stay in one piece..." she laughed to try to soften the blow.

Kurt breathed a sigh of relief.

Dimitri shrugged, running a hand through his thick, curly hair. "No big deal. We'll go another day."

Smiling, Grizz nodded. "Sounds great."

Kurt frowned. *So much for us surfing together...* he thought dejectedly. *Here they are, making dates as if I don't exist. Why hasn't the potion kicked in yet?* "Have fun," he muttered, turning away from them.

Grizz cocked an eyebrow, watching him walk away. "Kurt...?"

"So, Grizz..."

Grizz turned her attention back to Dimitri. "Hm?"

"I looked at the schedule," Dimitri began, taking a step closer to her, "And I couldn't help but notice that you and I are both off next Saturday..."

Her heartbeat quickened. *He looked to see if I was free?* she thought numbly.

"Do you have plans that day?" he asked.

Licking her lips, she fought to play it cool. "No, no plans."

Dimitri grinned. "What do you say to meeting me at the Boardwalk around 1? We can eat, walk around..."

Grizz nodded enthusiastically. "That sounds awesome!" She twirled a lock of hair around her finger, biting her lip as Dimitri smiled at her. *I can't wait to tell Patricia!*

≈

Kurt walked briskly through the Torres' backyard, head on a swivel as he searched for Tuck.

"Yo, Kurt!" Quincy called out to him as he passed the pool. "There you are! We were going to start racing." Quincy folded his burly arms across his chest. "What do you think—you go against Nick first, or…?"

"Where's Tuck?" Kurt interrupted him.

Quincy furrowed his brow. "I'm not sure…"

"I saw him in the kitchen," David, another one of Kurt's teammates, spoke up from his spot in the lawn chair.

"Good. Thanks." Kurt turned and walked back to the house.

"Wait—what about racing?" Quincy called after him.

"Later!"

Pushing through the crowd of people talking and dancing in the house, Kurt wove his way down the hallway. He saw Tuck talking to a girl in the kitchen.

"Found you." Kurt strode up to him.

Tuck frowned. "Hey, dude. I'm kind of busy here…" he tilted his head to the girl he was with.

"Sorry, I need Tuck for a second," Kurt said to her, grabbing Tuck by the elbow.

"Hey! What the—" Tuck cried in dismay, trying to pull free from Kurt's grip.

Kurt ignored him, dragging him to the back corner of the kitchen.

Seeing Kurt's severe expression, Tuck cleared his throat nervously. "What's up?"

"Nothing much," Kurt hissed. "Except that I just tried out the love potion on Zelda, and she's still flirting with Dimitri!" He lifted his eyebrows at Tuck. "Why didn't it work?"

Tuck straightened his shirt, sighing under his breath. "Oh, is *that* all? It just takes time, man!"

"Time?" Kurt repeated, giving him a skeptical look.

"Of course." Tuck paused. "Since she likes someone else, the properties of the pro pheromones are going to have to disable and destroy the pheromones that are attracted to Dimitri! Pretty soon, her system will be overflowing with *Kurt* pheromones."

Kurt stared at him, Tuck's nonsense science completely going over his head. "So, if I give it to her again…"

"Yeah, man, try, try again!" Tuck said, punching him in the arm lightly. "I'm sure you'll see results."

Kurt nodded slowly, calming down. "Okay. Oh, we were going to race. You in it?"

Tuck smiled, green eyes glinting. "To win it."

Chapter Fourteen ♡

Ben chuckled as he stared at the television in the Minolas' living room. "Man, these people are obsessed with the 'theater'," he commented, putting on a phony British accent for the last word. "Maybe you should re-think your intended major, Patricia; you might be stuck with weirdos like these."

Patricia made a face and nudged him. She was having Ben watch her favorite movie, *All About Eve*. Despite his remarks, he seemed to be enjoying it.

Ben frowned as the titular character spun yet another sob story to her audience. "Can't any of them tell this girl is… well, evil?"

"Just keep watching, her little followers drop off, one by one," Patricia murmured, eyes glued to the screen. She was absentmindedly petting Marmalade, who was perched on the arm of the couch, purring like an outboard motor.

Ben laughed, taking a handful of popcorn. "George Sanders' character is like, 'A woman after my own heart. A kindred spirit.' They should get the hook-up."

Patricia tapped him on the arm, wiggling her eyebrows. "Just watch!"

"Did I just make a prediction?" he asked excitedly.

Patricia held a finger to her lips and smiled, popping a piece of popcorn in her mouth.

Some time later, Ben groaned at what was unfolding in the movie. "Oh, don't tell me he dumps Margo and goes for this viper! Dude, Bill, are you stupid?! You all should have listened to the maid."

Patricia laughed and poked him. "Ssh!"

Ben playfully poked her back. "You wanted me to watch it! Can I help it if I'm getting into it?" He grinned. "Want me to start calling you 'the kid' —?"

Patricia pouted her lips and poked him again.

Grinning, Ben shot his hands out and began tickling her.

Patricia leaned against the arm of the couch to try to wriggle out of his grasp, and felt a furry body under her head. Marmalade hissed and tore away from the couch. "Oh, Marmalade! I'm so sorry!" She glared at Ben as best she could in the midst of her giggles. "It's your fault!"

"Should have thought about that before you poked me!" Ben said mercilessly. "I will not take being poked lying down."

"You kind of are lying down, now," Patricia choked out, feeling tears of laughter spring to her eyes. Holding up her hands, she decreed, "I surrender!"

Ben laughed, helping her sit upright as he ceased tickling her.

Their laughter was interrupted when the lights, which had been dimmed, were turned up all the way.

Patricia turned to see Kurt shuffling into the living room in pajama shorts and a tee shirt, his hair sticking up in different directions.

Ben glanced incredulously at the clock on his phone. "Did you seriously just wake up?"

Stifling a yawn, Kurt nodded. "Yeah, bro, it's my day off." He squinted bleary-eyed at Patricia. "Hey, Patty."

Patricia waved, pausing the movie. "Hi, Kurt."

"What are you two up to?" Kurt asked, plopping heavily into the armchair across from them.

Ben frowned. "Well, we were watching a movie, so…"

"Oh, sweet." Kurt reached for the large bowl of popcorn on the coffee table.

With lightning reflexes, Ben snatched the bowl away from him.

"Aw, man," Kurt leaned back in the chair, pouting.

Ben and Patricia shared a look. *Is he not going to leave?* Patricia wondered in annoyance.

Drumming his fingers on the arm of the chair, Kurt heaved a sigh. His hazel eyes flicked to Ben, then rested on Patricia.

Patricia squirmed under the intensity of his stare. "What?"

Sighing again, Kurt said, "Here you guys are, having a nice date…"

Ben set his elbow on the arm of the couch, his chin in his hand. "You mean we were…" he grumbled.

"Meanwhile, my love life is in the chowder, because Zelly is mooning over that douchebag Dimitri," Kurt went on with a frown, running his hands through his disheveled hair. "I've got drive! Goals! Why is she still all over him?"

Because she likes him? Patricia wanted to say, but held her tongue.

Not really sure why, but I can't change who she likes. "I'm going to grab some more soda," she mumbled to Ben as she stood up.

Kurt leaned forward and said to Ben, "I just don't get it, man. She should be crazy about me by now."

Ben crossed his arms across his chest as he began, "Um, Kurt, it doesn't always work that way. If Grizz doesn't like you, she's just not interested in you..." He tilted his head sympathetically. "Sorry, man. That's gotta suck."

Kurt shook his head impatiently. "No, but she *should* now! I've been putting the potion in her drinks..." Kurt's eyes widened as he saw Ben's expression.

"The what?" Ben asked cautiously, a feeling of dread washing over him.

Patricia, who had made it to the edge of the room, slowly turned around. "What are you talking about?"

Kurt clammed up, casting his gaze to the side. "Nothing..."

Patricia stomped back over to the chair, looming over Kurt as she demanded, "*What* have you been slipping Grizz?!"

Kurt leaned around Patricia to look imploringly at Ben. Ben stared stonily back, and Kurt shrugged sheepishly. "Well, I..."

Patricia rolled her sleeves up, putting her fists on her hips. "You'd better spill *right now*, KIRK!"

Kurt leaned back as far as the chair would allow. "A love potion," he mumbled.

Ben rose to his feet. "I'm sorry, I must be hard of hearing. I did not just hear what I think I did."

Patricia turned to him. "Oh, you did. We both just heard your brother say that he's been giving Grizz a love potion." Whirling back on Kurt, she hissed, "What the hell are you talking about?" She wanted to believe Kurt was pulling a prank on them, but, sadly, she knew he was too dumb.

"Stop yelling," Kurt whined, head falling into his hands.

"Then *speak*," Patricia hissed between clenched teeth.

Running his hands through his hair, Kurt began, "Um, Tuck kinda sorta gave me a love potion…"

Ben blew out a puff of breath. "Robinson. I should have known. That—"

Patricia cut him off. "You *do* realize there's no such thing as a love potion, right, Kurt?"

Kurt scoffed. "Of course there is! I paid good money for it! Tuck wouldn't lie to me."

"You *paid* for it?" Ben asked incredulously.

Kurt shook his head, pinching the bridge of his nose. "Stop grilling me! Ugh, I've gotta go. All of this yelling so early in the morning is too intense, man." He rose to his feet and fled the room.

"Kurt! Get back here!" Patricia called after him.

Ben sank onto the couch. "There goes our date! He's so annoying sometimes," he muttered.

"Think of it this way," Patricia began, joining him on the couch. "Soon you two will be in separate states."

Ben froze. "I know I'm going to be sad when it happens, but right this second that seems really, really appealing." Sighing, he cracked his knuckles. "But first things first. I want to have a little talk with Tuck."

Grizz adjusted the hem of her short jean skirt as she checked the time on her cell phone. She hadn't meant to be a few minutes late, but her bus had run behind schedule. She couldn't wait until she had enough money for her car to be out of the shop, then she'd have her freedom back. After a few more minutes passed, Grizz frowned. Maybe Dimitri was running late, too. She began to type out a message to him just as her screen lit up. Heart skipping a beat, she eagerly opened the text.

"Sorry, Grizz, I can't make it after all. Rain check?" This was accompanied by a winking emoji.

Grizz couldn't take a full breath for a moment, unable to process the words. Then her heart sank. Dimitri was bailing on her, again. *He offered to drive me home. He asked me out. What the hell? He doesn't even have a reason!* She felt hot tears sting her eyes, but she willed herself not to cry. It was his loss! Her shoulders slumped. So much for her perfect date outfit. "And what am I supposed to do with myself? Dimitri was going to take me home, I don't want to get right back on the bus..."

Dejectedly, she shuffled her plaid Converse to the nearest bench and sank with a heavy sigh. She dully stared at the crowds of people as they milled by, eyes narrowing at saccharine couples who stood in line for a Boardwalk game. "Oh, you think he's going to win a prize for you, do you?" she muttered spitefully. "That's a cute thought. 'Oh, you don't have to, babe!'" She lowered her voice several octaves. "'Hey, for you, baby? Anything.' Even if he manages to win that rigged game, your perfect little fairy tale won't last. Just wait until he dumps your ass. Then you'll be sorry, your pretty face melting as your makeup runs and your skin puffing while you binge on junk food, you—"

"Hey, Zelly!"

Grizz paused in her diatribe as she lifted her eyes to see Kurt standing before her, holding his skateboard casually over his shoulder. She opened her mouth, but no words came out.

"What a coincidence, man," Kurt said, trying to remain cool even though he was bubbling with excitement. "I was just going for a board." He tapped his skateboard affectionately. "What are you doing here?"

Grizz found her voice. She sighed heavily, shoulders drooping. "Well, I was meeting someone here, but he couldn't make it, so…"

Kurt felt a pang of jealousy, realizing that the "he" was Dimitri. Just how much time was that love potion going to take? "Oh, bummer." Then he brightened. "I'll hang out with you, Zelda! Are you hungry?"

Grizz stared at him, stifling a groan. *Could this afternoon get any worse?* Seeing the puppy-dog look in his hazel eyes, she considered his offer. What were her plans, anyway? She was going to have to wait for the next bus, and she *was* pretty hungry. Pouting her lower lip, she nodded.

Kurt grinned, face flushing in excitement. "Awesome! Let's head to the Wharf and scope out the options!"

"Sure," Grizz muttered, rising to her feet and trailing after him. They made their way from the Boardwalk to the Wharf in silence, Grizz inhaling deeply and taking in the scents of fried food, fish, and the ocean. She tossed her head back, basking in the refreshing breeze coming in off the water.

Kurt glanced at her and blushed. He quickly pulled his sunglasses from the pocket of his cargo shorts and slid them on his face. "The sun is wicked bright today, man. Need my shades."

Grizz snickered, looking up at him. She immediately wished she hadn't. His profile was thrown into relief in the sunlight, the faintest hint of dark stubble on his chin. She frowned and ducked her head.

"What are you in the mood to eat? There's fish and chips, burgers, corn dogs..."

Grizz's stomach rumbled, and she covered it self-consciously with her hand. "Fish and chips sounds pretty good."

Kurt nodded, pointing to a food stand. "Let's go here! I think I'll get a burger and fries."

As they stood at the end of the line, Grizz tried to settle her frustration. It wasn't Kurt's fault that Dimitri stood her up. She would get to go out with Dimitri soon—he said he wanted to do a rain check, after all.

"When's your next shift, Rizzo?" Kurt asked as they waited.

Grizz went over her schedule in her mind. "Monday."

Kurt nodded. "Mine's tomorrow. I don't know if it's going to be on bar or if I need to suit up, haha."

Grizz poked him with a hot pink polished nail. "Well, it all depends if Obe values his customers. That last Shot in the Dark you made—"

"Hey, it says 'In the dark.' How was I supposed to know I needed my eyes open?"

Grizz giggled, glancing at him out of the corner of her eye.

"Hey, Kurt!"

Grizz turned her head to see Sophie Sinclair from her cooking class waving at Kurt. She skipped over to them, completely ignoring Grizz as she said, "Wow, Kurt, fancy seeing you here. It's been fo-re-ver."

"Oh, hi Sophie," Kurt replied, taking a step forward as the line went up.

Sophie giggled, twirling a lock of hair around her pointer finger. "So, what are you up to?"

"Riz and I were just grabbing lunch," Kurt said with a nod to Grizz.

Sophie barely glanced at Grizz before she said, "Oh, that sounds great! Could I join you?"

Grizz had to fight to keep a calm, relaxed expression and not show her distaste at the idea of eating with Sophie. In their four years at Vista, Sophie had never so much as had a smile or a civil word for Grizz. This was what came from hanging out with Kurt Minola! She would always be surrounded by rude people who ignored her very existence just to bask in the water polo god's aura.

Kurt glanced at Grizz and shifted his weight, his skateboard touching the ground. "Maybe some other time."

Grizz closed her eyes in relief, then opened them to see Sophie's cheeks flushing. "Oh, sure, I understand, Kurt," she cooed, still pointedly acting like Grizz wasn't even there.

The nerve! *Why can't she get lost?* Not that she and Kurt were on a date or anything…

"Um, listen, that new comedy is coming out this weekend, and I was hoping," her petite form began to wiggle nervously back and forth, obviously trying to look cute. It wasn't working, in Grizz's opinion. "That you could go with me?"

Kurt paused, eyes softening as he said gently, "Sorry, Soph. I don't think I can."

Sophie froze, stammering, "O-oh, is this weekend bad? Because—"

Kurt shook his head. "No, I can't go out with you at all. I'm sorry." He shrugged, putting one hand in the pocket of his khaki cargo shorts. "I'm a one-woman man, now."

Grizz stared at Kurt in surprise. Did he mean…? *Oh, gag me with a spoon! He thinks this is a date?!* She wanted to shake her head, tell Sophie to flirt with Kurt all she wanted, because... *I'm not interested!* Yet she found she couldn't speak, couldn't move.

"Oh..." Sophie's large blue eyes grew suspiciously bright as she stepped away from them, looking at Grizz as if seeing her for the first time before she turned back to Kurt. The meaning of his words seemed to dawn on her. "Um, okay. See you later." She threw Grizz a furious glance before she walked away.

What are you glaring at me for? It's not my *fault that he's got the hots for me,* Grizz thought in irritation as she watched Kurt out of the corner of her eye. There he stood, smiling at her like an idiot, the tips of his ears slightly pink at his confession.

"The line is moving," she said after a few moments.

"Oh, oops," Kurt turned away from her to move up in the line.

Once she placed her order, Grizz turned and scanned the area for Kurt. She spotted him perched on the rail, tanned arms flexed as he leaned back and basked in the sun. He lowered his face and caught her eye, waving enthusiastically.

Grizz blew her bangs off of her forehead in annoyance and made her way to him. She lifted her receipt. "Now just have to wait for the food," she said once she'd reached him. She noticed Kurt was staring at her, mouth agape. "W-what?" she asked self-consciously, glancing down to make sure she didn't have something on her clothes.

Kurt cleared his throat, wiping his palms on his knees. "Your hair—in the sun..."

Grizz cocked one eyebrow. "Speak English?"

Kurt broke into a slow grin, ducking his head as he chuckled. "The aqua streaks are super vibrant in this light. You're a total mermaid,

Zelly."

Grizz felt her cheeks grow warm at his surprisingly sweet pronouncement. "Aw, shucks," she said nonchalantly, turning her head away from him to hide the fact that his compliment had pleased her.

"Where do you want to sit?" Kurt asked, hopping easily off the railing and reaching for his board.

Grizz glanced around, pointing to an empty table near the railing. "Over there looks good."

"Choka." Kurt followed her and sat at the small table.

Their bare knees brushed, and she bristled, scooting away from him. It was difficult since the table was so small and they both had long legs, but she refused to touch Kurt Minola. She leaned back in her chair and played with her receipt, not sure what to say. *I never used to have this problem around this idiot,* she thought with annoyance.

"Number 238! Number 239!"

Grizz began to stand up, but Kurt leapt to his feet first. "I'll get our stuff, Zel!"

"Oh, um, thanks," Grizz murmured, staring after him as strode easily to the stand in his black tee shirt. She pulled out her phone and texted Patricia.

"Dimitri stood me up, and guess who I'm stuck with now?"

Kurt snuck a glance at Grizz and saw that she was engrossed in texting on her phone. "Now's my chance!" He pulled the small purple bottle Tuck had given him from his pocket and squeezed a few drops into both his and Grizz's soda, stirring it in with the straws. "Sweet."

She lifted her eyes to see Kurt walking toward her, holding his skateboard in his hands by the wheels, turned upside down like a tray. Their food was carefully arranged on it. Her cheeks puffed as she held in her laughter, before she let out a huge guffaw. "Wow. Just—wow." She held her stomach as he set the board on their table. "I've got to admit, that's clever," she breathed as she burst into a fit of giggles.

Kurt stared at her, scratching the back of his neck as he chuckled. "Thanks, Rizzo. Here's your food." He set her soda and basket of fish and chips in front of her.

"Why thank you, Kirk," Grizz said, reaching for packets of ketchup. "Mm!" she declared after a few moments. "Delish!"

Kurt took a swig of his soda and nodded. "I don't know about you, but the salt air really makes me hungry."

Grizz laughed. "Yeah." She reached for her soda, and Kurt watched her intently. "What?" she demanded, holding the cup aloft.

Kurt cleared his throat. "Uh, nothing. You-your bracelet is cool," he commented, pointing to the many chains adorned with beads that crisscrossed on her wrist.

Grizz eyed him suspiciously, lifting the straw to her lips. "Thanks…"

Kurt crossed his fingers under the table, pretending to be staring at his food while watching her drink the soda. Grizz lifted her eyes after a few moments and met his, and he held his breath.

She gazed away, irritation bubbling in her stomach once more.

Silence followed for a few moments as Kurt watched her out of the corner of his eye. *She's not looking at me… maybe the potion is taking effect and now she's too shy! Poor girl.*

Dipping a fry in ketchup, Grizz finally said, "So, which do you prefer? Working on bar or being the company mule?" She slapped her knee at her own joke.

Kurt's shoulders sagged. *That's not the question of a babe in love…*

Then he looked at Grizz sitting there, eyebrows raised as she waited for his response. *I guess I should consider it lucky that I get to hang out with her for a little bit.* Trying to smile, he replied, "Well, I love to groove to the tunes in the suit. All of the people who walk by get really into it. It takes a lot out of you, though. That costume is hard to breathe in."

"Well, we definitely don't want you to expire," Grizz laughed, munching her fish sandwich. "When you start to overheat, take the 'grooving' down a notch or two. Or else we'll have the forest rangers out to peel a collapsed mule off the street."

Kurt felt his heartbeat thudding in his ears. "That's sweet of you to worry about me, Riz, but I'm tough, I'll be fine."

Grizz lifted her chin. "That's not what I was saying," she said with an annoyed sniff.

Kurt leaned back in his chair, her words not appearing to faze him as he grinned lazily. "Aw, aren't you a cute little guy," Kurt said to the seagull that landed on the railing near their table. He pulled a french fry from his basket. "Here you—"

"Don't feed the seagulls!" Grizz screeched, slapping the french fry from Kurt's large hand.

Kurt looked at her with confused eyes. "But the little guy is hungry..."

Grizz exhaled and leaned forward, running her hands through her bangs before saying, "You have lived here your *entire life*, and have never *once* read the signs?!" She pointed to a sign posted several feet away from them that read, "Please do not feed the seagulls."

Kurt glanced to where her hot pink polished finger indicated and shook his head. "Man, Zelly, people are mean. These poor little gulls have a hard day's work on the ocean, and are surrounded by tantalizing good food."

Grizz rolled her eyes. "Look, I get that your heart is in the right place, but human food can make them sick." *You moron,* she thought.

Kurt's hazel eyes widened, and Grizz realized that this thought had truly never occurred to him. "Oh, okay. Sorry, bird, none for you." Kurt scooted his chair so that his will wouldn't be broken by the seagull's cute face.

Grizz reached for her soda, smirking triumphantly.

When they'd finished their lunch, Grizz stood up and threw away her trash, wondering what was in store next. Should she try to ditch him, or suffer a little longer? Watching him leaning back in his chair, staring out over the ocean, she smiled to herself. *I guess I can put up with him for maybe another half hour or so.* She walked over to him. "So, what do you want to do now?"

Kurt sat up eagerly. "Whatever you want to do, Gwendolyn."

Grizz closed her eyes for a moment. *Nope, I was wrong. I should have ditched him while I had the chance.* "Um, maybe let's walk around or something..."

Kurt stood and picked up his skateboard. He snapped his fingers. "Hey, do you want to check out the sea lions?"

"Sure, I haven't gone to visit them in awhile." Remembering his Sea Lion pride, Grizz added, "Besides, we should see how our official animal is doing."

Kurt chuckled. "You know it."

They made their way down the steps to the sea lion viewing deck. Grizz glanced around at the wood beams. *It's kind of cool down here, but a little spooky...* She felt like a ghost could appear at her elbow any minute. Then she glanced at Kurt, who was peering around for sea lions. *Nope. No ghosts. Just a goon.*

"Oh, there's some!" Kurt pointed to three sea lions lounging on the beams under the Wharf. "Whoa, they're so cool. Chilling, man. Don't mind the land walkers. In harmony with the sea."

Grizz snorted. "You're hilarious."

Kurt flushed, feeling like an idiot. He glumly watched the sea lions for a few minutes in silence.

Suddenly another pair of sea lions who were on the scaffolding further back snarled at each other. Grizz gasped and involuntarily grabbed Kurt's arm at the sound.

"Whoa!" His eyes bugged out as he watched one sea lion knock the other into the water. "Lions came to play!"

Grizz put her hand on her chest to steady her heartbeat. "And this is why we don't get to feed the sea lions," she said with a breathless laugh, glancing at Kurt.

"I wouldn't mind feeding them a cardinal," Kurt laughed with a shrug, turning to face her.

Ba-dump. Ba-dump. Grizz's heartbeat pounded as she looked up into his hazel eyes, the beams of the deck above casting shadows on his face. She removed her hand from his arm and stepped back, trying to clear her senses. "Race you to the Boardwalk!" she called as she hurried up the steps.

Kurt stared after her for a moment, his cheeks flushed. "Wait—what? Rizzo! Come back!" He picked up his skateboard and hurried after her.

Chapter Fifteen ♡

B EN LED PATRICIA THROUGH THE GATES OF THE COMMUNITY pool, glancing around as he signed them in.

"Are you sure he's here?" Patricia asked in a whisper.

Ben turned to her and nodded as he walked to the spacious grassy area. "Trust me. If he's not working, he's here swimming. Every time I come to use the pool, Tuck's here. Like clockwork."

Sure enough, when Patricia scanned the poolside, she saw Tuck, wearing the telltale red swimming trunks and white tee shirt of a lifeguard. "Target acquired," she murmured to Ben, setting her jaw as she made her way toward him. Tuck didn't appear to notice their presence, focused on the pool full of people.

"Hey there, Tuck."

Tuck turned his head, eyebrows lifting as he saw Patricia standing next to him, hands on hips. "Oh, hi, Patricia. What's up?"

Patricia didn't waste time with pleasantries. "Would you like to explain to me why Kurt thinks he has magical powers?!"

Tuck shrugged his shoulders, looking at her skeptically. "I think you've been hitting the caffeine a little too hard."

Patricia folded her arms across her chest. "Don't play dumb. Answer my question."

Tuck laughed, turning away from her to face the pool once more. "I don't know what you're talking about. And honestly, I can't talk to you. I have to be focusing on the people in the pool. You know, so they don't drown?" A shadow fell in front of him, and his eyes flicked back to Patricia to see that Ben had joined her.

Ben smirked just as the whistle signaling break time sounded. He looked at his watch. "What do you know? You're free from that task for a little bit, so you can't ignore Patricia's question."

"Uh..." Tuck faltered, his ruddy complexion paling. "Hi there, Ben. Um, sorry Patricia, could you, ah, repeat the question?"

"Kurt seems convinced that Grizz will fall in love with him because of some sort of concoction. One he purchased from *you*." Patricia poked him in the arm with the last word.

Tuck opened his mouth to deny it, but one look at the grim expression on Ben's face changed his mind. "Oh... *oh!* That. It was just a little joke... anyone can see he's mooning over Grizz, and I figured, heh," the mischievous glint was back in Tuck's bright green eyes, "I'd mess with him a little."

Ben shared a look with Patricia.

Tuck glanced between the two of them, sensing their hostility. "Oh, come *on*, guys, you have to admit Kurt is a huge jerk, strutting around the school acting like he's all that and a bag of chips. There's other guys on the water polo team, too, and we're not *all* as tight-knit as you'd think." He smirked. "He deserved it."

"Listen, Robinson, Kurt may be a moron at times, but he's not a malicious ass," Ben began, setting his jaw. "He thinks of you as a friend. I don't know how he could actually believe in that mumbo jumbo, but he does, and he's going to be hurt that his friend tricked him. You mess with my bro? You mess with me."

Tuck looked to Patricia imploringly, but she glared back haughtily, hands on hips. He sighed. "I don't know what you want me to do about it," he grumbled, tugging helplessly at the whistle around his neck.

"How about you, oh, I don't know," Patricia lifted her eyebrows, "Apologize to Kurt and explain that there's no love potion, it was just *you* being a jerk?"

Tuck squirmed, not seeming to like that suggestion. "But…"

Patricia's phone began to chime, and she habitually slid it out of her pocket. She saw that she had several unread text messages from Grizz. Scanning the texts, she groaned. "Oh, great!"

"What?" Ben asked.

"Grizz apparently has been sending me SOS texts that I missed. She said over an hour ago that Dimitri ditched her for their Boardwalk date…"

Ben grimaced. "Yeah, not a big fan of that Dimitri."

"And then she texted me that Kurt is with her! And not planning on leaving anytime soon." Tuck snickered, but Patricia and Ben silenced him with glares. "I'm putting an end to your little scam right now, Tuck. I'm going to call her."

"Aw, man," Tuck whined, stamping his foot. "You two are no fun."

Patricia bounced on her heels as she waited for Grizz to pick up. She was not going to be happy.

Kurt walked quickly down the Wharf, looking all around for Grizz. He'd lost sight of her when they were watching the sea lions. *Where did she go?* he wondered, half-tempted to take to his skateboard to search for her.

He spotted aqua-tipped hair, and saw that Grizz was hunched over her phone, rapidly texting as she perched on a bench.

"There you are, Zelly," he said in relief. "Why did you run off?"

Grizz willed herself not to look at him. She weighed her options. She could lie and say she felt sick and wanted to go home, or she could hang out with him a while longer. It was strange, but though she couldn't stand the thought of hanging out with him another minute, there was a part of her that didn't want to leave. Maybe she was getting a sick kick out of teasing him. "Oh… I needed to make a phone call," she lied.

"Oh, okay." Kurt beamed at her, and she foolishly chose that moment to look at him. Though his hazel eyes were shielded by his sunglasses, she had a feeling they'd be sparkling, turning amber in the sunlight. "Do you want to go on any rides now?" He snapped his fingers. "Hey, I know! I won a free pass to Neptune's Kingdom for mini golf at Grad Night! Do you want to do that? You can have the pass."

Grizz blinked, surprised by his sweet offer. "You don't have to do that…"

Kurt shifted his weight, casting his eyes to the ground. "It's my way of saying thank you for spending time with me."

Grizz suddenly felt warm, and she knew it wasn't from the sun. She stared at Kurt before finding herself saying, "Okay, thanks. Sounds fun."

Kurt lifted his eyes and grinned, and Grizz rose to her feet, following him to the Boardwalk.

They walked in silence for several minutes, and Grizz found herself thinking about Dimitri. *What would our date have been like?* she wondered. *Would we be doing basically what I'm doing with...* she glanced at Kurt and suppressed a shudder, *Or would we be doing something totally different?* Based on his track record, she wondered if she'd ever have the chance to find out.

"So, Gwen," Kurt began, pivoting on his heel and walking backward as he focused on her. "What are you looking forward to most about ASU?"

It took all of her control not to curl her lip and snarl at him. *It's not his fault, it's normal to bring up college,* she told herself. "I don't know... I'm excited about living on campus, and joining some clubs... meeting new people..."

"Yeah, it will be so cool. But kind of nerve wracking as well," Kurt replied.

Grizz was surprised. "You're nervous, too?"

Kurt nodded, still walking backward. "Definitely. I've hardly ever been away from home without Ben or my parents. I mean, Ben and I aren't like this," he stuck his middle and forefingers together tightly, "but he's still my bro, you know? I'll miss him."

"I'll miss my parents, and my dogs. And all of my friends!" Grizz said in a rush.

"We'll be home for Fall Break, though," Kurt said encouragingly. "Just enough time to recharge before we have to get back to the old grind."

Grizz sighed with satisfaction. "Sounds good to me!" Her eyes locked with his, and he grinned from ear to ear. Her eyebrows lifted as she gazed past him. "Look out!"

"Wha-?" Kurt walked back-first into a bench. "Ack!" He wobbled slightly and almost dropped his skateboard.

"You should really watch where you're going," Grizz scolded with a giggle. "Are you okay?"

Kurt waved his free hand, seeming embarrassed. "I'm cool." He looked over his shoulder. "Oh, sweet, we're almost there."

Grizz noticed Kurt was quiet as they approached Neptune's Kingdom. *Probably embarrassed by his near wipeout,* she thought.

Stopping in front of the building, Kurt said, "Here, I'll give you the pass, Grizzy."

Grizz rolled her eyes, her annoyance toward him building again.

Kurt held out his skateboard to her. "Um… can you hold this for a second?"

Grizz narrowed her eyes at his skateboard. "What am I, your devoted fangirl? No way."

"Oh, okay. Um…" Kurt balanced his skateboard on his arm, unbuttoning the pocket of his cargo shorts. Opening the wallet, he frowned as he tried to wiggle the pass out with one hand.

Heaving a sigh, Grizz held out her arms.

"Oh, thanks, you're a lifesaver." Kurt handed her the board before digging through his wallet.

Grizz tossed her head to get her bangs out of her eyes, studying the skateboard, then turning to look behind her. A wicked grin graced her lips as she set the board down, stopping it in place with her plaid sneaker.

Kurt turned his head at the sound of wheels fading away. "Whoa—wait!" he called after Grizz as she rolled down the street. "Rizzo! Come back!"

"Whee!" Grizz threw her arms out as she rode away, Kurt's cries fading in the background. "I'm free as a bird!" She rode the board for several minutes, the wind through her hair just the thing she needed to clear her head.

Her reverie was broken by the sound of her ring tone. "Whoa, whoa," she muttered, the skateboard wobbling slightly as she rolled to a stop.

She dug through her bag, her hands finally closing over her phone just as the refrain of her favorite song was ending. "Argh! Wait!" She swiped just in time. "Ha, ha, got it! I almost missed you, Patricia."

"Grizz, I'm glad you picked up."

Grizz heard the urgency in her friend's tone. "What's the matter?"

"Well…" Patricia's voice was barely audible amidst the hubbub of children's squeals and people talking. "I'm not sure how to relay this to you… it's going to sound awfully stupid, but as your friend I—" She broke off, murmuring something to someone else, and Grizz thought she heard Ben's voice. "Um…"

"Spit it out, would you?" Grizz demanded.

"So, you know how Kurt likes you? Well, he may be acting extra weird recently because Tuck found out that Kurt likes you, too, and decided to play a trick on him," Patricia babbled.

Grizz lifted her brows. "Okay…"

"And he sold him a love potion and Kurt is convinced that if he gives you some in like, your soda or something, that you'll fall head over heels in love with him," she finished in a rush.

Grizz pulled the phone away from her ear for a second, feeling dumbfounded by Patricia's tale. "What?"

"I know, it's really stupid. I'm just telling you this to put an end to Tuck's joke," she said so fiercely that Grizz wondered if Tuck was there with her. "Ben is going to tell Kurt about the prank. I can't believe he fell for it, but..."

The wheels in Grizz's head began to turn as she thought about the sheer stupidity of it all. *He wanted to make me fall in love with him with a potion, eh? Well, be careful what you wish for, little Kirk...*

"Kurt's with you, right?" When Grizz didn't answer, Patricia repeated, "Right?"

"Oh. Um, yeah," Grizz replied, glancing back to where she'd left him.

"I'll have Ben call him," Patricia said.

"No!" Grizz cried out. "Don't."

"Why not?" Patricia asked in surprise.

"Do not say anything to Kurt about this," Grizz told her.

"But..." Patricia's voice was skeptical.

"I'll take care of it," Grizz insisted. "Gotta go." She hung up to the sound of Patricia's protests.

Putting the skateboard under her arm, Grizz jogged to the nearby restroom. She dug through her purse and pulled out a few things, looking at herself critically in the mirror before she brushed her hair. When she was satisfied, she put on a fresh coat of lipstick, kissing the air dramatically. "Why yes, you *femme fatale*," she said to her reflection, "You'll pull this off perfectly."

She stepped out onto the Boardwalk once more, tossing her hair over her shoulder as she strolled back to Neptune's Kingdom. Puzzled, she craned her neck to search for Kurt when she didn't see him where he'd been standing just a few minutes before.

"Rizzy!"

Grizz smiled to herself. *It's show time.* She turned slowly to look at him, widening her eyes dramatically.

"Took a ride down the Boardwalk, huh?" Kurt asked with a chuckle. "It's really a great day for it."

Grizz staggered back, putting a hand to her chest. "I may need to sit down for a second," she said, her voice coming out light and breathy.

"Whoa, did you overdo it?" Kurt asked in concern, reaching out to steady her. "Here, let's get you out of the sun…"

Grizz pressed her lips together in frustration. *Now's not the time to get all sweet and concerned on me!* "No, no," she said, looking up into his eyes. "It's just that never in my life have I beheld such manliness!"

Kurt furrowed his brow, looking over his shoulder. *Wait—could she mean me?*

She latched onto his muscular arm, ignoring the little thrill it sent through her. "Do you work out every morning to be this hot, or is it a natural gift?" She was determined to keep a straight face, even though the words made her want to gag.

Taking in her shining eyes and pouting lips, Kurt glanced down at where she gripped his arm and felt himself flush. "Um… are you okay, Zel?"

Grizz tossed her head and batted her eyelashes, trying to imitate all of the girls she'd seen flirt with him. "Of course I'm okay, silly! I'm just blown away by your studliness, that's all!"

Kurt stared at her, dumbfounded. *What the hell? Did…* He grew excited as a thought came to him, *Did the potion work?* He couldn't control the grin that was spreading across his face. *Tuck was right—it builds up in her system slowly.* He croaked in a squeaky voice, "So..." he paused and cleared his throat. "So, do you still want to play miniature golf, or...?"

Grizz giggled exaggeratedly. "What-ev-er *you* want to do, stud muffin!" She found herself chanting internally, *The show must go on!*

Kurt ducked his head. "Okay, then let's go! Oh, I can take my skateboard now," he said, holding his free hand out.

Grizz smiled sweetly and handed him his skateboard, batting her eyelashes again. She figured she looked pretty stupid, but Kurt was eating it up.

They walked arm in arm to Neptune's Kingdom, and Grizz finally let go of his arm to allow him to go to the counter. "Two please," Kurt told the man at the register, handing him cash and the coupon.

After they got their drivers and balls, Grizz followed Kurt to the first hole. "I'm not sure if I can do this..." she said in mock-shyness.

"You've never been mini-golfing before?" Kurt asked in surprise.

In reality, Grizz had played miniature golf more times than she could count, and she was pretty good at it. Yet she couldn't resist the urge to play dumb and mess with him some more. "We-ell, I *have*, but it's been so long I don't remember."

"There's nothing to it!" Kurt said encouragingly, resting his club over his shoulder.

"Just to be sure," Grizz hummed, shifting her weight like she'd seen Sophie do at lunch, "Why don't you go first?"

"Sure," Kurt agreed with a shrug. Setting his red ball on the ground, he took aim and knocked it across the small patch, causing it to land just a few feet from the hole.

"Oh, Kurt," she cooed, flipping her hair over her shoulder and batting her eyelashes. "You're so strong!"

Kurt chuckled awkwardly. "Not really… I'm sure you can hit it just as far."

Grizz was sure she could, too, but hadn't expected him to admit it. "Oh my, no," she murmured, impressing herself with the fact that she wasn't laughing, "I could never hit this little old ball all the way over there! I mean, how do you even *hold* this here thing?"

"Is something wrong, Zel?" Kurt asked with his eyebrows pinched together. Her voice suddenly sounded Southern.

Grizz shook her head. "How do you hold it?"

Kurt felt his heart begin to speed up. "Well, um…" He took a step closer to her, awkwardly holding out his hands. "You—you kind of…"

Grizz cocked her head his way, trying to look doe-eyed and coy. "Hm?" When Kurt didn't move, she stepped backwards so that she was in his arms. Ignoring her racing pulse, she said, "I what?"

Kurt swallowed hard, reaching for her hands. "First of all, you hold it like this…" He turned the club right side up, furrowing his brow in confusion. *Did the love potion affect her brain?* he worried. *She's usually not mixed up like this. Is that a side effect?*

When he didn't continue with the lesson, Grizz elbowed him a little too roughly.

"Ow!" he exclaimed.

"Oh, sorry, cutie," Grizz cooed. "You were saying?"

Blinking rapidly, Kurt said, "Stand like this." He turned her gently so that her left side was facing the hole. Then he swung her hands in his backward. "Just hold it like this, aim for the ball, and swing." He chuckled. "You can do it easily."

Grizz pretended to concentrate hard for a moment, before smiling brightly. "I'll try it."

She swung wildly, and Kurt had to tighten his grip. "Whoa, whoa! Just use a little of that strength; it goes a long way. If you hit it with that much force, it's going to go wild and knock someone out."

Grizz bit her lip and tittered like a chipmunk. "You're so right. Better guide me, just to be sure."

Flushing, Kurt nodded. "Okay, ready?"

Grizz swung her club exactly as she would have done if Kurt hadn't been holding onto her, trying not to think about how his touch made her feel warm all over. Just as her club was about to make contact with the ball, Grizz felt someone's eyes on her. Looking up, she saw Stacey standing across the way, jaw dropped as she stared at them.

Grizz leapt in surprise, swinging a lot harder than she meant to. She sent the ball flying through the air. It hit an animitronic pirate in the face.

"Gnarly," Kurt commented with a grin.

Grizz quickly stepped away from him, hurrying across the bridge. "I'll get it!"

"Hi, Grizz," Stacey greeted her with a smile.

"Hi, Grizz," Stacey's little sister, Jamie, said shyly.

"Hi girls," Grizz said hurriedly, glancing over her shoulder at Kurt, who thankfully wasn't looking their way.

"Looks like you're having a fun date," Stacey commented, wiggling her eyebrows.

"I can explain," Grizz whispered desperately.

"Don't bother!" Stacey said knowingly. "I saw the way you two were acting at Grad Night."

Cheeks flaming, Grizz knew it would do no good to argue right then. "I've got to grab my renegade ball." She pushed past them, ignoring Stacey's stares.

Crouching to collect her green golf ball, Grizz took a deep breath. *Don't act too weird,* she scolded herself, *Or this prank won't last much longer.* Turning to walk back to Kurt, she groaned when she saw Stacey was rabidly texting someone while Jamie putted.

She could only guess what it was about.

Chapter Sixteen ♡

THE FOLLOWING MORNING, PATRICIA KNOCKED ON THE Minolas' front door. Ben opened the door, his lips drawn together in a frown.

"Hi," Patricia greeted him, not cracking a smile. "I have a sneaking suspicion why you wanted to see me so early…"

"Kurt came back… very happy last night," Ben told her, his eyebrows pinched together.

Grumbling, Patricia passed Ben into the Minolas' house, then followed him down the hall and up the stairs.

Ben beckoned her into his bedroom, and she slid her purse off her shoulder, sinking in the desk chair. She stared absentmindedly at the opposite wall, focusing on a video game poster with dragons on it.

"Have you talked to Grizz?" Ben asked after a long moment.

Patricia sighed, pulling out her cell phone. "Stacey texted me yesterday that Kurt and Grizz were on a 'date' at Buccaneer Bay," she began, making quotation marks with her fingers. "At first I assumed Stacey had it wrong, because of course I knew that Grizz was with Kurt at the Boardwalk, but it wasn't a date. I told her as much. But then Stacey sent me *this*," Patricia tapped on her phone, holding it up for Ben to see.

Ben's eyes bugged out at the picture of Kurt—looking embarrassed yet pleased—with his arms around a smiling Grizz. "What the actual—"

"So then I remembered how Grizz said *she* would take care of the love potion," Patricia went on, sliding her phone back in her purse. "I sent her about a million texts until she answered a couple of hours later."

"I can't believe she spent that much time with him, even for a joke," Ben said with a frown.

"I know," Patricia exhaled. "When she finally replied, she just said that she was handling it, and was going to teach him a lesson he won't forget." Her shoulders slumped. "She didn't answer the phone when I tried calling her."

Ben crossed his arms over his chest. "We should tell Kurt."

"I..." Patricia paused, her long hair cascading over her shoulders as she put her head in her hands. "I don't know. Grizz would be so mad if I went behind her back."

Ben sighed. "But if Kurt thinks she genuinely has feelings for him..."

"I know, Ben, but she's my best friend!" Patricia cried out, feeling on the verge of tears. "And she's been acting *so* touchy about Kurt."

Ben nodded, crouching in front of her. "It sucks being caught in the middle, huh?" he asked quietly.

Patricia sniffled, tucking her hair behind her ears. "Between a brother and a bestie," she quipped. Ben reached for her hand, and she went on, "I just worry that she'll get so mad that she won't speak to me. And when we go off to college, it really *will* be friendship over."

Ben thought for a long moment, then replied, "Yeah, in the end, I think you're right. Tuck shouldn't have sold him that potion, Kurt shouldn't try to control her feelings, and Grizz shouldn't pretend she likes him. We've got to let them sort it out for themselves." Seeing Patricia's expression, he squeezed her hand. "Cheer up!" He gave her a quick kiss on the lips.

She blushed. "Okay. I'll try not to dwell on it."

"But there is something that I *would* like to do," Ben continued, rising to his feet.

Patricia stood as well. "Hm?"

Ben held up a hand, striding to the door and poking his head out. He saw the door to Kurt's bedroom was wide open, and heard the shower running in the bathroom. He swiftly beckoned to Patricia. "Follow me. I want to analyze that love potion," he told her quietly. "I don't trust Tuck, who knows what kind of crap is in that thing?"

"Good idea," Patricia said, following him across the hall into Kurt's bedroom.

When she stepped through the doorway, she gazed around at the ocean blue walls. Like Ben, Kurt had a few posters up, but he also had a wooden surfboard that looked handmade hanging over his bed, plus a Vista High pennant, framed photos of the ocean, and a few carved signs that had sayings like, "If you need me, I'll be at the beach."

"Surfer dude central," she whispered under her breath.

Ben laughed. "Yep. Now, if I were a love potion, where would I be…" Ben muttered to himself, lifting one of Kurt's sweatshirts off of the floor.

"In a safe place... unless he's been keeping it on him," Patricia mused.

Ben rummaged through the pockets of Kurt's beloved Santa Cruz sweatshirt. "Not here..."

She stepped over to the unmade bed where a very content-looking Marmalade was curled. "Oh, hi sweetie," Patricia whispered to the cat. "Do you know where that stinky love potion is?" Marmalade opened her blue eyes and stared at Patricia unblinkingly.

Patricia laughed and scratched her behind the ears. "You're no help."

Ben began rooting through Kurt's closet, and Patricia walked over to his desk, which housed his laptop, oversized headphones, some papers, and a few framed photos. Scanning the surface, she paused when she saw that he'd framed the cast photo they'd taken the night of the theater festival. Patricia and Grizz stood in the center of the picture, flanked by Peter, Phillip, Nicole, and Natalia. Kurt, to Grizz's annoyance, had been sort of squished between her and Natalia. She took in Kurt's smiling face in the small photo and shook her head. Lifting her eyes, she saw that the pamphlet from Grad Night was propped against the frames, as if also on display.

She abandoned the desk to wander again, pausing to sort through the CDs tossed on top of his stereo. She crouched to see if the potion was stashed on any of the shelves, noticing that the stereo stand was handmade as well, a chain of seashells dangling from one of the racks.

"Ah-ha!" Ben lifted the bottle triumphantly out of a small wooden box on one of Kurt's bookcases.

Patricia came over to inspect the box, which was plain wood with

"VHWP" engraved on the top. "I'm noticing a theme in this room," she joked. "Let me guess—handmade?"

Ben chuckled, setting the box back on Kurt's shelf. "He made it a couple of years ago for his keys, because he kept misplacing them. You know his obsession with his car."

"Don't you mean Kahuna?" Patricia teased.

Ben squinted at the purple liquid. "I'm going to the lab to analyze this," he muttered, heading to the doorway. He turned to Patricia, eyebrows lifted expectantly. "Well, little Wahine? You coming?"

"You dork," Patricia laughed, darting over the threshold and hurrying down the stairs after him.

Ben squinted at the test tube, shaking the small amount of potion he'd poured into it.

Patricia hunched over the counter of the Vista High chemistry lab, studying the label on the potion bottle. "Check this out," she said with a scoff. "'Love Potion Number 9: Guaranteed to Wow the Person of Your Dreams.'" She squinted to read the fine print at the bottom of the label. "'From the Dreams and Things Company. Patent pending.'" She turned to Ben. "You know, you have to hand it to Tuck. He sure put a lot of thought into this." She sighed. "And poor Kurt fell for it."

Slipping his goggles over his eyes, Ben began collecting his equipment. "I wonder just how long he had this in the works," Ben muttered. "Oh, put on these goggles."

Patricia looked at the goggles he held out to her skeptically. "Seriously?"

Ben put on a severe expression. "Mr. Johnson would flip his lid if he found us breaking the safety goggles rule!"

"Even though we no longer go here?" Patricia huffed, taking the goggles from him. "What would he do? Arrest us?"

"You're speaking of my employer," Ben replied, collecting beakers and droppers. "It's very nice of him to let me use the lab without supervision."

"It doesn't hurt that you were one of his best students," Patricia teased, coming to stand by him in front of the counter.

"I don't want your eyes getting splashed with chemicals," Ben insisted, pausing in his work expectantly.

Patricia gave in. "All right, all right." She slid the goggles over her head. "But was the lab coat really necessary?" she asked skeptically, eying the long white coat he wore.

Ben lifted his chin with an air of authority. "I am conducting an important experiment in the interest of science."

Patricia rolled her eyes, perching on a lab stool.

"Anyway, like I was saying, Tuck must have been planning to spring this on Kurt," Ben continued.

"I wonder how he knew Kurt liked Grizz?" Patricia wondered.

"Don't put anything past Robinson," Ben muttered as he set up the tools for the experiment. "Haven't you ever noticed?" He paused. "He's always listening, always watching."

"Yeah, especially when he wants to troll someone," Patricia said with a shudder. "I mean, Kurt shouldn't have taken the love potion anyway, even if he's stupid enough to believe in such things," she added wryly. "Trying to make Grizz like him is a little..."

"Pretend you've got Kurt's pea brain, Patricia," Ben replied as he squinted at the measurements.

Sticking out her tongue, Patricia hissed, "Don't even suggest such a horror!"

Chuckling, Ben went on, "He thinks it's magic. He's not applying logic or conscience to it. Tuck probably sold it to him pretty good."

"It's kind of weird to think that Kurt likes Grizz so much..." Patricia mused, running her fingers absentmindedly over one of the empty beakers.

"Yeah," Ben agreed as he took notes on a pad of paper. "I've never seen him so depressed over a girl before like he was the other day... except when he liked you."

Patricia flushed, not wanting to be reminded of those weeks when she was the object of Kurt's affections. "So, he's never really liked a girl that seriously before?"

Ben shook his head as he took a dropper out. Patricia looked at all of the equipment and furrowed her brow, not sure what he was doing, but glad he seemed to know. "Hm. Grizz told me he said that it 'was her all along' ...Is it wrong that I feel relieved he stopped liking me?"

Ben paused, lifting his eyes to glance at her. "I don't think anyone is more relieved than I am."

Patricia lifted her eyebrows dubiously, feeling her heartbeat speed up. "Don't tell me you seriously worried that I'd start liking Kurt?"

"I don't know, you were awfully close during the theater festival..." Ben mumbled with a flush, dropping his eyes back to the counter.

Patricia stared at him, realizing he was serious. "You thought I liked Kurt?" She burst into giggles.

Ben crossed his arms and looked away, pretending to be indignant. "You two were always together, late into the night, alone in his workshop."

"Oh, so that's why you insisted on staying during every rehearsal!" Patricia teased. She'd secretly hoped it was to spend more time with her, but she never realized that Ben had been jealous of Kurt.

"If I hadn't asked you out when I did, it may have been too late!" Ben said earnestly.

"Oh, whatever!" Patricia snorted. "I liked *you*, you dork! I wasn't about to go out with your brother."

Ben couldn't help but smile at that, but went on, "I thought all girls were irresistible to his wiles…"

"If that were true, Kurt wouldn't feel the need to rely on this potion, would he? Besides," she continued, wiggling her eyebrows, "just because you two are twins doesn't mean he's interchangeable for you."

Ben grinned, and the two stared at each other for a moment before he broke her gaze. "Um…" he cleared his throat, focusing on the equipment, "let me just finish this up…"

Patricia laughed, pulling out her phone while he worked. After a few minutes of debating mentally, she finally texted Grizz, *"Let's have a girl's night this week. Pizza and a movie?"*

She swung her legs impatiently against the bars of the stool as she waited for her reply. She vaguely wondered if Grizz was at work, or if she would just avoid her from now on.

Her phone dinged. She read the text from Grizz and sighed with relief. *"Sure! Want to do Friday?"*

Patricia grinned and replied that Friday was perfect. She locked her phone and smiled. At least Grizz didn't seem mad.

"Eureka!" Ben cried at that moment, lifting his hands in the air.

"You've made a new discovery?" Patricia asked, pushing herself off of the stool.

"No. I'm just done," Ben replied with a grin. Lifting his notepad, he read, "It's composed of water, sugar, vanilla syrup, some club soda, which explains the slight fizz..." He chuckled. "Oh, and get this—I figured out the secret ingredient. Passion fruit juice."

Patricia giggled. "Well of course, it's a love potion!"

"And finally, food coloring," Ben finished, setting the pad down with a sigh. "So, we've learned that if nothing else, Tuck can always go into the soda business."

"You probably could have figured that out from tasting it," Patricia said with an eyeroll. "Was it really necessary to come to the lab and do all of this?"

"It was scientific inquiry," Ben insisted.

"Are you sure it wasn't just so you could show off your mad science skills in front of me?" Patricia asked, taking a step closer to him.

"Did it impress you?" Ben asked hopefully, not denying it.

Patricia tilted her head, acting like she was thinking hard about it. She put her thumb and forefinger together. "Just this much..."

"Good." Coming closer to her, Ben asked in a low tone, "After all, weren't you saying something about me being the 'better' twin? I thought that meant you were after me for my brains." When she shook her head, Ben widened his eyes and laughed incredulously.

"Being better in *both* the brains and looks department in your girlfriend's opinion can't be something to complain about," Patricia told him, eyes dancing mischievously.

Ben wrapped his arms around her and leaned down. Patricia's eyes began to close just as she felt a jolt when their goggles knocked together.

Ben pulled back, blinking in surprise.

Patricia giggled, taking her goggles off and setting them on the counter. She reached up to slide Ben's pair from his head, before tugging on the front of his lab coat to draw him in for a long kiss.

Chapter Seventeen ♡

GRIZZ STIFLED A YAWN AS SHE WALKED TOWARD THE MERRY Mule on Monday, hoping that she had enough time to make herself a mocha before the doors opened.

She blinked when she caught a flash of blue to the side of the building. *No, no!* Her eyes widened, focusing on Kurt's Jeep Wrangler in the parking lot. *I didn't think this through. Did not think this through.* Her stomach twisted when she remembered how Stacey saw them at Buccaneer Bay. Pretending to be in love with Kurt was fine when there were no witnesses, but what would her coworkers think?

She paused. *I wouldn't mind if that jerk Dimitri saw us together, though.*

This thought gave her a burst of courage, and she steeled herself before walking through the french doors.

"Hi, Grizz!" Hayley greeted her with a smile, tying on her apron as she approached.

Grizz forced her lips upward as she looked past Hayley. "Hey, girl." Still no sign of Kurt. *Act normal.* This time she genuinely smiled and focused on Hayley. "How was your weekend?"

"It was awesome!" Hayley told her excitedly. "I went to the Marine Discovery Center on Saturday."

"That's cool," Grizz replied.

"Yeah, it was so much fun! Plus the weather was *gorgeous* that day," Hayley enthused. "What did you do?"

The memory of her impromptu "date" with Kurt hung around her like a stifling cloak. She tugged self-consciously on the end of her aqua-tipped ponytail. "Oh, just went to the Boardwalk."

Hayley smiled and walked to the counter. "Cool!"

Grizz blew her bangs off of her forehead with a frustrated huff, tiptoeing to the break room. She could do this—she could totally do this. *Who cares what Hayley or anyone else thinks? I'm not that close with them, anyway.*

When she walked through the doorway, she frowned when she didn't see Kurt. *He's got to be around here somewhere…*

"Hey, Zel."

Jumping slightly, she turned to see Kurt emerge from behind a tall shelving unit, wearing the body suit of Flute the mule.

"Kurt," her voice came out unintentionally breathy due to him startling her, but it worked in her favor. She thrust out her hip and tossed back her hair. "Ha, ha. I didn't see you."

Kurt pulled on his furry gloves, not looking her in the eye. "How was the rest of your weekend?"

Grizz blinked. Was he being shy? Just that fact alone was enough to boost her confidence. *The show must go on.* "It was great!" she said with an overzealous grin. "I just rested and caught up on some crafting."

Daring to look up, Kurt asked with a small smile, "What are you working on?"

Grizz felt her breath hitch when their gazes locked. "Um, I'm making Patricia a flip book..." she replied, her voice coming out much softer than she'd meant it to.

"One of those books where when you flip the page, there's a picture of a mouse running or something?" Kurt asked eagerly. "I didn't know you could draw!"

Grizz waved her hands. "I can't. Well, I mean, I do, a little, but..." she paused and laughed. "It's a different kind of 'flip book.' It's a little book I made out of cardboard and scrapbooking paper. Then you make pages out of more paper, but they flip in different directions—"

"Oh, kind of like a pop-up book?" Kurt leaned against the shelving unit, letting the hand that held his mule head dangle at his side.

Grizz nodded, forgetting to act crazy about him for a moment. "Yes! And then you can put all sorts of pockets and little notes that fold out and stuff. I'm making it as a memory book for our senior year." She ticked off her fingers. "Photos, tickets, fliers from the theater festival, favors from Homecoming, that sort of thing."

Kurt straightened, taking a step closer to her. "Wow, that sounds really cool! Can I see it when it's done?"

Grizz faltered, surprised he seemed genuinely interested. "Sure. But keep it a secret from Patricia, okay?"

Kurt nodded, pulling his fingers across his mouth as if he was zipping them. "Got it."

Remembering the love potion, Grizz reached out for his arm. Though it was covered in brown fur, she still felt heat beneath her fingertips. "Thanks, cutie," she said with a giggle.

The tips of Kurt's ears turned pink as he stared down at the hand on his arm. "Um, Zella…"

Grizz started when she heard someone clear their throat loudly. Turning, she saw Obediah standing in the doorway, holding a large cup of yogurt.

He peered suspiciously at the pair. "Hello, Kurt. Grizz," he said as he spooned his yogurt, gray eyes riveted on her.

"Oh, hello, sir," she stammered, withdrawing her hand and stepping away from Kurt.

"Shouldn't you two be running along to start your shifts?" Obediah asked.

Realizing she hadn't clocked in, Grizz nodded hurriedly. "Right."

"Sure thing, boss!" Kurt said, casting a look at Grizz before he donned his mule head.

Grizz signed in on her time card, yanking her apron on over her head. *Thank goodness he's gone,* she thought with a sigh.

"Hi, sorry, sorry," Frank mumbled as he skidded to a halt in the break room.

Obediah looked at the clock, then back to Frank. "You're just in time."

Frank breathed a sigh of relief, hurrying over to sign in. "Hey, Grizz!"

"You'd better be careful, or Obe will give you the heave-ho," Grizz whispered when she saw their boss disappear into the cafe.

Frank stifled a yawn, pinning his name tag on as they walked to the front counter. "I know. I hate getting up early."

As they set to work, Grizz found herself looking out the front window for Kurt. He danced on the sidewalk, waving a poster board vigorously. He didn't seem to have many takers at the moment, but that didn't faze him.

"Grizz?" Hayley asked expectantly. "The machiatto?"

Snapping back to attention, Grizz picked up the cup Hayley had set on the bar for her. "Right." *This is perfect,* she thought as she made the espresso shot. *I can act lovey-dovey with him behind the scenes, and no one will notice! I won't have to deal with him for awhile anyway.*

When the opening rush was over, Grizz wandered to the seating areas, sweeping up crumbs and wiping down tables. She stepped out to the patio, crouching to lift wadded napkins that had missed the trash bin.

"Brr." She rubbed her arms as the wind picked up. *I better go put on my sweatshirt,* she thought, glancing at the gray sky.

Kurt was dancing a few feet away from her, pulling a flier out of the pocket of his apron to hand to a woman walking by with her children. The little girl giggled and reached out to him, and Kurt crouched to pat her on the head. Grizz found herself smiling as she watched them. The little boy, whom Grizz guessed was probably three, hid behind his mother's legs. When Kurt waved and said hi to him, his face crumpled, and he burst into tears.

"I'm so sorry," the woman said, scooping the boy into her arms.

"It's okay, sorry I scared him!" Kurt said, waving good-bye to the little girl as she walked off with her mom and brother. He sighed. "Oops."

Grizz walked over to him, patting him on the shoulder. "Don't feel too bad. When they're that small they always run in terror from people in animal costumes. When I went to Disneyland when I was four, apparently I cried anytime a character waved to me."

Kurt cocked his head in sympathy, the effect hilarious with his costume. "Aw, poor kiddies. I get it, though."

Grizz folded her arms across her chest, rocking back and forth on her heels. "Not too cold out here for you?"

"No. This suit keeps me toasty. When the weather is cooler it's actually a relief. But you should go in, Zelly," he added, nodding toward the french doors. "You're chilly."

Grizz smiled at his sweetness, then caught herself. "You're right, I shouldn't keep talking while we're supposed to be working," she told him in a stage whisper.

Kurt nodded, and though she couldn't see his face, she was sure he was blushing. *Sucker.* "I'll leave you to it, Flute!" She waved to him with a forced giggle, and went to collect the dustpan and hand broom.

"Hi, what can I get started for you?" Hayley asked when a woman came to the counter later that day.

"A mocha please, extra hot," the woman replied, brushing raindrops off of her shoulders. "The sky finally gave way."

Grizz paused in making a cappuccino, looking out the windows. It wasn't just raining, it was pouring raindrops practically the size of golf balls. Yet Kurt still danced on, his poster board becoming soggy in the downpour.

Grizz hurriedly called out the drink and rushed to the french doors. "Flute!" When he didn't react, she sighed and shouted, "Kurt! Get in here!"

Kurt turned and shrugged his sodden shoulders. "The show must go on!" he called back.

Grizz rolled her eyes.

Obediah appeared at Grizz's side, hurrying out to the covered patio. "Kurt! Get inside quickly!" Thankfully Kurt listened to Obediah, jogging to the shelter of the patio.

Grizz joined them, pulling her sweatshirt tighter about her body as she frowned at the rainstorm. The wind was hurling the rain every which way, the cobblestones of the patio already damp.

"I could keep dancing, boss," Kurt said, pulling the sopping mule head off.

Obediah shook his head. "That's admirable of you, Kurt, but not only is your costume and the boom box going to get ruined, but you can't hand out fliers when they're soaked through."

Kurt lifted a piece of paper, now see-through and soggy, the ink running. "I see what you mean."

Grizz wrinkled her nose. "And no offense, but you're starting to smell like wet dog."

Kurt laughed. "Don't you mean, 'wet mule,' Gwen?"

Grizz shook her head. "Silly."

Obediah lifted his precious boom box off of the table, drying it with a rag. "Go get changed, Kurt."

"I'll make you a Mexican mocha to warm you up," Grizz told him, taking in his soaked appearance. She turned to go back into the shop, then stopped short. *Why did I just do that? Oh, that's right, the love potion. I guess I'm getting the hang of fawning over Kurt.* She stuck her tongue out at the thought. *Ick.* Thankfully, her back was to Kurt, so he didn't see it.

Kurt grinned as he followed her inside. "Wow, thanks!"

Frank peeked from around the bar as the trio approached. "I'll go get the mop," he said when he noticed the giant, wet footprints Kurt was leaving in his wake.

Obediah sighed, staring at the downpour through the windows. "I'll lower the umbrellas. Hayley, could you close the side doors, and those windows, please?"

"Sure thing," Hayley said as she hurried to the far side of the shop.

Once the doors and windows had been closed and the water mopped up, Frank and Grizz set to making drinks again.

Grizz was just shaking cinnamon atop the whipped cream of a drink when Kurt emerged from the back room, once again in his street clothes. "Whew, it's good to be free," he exclaimed, stretching his arms.

Grizz set the mug on the counter and gestured to him. "Here you are, Flute. A Mexican mocha."

Kurt lifted the mug. "Wow, Zelly, it's bodacious!" he exclaimed, admiring the cinnamon sprinkled on the generous amount of whipped cream.

Grizz felt her face scrunch as she held in her snicker as best she could. "Oh, you're sweet," she said coyly. "Drink it up before the whipped cream melts."

Frank coughed loudly, eyes wide as saucers as he watched them.

Grizz reddened when she realized she had just flirted with Kurt in front of an audience. She dropped her gaze to focus on making the next drink.

Obediah came back into the cafe, stomping his feet on the mat. "I don't want to ruin Frank's mopping," he said with a smile.

Frank chuckled. "Thank you, sir!"

"Hey, Obe, maybe we could get lollipops or something for the kids," Kurt said, turning to face his boss.

Obediah looked at him curiously.

"Well, this little kid cried when he saw me. Maybe a lollipop would have made him feel better. And since I'm working with the Merry Mule, parents wouldn't be creeped out, 'cuz it's not like taking candy from strangers or whatever."

Obediah lifted his brows, and Grizz could see that he was impressed by Kurt's suggestion. She hated to admit it, but so was she. "That's a good idea, Kurt," he said finally. "I'll make sure to have some in stock next time you come in. Since you can't be Flute today, you can stay by the doors and hand coupons to customers who come in, and help make coffee when the others get backed up."

Kurt stood rigidly straight and saluted him. "Aye, aye, Captain!" He hurried to the back room.

Grizz sighed with relief. *Maybe for the most part he'll be over there, and I'll be over here.*

The cafe soon became crowded as people who'd been shopping nearby sought refuge in the warm, dry cafe. To her annoyance, Kurt had to come prepare drinks so that they could keep up with the rush.

Kurt stopped by Grizz's elbow at the espresso machine as she pulled a shot. "So, do you need a ride home later, Rizzy?"

Grizz felt goosebumps pop up on her skin when she thought of being alone with Kurt, yet again.

Frank paused in his work, turning to face them with interest.

Shooting Frank a quick look, she began, "Oh, you don't have to do that!"

Kurt scratched the back of his neck, causing his bicep to bulge slightly. Grizz dropped her eyes to the counter. "I don't mind! It will save your parents a trip."

Got to keep up the act, Grizz chanted to herself. Though she could feel Frank's eyes boring into her, she shrugged and said, "If it's no trouble, then that would be awesome."

Kurt grinned. "Sweet."

Grizz lifted her eyes only to find herself rooted in place by Kurt's stare. Though she tried, she couldn't find the will to tear her gaze from his.

She jumped when Frank cleared his throat, looking at him with alarm. "I need to make a shot," he explained, holding up the coffee he was making.

"Oh, sure thing," Kurt stepped away from Grizz to give Frank room, and Grizz felt her muscles relax. She tried to focus on finishing the white mocha she was making, but she felt an odd surge of adrenaline that made her want to dart through the doors and run a marathon.

"Blue straws for the mocha with no whipped cream," Kurt muttered under his breath, pulling one skinny straw from the large mug on the counter. "Where's another one?" His fingers maneuvered through the cluster of straws. "Ah-ha! And a pink straw for the strawberry smoothie. Red straws for the cinnamon latte..."

Grizz paused in her work to stare at him. "Um, what are you doing?"

"This lady ordered four coffees," Kurt explained as he hunted for another red straw. "And I'm color-coordinating the straws so that she can tell which is which."

"She *could* just read the sides," Grizz pointed out.

"The hot drinks have sleeves! They cover the order. Besides, have you ever tried to see what was written on the side and tipped it?" Kurt mimed spilling coffee. "It offsets the balance."

Grizz put her hand over her mouth to cover the giggle that escaped. "Very smart," she choked out in a breathy voice.

Kurt smiled. "Thanks!"

Grizz felt a little guilty that her praise was in actuality sarcasm, but she tried not to dwell on it.

"Molly mocha, John strawberry smoothie, Molly Irish latte, and a Foal cinnamon latte!" Kurt called out.

The woman approached the counter, smiling warmly at him. "Thank you!"

"Oh, would you like a drink carrier, ma'am?" Kurt asked, realizing the woman was unaccompanied.

"I'll grab it," Grizz told him, crouching to retrieve one from beneath the counter.

"Thanks, Zel!" Kurt placed the four drinks into the carrier.

"Oh, thank you so much!" the woman said, shouldering her purse as she reached for the carrier.

"Kurt color coordinated the straws, so you can tell which drink is which," Grizz added.

"Red for the cinnamon latte, green for the Irish, and blue for the mocha," Kurt listed with a nod.

The woman smiled. "Thank you very much, young man. Have a wonderful day, you two," she said, passing her hand over the tip jar and dropping two dollar bills inside it.

Grizz lifted her eyebrows at Kurt after the woman had left. "Hey, what do you know? Your obsessive colored straw labeling paid off!"

Kurt beamed with pride. "I'll say!" He lifted the tip jar and jangled the money inside, causing the drawing of Flute on the glass to look like he was dancing.

≈

The rain pelted the windshield of Kurt's Islander, the wipers barely fast enough to make the road visible.

Kurt leaned forward over the steering wheel. "It's gnarly out here!"

Grizz nodded, staring at the raindrops collecting on her window. "I'm glad I didn't ride my bike," she said frankly, clucking her tongue.

"Me, too," Kurt agreed.

Grizz smiled at that, watching him as he furrowed his brow, focused on the road through the small clear patch on the windshield. After a long moment, she caught herself. "I like the rain, though," she commented.

"Y'know, I do, too," Kurt said, adjusting the speed of the wipers when the downpour lessened slightly. "Blue skies are great, but rain makes everything so…"

"Fresh and alive," Grizz finished for him. "Have you ever noticed that colors seem brighter during a rainstorm?"

"Yeah!" Kurt grinned. "And the ocean is so sick when it's stormy. It's awesome to be out there."

"You don't try to surf in it ever, do you?" Grizz asked in alarm.

Kurt shook his head. "Nah, man, I'm not bonkers."

Grizz leaned back in her seat. "Oh, that's good." *Wait—why do I feel relieved? I don't care if he does moronic crap!*

"Speaking of surfing," Kurt began, glancing at Grizz for a moment before returning his attention to the road, "Would you like to hit the beach again soon?" He held his breath, hoping she wouldn't turn him down.

That's right, I haven't gone for awhile… not since Dimitri wanted to go to lunch. Remembering how Dimitri stood her up not once, but twice, made her bristle. *Jerk.* She noticed that Kurt kept stealing glances at her, and she found herself saying, "Sure."

Kurt exhaled, a grin replacing his pensive expression. "Really? Awesome. I checked my surfing app, and there should be primo weather this Friday."

"That'll be fun!" Grizz said, accompanying it with a giggle.

Kurt prattled on in excitement, and Grizz felt a sick feeling in the pit of her stomach. Turning her gaze from him, she leaned her head against the window, staring at her reflection. *What am I getting myself into?* she thought, the raindrops making her look more dismal than she already felt.

Chapter Eighteen ♡

"SHOULD I DO PURPLE, PINK, OR GREEN?" GRIZZ MURMURED that Friday evening, rooting through her stash of nail polish.

"You could do blue. It would match your hair," Patricia pointed out, setting a towel down on her bedroom carpet. She eyed her toes. "I don't relish prepping you," she grumbled.

"Nah, that's what I already have on. See?" Grizz held her foot aloft and wiggled her toes.

"Oh, that's pretty," Patricia commented, taking a sip of soda.

Grizz frowned at the chipped polish, remembering how earlier that day, when taking off her flip flops to join Kurt in the water, a huge chunk of polish had peeled off of her big toe. She grunted.

"You should make a rainbow then," Patricia decided. "Your toes can look like Skittles."

"Very well," Grizz agreed, pulling her cell phone from her purse.

"But first, we need some music! Maestro, do the honors?"

Patricia reached for Grizz's phone, crawling towards the nightstand where she kept her speakers. "Any requests?"

Grizz shook the bottle of hot pink polish, lifting her eyebrows. "Girl, you know I have impeccable taste in music. Put it on shuffle!"

Laughing, Patricia obeyed, bobbing her head to the music as she got to work painting her toenails.

When Grizz was done with her left foot, she leaned back and admired it. "You, my little tootsie, are gorgeous."

Patricia frowned when the music went silent for a moment. "You have a text or something," she said, moving to retrieve it.

Grizz nodded, eyes focusing on the lighted screen of her cell phone. She felt seized with panic when she read who the text was from. "I've got it!" she cried, snatching the phone out of Patricia's reach with lightning speed.

Patricia shrugged, returning to her polish. "Cool."

Grizz breathed a sigh of relief, thankful Patricia's back had been to the phone. Sure enough, when she unlocked it, there was a text from Kurt.

"So, Zel, had a lot of fun surfing. U were choka out there!"

Grizz smiled to herself, remembering how she'd been able to stand up and ride several waves in to shore—small as they may have been—all on her own that afternoon.

Just as she began to write a response, another text came in. *"Want 2 check out the Surfing Museum at Lighthouse Point?"*

He's asking me on another date, she thought, swallowing the lump that had appeared in her throat. Smirking, she texted back, *"Don't you make a regular pilgrimage there?"*

"*Not for years,*" he replied.

She tapped her finger against her phone. *Lighthouse Point… wait! That's that cool old lighthouse I've always wanted to explore!* She texted back, "*Is that off of West Cliff Drive?*"

Kurt responded immediately. "*Yep!*"

"*There's a museum there too?*" she asked.

Patricia looked at Grizz, who was staring at her phone and texting rapidly. She shrugged, reaching for a bottle of polish from Grizz's stash.

"*The mus. is in the lighthouse,*" Kurt explained. "*Not super big, but we can walk around the beach, & check out Seal Rock…*"

Grizz tapped the phone against her chin thoughtfully. She loved museums, and had always wanted to see Seal Rock. Besides, it went along with her plan perfectly—and if she had to be stuck with Kurt, she may as well enjoy herself. "*Okay! Sounds fun,*" she began to type, then added, "*Stud muffin.*" She hit send before she could change her mind, then placed the phone back on the speakers. She sighed under her breath, focusing on her toes once again.

After fifteen minutes of silence, Patricia stole another glance at Grizz, wondering why she was so quiet. Finally, her curiosity got the better of her. "So…" she began, trying to keep her tone light, "how's operation: love potion going?" She cringed, wondering why she'd thought that was a good idea. She braced herself for an explosion.

Grizz glanced up from her pedicure, recalling the past week with Kurt. "It's going great. He's putty in my hands. Ooh, Kurt, you're *so* strong," she cooed. "You and those man muscles! I'll do what-ev-er you say!*"

Patricia dropped her handful of chips and stared at Grizz in horror. "Whatever he says?" she repeated carefully.

Grizz snorted, setting down the bottle of electric blue polish. "Oh, relax. I'm not even going to kiss him." The thought of that, however, made a funny chill run down her spine. She shook it off. "I'll just follow him around with big puppy dog eyes and be really annoying."

"I didn't think following Kurt around all day was the way you'd dreamed of spending the summer," Patricia said with a frown, popping a chip in her mouth.

"It's not," Grizz snapped back. "But it's necessary."

Patricia didn't agree, but decided not to say anything. She pretended to be very interested sorting through nail polish.

"Besides, there's no way it will last long," Grizz reasoned, holding her foot in mid-air and admiring her rainbow toes. "Like he's been with any other girl who gets too ga-ga over him—as soon as he's 'got me,' he'll get bored and won't be interested in me anymore." She spread her hands. "It'll be over in less than a week."

Patricia frowned, recalling what Ben had said. *"I've never seen him so depressed over a girl before like he was the other day..."* Fiddling with the bottle of purple polish she held, she began, "But he seems to *really* like you..."

Grizz scoffed, reaching for a handful of M&Ms. "Oh, please. His crushes are shallow as a tide pool."

"You're using surfer speak," Patricia said slyly.

Grizz's eyes bugged out dangerously, and she threw a pillow at Patricia.

"Ack!" Patricia ducked, the pillow swiping her hair. "Okay, this means war!" She stretched out her arm and grabbed a pillow off her bed, sending it straight for Grizz.

"Hey, no fair!" Grizz exclaimed, holding up her hands as shields.

Patricia was grateful for the distraction. The tension seemed to melt away, and they enjoyed their sleepover without any more mentions of Kurt or the love potion.

The following afternoon, Grizz stood in front of the espresso machine at the Merry Mule. For practically the first time since she'd started the love potion charade, Kurt was not sharing her shift, and she was enjoying the peace of mind.

"I'll get that started for you," she said to the man who'd ordered a blended latte. She glanced at the clock. "Almost my break time," she muttered to herself, stomach growling. "Maybe I'll have one of those chocolate muffins…"

"Hey, Grizz."

Grizz felt her spine tingle. Turning, she saw Dimitri had appeared behind the counter. "Dimitri," she said with little enthusiasm. "I didn't know you were working today." It had been a while since she'd had a shift with him, which was a blessing in disguise.

"Yeah," Dimitri replied with a shrug, walking to the pastry cooler.

"And once again, I've been blown off," Grizz hissed under her breath, pouring ice into the blender with such force that some cubes flew over the sides.

"Molly blended latte for here!" Grizz set down the mug forcibly on the counter, wiping her hands on her apron before starting on a new drink.

Dimitri appeared at her side. Stiffening, Grizz stepped away from the bar. "Be my guest." He made no move, and Grizz realized belatedly that his hands were empty. Grunting, she resumed mixing the syrups.

"So, Grizz," Dimitri began, leaning against the counter while she refused to look at him. "How have you been?"

Chill, girl, you've been waiting for this moment, Grizz instructed herself. "Oh, I've been fantastic. This summer is *flying* by with all of the fun I've been having." She tossed a scoopful of coffee beans into the espresso grinder with a flourish to accentuate her fake happiness.

"Oh." Dimitri's voice held a tinge of disappointment.

It's working! Grizz thought, stealing a glance at him and noticing that his eyebrows were furrowed.

Tapping his fingertips on the counter top, Dimitri asked, "What have you been up to?"

"Oh, you know, going shopping with my friends. Hanging at the Boardwalk with Kurt. Surfing with Kurt." Dimitri's eyes widened, and Grizz realized with glee that she'd hit a sore spot. *You snooze, you lose!*

"Wow, sounds like you've been having a blast," Dimitri mumbled. "But, listen, Grizz—"

Grizz chose that moment to start the espresso grinder.

Dimitri flinched.

"Oops, sorry," Grizz said innocently. "What were you saying?"

"I just wanted to say how sorry I am about bailing on our date," Dimitri said quietly.

It took you over a week to say that? Grizz thought. She shrugged. "No big deal."

When she turned her back to him, Dimitri put his hand on her elbow. "Please Grizz, don't be like that. I'm really sorry, I was super sick."

His touch sent a jolt of electricity all the way up her arm, and she felt her cheeks redden. "You—were sick?" she repeated.

Dimitri nodded. "Bad case of food poisoning." He chuckled, causing another tingle down her spine. "Never eating shrimp again. It made me miss out on an awesome date with you."

Grizz bit her lip, forgetting all about making coffee for a moment. She turned slowly, eyes locking with his. *Why was I so annoyed with him?* she wondered wildly. *It's not his fault he got food poisoning.*

"So," Dimitri began, lifting his eyebrows, "do you forgive me?"

"S-sure," Grizz stammered, feeling her heart pound.

"And maybe I can cash in that rain check?" he asked hopefully.

Face flushing, Grizz nodded, turning on the steamer. "Yeah!"

"Great, let me know when you're free," Dimitri whispered in her ear, before walking away.

Grizz took a deep breath to calm her racing heart. *He's so hot,* she thought with a little squeal. "Here's your coffee," she told the girl who was waiting, before looking at the clock. "Break time!" She took off her apron and hurried to the back room, feeling practically giddy.

"This is awesome," she whispered to herself, pulling her cell phone from her locker. "He wasn't being a jerk after all—he was just sick! He likes me—he really likes me!" When her phone turned on, she sank to the couch and began to web-surf. *I should go grab a muffin, but I feel too charged to see him again so soon,* she thought. *I wonder when we can go on our date?*

Music hit her ears, and she realized with a jolt that her phone was ringing. She swiped her finger across the screen absentmindedly. "Hello?"

"Yo, Rizzy!"

Grizz felt as if her heart stopped. Why hadn't she checked before she answered the phone? Taking a deep breath, she said, "Oh, hi, Kurt."

"What's up?" Kurt asked cheerfully.

"Not much, I'm at work on my break," Grizz answered, tucking a strand of hair behind her ear. She stifled a groan. Was he calling her just to chit-chat now?

"Cool. I have the day off," he told her unnecessarily. "So, what day do you want to go?"

Grizz pinched her eyebrows together. "Go where?"

"To the Surfing Museum!"

All of her happy thoughts about Dimitri went out the window. She'd completely forgotten about making that date with Kurt. How could she go out with both of them? *This is the moment I've been waiting for,* she reasoned. *It's time to call it quits with Kurt.* "Listen, Kurt, the thing is…"

"I was thinking I could pick you up," Kurt went on, "and then we could go to lunch after the museum? Is that okay? Unless, like, you want to go later in the day…"

The words died in her throat. Something about the happiness in his voice told her she couldn't go through with it. Telling Kurt that she didn't actually like him would *crush* him. *Wait—why do I care about this doofus' feelings? I'm out for revenge! That's right. I'm allowed a little more fun, aren't I? I'm young, I can swing this!* "Let me check my schedule really quick," Grizz mumbled to him, wandering over to the posted calendar. "Oh, I see we're both free on Monday. Work for you?"

"Awesome!" Kurt declared. "So, what are you up to?"

Irked, Grizz replied, "Well, like I said, I'm on my break, and I'm kind of hungry…"

"Oh, you should definitely eat, Zelda," Kurt interjected, a worried note in his voice. "I'll let you go."

"Yeah, thanks," Grizz stammered. "Talk to you later." She lowered the phone from her ear, staring at the calendar in front of her as she processed what was happening. Did she seriously just make a date with two guys? "Argh, what are you doing?" she whimpered, digging her fingers in her hair.

Her eyes focused on the dates in front of her, and she let out a strangled cry.

"Whoa, what happened?" Frank asked in a panic, having appeared behind her.

Grizz gasped, then pointed to the schedule with a shaking finger. "Loo-look," she breathed.

"Wednesday: 9 AM–1 PM. Grizz Sheridan, Kurt Minola, and Dimitri Russell." Frank frowned. "So...?"

Wide-eyed, Grizz turned to Frank and gripped his shoulders. "All three of us will be working *at the same time!*"

"So? You've done that before," Frank said with a frown.

Grizz gave his shoulders a shake. "That was before! Now it must never happen! What am I going to do?"

"Listen, you're on your break, but I'm not," Frank said, wiggling out of her grasp and pulling a sweatshirt from his locker. "So, I've..."

Grizz ignored him, snapping her fingers. "That's it! Switch shifts with me."

"Grizz, I have to get back out there before Obe—"

"This is an emergency!" Grizz half-shrieked. "I just made a date with Dimitri *and* Kurt. We *cannot* all have a shift together."

Frank's eyebrows lifted so high they disappeared behind his thick bangs. "What? I thought you were going out with Kurt! Why did you say you'd go out with another guy?"

His words made Grizz feel a pang of guilt, but she tried to ignore it. "I'm not going out with Kurt."

"What?" Frank exclaimed. Grizz held a finger to her lips. "But you've been all over him," he whispered. "Calling him 'handsome,' and 'hunk'…"

Grizz lifted her hand to stop him. "Don't remind me, please."

"That *was* pretty weird considering you couldn't stand him before," Frank said thoughtfully.

"I was just messing with him, because he was trying to control how I feel," Grizz whispered back.

"What the hell?" Frank asked, looking utterly baffled. "I don't follow."

"What aren't you following, Frank?!" Grizz demanded, all thoughts of whispering flying from her mind.

"Okay, okay, don't freak out!" Frank implored. "So, you like Dimitri?"

Grizz looked over her shoulder to make sure they were still alone. When she saw the coast was clear, she nodded. "Yes."

"And you don't like Kurt."

Another nod. "Correct."

"But you're *pretending* to like Kurt," Frank said, a crease forming between his eyebrows.

"Yep." Grizz pressed her lips together, the frustration of the situation getting to her.

"Why?"

Grizz shot out a puff of air, throwing her hands up. "He was being a jerk and needs to be taught a lesson. Can we continue?"

"Okay! You want to go out with Dimitri," Frank finished.

Grizz held up her thumb. "You're with me. So they can't be in the same place with me. There's no way I can pull off pretending to like Kurt in front of Dimitri; he'll get the wrong idea."

"What would the *right* idea be?" Frank muttered. Seeing her glare, he said hurriedly, "Either way, you've got yourself a problem, Grizz."

"Not if you switch shifts with me," she said in a sing-song voice.

Frank frowned, looking back and forth between the schedule and her. "Okay, fine, I'll help."

Grizz threw her arms around him. "Oh, thank you! You're a lifesaver."

Frank smiled, zipping up his sweatshirt and walking away. "Anything for a friend."

"One more thing."

Frank slowed his steps, turning to her with interest.

"Don't tell Dimitri *or* Kurt," Grizz said imploringly.

Frank looked skeptical, but nodded.

"Thank you." Grizz put her phone back in her locker and followed him back into the cafe. "I have just enough time to wolf down a muffin!"

She caught Dimitri's eye as she headed for the pastry shelf, and he winked at her. *I can handle this,* she told herself, trying to calm her racing heart.

Chapter Nineteen ♡

T HAT MONDAY, GRIZZ STROLLED THROUGH THE SURFING Museum, pausing to admire a vintage wooden board, eyes scanning the information sign next to it.

She hated to admit it, but she was enjoying herself. She liked museums in general, and was having fun reading about surfing and looking at all of the photographs of the ocean.

She cast a glance at Kurt, who stood several feet away from her, engrossed in staring at the various boards that hung on the walls, reading the signs underneath each one under his breath. She smiled to herself.

Since the museum wasn't very big, they soon finished and went to meander through the gift shop. She lifted a photo book from a shelf and thumbed through it.

"Those were some sick boards, huh, Zelly?" Kurt asked, stopping to look at a rack of keychains.

Grizz put the book back on the shelf. "Yeah, the old-fashioned ones are pretty cool, but I don't know if I'd be able to carry them."

Kurt nodded. "I know what you mean. Some of them were huge!"

"You could probably handle one, since you're so tall," Grizz began, eyes dancing. "They'd only be *half* your size."

Kurt chuckled.

"Oh, these are cool!" Grizz exclaimed, unhooking a keychain shaped like the lighthouse off of the rack. "They have all kinds of stuff— ooh! Little surfboards!" She ran her fingers through the rack, looking at the different styles and colors. "Whoa..." Carefully she pulled one free, holding it close to admire it. "This looks like my surfboard!" Pausing, she continued, "Okay, it's not really *my* surfboard, but, you know."

Kurt watched her with a smile on his face. "That is an awesome keychain. You should get it!"

Grizz bit her lip, running her thumb over the aqua plastic, turning it over in her hand. Her heart sank. "That's a little too much for a keychain," she sighed in disappointment, placing it back on the rack. "That's okay."

She meandered over to another bookcase, glancing at the mugs and hats. "I think I'm going to go outside," she told Kurt, pointing to the door.

Kurt caught her eye and nodded. "Okay, be with you in a few."

Grizz walked out of the museum, inhaling deeply as the sea air hit her nostrils. She was glad Kurt was still browsing, needing a little time away from him.

Walking to the edge of the path, Grizz pulled her cell phone from her pocket, taking a few pictures of the breathtaking view. "Lighthouses rock," she murmured to herself, resting her arms on the railing.

She was so lost in her reverie that she didn't notice Kurt until he had come up beside her. "Choka view," he commented, hands curling over the metal railing.

Grizz laughed to herself at his surf-speak, pushing her hair away from her face as the wind picked up. "Yeah…" She focused on someone wind surfing in the distance, their board bobbing in the waves. Her sight was obscured when a blue object was dangled in front of her face.

Blinking, Grizz lifted her hand to grasp the keychain. "What…" She looked at the little aqua surfboard in her hand, then at Kurt, who was watching her, trying to hide his smile. "You bought it?"

Kurt nodded. "You liked it so much, I thought you should have it."

Grizz felt at a loss for words. "I wasn't trying to hint that you needed to buy it for me," she stammered at last.

Kurt leaned back against the railing, shaking his head. "You didn't! I just figured it's your surfboard, you know, you should have it."

Grizz felt her cheeks grow warm, dropping her gaze to the keychain once more. "Thank you. Look, it's got the little yellow flowers and everything!"

Kurt broke into a grin. "Is blue your favorite color?" he asked, taking in her hair and purse.

"One of them, yeah," Grizz told him with a shrug. "Hey, it will look great on my bag!" She slid her purse off of her shoulder and hooked the keychain onto one of the large metal rings on the front of the bag. "There."

"Looking good!" Kurt pushed away from the railing. "Want to check out the seals?"

Grizz found herself grinning from ear to ear, falling into step with him. "Sounds fun!"

Kurt glanced at her as they walked, the wind running through her hair. She smiled and tilted her chin up, the sun casting a glow on her features. He looked away quickly, feeling his breath catch.

When the rock came into sight, Grizz broke into a jog until she reached the railing. "Wow!" There were several seals gathered on the rock, sunbathing, and a couple dove into the waves as she watched them. "They're *so* cute," she sighed, pulling her phone out of her purse and focusing the camera on the rock.

"Yeah, look at them, totally in tune with the waves," Kurt said, hands in the pocket of his hoodie as he joined her.

Grizz took a few pictures, admiring how they turned out. "Oh, you can see them really good in this one," she said.

Kurt leaned closer, and she tilted the screen in his direction. "Those are *sweet*!" Kurt declared. "Will you text me some?"

Grizz lifted her eyes and jumped slightly when she realized how close his head was to hers. "Sure," she mumbled, taking a step away from him and setting her phone on the railing.

They stood side by side in silence for a few minutes. Grizz tried to focus on the seals, and not the fact that Kurt was mere inches from her.

Kurt stared at the waves crashing against the rock and muttered, "Man, the waves are going off today. I need to get out there and practice."

Grizz cocked her head with interest. "Practice for what?"

"There's a surfing competition this Saturday," Kurt explained.

"Oh, that's cool," Grizz replied. "How does it work?"

"There are different kinds of competitions, but, basically, there's several heats divided by age, and people get eliminated each round." Turning to face her, Kurt began, "Actually, would you be interested in going?"

Grizz didn't follow. "I can't enter," she said, shaking her head.

"No, I mean, do you want to come watch me? If you don't think you'd be bored," he added hurriedly.

Thoughts racing, Grizz realized he was asking her on another date. She tucked a strand of hair behind her ear as the wind whipped around them, Kurt's eyebrows lifted hopefully as he waited for her answer.

"Sure, why not," she said, shrugging lightly. "Sounds fun." *And if I'm bored out of my mind, I'll just ditch him,* she thought.

Her heart fluttered when Kurt's features broke into a relieved grin. "Awesome!"

Grizz resumed watching the seals, leaning over and resting her elbows on the railing.

Kurt mimicked her, and she noticed with a jolt that his elbow brushed hers. She scooted away from him as inconspicuously as possible.

"How's Patricia's pocket book going?" Kurt asked, breaking the silence.

"Flip book," Grizz corrected him. "It's going," she said with a shrug. "I'm just a little stuck on it. There's several blank pages that I don't know how to fill."

Kurt straightened and turned his back to the railing, crossing his arms. "Yeah, that's kind of like life."

Grizz took a step away from the rail, staring at him with a wrinkled nose. "Huh?"

"Like, life is a blank book, right?" Kurt said earnestly, draping his arms over the edging. "We each have our own pages to fill. Tomorrow stretches before us like, 'Dude, I can do *anything*. I can go to work or school, or I can become world-famous. Anything can happen, and it's all up to me.'"

Oh, great. He's a philosopher now, Grizz thought, though what he said actually spoke to her. "That's a nice way to think about life," she murmured.

"Especially since you're a writer, Grizzy," Kurt went on with a grin.

If only he could cut off that last syllable, she thought in annoyance. Their eyes locked, and her heart pounded. "Yeah, life's my book…"

Grizz tore her gaze him when she heard her phone chime. Glancing at it, she saw Dimitri had texted her.

Kurt looked curiously to the phone on the railing between them, and Grizz was seized with panic. With no time to think, she shot her hand out and grabbed a fistful of his sweatshirt, tugging him toward her.

Kurt caught himself as they collided, hands resting clumsily on her arms. Grizz flushed, eyes locking with his, hand unconsciously curling around the fabric at his chest.

Kurt stared back at her, swallowing hard. "Um…"

Snapping back to reality, Grizz snaked her arm around his back, a whiff of his aftershave overwhelming her senses as she did so. "I…" she began breathlessly, hand clumsily searching for her phone on the railing, "I lost my balance," she lied, squeezing her eyes shut to pretend she was dizzy, but, in reality, it was so she didn't have to keep looking at him. When her fingers curled around the familiar soft rubber of her cell phone case, she smiled in relief. Pulling back, she casually slipped her phone into her pocket, batting her eyelashes at him. "Thanks, hero."

Kurt stared at her for a moment, lips parted as if he wanted to say something. Finally, he cleared his throat and faced the water once more. "No problem."

Good, he fell for it, Grizz thought, sliding her phone out from her pocket while Kurt's back was turned. She slid her thumb across the screen and read the message.

"Are you free this weekend?"

Grizz felt her heartbeat speed up, and she glanced around to make sure Kurt still wasn't looking. Hands shoved in his pockets, his brown hair was being ruffled in the breeze as he stared out at Seal Rock.

Her stomach gave a funny twist, and she remembered the surfing competition. *"I'm busy this weekend, sorry!"* she typed in response. *"I'll see when I'm free, and let you know."*

Locking her cell phone, Grizz tossed it into her shoulder bag, finding herself staring at Kurt again. She had the sense that she was digging herself deeper and deeper into this lie, and wondered how she would ever get out.

Chapter Twenty ♡

W HEN GRIZZ ENTERED THE BREAK ROOM OF THE MERRY Mule Thursday afternoon, she lifted a hand to greet Hayley, who was leaning against one of the bookcases, her cell phone pressed to her ear.

"Yeah, that sounds fun," Hayley said with a giggle, flipping her long hair over her shoulder. "Mm-hm. You're awful," she said in a tone that implied she didn't think the person she was talking to was awful at all.

Grizz set her purse and sweatshirt in her locker, trying unsuccessfully not to listen to Hayley.

"No," Hayley said with a giggle. "I'm at work! Well, maybe later..." She giggled again.

Grizz paused as she was tying on her apron, cocking an eyebrow with interest.

"That sounds fun," Hayley said, twirling a lock of hair around her finger. "But I've got to go now." She laughed, covering her mouth. "Stop! You know how he gets. I'll see you tonight. Bye."

Pivoting on her heel, Grizz was poised to pounce like a cat. "So, Hayley," she began nonchalantly, "how have you been?"

Hayley reddened, ducking her head to let her long hair swing like a curtain over her face. "Good."

"Sounds like better than good," Grizz teased, following her into the cafe. "Hot date?"

Hayley giggled, waving to Mia, one of their coworkers. "Well…"

"That giggle betrays you," Grizz said knowingly.

Hayley nodded shyly. "I'm going to the movies."

"Who's the guy? Is he cute?" Grizz asked, leaning toward her and wiggling her eyebrows. Hayley glanced around in embarrassment, putting a finger to her lips.

"Sorry," Grizz whispered sheepishly, mirroring Hayley's shushing gesture. When Hayley still didn't answer, she prompted, "Well?"

Hayley laughed. "Actually, it's—"

"Hey Grizz!"

Grizz turned her attention to the counter, where Ben and Patricia now stood.

"Hi Patricia! Ben," Grizz greeted, poised to take their order. "What would you two like?"

"I'm ready this time, I promise," Ben teased, pulling out his wallet. "Can I get a Molly iced tea?"

"Sure thing." Grizz paused. "Do you want the black tea, the mint, or the peach?"

Patricia playfully rolled her eyes. "Don't give him options!"

Ben flicked his gaze to her, pretending to be indignant. "For your information, I'll try the mint."

"Excellent choice," Grizz replied, typing it out on the register as he handed her his money.

"How's it going?" Ben asked.

Grizz shrugged, taking his punch card from him. Things had been tense for a few days; the situation with Kurt and Dimitri weighing heavily on her mind, but she was beginning to relax. "Good. How's being a lab rat?"

Ben cocked an eyebrow. "You do know that's not what that means, right?"

Grizz laughed and passed the card back to him, handing the plastic cup to Hayley. "What about you, Patricia?"

"Can I get a raspberry Italian soda?" Patricia asked.

Mia leaned against the counter. "Sorry, we're all out of raspberry syrup."

Patricia frowned. "Really? Well, then maybe I'll get..."

Ben nudged her. "How's it feel now that the shoe's on the other foot? Tick-tock, tick-tock."

Patricia stuck her tongue out at him. "Shush. Do you have cherry?"

Mia smiled. "Sure thing!"

Grizz waved to them as they walked through the french doors onto the patio.

"There's a good spot," Patricia said, making a beeline for a white wrought iron table with a blue and pink umbrella.

"Prime mule viewing," Ben agreed, positioning his chair to face Kurt, who was lifting his poster board to the rhythm of an upbeat pop song.

"Whoo! Dance, baby, dance!" Patricia hooted.

Kurt turned and waved at them. "Hey, guys! I didn't see you come in."

Ben shrugged. "We used the side doors."

"Oh, sneaky," Kurt said, handing them each a flier.

"'Buy one muffin, get one free,'" Patricia read aloud. "What say you, Ben? Feel like a muffin later?"

"Twist my arm," Ben replied.

Kurt resumed dancing, turning back to face the street.

Patricia pulled out her smart phone and web-surfed while they waited for their coffee. "Oh, look! Holly finally uploaded her prom pictures to Facebook," Patricia said, turning her phone to Ben so he could see.

"Ha, that one's great," Ben chuckled, pointing to the picture of Teddy holding five fondue skewers with a crazed look on his face.

"Prom was fun," Patricia said with a wistful sigh, flipping through the album. "She got lots of good pics!"

"Speak of the fondue hog," Ben said, pointing behind Patricia.

Patricia turned to see Teddy sneaking up behind Kurt, back hunched and hands curled like claws.

"Boo!" Teddy shouted, pouncing on Kurt.

Kurt leapt in terror, dropping his poster board. "Shit!" He put a hoof to his chest. "You scared me!"

"Sorry, dude," Teddy playfully punched him on the arm.

"You better watch it, Teddy, there was about to be a report of a giant mule attacking a civilian," Ben chuckled.

Kurt pulled a flier out of the pocket of his apron. "I'm not sure if you deserve this, but..."

Teddy's lips spread into a grin. "Two for one large muffins? Sweet! Be right back, guys."

"Hey, Teddy," Grizz said as she passed him on her way out of the cafe. When she reached Ben and Patricia's table, she said, "A Molly mint tea for Ben, and a Molly cherry Italian soda for Patricia."

"Zelly! Those drinks look extra refreshing," Kurt said, fanning himself.

"Do you want me to get you something?" Grizz asked him.

Kurt waved his hand. "Nah, my break is in just a few minutes. Besides, I have no way to drink it." He poked his mule head to demonstrate.

Grizz giggled, tucking a strand of hair behind her ear, and Kurt chuckled with her.

Ben shared a look with Patricia. "Give me strength." Patricia patted his arm soothingly.

"Back!" Teddy announced, double fisting a poppyseed and chocolate chip muffin. He took a bite of each one, struggling to chew the large mouthful.

Patricia snorted, and Teddy shot her a scowl. "What? Did you expect me to pass up on a deal like this?" he asked.

Kurt said something, but it was muffled due to the loud music and his mule head.

"What?" Ben asked, leaning in a little closer.

Kurt chuckled and held out the poster board for Ben to take. He pulled off the mule head and rested it on his hip, running a gloved hand through his hair. "Phew! Anyway, I was saying you guys should come to the surfing competition this weekend! I'm already going to have my lucky mermaid in the audience," Kurt said, looking at Grizz with a smile.

Teddy coughed, fighting to not choke on his muffin.

Grizz blushed, feeling a little thrill at being called his "lucky mermaid." Looking between Ben and Patricia, who were watching with keen interest, and Teddy, whose brown eyes were so wide he looked like a bullfrog, she realized that Kurt was totally flirting with her in front of all of their friends. She wanted the earth to open and swallow her up. When her eyes landed on Kurt, however, taking in his innocent expression, hair sticking up slightly from the costume head, she felt herself relax. "Yeah, you should totally join us, guys!" she said with enthusiasm.

Coughing slightly, Ben said, "You know I will. You want to come, too, Patricia?"

Patricia sipped her Italian soda and shrugged. "Why not? It sounds fun."

Kurt turned to Teddy. "What about you?"

Teddy blinked, shaking off his initial shock. "Should I brush up on my surfing skills and join?"

"Sure, dude, there's still time!" Kurt replied.

Teddy waved a hand, chuckling in embarrassment. "I was just kidding. But I'll definitely go and root for you. And I'll text Lita and ask her to come, too."

"Sweet!" A beeping sound went off, and Kurt pulled off his glove, lifting his digital watch. "Break time. See you guys in a bit."

"Yeah, I have to go in, too," Grizz said, waving to them as she fell into step with Kurt.

When Kurt and Grizz were out of earshot, Teddy sat down in the free chair next to Ben. "Whoa, I didn't know they were going out."

Ben grimaced, sharing a look with Patricia. "They're not."

"Are the kiddies not calling it that anymore?" Teddy said in a mock old-man voice. "Because dude, that's going out! Is Kurt stringing Grizz along?" He rolled up his sleeves. "Because I'll kick his—"

"No, no," Ben interrupted him. "It's kind of the opposite."

"That's not like Grizz," Teddy said with a frown.

"It's complicated," Patricia chimed in, glancing around to make sure no one was listening. "She's exacting 'revenge' on him. Kurt really likes Grizz, but she doesn't like him back."

Teddy's dark brows knit together. "Go on."

"So Tuck caught wind of that," Ben added, "and made up a little sugar water formula that he claimed was a 'love potion'."

"What a troll!" Teddy exclaimed. "Don't tell me Kurt was dumb enough to..."

"Yep." Ben cut him off with a single nod. "He fell for it, hook, line, and sinker."

"Whoa." Teddy whistled, sitting back in his chair. "You and your brother are like total opposites in the brain department. Not that Kurt isn't smart in some regards," Teddy added hastily. "But, man, how could he fall for something like that? You set him straight, right?"

Taking a sip of his soda, Ben admitted, "Um, no."

"Grizz *begged* me not to," Patricia whispered. "She said she wanted to deal with it herself."

"Drooling all over him is dealing with it?" Teddy asked skeptically.

"She's pretending the love potion worked," Ben said. "We both feel caught in the middle."

"Grizz has been really sensitive and acting kind of weird recently,"

Patricia confessed. "I think it's better if we let them deal with it on their own. That's just my gut feeling."

Teddy lifted his eyebrows, processing it all. "We may not be able to do anything about Grizz and Kurt yet." He smiled mischievously. "But we can still deal with Tuck."

"How do you know this is going to work?" Patricia asked Teddy as she and Ben followed him through the community pool parking lot.

Teddy's mouth curved into a smile. "Don't worry about it! Just let me do all of the talking."

Patricia sighed. "Well, the less I have to interact with Tuck, the better."

"Game faces," Teddy muttered to Ben and Patricia, strolling casually up to Tuck, who was sitting on a bench, apparently taking a break from swimming.

Good, he's not working, Patricia thought.

"Hey, Tuck! My man!" Teddy waved to him enthusiastically.

Don't lay it on too thick! Patricia bit her lip, trying not to cringe.

"Hi, Theodore," Tuck said with a smirk, eyes landing on each of them in turn. "Patricia. Benjamin."

Patricia rolled her eyes, setting her bag down on a bench on the pretense that she was about to swim.

"So, how's your summer going?" Teddy asked, sitting next to him and pulling off his shoes.

Tuck shrugged. "Good. Just trying to stay in shape. The tryouts for the water polo team are the first week of school."

"Got any side projects going on?" Teddy pressed, not looking at Tuck.

Tuck pressed his lips together and threw up his hands. "I knew it! If this is about the love potion, you already caught me!" He threw an accusing glare at Ben. "What am I supposed to do, grovel on my hands and knees to that jackass?"

Patricia snorted at his choice of words.

"No," Teddy began, "But what you *could* do is give back the money that you weaseled out of Kurt."

"Hey! Unlike Kurt, I'm not made of money," Tuck said with narrowed eyes. "That fifty bucks was probably his daily allowance."

Patricia's jaw dropped. "Fifty dollars?" she mouthed to Ben.

Tuck rose to his feet. "I'm not sticking around for this."

Teddy wasn't about to be swayed. He and Ben each took a step until they were shoulder to shoulder, blocking Tuck's path. "I'm sure you'll see things our way," Teddy said innocently. "That is, unless you want your dad finding out about... a certain little incident." Teddy cocked an eyebrow.

Tuck faltered. "You wouldn't."

Ben and Teddy glanced at each other and shrugged.

Tuck scowled, pivoting to retrieve his wallet. "I have to go practice. We don't all get handed a position on the team with a shiny scholarship like some people," he huffed, slapping the bills onto Ben's open palm.

"Thank you for your cooperation," Teddy called after him as he stomped away.

"That was awesome, bro!" Ben exclaimed as they left.

Teddy bumped fists with him. "Thanks. It was *so* satisfying telling that creep off."

Patricia paused, Tuck's words ringing in her ears. "I *do* feel a little sorry for him, though," she was forced to admit.

"I suppose Kurt does cast a big shadow," Teddy said thoughtfully, shoving his hands in his pockets as they walked down the street. "But that's no excuse to be a jerk."

Ben sighed. "Well, it's all over now."

"Just one question," Patricia began, slowing her steps. "How are you going to give the money to Kurt? I thought we weren't supposed to let on that the love potion is a prank."

The trio was silent for a few moments.

Teddy snapped his fingers and caught Ben's eye. "I *bet* I can think of a way."

Ben pointed at him, nodding slowly. "Ah!"

Patricia pursed her lips. "Are either one of you going to tell me what you're planning?"

Ben put his arm around her as they resumed walking. He whispered in her ear, "Listen and learn."

Chapter Twenty-One ♡

"**A**LL RIGHT, SURFERS," THE ANNOUNCER CALLED OVER THE loudspeakers, "*It's almost time for the first heat of the day. First up is our Junior Men's Division.*"

Kurt took a deep breath, trying to psych himself up like he did for a water polo match. "Don't think too much, just feel the water. You've got this." He absentmindedly looked at the other surfers he would be competing against, waving to a few of his friends.

He froze, lowering his hand when he saw Dimitri further down the beach, deep in conversation with another surfer. *I guess he was serious about entering,* Kurt thought, recalling his bragging at Teddy's party. *Is he the real deal, or a fakie?*

"Ready to rock?" his friend Brody asked him, holding out his fist.

Kurt grinned, grateful for the distraction from Dimitri. He bumped Brody's fist with his. "You know it." He felt the hairs stand up on the back of his neck, like someone was watching him, and turned to see Dimitri's gaze riveted on him. Dimitri smirked, turning away to watch the incoming waves.

What is with that guy? Kurt thought. He tried to shake it off. *Don't think about it, who cares what his problem is,* he told himself firmly. *Besides, you've got Zelda in the audience. Can't screw up and let her down.*

"Good luck out there, dude," Brody called to him when the announcer signaled for them to begin paddling out.

"You, too," Kurt said, turning all of his focus to the heat.

Saturday greeted them with sunshine as Patricia, Ben, and Grizz arrived at the beach.

Patricia checked her phone. "Lita said she and Teddy are in front of one of those big tents in the middle."

Grizz looked out at the sea of tents, and the even bigger sea of people standing around laughing and talking. She'd had no idea just *how* popular these surf meets were, although she should have guessed. "That's helpful."

Ben shrugged, heading for the tents. "We'll find them."

"Glad you're confident," Grizz muttered under her breath. As they neared the shore, her gaze wandered to the water. She knew that Kurt had arrived earlier to practice.

"Hey, guys!" Teddy called out, squeezing between people to meet them.

"Have you talked to Kurt yet?" Ben asked as the trio fell into step behind Teddy.

"No," Teddy replied with a shrug. "I hope we get to at least wish him luck before the meet if nothing else."

"Hi, you two!" Lita said, holding out her arms and embracing both Grizz and Patricia. "Now, I don't know a lot about these things, but see that big, burly guy?" She pointed to a surfer on the shore line with broad shoulders and huge muscles. "He was sharing a wave with that girl," she pointed to a much shorter girl who was currently doing a series of stretches. "And he totally wiped out, while she rode it like a dream!"

"Yeah, brawn doesn't always help with surfing," Ben commented, crossing his arms over his chest.

Patricia glanced at his muscular arms, poking him in the shoulder. "Have *you* ever tried surfing?" she asked with a twitch of her eyebrow. Ben looked at her, cheeks tinging red. He cleared his throat.

"Aw, you embarrassed him," Grizz teased.

Ben frowned, ducking his head. "Shut up," he whispered out of the corner of his mouth.

Grizz smiled sweetly. "Sorry. Now where is our star?" she wondered, turning to scan the beach. She thought she could spot him by his red surfboard, but, unfortunately, there were a lot of red surfboards.

"There he is!" Lita exclaimed, pointing to a figure in the whitewater. "Hey, Kurt!"

Kurt heard the voice and waved, lifting his board and heading inland. Grizz found herself drinking him in as he walked up the sand, his golden physique glistening from the waves, soaking swim trunks hanging low on his hips. She felt like she was watching him in slow motion as he closed his eyes and ran a hand through his wet hair, whipping drops of water everywhere. Her heartbeat sped up, and she shook her head. Was she checking out Kurt Minola? She squeezed her eyes shut, then, despite her best efforts, found one eye opening slowly to peek at him again.

"Hey, dudes, you made it!" Kurt said enthusiastically once he'd reached them.

Grizz averted her eyes, hoping her friends hadn't noticed how she'd been staring.

"When does the heat start?" Ben asked.

Kurt checked the time on his digital watch. "In fourteen minutes." He bounced on his heels. "Getting a bad case of the jitters."

"Don't be nervous!" Lita said.

"You'll be great," Patricia agreed, giving him the thumbs up sign.

"Thanks," Kurt said with a chuckle, rubbing the back of his neck. He looked to Grizz, eyes shining hopefully.

Aware that all of her friends were watching them like hawks, Grizz flushed, but said, struggling to look him in the eye, "Knock 'em dead."

Kurt grinned, pumping his fist. "Okay, I should get ready. See you later."

"Bye!" Ben, Teddy, and Lita called after him while Patricia waved. Grizz, however, was silent as she watched him disappear into the crowd of people.

"I'm going to go get something to drink," she said a few minutes later, shouldering her purse. "Anyone want anything?"

Teddy opened his mouth, but Lita elbowed him. "If you make her get you snacks, she won't be able to carry it all."

Teddy pouted. "Ah, I guess I'll wait until after the first couple heats."

"We'll celebrate Kurt racking up the points," Ben told him.

Lita laughed. "Good answer."

"Okay, I'll be right back." Grizz weaved through the crowded beach to the snack stands that had been set up.

"Something cool and refreshing," Grizz whispered to herself as she perused the tables. "Ooh, strawberry soda!" She hurried to the table that was selling hot dogs, their available sodas lined up in front of the sign. "I'll take one strawberry, please."

"Two dollars, please," the man said, turning to pull the soda out of the cooler.

"What can I get for you?" the girl beside him asked the next customer.

"Just water, thanks," a familiar voice said.

Grizz froze, and felt her heartbeat spike when someone tapped her shoulder. She turned. "Dimitri!"

"I didn't think I'd see you here," said Dimitri with a smile. "Where are you watching?"

Her throat dried up, and she took a large gulp of her soda. *I can't let him sit with me,* she thought wildly. "Over there," she muttered, pointing vaguely to the crowd.

"Great, then you should have a good view of me!"

Blinking rapidly, Grizz asked, "You're competing?"

"I'm dominating," Dimitri countered with a grin.

Grizz closed her eyes for a second, feeling like an idiot. *Of course! He and Kurt were talking about an upcoming surfing competition when we were at Teddy's party!* With all of the excitement that had happened since, she'd forgotten.

Dimitri winked. "Wish me luck."

"Good luck." The words came out as little more than a croak, but

Dimitri had already begun to walk away.

"I'll see you in a few!" he called, lifting a hand before he jogged toward the shore.

Stricken, Grizz strode swiftly back to her friends.

"Hey, check it out, Grizz," Patricia said eagerly. "Lita was just teaching me a cheer!"

"Go—go Kurt, go, we—want—a—ten!" Lita chanted while Patricia did the arm movements she'd been taught.

Patricia smiled breathlessly as Ben and Teddy whooped. "See?"

"Come with me—now," Grizz demanded, voice strained.

Patricia yelped as Grizz dragged her off by the wrist.

When they were well away from the others, Grizz slowed her steps and looked around wildly.

"What's the matter?" Patricia asked, taken aback by Grizz's demeanor.

Grizz sighed. "Dimitri is here."

"That asshole," Patricia snarled, punching a fist into her palm.

"No!" Grizz protested.

Patricia looked at her quizzically, and Grizz realized all too late that she hadn't told her about the latest development with Dimitri. Shrugging helplessly, she said, "He and I talked. It turns out he was super sick, and that's why he bailed on me."

"So… you still like him," Patricia said, her voice sounding funny.

"Yeah, I mean he's so cute, and cool, and…" Grizz fanned herself. "And—he's here, but Kurt's here, and I'm supposed to sit with you guys, and Kurt is going to be hovering over us, but…" Her mind filled with static. "Dimitri saw me. He's going to want to talk to me more." Her breathing became ragged, and she flailed her hands in the air.

"Help, I think I'm having a heart attack!"

Patricia put both hands on Grizz's shoulders. "No, you're okay, it's a panic attack, not a heart attack. Thankfully not life-threatening. Take a deep breath." When Grizz held still, tight lipped, Patricia gave her shoulders a little shake. "GRIZZ!"

"Okay," Grizz stammered, breathing in deeply.

"Inhale, exhale. Inhale, exhale," Patricia coached, her voice soothing.

Grizz exhaled slowly, posture relaxed as she opened her eyes slowly.

"Better?"

"Yeah, thanks," Grizz patted her cheeks, feeling much calmer. "But what do I do?"

"Why don't you just tell Kurt that the love potion is bogus?" Patricia asked.

Grizz felt a shot to her gut, a vision of Kurt's hazel eyes widening in betrayal and shock coming to her. "I—er—no…"

Patricia closed her eyes for a brief moment to keep her temper. "Okay, so you want to string them both along?"

"I'm not stringing Dimitri along," Grizz snapped defensively. "I genuinely like him."

Patricia folded her arms across her chest, a definitive sign of her annoyance. "Then how exactly are you going to balance pretending to be in love with Kurt and flirting with Dimitri?"

Feeling irritated at Patricia's incessant questions, Grizz felt renewed fire to keep her plan in motion. "Piece of cake! Kurt the Jerk is too dimwitted to notice what I'm doing behind the scenes. Just leave it to me."

Patricia grimaced, glancing over her shoulder to make sure they were still alone. "I don't know, Grizz, that seems kind of mean… would you like it if you were dating a guy who turned out to be seeing someone else behind your back?"

"I like how virtuous you're being now, when we screwed with him during the play," Grizz snapped, narrowing her eyes. "What, it's okay when you're mad at him, but not when I am?"

"I didn't pretend to be in love with him during rehearsal," Patricia said quietly.

Grizz wrinkled her nose. "Whose side are you on? Have you forgotten that Kurt has bothered me nonstop since school got out?" The more she thought about it, the more she decided Kurt deserved it. "Cock-blocked my chances with Dimitri at every turn? Tried to control my emotions with a love potion? I'm teaching him a lesson he won't soon forget."

"Okay," Patricia agreed, mouth twisted in a frown.

"Good. Let's get back," Grizz said, heading back down the beach.

Patricia followed her slowly, conscience still not at ease.

"Which one is Kurt?" Lita asked, squinting at the lineup.

Ben started to point, but Grizz said, "He's the one with the red board and the blue trunks."

Patricia lifted her eyebrows, trying to hide her smirk.

"Oh, I see him!" Lita said with a grin.

And Dimitri is the one with the yellow board and plaid trunks, Grizz added mentally, hoping no one would notice how her eyes kept flicking to him.

"Come now, Grizz," Teddy teased, holding out his hand to the waves incredulously. "Any surf fan *knows* those are board shorts."

Grizz rolled her eyes, poking him. "Thank you, Teddy, fashion guru."

Teddy folded his arms, pretending to be offended.

As a large wave rolled in, the surfers all began to turn and paddle, and Grizz felt her stomach clench with excitement.

"An awesome aerial from Kurt Minola with a clean landing," the announcer said with enthusiasm.

Ben cupped his hands around his mouth. "Go, Kurt!"

Grizz fully focused on him in the water, holding her breath as he carved the large wave. She gasped when another surfer suddenly veered into his path, looking like he was going to run into him.

"Interference from Dimitri Russell as he drops in."

Dimitri shifted his weight and swept past Kurt, lifting his hand in apology.

Teddy's eyes widened in surprise. "I didn't know Dimitri was in the competition, too!"

Grizz felt her palms begin to sweat.

"He is?" Ben asked, squinting at the surfers in the water.

"Dimitri Russell gives us snaps—pardon the pun, ladies and gentlemen— as he backside snaps on the wave!"

Teddy clapped, staring at the waves with a puzzled expression.

Lita looked at them curiously. "Dimitri?"

"You remember, Lita, he came to the party," Teddy told her. "We went to grade school together."

Lita's eyes lit up with recognition. "Oh! Okay. I only spoke to him for like, a second," she said with a laugh. "So I only have a vague idea who you're talking about."

Grizz bit her lip nervously. *Can we steer the conversation away from Dimitri?* "So, I wonder how Kurt will do," she said with enthusiasm. She could feel Patricia's eyes boring into her.

"Brody Hutchins is hanging five," the announcer said, and Grizz turned her attention to a guy with a shaved head and a tan surfboard.

"Look at him charge that wave!" Teddy exclaimed, pointing to Kurt.

Grizz watched as Kurt rode the inside of the wave so far up that he looked like he was going to fall head-first into the surf. She gasped when he sharply rotated and rode the wave back down effortlessly.

"Whoa! Kurt Minola pulls off a wicked backside tail-slide."

"Yes!" Grizz exclaimed, leaping up and down as she clapped enthusiastically. "Go, Kurt!" Her face flushed when she realized what she'd done, and she took a swig of soda to calm herself.

"That finishes it up for this heat," the announcer called several minutes later. *"Surfers, come on back. Next up is the first heat for the Junior Women's Division."*

"I'm going to get something to eat," Grizz said, crunching her empty soda can in her hands.

"I'll come with you!" Teddy said eagerly, rubbing his stomach. "See you guys in a bit."

"Or never!" Lita taunted, knowing her boyfriend's appetite.

"There's Kurt!" Ben made his way through the throng of people to where Kurt stood on the beach.

"Hi, guys!" Kurt greeted them, wiping the water from his eyes.

"You did great, dude," Ben said, giving Kurt a high five.

"Thanks, bro," Kurt grinned.

"I loved that move you did toward the end," Patricia told him.

Kurt ducked his head, waving a hand. "No big deal, but I'm glad you liked it." He glanced around. "Er... where's Rizzy?"

"Getting food," Lita told him. "Teddy, too."

Kurt frowned, seeming disappointed. "Bummer." His eye caught movement as Dimitri staked his board in the sand right next to a few other surfers, then strode up the sand. *Damn, he's cocky,* Kurt thought in agitation. "I don't know what that guy's problem is."

"Who?" Lita asked curiously.

"Dimitri," Kurt said, turning his attention back to the group. "He has some major aggro."

Ben frowned. "Monsters chase him?"

"That's video games, man," Kurt said. "He charges!"

Patricia and Lita exchanged confused glances.

"He doesn't respect the priority at *all,*" Kurt went on. "He dropped in and almost knocked me off of my board!"

"Maybe he didn't do it on purpose?" Lita suggested with a confused shrug.

Kurt looked at her, not seeming convinced. "Maybe..." he sighed. "Oh, well. I think I'll get some water and try to clear my head. See you guys later."

"Good luck!" they called after him as he trudged down the beach.

Chapter Twenty-Two ♡

"DO I WANT NACHOS…OR CORN DOGS…OOH! THAT BOOTH has shaved ice!"

Grizz laughed at Teddy's enthusiasm as his head swiveled back and forth. "Shaved ice isn't very filling," she pointed out.

Teddy stroked his chin thoughtfully. "Good point. Nachos it is!"

"Okay, I think I'll get a hot dog," Grizz called after him as he hurried to get in line at the nachos stand.

She slowed her steps when she saw Dimitri was in the hot dog line. Looking around to make sure she wouldn't be seen, she skipped over to him. "Hi, Dimitri."

Dimitri turned in surprise. "Oh. Hey, Grizz," he replied.

"You did great in the heat," she continued as the line moved up.

Dimitri's eyebrows pinched into a scowl. "Not as great as some people."

Grizz faltered, knowing that Kurt had ranked several places above Dimitri. *That's not who he's talking about, though, I'm sure,* she told herself.

"I usually score a lot better," Dimitri leaned close to her to confess.

Blushing, Grizz tucked a strand of hair behind her ear. "You were probably just nervous," she reasoned.

"Yeah…" Dimitri nodded slowly, before stepping up to the table. "Can I have a bag of trail mix and some coconut water?"

Grizz felt a tinge of shame that she was going to order a hot dog with all of the works and a soda. *But he's competing,* she reasoned. *He can't eat anything heavy, or he'll cramp up and drown.*

Ripping open the bag and throwing some trail mix into his mouth, Dimitri stepped away so that she could order. To her delight, he waited while she ordered her food. *This is great,* she thought happily. *Just Dimitri and me.*

"Is this your first time seeing one of these?" Dimitri asked as they walked away from the line.

Grizz took as dainty a bit of her hot dog loaded with mustard, relish, and ketchup as she could manage, hoping she still looked alluring. "Mm-hm."

"How are you liking it?" Dimitri asked, screwing the cap back on his coconut water.

"It's a lot more fun than I expected," Grizz said with a smile.

Dimitri chuckled. "Oh, so you were dragged into coming, huh?"

Oh. My. God. Grizz felt that panicky feeling again. She had to think of something, before he asked more questions. "Oh, yeah, a couple of my gal pals really wanted to see the hot surfers." Since both of her "gal pals" were in relationships, this was a lie, but the less she said, the better.

Luckily, Dimitri seemed to find that hilarious. He threw his head back and laughed. "So you guys are having a good time?"

"Uh-huh," she said in a noncommittal way. "I love all of the tricks you guys do."

"Then stick around for this next round, I'll blow you out of the water," Dimitri said with a confident grin.

Grizz felt her heartbeat spike.

"Wish me luck!" Dimitri said, pivoting and walking away from her.

"Good luck," Grizz told him with a smile and a wave. She began to stroll back to Patricia and the others, humming under her breath.

"Hey, Grizz!" Teddy called to her.

She froze, turning to see him coming toward her, holding nachos in one hand and a chocolate bar in the other. *Did he see me with Dimitri?* she thought, feeling sick.

"Your hot dog looks epic. Does it taste epic to match?"

Grizz relaxed slightly. "It's really good. How are your nachos?"

"Tasty, tasty. I got them with all of the works." He held it aloft for her to see. "And some candy to wash it down with."

Grizz laughed, feeling a lot calmer as they walked toward Ben, Patricia, and Lita. "Yum!"

"You guys are back just in time to see the results of this round," Patricia told them.

"The lines were long," Teddy said with a shrug.

Lita smiled mischievously and took a nacho. "These are really good!"

Teddy grinned. "Have as many as you want. I'll just get more later."

"It's almost time for the second heat of the Junior Men's Division. What sweet moves will they bring to the waves?"

Heart pounding, Dimitri's words rang in Grizz's ears. *"I'll blow you out of the water."* She found herself craning her neck to see where Dimitri was on the beach, hoping to catch a glimpse of him.

Kurt held a hand above his eyes to gaze out at the waves rolling in. *That perfect wave is just calling to me.* Glancing down the beach, he saw that Brody was talking to some of their friends, and Kurt made his way toward them.

His steps slowed when he saw Dimitri standing right next to Brody and the others. He pinched his brows together. "I do *not* want to deal with this dude," he muttered.

"Maybe he didn't do it on purpose?" Lita's words flashed in his mind, and he felt a pang of guilt.

I'm not being fair, Kurt thought with a sigh. *It had to have been an accident. I could still be prickly because Rizzo used to dig him.* Kurt nodded to himself. *Yeah, that's all it was.*

"Good luck in the heat," Kurt said amiably, holding out his hand to Dimitri.

Dimitri lifted his eyebrows incredulously at Kurt, then stared at his outstretched hand. Grunting, he turned away from him without a word.

Kurt stood as if frozen for a moment before slowly curling his fingers and dropping his arm to his side. *Major aggro.*

Drawing in a sharp breath, Grizz watched unbelieving as Dimitri made a face at Kurt and turned away from the hand he'd offered. *That was rude,* she thought. *But maybe Kurt said something cocky...*

She didn't have much time to dwell on the situation as the announcer told the surfers it was time to get out in the water.

"All right, here comes a good wave, let's see what our contestants have in store!"

Dimitri popped up on his board and soared through the water, shifting his weight to cause his board to arc in the wave.

"Dimitri Russell does a strong roundhouse cutback," the announcer said over a chorus of clapping.

Grizz giggled in excitement, clapping enthusiastically. Luckily, Teddy and Lita were clapping just as loud, so it drowned her out.

"Jake Swanson pulls off a sharp frontside carve."

Patricia lifted her eyebrows, impressed. "They make it look so easy!"

"I know, right?" Lita agreed.

"Check it out, dudes, Kurt Minola is hanging ten!"

Ben whistled, keeping his fingers crossed. "Go, Kurt!"

Grizz couldn't take her eyes off him as he rode the wave perfectly balanced on the edge of his board. *That's awesome,* she thought with a dazed smile.

Kurt switched his stance effortlessly, before a figure swooped in front of him.

Grizz leapt, startled, as the surfer crouched down low and rode out of Kurt's way. Kurt wobbled for a moment before steadying himself and turning on the wave.

"Interference from Dimitri Russell," the announcer called over the

loudspeaker.

Grizz blinked, squinting out at the surfers. Sure enough, Dimitri stood up fully on his yellow board and continued carving the water.

"He really *does* charge," Ben commented, shaking his head in disgust.

Grizz frowned. She thought back to how he'd turned away when Kurt tried to shake his hand. Was it just her, or did Dimitri have something against Kurt?

Kurt didn't seem to let it faze him, bending his knees before lifting off and spinning mid-air.

"Whoa! Kurt Minola just did a backside air off the lip!"

Grizz squealed, leaping up and down as she clapped her hands. The entire crowd seemed to feel the same way, whooping and cheering.

She didn't notice at first how fast Dimitri was barreling toward another surfer.

Brody had bent his knees, board tipping upwards as he was opening for a trick, when Dimitri's board slammed into him, knocking them both into the water.

"Interference from Dimitri Russell to Brody Hutchins!"

The din of the crowd became unbearable as people shouted. Dimitri and Brody both surfaced, Brody looking angry as he spoke to Dimitri.

Grizz watched dumbfounded as Dimitri seemed to be equally angry, shoving Brody back as he pushed him.

"Damn!" Teddy exclaimed in surprise. "What is Dimitri's *problem?*"

Grizz found herself thinking the exact same thing.

Sharp whistles rang through the air, causing Grizz and Patricia to wince and cover their ears.

Two contest officials had run to the edge of the surf, blowing on their whistles and gesturing to Brody and Dimitri, who were trudging slowly toward the shore.

"Time is up for this heat. We had more of an exciting finish to this one than we normally want. Surfers, come on in."

The shoreline became very crowded, the contestants soon lost in the throng. Grizz felt her ears ring, unable to believe that Dimitri could do something like that. Yet she couldn't deny that he had all the same.

"This is getting intense," Lita said with a nervous laugh.

Ben, Teddy, and Patricia all started talking at once, and Grizz couldn't take it. "I'll be right back," she stammered, hurrying up the beach and away from them.

Once she'd reached the restroom, she headed for the sink, gripping the sides of the white porcelain and ducking her head. "Remember what Patricia said," she whispered, feeling sick. "Breathe in, breathe out. Breathe in, breathe out." Once her stomach had settled, she ran the water, splashing her face and trying to calm her racing thoughts.

Patricia stood on her tiptoes to see over the crowd. "Have they finished settling it yet?"

Ben shrugged. "This whole Dimitri-Brody thing is holding up the event."

"Oh, look, here comes Kurt!" Lita said.

Kurt pushed his way past several people, stopping in front of his friends and sighing.

"Hey, man, what's going on?" Teddy asked him.

Ben asked hurriedly, "Is Brody okay?"

"He's fine, but I don't know if he's going to do the next heat," said Kurt. "He's pretty shaken up. Had the wind knocked out of him."

"Poor guy," Patricia said in sympathy.

"What the hell was Dimitri doing?" Ben asked angrily.

Kurt scowled. "I don't know, but he's disqualified."

Patricia sighed in relief. "That's good, at least."

"I didn't think he'd be so aggressive!" Teddy exclaimed.

"Probably the truth is he's a total fakie and tries to take out the others so no one will find out," Kurt said with a smirk.

Ben clapped him on the back. "Good one."

Kurt glanced around. "Where—"

"Oh, dude, I almost forgot!" Ben began with a forced chuckle. "Teddy and I had a bet going."

Teddy's eyes lit up, catching on.

"What kind of bet?" Kurt asked eagerly.

"He thought that you couldn't score higher than Jake," Ben said hurriedly.

"He thought *what* now?" Kurt raised his eyebrows.

Teddy cleared his throat. "Yeah, yeah, I totally was wrong man. Sorry 'bout it."

"What's going on?" Lita whispered to Patricia.

Patricia cupped a hand over Lita's ear. "Tell you later!"

"So you won fifty bucks!" Ben continued. "Here ya go!" He eagerly grabbed Kurt's hand, slipping him the bills.

"Wait, if you won it…" Kurt began, holding the cash out to Ben.

Ben held up his hands. "No, man, it was a bet on you. So that means *you* get the money," he said, trying to sound like an expert on the subject.

"Dude, I didn't know that was how it worked…" Kurt said slowly, folding the bills before slipping them into his pocket. "Uh, thanks guys." He turned his focus on Patricia. "Where's Zelly?"

Patricia dropped her eyes to the sand, worried that she'd gone to look for Dimitri. "I'm not sure where she went—maybe to get some water?"

"That was awhile ago, though," Lita commented.

"Oh." Kurt frowned thoughtfully, breaking away from the group. "I'll go look for her."

Patricia winced, hoping it wouldn't end badly.

Grizz strode quickly along the beach. The second round of the Junior Women's division had already started, and so most of the hubbub over Brody and Dimitri's incident had died down. Shielding her eyes, she tried to find Dimitri standing in the crowd with the other surfers waiting for their round, but she came up empty.

Grizz sighed, slowing her steps. It looked as if Dimitri had left. Thinking back to his attitude during the competition, she couldn't say she was sorry. Yet a part of her had wanted to talk to him—find out what was going on. *I'm so confused,* she thought, exhaling in aggravation.

She turned her back on the surfers, crossing her arms. *I guess I'll go back to Patricia and the others.*

Eyes cast to the sand, she didn't notice that someone was standing in front of her until she almost rammed into them. "Sorry," she muttered, lifting her head.

"There you are," Kurt smiled in relief.

"Oh, hi Kurt," Grizz dropped her gaze, only to focus on his sculpted, bare chest. She pointedly chose a spot over his shoulder to stare at. "How did you place?"

"Second. I'm moving on up!" Kurt's expression grew somber as he added, "But poor Brody, man. He was doing just as good."

Grizz gasped. "Is he badly hurt?"

Kurt waved a hand. "He'll be fine, no damage done, but he may not surf the next round."

"I can understand that." Grizz began absentmindedly picking at one of her bracelets.

"Dimitri got disqualified," Kurt said off-handedly.

Her pulse quickened, feeling a sense of guilt. *Does Kurt realize I was looking for him?*

"What?" Grizz squeaked. "Oh, wow. Not that I can say I'm sorry," she added gruffly.

"Yeah, that was totally screwed up," Kurt shook his head. "I never really liked him, but to think he'd be a kook…"

Grizz furrowed her brow. "Kook?"

"Basically, a bad surfer who doesn't follow the rules," Kurt explained.

"Oh." Grizz was silent, thoughts racing.

Kurt studied her face. "Are you okay, Zelda?"

"Who, me? What?" Grizz asked wildly, locking eyes with him.

"Is something wrong?" Kurt pressed, reaching out to touch her arm. "You look kind of…"

Very aware of his fingertips brushing her skin, Grizz said quickly, "No, I'm fine! It's just… I saw what a jerk he was being to you earlier, so I'm kind of pissed off."

Whoa. Where did *that* come from?

Kurt grinned, leaning down and kissing her cheek.

Eyes widening, Grizz froze, feeling flushed all over.

Pulling back and dropping his hand from her arm, Kurt beamed at her. "You're the best. Wish me luck!"

He took off before she could say another word. Slowly, she lifted a hand to her cheek, the spot where his lips had been warm to the touch.

After standing still as a statue for a solid minute, Grizz shook her head. "I need to get back to the others," she told herself, hurrying up the beach.

"There she is," Grizz heard Patricia say as she neared the group.

"Hey, where have you been?" Lita asked, bumping shoulders with her. "It's almost time for the boys' third round!"

"We're down a few extra players than normal," Teddy said darkly. "Thanks to a two-faced jerk."

Patricia looked sharply at Grizz to gauge her reaction, but Grizz was silent, looking dazed as she watched the contest. "Are you okay?" Patricia whispered to her.

Grizz nodded curtly, grasping the strap of her shoulder bag. "Yep. Just peachy."

Patricia frowned but kept silent.

"Ooh!" Lita squealed, reaching out and touching the surfboard keychain that hung from the metal loop of Grizz's purse. "This is so pretty! Where did you get it?"

Brushing a bang from her eye, Grizz began, "Kurt bou—" She was hit with a visceral memory of Kurt kissing her, and felt her cheeks flush. She cleared her throat. "Um, I bought it at the Surfing Museum gift shop." She could feel all of her friends staring at her, but pointedly ignored them.

"Cowabunga! The third round of the Junior Men's Division is here!"

"Look, they're starting," Grizz said with a fake laugh, hoping Patricia and the others would become absorbed in the competition and stop boring their eyes into the back of her head.

Kurt swiveled in the water and began gunning for an incoming wave.

Grizz lifted her eyebrows. "That's a really big wave," she said, her voice coming out louder than she'd meant it to.

"Kurt's going for it, though," Teddy said enthusiastically.

They watched in amazement as Kurt's board was picked up by the wave, and he leapt to a standing position.

"Kurt Minola is wowing us already with his awesome choice of wave!"

The crowd cheered, and Grizz felt tingles of excitement. *Go, Kurt!*

Kurt bent his knees and shifted his weight, hurtling toward the curve of the wave.

"Looks like he's trying a layback snap. Can't wait to see if he can pull it off."

Grizz found herself crossing her fingers and chanting under her breath.

Her eyes widened when the wave twisted Kurt's board out from under his feet, slamming into him as he fell backwards into the water.

Chapter Twenty-Three ♡

"**K**URT!" BEN SHOUTED IN TERROR, HIS VOICE ABSORBED into the din of the crowded beach.

Grizz stared disbelieving out over the water, unaware that she'd seized Patricia's arm in a death grip.

"Come on," Teddy choked out, breaking into a run down the beach.

Grizz felt her ears begin to ring as she and the others staggered to the shoreline.

Patricia stumbled along, being held on both sides by Ben and Grizz. She was grateful for the support, afraid her knees might give out from the shock.

Grizz prayed silently as she scanned the endless waves for Kurt, the seconds stretching like hours. Where was he? Where was the medical team? Dully she caught red out of the corner of her eye and saw lifeguards readying themselves to go out and rescue him.

"There he is!" Lita shrieked, pointing to a familiar figure in the water who had stood up, thrusting his thumb in the air.

"It looks like Kurt is all right, but our first aid team will check him out, just to be sure."

Ben pumped his fist in the air, giving Patricia's hand a squeeze as he headed for the shoreline, pulling her along with him. Heart still hammering, Grizz followed them, eyes never leaving Kurt's form as he paddled inland.

Reaching the whitewater, Kurt hopped off his board and picked it up, still coughing up salt water. Ben released Patricia to wade into the water. He pulled Kurt into a tight hug, patting his back as he coughed. "Kurt! Are you okay?!"

Kurt pulled away, nodding. "Sorry, bro. I thought I'd nailed that one." He laughed, running a hand through his wet hair. "Got stuck in the washing machine and couldn't find my way out for a little bit."

"I'm glad you're all right," Patricia said with a shaky smile when Ben and Kurt stepped onto the sand.

"Yeah, that was not cool, bro," Teddy teased, his smile not quite reaching his eyes.

"Sorry, guys." Kurt's eyes widened as they landed on Grizz. "Oh!" he began, wiping the water from his eyes. "Y-you saw me eat it?" He chuckled, feet shuffling awkwardly in the sand. "Aw, how lame, I wanted you to see the layback snap..."

Grizz stared at him silently, tears in her eyes. Slowly, she lifted her fist and punched him in the shoulder.

"Hey—" Kurt exclaimed. He dropped his surfboard in surprise when she flung herself against him.

"You're okay, right?" she asked in a very un-Grizz like squeak, eyes squeezed shut as she rested her forehead against his chest. Her shoulders shook as she began to sob.

Kurt furrowed his brow in concern, wrapping his arms around her. "I'm fine," he whispered, rubbing her back gently.

"You didn't come up for the longest time," she whimpered, dully aware of his heart thudding against her ear.

Kurt chuckled, pulling back slightly to look at her. "I've wiped lots of times before, Zelly. I probably should have bailed, but, I…" he began to cough, having to cover his mouth and turn slightly away from her.

Grizz sniffled, poking him. "See? You'll be coughing up sea water for a month now," she said sternly. "You shouldn't have tried to take on such a big wave."

Two people from the medical team jogged up to the group. "How are you feeling?" the woman asked, scrutinizing Kurt as she lifted her sunglasses.

Eyes widening, Grizz realized in horror that she and Kurt were hugging, not just in front of their friends, but the *entire beach*. She pushed herself out of his arms and quickly wiped her face.

Kurt reddened, clearing his throat awkwardly.

The medic didn't seem to notice, continuing briskly, "Let's get you to the tent to make sure everything is all right."

Kurt glanced at Grizz, who was pointedly not looking at him. "Oh, um, sure."

"I'm glad you're not hurt," Lita told him.

"Thanks." Kurt turned his attention from Grizz to kneel and retrieve his surfboard from the sand. "Um, see you later, guys."

"Well, that was fun," Teddy said sarcastically, his laugh sounding forced and hollow.

Ben sighed. "Yeah. Surfing is cool, but it can get scary as hell."

"Aw, man, I dinged my board," they heard Kurt whine from up the beach on the way to the medical tent.

Patricia giggled, relaxing a bit. "Well, sounds like he's fine."

"Classic Kurt," Lita added with a grin. "Right, Grizz?"

Grizz didn't answer, staring after Kurt's retreating form with glassy eyes, heart thudding in her chest.

A few days later, Grizz was finishing up her shift with Mia at the Merry Mule. She finished mixing a drink, placing the spoon in an ice bath.

"Mexican mocha for he-ere," Mia sang to Grizz.

"I love Mexican mochas. They're not too hot to handle for me." Kurt's words, for some reason, came to mind.

Grizz felt her cheeks grow hot as she just stared at Mia.

Mia lifted her eyebrows. "Grizz?"

Blinking, Grizz snapped to attention. "Sorry. Mexican mocha for here. Got it." She turned her back on her coworker and pulled a large mug with a pale blue seahorse from the peg on the wall, muttering the ingredients under her breath to try and stay focused on the task at hand. Her thoughts the past few days had, to her utter confusion, been filled with Kurt. He hadn't been seriously hurt, but had been forced to drop out of the competition due to pulled muscles and some bruised ribs from being hit full-on by his board.

Grizz sighed, starting the steamer. She hadn't spoken to him since, and was glad; the surfing competition was an entire experience she wanted to block from her memory. "Mexican mocha for here!" she called, setting the steaming mug on the end of the bar.

The jingle of the front door caused her to glance up, and she froze when she saw Dimitri walk into the store. *He must be replacing one of us for our shift,* she thought with a groan.

Grizz had felt a little weird about Dimitri since the competition—she'd seen a side of him she hadn't liked, and then he left without a word. It had been radio silence from him since then—not a word or a text. She ducked her head and focused on wiping down the equipment, praying he would go into the break room without stopping.

The door jingled again, and Grizz looked to see Frank hurry into the cafe. "Hi, Frank," she said with a wave, grateful to see that Dimitri was gone for the moment.

"You're here early for once," Mia teased.

Frank came behind the counter. "I have to talk to you," he whispered to Grizz in an urgent tone.

"So talk," Grizz waited expectantly.

Frank glanced around, eyes widening as Dimitri came out of the back room. "Alone. Now."

"But there's still a few minutes left of my shift," Grizz whispered to him. "I'll get in trouble if I take off now."

"Hey, Frank, Mia," Dimitri said, strolling behind the counter. "Hi, Grizz," he said silkily, eyes landing on her.

"Hi." Grizz decided that potentially getting in trouble was a better option than having to be around Dimitri. She nudged Frank. "Okay, come on."

When they'd reached the back room, Grizz ducked behind a shelving unit. "Okay, what is it?"

"I'm sorry for telling you this now, but I don't have your number, and I wasn't sure when I'd see you next—"

Grizz put her hands on her hips impatiently. "Spit it out, Frank!"

Frank took a deep breath, pulling his smart phone from his pocket. "Okay. I haven't been on my Facebook for awhile, but I was going down my feed…"

Grizz pursed her lips, wondering where this was going.

Frank tapped his phone a few times, then turned the screen to face her. "Look at Hayley's post."

Grizz peered at the photo. It was Hayley and a guy taking a selfie. They were kissing on the lips. She wrinkled her nose. "Who's she making out with—" She froze, eyes widening in recognition. Clumsily she reached for the smart phone, holding it closer.

Frank's face twisted into an apologetic grimace. "Dimitri got rid of his Facebook account awhile ago, but…"

"That's him." Grizz said flatly, squinting her eyes at the date of the photo, thinking desperately it may have been an old picture. She read and re-read the date under her breath, wondering why it was ringing a bell. "Oh, my God." She realized that it was the day he'd promised to go to the Boardwalk with her. It had a location, as well—Hayley had uploaded it the moment they took it.

"*I went to the Marine Discovery Center on Saturday. The weather was gorgeous!*" Grizz recalled how Hayley had chatted about her weekend a few weeks back. "Wait—why was he going out with Hayley when he'd made a date with me?"

Frank shrugged apologetically. "Because he's a two-timer?"

Grizz exhaled sharply, feeling like such an idiot. "Apparently, yeah." She began to scroll down Hayley's page with her finger, seeing more posts with Dimitri, up until just the day before. "And he's still flirting with me?" she asked in disbelief and disgust.

"I'm sorry, Grizz," Frank said sincerely. "I just thought you should know."

"No, you did the right thing," Grizz assured him, handing his phone back. "It wouldn't have been good for me to keep liking him without knowing his true colors." All at once, she felt an overwhelming sense of guilt, realizing that she'd essentially been doing the same thing to Kurt. How would he feel if he found out she'd been trying to go out with him and Dimitri at the same time? *Patricia was right.*

"I'll let Hayley know what Dimitri has been up to," Frank went on. "She doesn't deserve to be two-timed."

"No one does," Grizz said softly, thinking of Kurt with a pang.

"Well, I'd better get ready for my shift," Frank began, looking at the clock. "I'm sorry again, Grizz."

Grizz folded him into her arms, giving him a warm hug. "Thanks, Frank."

Frank pulled back, smiling. "No problem."

Once Frank clocked in and left the back room, Grizz sighed, walking to her locker. "At least I don't have a shift with him right now."

Shouldering her purse a few minutes later, Grizz came out into the cafe and began to walk to the front doors.

"Grizz!"

She stopped in her tracks at Dimitri's voice.

He jogged toward her. "Sorry I took off so quick the other day," he began.

"You mean, when you got disqualified for surfing like a kook?"

Grizz quipped, surprised that she'd used Kurt's term, but pleased by the reaction it got from Dimitri.

Frowning, he stammered, "It was just the gnarly waves that day." He cleared his throat. "Anyway, I was hoping I could cash in that rain check? Say, dinner later?"

Grizz felt anger bubble in her chest, but she shrugged as casually as she could manage. "That's not going to happen."

Dimitri's brows knit together. "Is tonight bad?"

"Nope." Grizz cut him off, flipping her hair over her shoulder. "Truth is, I just have no interest in going out with you." She turned on her heel and strode out of the cafe before he could reply.

Once she was outside, she pumped her fist, feeling a rush of pride for telling him off. She exhaled, walking to the bike stand and pulling out her keys. It was weird. She thought she would feel more upset about Dimitri's cheating, but all she felt was… relief.

"What the hell?" Grizz mumbled to herself, unlocking her bike and wheeling it toward the street.

Her phone began to ring in her purse, and she pushed the kickstand into place. Her heart gave a strange little flutter when she saw the caller ID was Kurt.

Hands shaking, she swiped the screen to answer the call. "Hi," she said, finding to her annoyance that her voice quavered a little.

"Sup, Rizzy!" Kurt's voice bubbled with enthusiasm. "I was wondering if you want to grab dinner tonight."

Given the Dimitri situation, she figured she owed herself some fun. "Sure. What do you feel like?"

"Are you in the mood for seafood?" Kurt asked. "I was kind of thinking of going to The Blue Sea."

Grizz rolled her eyes. The Blue Sea was Patricia's family restaurant. She debated mentally for a few moments, then gave in; it was her favorite seafood place, after all. "Yeah, sure," she replied.

"Awesome! I'll pick you up at five thirty!"

Feeling an entirely new set of jitters, Grizz said, "See you then," before hanging up and taking the scenic route home. She needed the fresh air to clear her head.

Chapter Twenty-Four ♡

RIZZ HUMMED ALONG TO THE UPBEAT TUNE PLAYING OVER Kurt's speakers. The top was down on his Islander, and she was enjoying looking up at the sky.

Playing absentmindedly with the key pendant she was wearing, Grizz cast her eyes to Kurt as he drove. She had chosen to wear an aquamarine sundress with a white shrug, and was pleasantly surprised to see that when Kurt picked her up, he was dressed nicely as well, with black pants and a dark blue button-down shirt rolled up at the elbows. The muscles of his lower arm looked taut and strong as he clutched the steering wheel, profile thrown into shadow.

Grizz caught herself and looked away. *Why do I keep checking him out?*

Because he's hot, a traitorous voice whispered.

Pouting her lips, Grizz stared out the window, trying to calm her racing heart.

"Did you hear what Obe wants me to do next week?" Kurt asked.

Grizz lifted her head with interest. "No, what?"

Keeping his eyes on the road, Kurt said, "There's a jogathon next week and the Merry Mule is one of the sponsors. He wants me to go in costume."

"And jog?" Grizz asked with a devilish lift of her eyebrow.

Kurt looked at her and smiled. "Hey that's a good idea!"

"No, in that boiling costume? You'll collapse," Grizz countered, playfully tapping him on the arm.

Kurt cleared his throat and smiled, turning his eyes back to the road.

Grizz paused and pulled her hand back. "So, how was your day?" She regretted the question the moment it left her lips. *Stop talking so much, he's going to think something is up!* She bit her lip. *Oh, right. He won't think anything of it because of the stupid love potion.* Her stomach clenched as she wondered how she would get out of this mess.

"It was good, I helped my dad with some yard work," Kurt replied. "Part of the fence was rotted, so we replaced it."

"That's good," she said absently, eyes glazing as her thoughts raced.

"Sweet, we're here!" Kurt cheered when they pulled into the parking lot of The Blue Sea.

Grizz took a deep breath and unbuckled her seatbelt, reaching for the purse at her feet.

She started when her door opened, Kurt grinning and extending a hand to her.

"I don't need help out," Grizz told him, but accepted his hand anyway, feeling a rush of adrenaline at his touch.

Once on the ground, Kurt relinquished her hand and closed the passenger door.

Grizz smoothed the skirt of her dress and fussed with her hair, hit with nerves. As they walked toward the building, she relaxed slightly. She always had loved the Veronas' restaurant, with its quaint Cape Cod style, complete with powder blue siding and white shutters.

Kurt passed her and reached for the handle of the large white door, holding it open. "Ladies first," he said with a smile.

Grizz ducked her head, saying a soft thank you before entering the restaurant.

Wow, it's crowded, she thought, looking into the filled dining area.

Kurt appeared at her side. "This dude is awesome," he said, pointing to the life-size statue of a pirate next to the front counter.

"Yeah, old Braided Beard is pretty cool," Grizz agreed, patting the pirate's shoulder fondly.

Kurt chuckled.

"Well, fancy seeing you two here!" Patricia said, coming behind the counter to grab some menus.

"It's a full house tonight," Kurt commented.

Patricia shrugged. "This tends to be our rush hour, especially during the summer. But I think I can manage a table for you guys." She waved for them to follow her.

She led them to a small table for two along the back wall of the dining room. "I hope this is okay," she began, throwing Grizz an apologetic smile.

"This will be fine," Grizz replied. She had gotten used to sharing cramped spaces with Kurt.

Once they were seated, Patricia set a menu in front of each of them and asked, "Can I get you started on something to drink, or is just water okay?"

Kurt was silent, gazing around the restaurant with a dreamy look on his face. "Something smells like low tide..."

Patricia's jaw dropped.

Grizz was about to snarl a comeback, but then remembered the love potion. She cleared her throat. "Kurt, babycakes, don't say that about Patricia's family restaurant," she scolded. Internally, she was gagging.

Kurt stared at her, ears turning red at being called "babycakes." "Oh, no, Patty, I didn't mean it as an insult—I like it. Reminds me of the ocean."

Patricia shrugged it off with an eye roll. "Okay, anything to drink? We're having a special tonight on Roy Rogers and Shirley Temples."

"I'll have a Roy Rogers," Grizz replied. "I just love the way those taste with seafood!"

"And for babycakes?" Patricia's cheeks puffed as she held in a snicker.

Grizz caught her eye and smiled.

"I'll have a Roy Rogers, too," Kurt said, grinning at Grizz. "Whoa, Zelly, we ordered the same thing!"

"Because you copied me?" Grizz teased.

"Oh yeah you're right," Kurt mused as though it had just occurred to him. He ran a hand through his hair. "I feel so dumb!"

Grizz felt a pang of guilt. "Oh, I didn't mean it like that," she said, reaching across the table to rest her hand on his forearm.

Kurt smiled, skin tingling from where she'd brushed his arm. "Roy Rogers was the coolest cowboy ever!"

Grizz was impressed that Kurt actually knew who he was, but then remembered his love of old Westerns.

"Okay, two Roy Rogers for the cowpokes," Patricia said, turning to head to the kitchen.

Opening her menu, Grizz browsed the options, not sure what she was in the mood for. Lifting her eyes, she saw Kurt was flipping through his menu as well. She rested her chin on her fist, studying his chiseled features. *Screw dinner. I'm in the mood for a tall, dark, and handsome hunk.*

She blinked, catching herself. She lifted her menu to hide her red cheeks. *What is* wrong *with me?*

"So, what are you thinking of having?" Kurt asked, raising his hazel eyes to look at her.

Grizz slowly lowered her menu, casually not meeting his eye. "Maybe shrimp of some kind. You?"

"Shrimp's awesome," Kurt agreed, turning one page of the menu back and forth. "I can't decide—Surf and Turf, or Catch of the Day?"

"Surf and Turf," Grizz replied. "Best of both worlds."

"You're so right," Kurt chuckled. "Land and sea."

Grizz giggled, not noticing that Patricia had reappeared.

"Here are your Roy Rogers," she said, setting the tall glasses with an umbrella in front of Grizz and Kurt. "Do you need a few more minutes?"

Kurt caught Grizz's eye. "I'm ready, are you?"

Grizz nodded. "Yep!"

She paused, until Kurt said, "You go ahead."

Blushing, Grizz focused on the menu. "Could I get the Ahoy, Mateys basket? Love these names, by the way."

Patricia giggled, writing down her order. "Would you like salad or chowder?"

"Salad, please," Grizz answered. "With ranch?"

"Okay. And what would you like, Kurt?"

"The Surf and Turf, medium rare, please," Kurt folded his menu.

"Chowder or salad?" Patricia poised her pen expectantly.

"Chowder sounds choka, Trix," Kurt said with a grin.

Patricia laughed. "Okay, I'll have that right out for you, Kyle." She took their menus and walked away.

Grizz wished Patricia didn't have to leave, not sure what to say to Kurt. She reached for her drink, taking a long sip from the straw.

Kurt followed suit, exclaiming, "I haven't had one of these in years, but I think this is the best Roy Rogers I've ever had!"

Grizz had to agree. "I love the drinks here." She pulled the umbrella out of the cherry. "They're cute, too."

Kurt admired the paintings of the ocean, the signs with carved fish, and the ship stern that hung on the wall. "The atmosphere in this place is bitchin'." He covered his mouth, looking around wildly.

Grizz cocked her eyebrow. "What?"

Kurt leaned closer and whispered, "I shouldn't swear in a family friendly place like this."

Grizz rested her elbows on the table, whispering back, "No one can hear you, it's too crowded."

Kurt nodded, staring at her intently. She was wearing really nice smelling perfume, and it was hard for him to pull away.

Grizz cleared her throat, sitting back in her seat and lifting her drink to her lips.

Kurt straightened, picking up the mermaid salt and pepper shakers from the table. "Uh, this is cool," he said, feeling awkward.

Grizz smiled in spite of herself. "I've always really liked those."

"So, how was work?" Kurt asked, trying to make conversation.

She recalled what had happened with Dimitri that afternoon. *I should have thrown coffee in that tool's face.* The thought gave her a twisted jolt of pleasure. "It was... eventful," she replied mysteriously.

"Cool," Kurt replied with that easy grin of his.

Grizz faltered, a heavy feeling settling in her gut as she thought about the mean trick she was playing on him. This wasn't fair. She had to put a stop to it. Taking a deep breath, she began, "Actually, Kurt, there's something I want to—"

"Okay, salad with shrimp and ranch dressing for Grizz," Patricia interrupted her, setting a ceramic bowl in front of her. "And clam chowder with a side of crackers for Kurt."

"Thanks!" Kurt inhaled deeply. "Smells so good!"

Grizz stared at him, closing her mouth and dropping her eyes to her lap.

"Want another one?" Patricia asked her.

Grizz blinked, realizing she'd stress-drank all of her Roy Rogers already. She numbly handed her empty glass to Patricia.

"Be right back!" Patricia said cheerfully, apparently not noticing her friend's stricken look.

"...good?"

Grizz stared straight ahead, mind whirling. Fingers snapped in front of her face. "Huh?"

Kurt chuckled, lowering his hand. "I thought I lost you for a second."

Shaking her head, Grizz mumbled an apology, picking up her fork. "Let's see how this tastes." She took a bite, wiping her mouth with the corner of her napkin. "Delightful!"

"Awesome." Kurt resumed eating his chowder.

"Here you go," Patricia said, setting a fresh drink in front of Grizz as she passed by. "We'll have your main course out in a few!"

"Thanks," Grizz waved to her. "How's your chowder?"

Kurt glanced up at her, mouth full. "Shgood," he mumbled.

Grizz laughed, feeling her nerves melt away.

"We're supposed to find out where we're living on campus pretty soon, right?" Kurt asked.

Grizz finished chewing her bite of salad. "Yeah. I wonder who I'll have for a roommate…" she began, feeling a rush of nerves. "I hope she's nice, and we get along."

Kurt smiled. "Of course you will. How could anyone not like you?"

Grizz blushed. "That's nice of you to say. I'm still pretty nervous thinking that in just a couple of months, I'm going to be so far away from everything I'm familiar with."

"After being at ASU for just a little bit, you won't even remember your jitters. You're one of the bravest people I know."

Grizz stared at him. "Seriously?"

Kurt nodded emphatically. "Of course! I've never known you to back down from a challenge. You'll be awesome."

Grizz blushed, feeling inexplicably happy. "Thanks." She speared her salad with a flourish. "We both will!"

The rest of their meal went by pleasantly, both of them talking and laughing so much that when Patricia brought the check, Grizz looked at the clock in surprise. "Wow, we've been here that long?"

Kurt smiled, reaching for both receipts. "Time flies when you're having fun."

I guess it does. She frowned when she saw her receipt was missing. "No, Kurt, I don't want you to pay for me."

"I want to treat you!" Kurt replied, lightly touching her hand when she tried to give him cash.

Grizz felt her skin tingle and found that she couldn't move her hand, though her brain told her to. This wasn't fair. Kurt shouldn't do sweet things like this. *He's getting the wrong idea,* she thought, heart pounding. *I can't use him like this. I need to tell him.* "That's really nice of you, but I'd like to pay for my share." Involuntarily, she felt herself squeeze his hand. *Why is my body betraying me?!*

Kurt blushed, nodding. "I totally understand."

Grizz stood up and shouldered her purse, making a beeline for the exit.

"Come again, you two!" Mrs. Verona called after them.

"Thanks!" Kurt replied with a wave, following Grizz out the door.

Grizz wrapped her arms around herself as the breeze picked up, bouncing in her heeled sandals as she waited by the passenger door. *Why didn't I bring something warmer than this?*

Kurt came to the passenger side, hitting the fob button to unlock the Jeep. "Whoa, are you cold?" he asked.

Duh, she thought, but just nodded.

Kurt hurriedly opened the door and rummaged in the back seat, draping his Santa Cruz sweatshirt around her shoulders. "I can put the top up, too," he said, heading to the back of the Jeep.

"No, no," Grizz told him, shoving icy hands through the sleeves. "I'll be fine now, thanks."

Kurt smiled happily, going around to the driver's side and starting the car.

Pulling the sweatshirt tight around herself, Grizz noticed that it smelled like his spicy cologne, and felt a spike of adrenaline. *There's no place like home, there's no place like home,* she chanted to herself as they drove to her house in silence.

Kurt pulled in front of her house a few minutes later, putting the Jeep in park. "Well," he began, turning to face her, "Thanks for coming to dinner with me. I had a lot of fun."

Grizz ducked her head, a strand of hair falling in front of her face. "Thanks for inviting me. I had fun, too."

Kurt found he couldn't tear his eyes away from her. Summoning up his courage, he reached out to tuck her aqua-tipped hair behind her ear, leaving his hand resting on her cheek. He inched closer, drawing his face close to hers.

Grizz swallowed hard, instinctively leaning toward him, as if mesmerized.

Kurt's kiss was hesitant at first, his lips hovering uncertainly above hers as his thumb stroked her cheek. Their lips brushed lightly, Grizz's heart pounding as her eyes slid closed. The kiss deepened as Grizz wrapped her arms around his neck, digging her fingers in his hair.

Kurt snaked his other hand to rest on the small of her back, pulling her in as close as he could with the center console in the way. His mind whirled, unable to believe that he was finally kissing the girl of his dreams, and she apparently wanted the kiss as much as he did.

He suddenly froze, realizing with a sinking heart that she *didn't* like him as much as he liked her. Not really. It was the love potion forcing her to do these things.

Kurt ripped his mouth from hers, breath ragged as the horrid truth of what he was doing hit him like a semi-truck. "I can't do this," he choked out, retracting his hands from her, resting them on the steering wheel.

Her heart was beating so loudly, she was sure he could hear it. "Wha-what?" she breathed, numbly aware of the absence of his touch.

Kurt shook his head. "This is so, totally *wrong!*" he exclaimed, refusing to look at her.

Wrong? What's wrong? Grizz tried to calm her racing heart and mind. *Did he not like kissing me?* Her mouth opened to protest, but no sound came out.

Kurt took a deep breath, thinking back to how concerned she'd been after he'd wiped out, how happy he seemed to make her. It was twisted of him to try to control her. *How could I have been so pathetic?* "I know this is going to be a shock, but try to snap out of it!" He turned back to face her, gently gripping her shoulders, and for one fleeting moment she thought—hoped—that he was going to kiss her again. "You're under a spell!"

Eyes widening, Grizz realized what was happening. Oh, she was under a spell all right—she actually wanted to kiss Kurt Minola!

He shook his head, eyes shining with regret. "You think you like me, but you don't! It's this stupid love potion, and I'm so sorry!"

Everything seemed to be crashing around her—this was what she wanted, wasn't it? To teach Kurt a lesson he wouldn't forget.

So why did it feel like it was *her* heart that was breaking?

"Kurt," she choked out, reaching out for him, but he pulled back, opening his door.

"No, Grizz. I can't mess with your feelings. It's not right. You like Dimitri... and I need to accept it."

Grizz fumbled with the handle to the passenger door, trying to follow him as he hopped out of the car. "But..."

Kurt ran his hands through his hair, leaning against his Jeep. "I don't know how to get this potion to wear off, but I'll find a way, I swear. You're not yourself if you go along with whatever I say—you're strong and independent, you made *me* want to be like that, too—that's why I fell for you in the first place."

Grizz felt fluttery inside at his confession, but he'd already opened the driver's side door and started the car. "I won't bother you ever again, I promise. I hope one day you can at least forgive me."

"Kurt..."

But he'd already driven away.

Grizz stood on the sidewalk, as if her legs were rooted in place, for what felt like an eternity. Numbly she noticed his spicy cologne lingered around her, and realized she was still wearing his sweatshirt. She'd screwed everything up—her life, Kurt's life, everything, with her stupid prank. She should have listened to Patricia and let Ben tell Kurt the truth.

She didn't even process for several more minutes that he'd called her Grizz.

Chapter Twenty-Five ♡

"SO THEN HE JUST GETS IN KAHUNA AND TAKES OFF, LEAVING me there like a stuttering fish!" Grizz told Patricia, ripping a licorice whip in half with her teeth.

"Wow." Patricia exhaled slowly. Grizz's story was a lot to take in. "Have you talked to him since?"

Grizz shook her head. "No, how could I? I've screwed everything up." She sighed, grateful that she hadn't had work for the past couple of days. "I'm sorry, Patricia."

"Why are you apologizing to me?" Patricia wondered, taking a handful of M&Ms from her desk. When Grizz had called, saying she needed some girl time, Patricia had gathered all of the comforting essentials.

Grizz hugged a pillow to her chest. "Because you wanted to tell Kurt about the love potion. But I had to take my hare-brained scheme and run with it. What I was doing was mean and two-faced." Kurt's words as he'd pulled away from her still rang in her ears.

Patricia reached over and squeezed her hand. "It's okay, Grizz. Your reaction was understandable, given the circumstances."

Grizz giggled. "Denial will do that to a person, I guess. Everyone else saw it first, huh?" she mused.

Patricia shrugged and smiled helplessly. "Yeah, we kind of did."

"A true friend knows you better than you know yourself," Grizz said sagely before she crawled toward her purse tossed in the corner of Patricia's bedroom. "Here," she began, handing Patricia a wrapped package. "For being such an awesome friend."

Wordlessly, Patricia peeled the tape off and pulled apart the paper, revealing a small handmade book with a photo of her and Grizz on the cover. "Besties" was spelled out in embossed, rainbow colored stickers. "Wow, Grizz," she breathed, carefully turning the embellished pages to find photos of their senior year. She ran her finger over the group shot they'd taken with their cast the night of the theater festival. A ticket for the festival was glued next to it. "This is incredible!"

Grizz shrugged, pleased that Patricia liked it. "I've been working on it all summer, but didn't finish it until yesterday."

Patricia clutched the book to her chest, sniffling. "I'll keep it forever!" she exclaimed, pulling Grizz into a tight hug.

Grizz grinned, a weight off of her shoulders now that she'd cleared the air with Patricia. "Now I think I feel brave enough to talk to someone else," she said, that fiery spark back in her eyes. *Even if he'll hate me forever,* she added silently.

≈

Grizz leaned against the railing on the Wharf, admiring how the dusk was casting dark orange tints on the water.

Clutching Kurt's folded sweatshirt to her chest, she checked the time on her cell phone for what felt like the thousandth time. Kurt should have been there three minutes ago. *If he's coming at all,* she thought, squeezing her eyes shut to try and calm her butterflies.

"Hi."

Grizz whirled at the hesitant greeting, feeling a new set of butterflies when she saw Kurt before her, wearing dark rinse jeans with a green tee shirt. "Hi," she said a bit breathlessly, faltering. She knew what she wanted to say, but had *no* idea how to even begin.

"You wanted to see me?" Kurt asked in a subdued tone, hands in his pockets.

Grizz swallowed hard and nodded. "Yeah. Here's your sweatshirt back," she began, holding it out to him.

"Oh. Thanks." Kurt shrugged the black fabric on, before shuffling awkwardly. "Well, if that's all…"

"No!" Grizz exclaimed, reaching out to stop him.

Kurt frowned, staring at where she held his arm.

Grizz took a step away from him, drawing back her hand and balling it into a fist. "I need to talk to you. Feel like going for a walk?"

Kurt was silent for a moment, then nodded. "Sure."

As they walked along the sandy beach, Grizz toyed with what to say to him.

"Look, Kurt—"

"Listen, Grizz—"

They looked at each other shyly and laughed. "You go ahead," Kurt said.

"No, you can," Grizz said, tucking a strand of hair behind her ear.

"I just wanted to say again how sorry I am. I—" Kurt rubbed his neck, struggling with the words. "I really liked you and wanted you to like me, too. So when Tuck suggested that potion, I thought, 'Dude! Here's my chance!'" He frowned. "But it was so messed up."

Grizz took a deep breath, steadying herself. "Kurt, I have something to tell you. That 'love potion' you got from Tuck? It was fake."

Kurt stopped in his tracks. "Wait—you're not still under the spell?" he asked curiously.

Grizz rolled her eyes, seeing he was missing the point. "I never *was.* There's no such thing as a love potion! Tuck was playing a dirty trick on you." How it took him this long to figure it out was anyone's guess.

"But all of that stuff you did..." Kurt began doubtfully.

"Guess maybe I should be a theater major too, huh?" she teased. Met by a blank expression, she went on, "I was faking it. I found out about the love potion, and wanted to teach you a lesson for trying to force me to like you..."

Kurt took a step back, letting her words sink in. "So... you never were under a spell."

Grizz fully faced him, shaking her head. "Nope."

That means she never liked me, even with magic. The thought was sobering. "Oh." Kurt shifted his weight in the sand. "I'm really sorry for all of this."

"I'm sorry, too, for tricking you," Grizz said, folding her arms to warm her hands in the chilly night air. "Spiking my drink with a love potion—real or not—was not cool, but I shouldn't have handled it the way I did. And—" Grizz bit her lip, voice growing quieter as she admitted, "I kind of flirted with Dimitri at the same time as I was going out with you…"

Though she'd braced herself, she wasn't prepared for the shot to the gut she felt when Kurt's face fell. "Oh." He sighed. "I guess I deserved it."

Grizz shook her head. "No one deserves that," she whispered. She took a step closer to Kurt, looking up at him. "I hope you can forgive me. And, I broke it off with him."

"You didn't have to do that because of me," Kurt told her with a frown. "You really like Dimitri."

"Actually, I don't," she said sincerely.

This whole thing was getting too complicated for Kurt to follow. Mind reeling, he stuttered, "What?"

Grizz shrugged, trying to ignore her thudding heart. "He's a jerk. Besides, there's someone else I like a lot more. It just took me awhile to realize it." She watched him carefully, waiting for his reaction.

Kurt stared at her, looking crestfallen. "Oh…" *Of course she likes someone else.*

"Don't you get it?!" she burst out after a long silence. Bravely she reached out and tugged on the edges of his sweatshirt, standing on her tiptoes and bringing his mouth to hers.

After a lingering kiss, Grizz finally pulled back, palms flat against his chest.

"Just to be, like, clear," Kurt began, his breathing ragged, resting his forehead against hers, "The guy you like is *me*, right?"

Grizz rolled her eyes, noting how her cheeks flushed and heart raced whenever she was around him. She wasn't sure whether to deck him or to kiss him again, but figured that was what came of falling for Kurt Minola.

Kurt wrapped his arms around her waist, resting his hands on the small of her back.

Arms locked around his neck, Grizz whispered as the last of the setting sun slipped away, "I may or may not be under your spell."

"Not funny," Kurt replied with a grin.

"'If you pardon, we will mend'," Grizz quoted teasingly, before pulling him in for another kiss.

ACKNOWLEDGMENTS

Thank you to my family, especially my mom, the biggest Grizz and Kurt shipper in the world. Without you, this story never would have made it!

Thank you to my amazing editor, Rose Anne Roper, and to Lyssa Chiavari for originally publishing "The Taming of the Dudebro" in *Perchance to Dream*.

A huge shout-out to Key of Heart Designs, who did the gorgeous cover and formatting.

Thank you to my BFF Poonum for your friendship and support while working on this story.

Thanks also to Cody, Kylie, Margaret, Matt, Meghan, and Shannon. You are the greatest besties a girl could ever have!

Finally, thank you to all of the amazing authors at Snowy Wings Publishing!

ABOUT THE AUTHOR

A voracious reader, Jane Watson has always been a fan of romance, fantasy, adventure and especially happy endings. She received her degree in Art History from the University of Puget Sound where she met many un-tameable dudebros. When she is not writing, Jane works at a museum. She likes to spend her free time doting on her menagerie of pets, riding her bike, crafting, and obsessively shopping for purses.

Visit Jane online at janewatsonauthor.com.

* 9 7 8 1 9 4 6 2 0 2 5 6 7 *